Discover more at millsandboon.co.uk

BIG SKY SLAYER

JUNO RUSHDAN

CHRISTMAS BANK HEISTS

R. BARRI FLOWERS

MILLS & BOON

First Published in Great Britain 2025
by Mills & Boon, an imprint of HarperCollins*Publishers* Ltd
1 London Bridge Street, London, SE1 9GF

www.harpercollins.co.uk

HarperCollins*Publishers*
Macken House, 39/40 Mayor Street Upper,
Dublin 1, D01 C9W8, Ireland

Big Sky Slayer © 2025 Juno Rushdan
Christmas Bank Heists © 2025 R. Barri Flowers

ISBN: 978-0-263-39731-4

1025

MIX
Paper | Supporting
responsible forestry
FSC™ C007454

This book contains FSC™ certified paper and other controlled sources to ensure responsible forest management.

For more information visit: www.harpercollins.co.uk/green

Printed and Bound in the UK using 100% Renewable Electricity at CPI Group (UK) Ltd, Croydon, CR0 4YY

BIG SKY SLAYER

JUNO RUSHDAN

To all those who have been burned by love.
May the right person walk into your life and convince
you to give love a second chance.

Chapter One

Parking in the heart of Bitterroot Falls was tricky in the morning and was the reason Winter Stratton typically avoided downtown at this time. Having lived in San Antonio, she was no stranger to tough traffic. She had moved to the small Montana town to be closer to her sisters—both had recently relocated there—to get away from high crime and congestion. To escape. Not to grit her teeth while trying to find a parking spot on Main Street.

Almost everything was nestled on this one four-lane road. Shopping. Public library. Bank. Playhouse. Restaurants. The newly built hotel hosting the annual Golf Course Superintendent Association fall meeting and trade show. This was also the peak time when people grabbed breakfast or coffee from the café or hit the only fitness center.

She was going to be late for a meeting she'd reluctantly agreed to and now dreaded. Was it a *meeting*? Sounded too formal, like networking. Coffee date?

Her heart skipped a beat at the thought of the four-letter D word. After her divorce, yet another D word, she'd taken a year to heal and recover and still had no idea why she was attracted to the wrong type. At thirty-two, she had to stop repeating the same mistakes.

This *appointment* was merely a conversation over coffee

with Chance Reyes. Yet, the prospect of being alone with Chance sent a wave of unwelcome butterflies through her belly.

Winter reminded herself she couldn't have a date of any kind with Chance. Not ever. Might be better if she was late. Then she could skedaddle quickly and go to work.

Two women in workout gear left Big Sky Fitness and waved goodbye to each other. One hopped into a car and pulled away, freeing a parking space close by. Convenient timing obliterated Winter's potential excuse. The universe was conspiring against her.

Sighing, she flipped on her turn indicator and squeezed her four-wheel-drive Bronco into the spot. Time was left on the digital meter. Twenty minutes.

A lot could happen in twenty minutes when it came to Chance.

She grabbed her dark gray blazer, jumped out into the crisp October air and hurried onto the sidewalk. The military had drilled into her that ten minutes early was late. Her army days were behind her, but old habits died hard.

Winter threw on her wool blazer, covering the holstered Glock at her side and the DOJ Division of Criminal Investigation badge hooked on her belt beside her law enforcement radio.

As she passed the fitness center, she glanced inside. The lobby was crowded with a sweaty crowd of spandex-clad people. Mostly female. Mostly young. The group buzzed around a woman in a formfitting purple outfit, her hair in a messy top knot.

Winter caught her reflection in the glass. Her honey-brown skin was dull. Dark circles shadowed her eyes from another restless night. She was coming off a major case, and work triggered nightmares. Wishing she'd bothered to put on makeup, she tugged her ponytail from her jacket and ran her fingers over the curly strands framing her face, ensuring it hid the scar near her hairline.

She quickened her pace. Whipped out lip gloss. Dabbed some on. Not that she should care what Chance thought of her appearance. But for some silly reason, she did.

Main Street was decorated with painted pumpkins, cornstalks, mums and colored light bulbs that gave a festive vibe at night. All a part of Bitterroot Falls's small hometown appeal. Along with the smiles and nods of greeting from passersby on the busy sidewalk.

Anxious energy bubbled inside Winter as she drew closer to the coffee shop. A man stood outside the café. His back was to her, but she didn't have to see his face to know it was Chance. If the instant tingle in her belly didn't give it away, then his sleek, muscular build would have. Tall. Solid shoulders. Great posture. Black Stetson. Curly, dark hair that fell to the collar of his leather jacket. Jeans hugged his hips, highlighting his long legs, and her mouth went dry in a way she hadn't anticipated.

Shake it off. Winter looked at his expensive Lucchese boots. No self-respecting rancher who got his hands dirty would be caught dead in the Rolls-Royce of cowboy boots. That snapped her back to her senses. Then he turned around—sharply hewn profile, olive complexion, his tan skin reflecting his Latino heritage—and his electric brown gaze met hers.

She was…ensnared. Pinned to the spot.

"Good morning," he said, flashing one of his devastatingly perfect smiles.

Instant regret socked her in the gut. Any time she spent near him only whetted her appetite for more. This was a mistake. "Morning." She kept her expression nonchalant, not wanting him to see the nerves trickling through her. "Why are you waiting out here?"

"The place is packed with people attending the GCSA powwow. I figured you'd make some excuse not to stay long, so why deprive someone of a table?"

She stiffened, disliking how he thought he knew her so well, and hating even more that he had pegged her correctly after less than six months in each other's orbit.

Her younger sister, Summer, had moved there and shacked up with a man she barely knew, Logan Powell—Chance's best friend. The two men grew up together in Wyoming, wealthy ranches adjoining. Logan was closer to Chance than he was to his brothers. Winter and Autumn relocated, worried about their sister. Now at family gatherings—weekly dinners, celebrations, drinks—Winter and Chance were thrown together. Stuck in each other's lives.

One more reason to avoid any doomed romantic entanglement with him.

"No need for me to make excuses. I have a job to get to." Winter pulled back her blazer and tapped her badge.

His gaze dropped to her hip. A grin tugged at the corner of his mouth. "Have I ever told you I have a thing for a beautiful woman with a gun? Intensely sexy."

He had. Many times. Repositioning her blazer, she concealed her firearm, not wanting to spoon-feed his little fantasy.

"We both have jobs, Winter, only I don't use mine as an evasive tactic. That's why I made this *coffee date* in advance, so we could clear thirty minutes from our schedules."

Thirty? And for a date? "First, you make your own hours and work when you want." Chance was an attorney, like Summer, but he didn't work in the field of law. Instead, he owned a small ranch that hired hands managed for him while he oversaw the Ironside Protection Services office in Bitterroot Falls, where Chance got to choose which cases his office took on. "I don't have the same luxury. Second, there's twenty minutes on the parking meter." She pulled out her cell phone and glanced at the time. "Make that seventeen. Third, this isn't a date."

"I'm happy to play this little game. A reliable source told me you're not working on any active cases now. You don't need to rush into the office or off to question a suspect, which means you do have the luxury of taking your time this morning." He gave her one of his sly, pleased looks that he got when he had the upper hand in a conversation.

Winter folded her arms. "Who's your source?" *More like snitch.* "Summer? Autumn?" She doubted her older sister disclosed such information. Maybe it was Declan Hart. A fellow DCI agent, he'd assisted Logan and Summer with a murder investigation that had brought the two to Bitterroot Falls and had somehow become part of the family. "Was it Declan?"

"If I divulged my source, I wouldn't be very good at my job, would I?"

Apart from the professional praise her younger sister and Logan showered on Chance, Winter had no idea whether he was good at his job. Might be lousy.

"As for your second point," he said, "I can accomplish more in seventeen minutes than most men can in thirty. So, I'm willing to take what I can get with you. For now. Third, despite this constant flirting from you—"

"From me?" Winter dropped her arms to her sides. "I am not the one flirting. This is repartee, light sparring for me. Nothing more."

"Potato, po-tah-to." He lifted a shoulder in a shrug. "For the record, a coffee date can be platonic. My goal this morning was not romantic in nature. When I do take you out on a date, there'll be no ambiguity, and my intentions will be crystal clear."

Her jaw dropped at his audacity, but just then a young

barista, wearing a green apron with The Beanery stenciled in white across the front, came outside.

"Here you go, Mr. Reyes." The perky young woman handed him two large disposable cups with lids. "Thanks again for the tip. We have a bet that it'll be the best one this week."

Another smile from him that was pure perfection. "You guys deserve it," Chance said, and then the barista went back inside. He turned to Winter. "I took the liberty of ordering since I recognize your time is valuable and I have no desire to waste it unnecessarily."

Her heart softened, only a skosh. "Did you ask your source what I might want?"

"I did not. How you take your coffee felt like an intimate detail I should discover myself, the morning after," he said, letting that dangle between them for a second or two as her stomach fluttered, "but I guessed a latte with soy milk, light foam." He extended the left cup. "And one sugar. A touch of sweetness to balance the flavors."

Insufferable and handsome, with toothpaste-commercial-worthy teeth—the only way to describe the man. Apparently, also a mind reader or a not-so-bad investigator since her idea of heaven was indeed inside the cup he offered, but she couldn't bring herself to admit it. "I'm not in a *touch of sweetness* kind of mood." Not a lie.

"Here, have mine." He handed her the other cup. "I prefer my coffee black and bold and nothing sugarcoated about it."

Was he talking about coffee or women, considering she was all three?

Then Chance winked. *Aha.* Incontrovertible proof he was the flirt. Not her. She narrowed her eyes in response.

He took a sip of her coffee and frowned. "Not awful. If you like your java watered down. I want the caffeine to hit me like a punch in the face."

No matter how great he was at pushing her buttons, she couldn't deny him his coffee. "Let me do you the favor of swapping." She reached for the other cup.

He rocked back, leaning away, and clutched the latte to his chest. "No, thank you." His tone held a hint of coolness. "I don't want any favors from you."

"Oh, really. Then what do you want from me?"

Chance raised an eyebrow. His dark gaze held hers before dropping to her mouth, and her stomach took a nosedive. "Oh, I have a list." He looked back up, meeting her eyes.

A jolt of yearning slid through her.

Something in his expression told her he felt it, too. Brimming with casual confidence she found far too alluring, he stepped so close she smelled his cologne—cedar and musk. "But I don't think you're ready to hear it," he whispered.

A grin surfaced, pulling at her lips despite her best effort not to let it. The man was a walking, talking warning sign: Danger High Voltage.

Erasing any hint of amusement from her face, Winter sipped the black coffee and gagged at the intense flavor.

"It's their ultra nitro blend," he said. "An acquired taste that becomes addictive. Not for the faint of heart. Like some women." His tone was cool, but his eyes were full of fire.

He was *still* flirting. Insufferable as well as incorrigible. If only he wasn't so compelling.

"Tastes like battery acid." Winter hoped that wasn't what he thought of her. She pried the sweetened latte that she was aching to drink from his grasp and shoved the turbocharged brew toward him, their fingers brushing in the exchange. Electricity traveled up her arm at the contact, and awareness sparked on his face, as though he'd experienced a similar jolt. "Why did you ask to meet over coffee when we could've spoken over the phone or at the barbecue Friday night if it had to be in person?"

"I have news, and I didn't want to be deprived of the look on your face when I shared it. I thought you might appreciate a heads-up that—"

Pop.

The sound was distinct. Unmistakable to a trained ear. Alarm streaked through her as shock swept over Chance's face.

People screamed behind her. Winter whirled around, and her gaze locked on a group standing outside Big Sky Fitness, shrieking and staring at the ground.

A body sprawled on the sidewalk. The woman in purple. Blood pooled beside her head.

Someone is shooting. Winter scanned the area. No gunman was in immediate sight.

"Get down!" She motioned frantically at everyone nearby. So many people out in the open. Dropping the coffee in her hand, she grabbed Chance's arm and tugged him low behind a parked vehicle.

Where is he? Where's the shooter?

"Get down! Now!" She instinctively drew her sidearm and then her cell phone to call it in.

Pop.

More screaming. People scattered, ducking and diving for cover.

But it was too late.

Chapter Two

Pop.

   Pop.

   Pop.

Gunfire echoed in the air. Bulbs from string lights burst. Storefront windows shattered.

Victims dropped like dolls onto the sidewalk. A young woman in purple Chance recognized—Lorelei...her surname escaped him. Then another woman in athletic attire with a long dark braid down her back. Killed, too. Next, a man, Ty Lee, hit in the leg and arm. Ty crawled to safety behind a parked van, leaving a trail of blood behind him.

Everything transpired simultaneously in a slipstream of chaos, in slow motion and at maximum velocity all at the same time.

Chance's heart jackhammered against his rib cage. His ears rang. His gaze bounced from a woman cowering behind a mailbox to another wearing a bright yellow dress lying on the ground beside a concrete planter—he knew her, Molly Finch—and then over to one of the dead bodies.

To the first person shot.

Lorelei.

Blood leaked from her head in a still-expanding pool, her eyes locked in a vacant expression. Across from her lay the other woman with the long braided hair. Shot in the chest, center mass.

"Attention all units," a dispatcher said over Winter's radio. "There's an active shooter on Main Street. Vicinity of Big Sky Fitness. DCI agent on the scene reported casualties. All units respond."

Chance couldn't tear his gaze away from the two dead women. Every nerve in his body pulsed with muted energy while a part of him was numb to the chaos and horror and death unfolding around him.

This was Bitterroot Falls, where things were quiet and slow. *Safe.*

He'd worked hard, doing his part to ensure public safety. Gone to considerable effort once—putting his life on the line, making himself bait and shedding blood to put away a bad guy who had been killing people not so long ago. Even that had been far removed from the center of town. Those murders had happened under the cover of darkness, in slaughterhouses scattered across the county.

Shootings on a busy street, in broad daylight, simply didn't happen here.

Winter spun in a crouched position. She eased up slowly, peered through the rear passenger window of the car beside them and looked around.

"What are you doing?" he asked.

"I need to find his position. See where the gunman is shooting from."

Chance wasn't risk averse. Sometimes you had to stick your neck out, literally. No one understood that better than him. But equally vital to one's survival was risk mitigation.

"You need to get down," he said, clamping a hand on the top of her head and forced her lower until she was completely shielded by the car door.

Pop! Glass rained on them as the car's rear window exploded. Their gazes collided, their faces nearly nose-to-nose. No hint of fear in her eyes. Only surprise. If he had hesitated for a second longer, the bullet would've killed her. He'd saved her life.

But no thanks came.

"I spotted a muzzle flash at the top of the hotel," she said. "Possibly from a room, I think. I need to get another look."

Chance cursed under his breath. "Progress," he muttered, half to himself.

"Huh?" She threw a confused glance at him. "What's progress?"

"Nothing," he said with a shake of his head. "The rooftop bar. It has a prime view of all Main Street." With the opening of the golf resort, the town council rushed the approval of the new hotel, with its swanky rooftop bar and heated infinity pool, calling the establishment progress. "The roof overhang provides cover, and the balcony has the perfect unobstructed line of sight to the street." Easier than getting into one of the sold-out rooms and breaking through the glass. "I would bet anything the gunman is there."

Movement on the sidewalk drew their attention.

The woman using a mailbox for cover leaped up out into the open and ran toward a store.

"No!" Chance cried out to her.

Pop.

A bullet struck her from behind with such force it spun her body 180 degrees, and she fell onto her back, the small gym bag in her hand dropping beside her. Still alive, she writhed on the pavement. Clutched her chest or her shoulder. He couldn't be sure at this angle.

"I need to get to the shooter and end this," Winter said.

What was she thinking? If they were right and the shooter

was at the top of the hotel, then the gunman had a clear advantage that made everyone within his line of sight an easy target.

Chance shook his head. "You already notified the police. We need to stay put until they arrive."

"I *am* the police."

Winter was prepared to run headlong into danger without caring for her own safety. He both admired and loathed such brazen boldness. "I mean you need to wait for backup."

Winter flattened her mouth in a grim line. "The longer I stay here, doing nothing, the more people could be killed or injured. There isn't time to wait for the Bitterroot Falls PD."

He couldn't deny it would take the BFPD at least ten minutes to arrive. The police station was clear on the other side of town. Logan was a detective on the force, and from what Chance knew of his schedule, the squad would have been in the middle of their morning muster, discussing the day ahead when the call came in. The closest SWAT unit, typically a necessity for this scenario, belonged to the county and was a ninety-minute drive away.

Chance took hold of her forearm and leaned close. "The sniper has got the high ground. Expose yourself again, and you could be the one killed or injured. You shouldn't try to apprehend him alone. It's less risky for you to hold off until the BFPD gets here and follow protocol." He might not be a cop, but he'd worked with enough to know about procedure.

"What if he wants to take out as many people as possible?" Her voice was calm yet firm. "When the ambulance arrives, the paramedics need to be able to help those people before they bleed out," she said, gesturing down the block at the wounded. "I have to do something. Now. Because if not me, then who?"

Winter was duty bound, sworn to protect and serve. Evidently, it was an oath she planned to keep no matter the personal cost. Even if it was her life. He understood all too well that level of commitment, embraced it himself and respected her for it, but they needed to weigh the options and make the smartest gamble.

A distant wail of sirens, still too far away. It was true, more lives could be lost in the next two minutes, let alone ten.

"I can't simply wait to do this by the book," she added. "More people might die. Better for him to shoot at me than pick off another innocent person. I need to take him down now."

As dangerous as her intention was and as much as he disliked it, Winter was right.

He met her determined gaze. "I'll go with you. Two moving targets are better than one." It might cause the shooter to hesitate long enough while he decided who to aim at first.

Winter rocked back on her heels. "You'll do no such thing. You're a civilian," she said, somehow making it sound like a dirty word. "If you want to help me, I could use a distraction. Something to refocus the shooter's attention, buying me enough time to get across the street without getting shot and without you endangering yourself."

That was a tall order. Why not ask him to pull a bunny from a magic hat while she was at it?

Chance hated the idea of her going after this guy on her own instead of waiting for units to arrive. He didn't want her to take such a risk, especially not on her own, but he couldn't stop her, either. Trying to change Winter's mind once she'd decided to do something was like trying to change the course of a Category 5 hurricane locked on a track set by mother nature.

Helping her was the only viable thing to do.

"A distraction. To keep you from getting shot." He nodded. "Okay. I can do that." *Think. Think.* Quick problem-solving was a hidden talent of his, one he needed now more than ever. Then an idea came to him—along with all the possible tactical errors that could get either of them killed. "Give me your car keys." He held out his hand.

Throwing a puzzled look at him, she dug her key fob out from her pocket and dropped it in his palm. "What are you going to do?"

No time to explain all the pieces of his plan. She simply had to trust him. Besides, she wouldn't like the part where he needed to make himself a moving target. Winter needed to reach the shooter without getting injured herself. The whole point of the diversion was for her to be able to take the sniper out. This was the only way to give her the best odds of crossing the street unscathed.

Chance was nothing if not a man of his word.

"Get ready to run." Panic shot a jolt of adrenaline through him. "On the count of three."

She scooted around him, drawing close—their bodies brushing in a way he had imagined many times but not under these circumstances—and repositioned herself toward the front of the car. Giving him a steely glance over her shoulder, she nodded to him to go ahead.

This had better work. Not only for both their sakes, but for everyone pinned down on Main Street.

He whipped out his own car keys. Hopeful as he might be in pulling this off, he had to consider the price of miscalculation, which meant that he had to be willing to sacrifice to achieve this goal.

"One," he said, beginning the countdown. "Two. Three." Hitting the alarm on her key fob first, he caused the lights on her vehicle to flash as the horn beeped down the street.

At the same time, Winter rushed out from behind the car.

Chance pressed the button on his keys next, setting off the

alarm on his truck parked farther down Main Street, in the opposite direction from where Winter had taken off.

A cold knot formed in the pit of his stomach as he bolted from the safety of cover, exposing himself, too.

Chapter Three

Running flat out, Winter shoved from her mind any thought of dying or the pain of being shot. The only thing that mattered was being as fast as possible.

Pop. Pop.

More gunshots.

No bullets hit her. None even came anywhere close. Chance's distraction was working. With the last round the sniper got off, she confirmed his location was indeed the rooftop balcony.

Winter made it across the street. Even after she knew for certain she was out of the gunman's line of sight, she still didn't slow down. She kept going, heading straight for the hotel.

Shooting from the rooftop bar made it easier to pinpoint the sniper, and it also made her wonder if his plan was suicide by cop. Maybe he wanted to go out with fanfare after killing only goodness knew how many others first.

Steady gunfire continued, directed across the road.

Winter glanced over at the other side of Main Street and faltered to a stop. Chance was running. Darting from one car to another. Making himself a visible target each time he moved.

No, no, no, no.

Concrete burst up from the sidewalk each time the gunman shot at him. Then a bullet struck Chance's hat, knocking the Stetson clear off his head.

Fear tightened her chest. Every life mattered out there, but Chance was different because of her sister. Logan was important to Summer and, by extension of the brotherly bond, so was Chance. That made both men important to Winter.

Chance ducked down behind a white sedan.

What was he doing? Why was he taking the risk of changing positions?

With a chill she remembered his words. *Two moving targets are better than one.*

Her heart sank. He was making himself a target, going through with his dangerous idea after she'd told him in no uncertain terms not to.

"Pigheaded. Stubborn," Winter muttered under her breath. She had asked for a distraction, needed his help, but not at the cost of putting him in jeopardy. The last thing she wanted was for him to be added to the list of casualties because of her.

Chance scurried from the sedan to the cover of a van, where a man had been wounded. Maybe he'd gone over to help him.

Right now, there was nothing she could do for Chance or the injured, other than reach the shooter and put an end to this assault. She had to make the most of the opportunity Chance had given her and ensure it was worth the risk.

Winter bolted down the street. She recalled a commercial for the hotel, featuring the rooftop bar. There was a large indoor portion that could be used year-round, but the balcony was spacious and even had a pool. It provided overhead cover and concealment making it the perfect sniper's nest.

Reaching the hotel on the corner of the block, she passed the sign welcoming people to the GCSA meeting and trade show, which was already underway. She yanked open the door and raced inside.

The lobby was filled with a stunned, murmuring crowd. She hurried through the throng, parting it in front of her with quick controlled sweeps of her gun hand, but she was moving too slowly. "Police! Make a hole!"

The sea of people split apart for her. She scanned the crowd, left and right. A hundred people easily, some with suitcases, duffels and golf bags. A shooter could slip out unnoticed among the attendees, hiding his weapon in luggage or a golf bag if suicide wasn't his end goal. The GCSA's big event was the perfect cover.

Was this shooting spree an act of an unhinged person who had snapped, or had this been planned far in advance?

Winter hustled to the bank of elevators and stabbed the call button, hoping it would be faster than the stairs. She grabbed her radio. "This is DCI Agent Stratton. Shooter is on the top of the Bitterroot Mountain Hotel! Rooftop bar. Heading there now. Request backup!"

With a chime, a set of doors opened. "I repeat," she said, jumping inside the elevator car and hitting the button for the upper-level bar, "the shooter is on the top of the hotel. Lock it down! No one leaves."

On the ride up to the fifth floor, she switched off her radio and silenced her cell phone. She'd seen a fellow officer take a bullet once when they crept up on a perp, and her partner's radio gave away his position. From what she'd seen in the advertisements, the indoor portion of the bar looked large enough to act as a buffer between the balcony, masking the audible signal of the elevator. With the element of surprise on her side, she wasn't going to waste the small advantage that was working in her favor.

What she wouldn't give to have her ballistic body armor

strapped to her chest. Instead, both of her vests, each with a level-four chest plate, were stuck in the back of her Bronco.

Sweat beaded her brow and trickled down her spine. She held her Glock in a two-handed grip and took a deep, fortifying breath. Her gaze bounced to the reflection in the shiny door of the hotel's slogan etched across the back wall of the car in bold white print: Untamed Adventures Await.

A soft chime dinged, and the doors opened onto the top floor. Adrenaline surged harder in her veins.

Stepping off the elevator, Winter scanned her surroundings. A sign pointed in the direction of the restrooms at the end of a quiet corridor beyond the stairwell. There was only one way in and out of the bar directly in front of her.

All the glass was intact; nothing had been smashed to break in. She tried the door.

Unlocked.

Winter opened the plate-glass door and crept into the enclosed portion of the bar that could be used year-round.

The indoor space was square with glass walls, and the wide, spacious balcony wrapped around the bar in a U, offering plenty of tables and chairs for lounging. Breathtaking panoramic views of the mountains, almost completely unobstructed, were visible from the rooftop. A few stone pillars lined the covered balcony, each a potential hiding spot that could conceal a person from view inside the bar, while still offering enough room to take aim with a rifle. Three doors led out to the expansive balcony.

Winter stood for a second and scanned the area in a full circle. From the center of the balcony all the way to the left corner of the U would've given the best line of sight to Main Street. The opposite side had a sizable pool and ran adjacent to an intersecting road.

She moved forward, keeping her head on a swivel. Pushing through the center door, she stepped outside. A strong gust of cold wind sent a slight shiver over her as the door softly closed shut. She hesitated, then proceeded to the left. Looked back over her shoulder. No sign of anyone lurking behind her.

Although the balcony was open air, the fire pits and the roof overhang that offered some shelter from the elements would make this a popular hangout spot in town one day.

Coming up on one of the stone pillars, she strode past a fire pit and chairs. Peered between the column and the glass balustrade with the steel railing, an optimal place for a shooter to be positioned.

Nothing. But she knew he was here...somewhere. Not only did the rooftop bar make the most sense—and she'd seen muzzle flashes from the top floor—but she felt it in her bones that he was still there.

Glancing around, she listened for any sound, the slightest movement.

Besides the whisper of wind and her heartbeat in her ears, there was only eerie silence.

No gunfire.

The shooter had ceased firing. Was he reloading? Did he stop because he had already hit every visible target below on the street?

Chance. Had he taken a bullet while she was in the elevator?

As quickly as the thought of him injured, bleeding or worse popped into her head, she blocked it out. Worry blurred the mind, not the kind of distraction she could afford. Chance was fast. Smart. Good fortune probably shone on him every day of his privileged life. People like him always had luck on their side.

Winter had to believe he was all right.

SO MUCH BLOOD.

There was so much blood, too much blood flowing from the wound in front of him. Chance had seized the moment to help the injured, starting with Ty.

Chance stared down at him. Ty had taken two slugs. Deep purple circles had developed beneath his eyes, and his skin was pale. Blood soaked his cycling pants and covered the sidewalk by his leg. Chance couldn't be sure if a main artery had been hit, or if Ty would be all right by the time paramedics arrived. A nick in the femoral artery could kill a person faster than some shots to the chest.

Either way, Chance had to do something to stop the bleeding or at the very least, slow it down. He unbuckled his belt, whipped the strap free from the loops of his jeans and wrapped it around the man's thigh. About two inches above the gunshot wound.

"I've got to tighten it, and it's going to hurt," Chance said, warning him that his pain factor was about to increase dramatically.

"O-okay," Ty said, trembling, probably on the verge of shock.

Chance slipped the belt through the buckle. "Here we go." He yanked on the leather strap, tightening it.

The man grunted but didn't scream as Chance secured the belt around the guy's leg. The improvised tourniquet wasn't ideal, but it would have to do until medical help arrived.

Chance took Ty's hand, lifted it to his arm and placed the palm over the gunshot wound. "Apply pressure to slow the bleeding," he said.

Ty nodded, clamping his hand down, and winced with a groan.

Sirens were drawing closer. Help would be there within minutes.

Chance realized there hadn't been any gunshots for several long seconds. Minutes even. *Winter.* She must've made it to the roof by now. Had she caught the guy?

He darted his gaze around and spotted the hat that had been shot off his head. Saw the hole through the top, mere inches from where his skull had been.

A close call. He had gotten lucky. *Very lucky.*

Main Street, bustling with activity only minutes ago, now appeared deserted aside from those stuck on the sidewalk where the shooter had been aiming.

An agonized scream echoed from down the block near the fitness center. He looked at the woman in the middle of the sidewalk, squirming in pain. He didn't know her name, but he had seen her around town, volunteering at charity events and helping out at the senior center. A nice woman, always with a smile, a little shy, but a kind soul.

She was losing a lot of blood. Perhaps if he was quick enough to reach her, he could help.

Movement from the corner of his eye drew his attention. Molly, the hostess at the Wolverine Lodge, lay flat on the ground behind a concrete planter nearby. She lowered her hands that had been clasped to her ears, raised her head and glanced around. Then she jumped up and rushed toward a store, running in high heels. A moving target in a bright yellow dress.

Impossible for a sniper to miss.

Yet, Molly made it inside the boutique. Not a single shot fired.

Maybe it was over.

Chance's gaze fell back to the other woman lying on the sidewalk. She was in urgent need of medical aid.

Not giving any thought to the statistical odds of taking a bullet, Chance patted Ty's arm and left him. He hurried to the injured woman despite the risk that perhaps the shooter had shown the lady in the yellow dress mercy that might not be given to him.

Taking a knee at the wounded woman's side, he looked down at her. "What's your name?"

Blood oozed from the gunshot in her shoulder. Thank goodness it wasn't in her chest and had missed her collarbone.

"N-Nora. Nora Santana. H-help. Help me," she said. Her cheeks were hollowed out, her light brown skin taking on a gray pallor from fear and blood loss. Tears leaked from her eyes.

Chance grabbed her gym bag, unzipped it and rifled through it until he found a towel inside. He pressed it to the wound. "You're going to be okay, Nora," he reassured her, replacing his hand with hers on the towel. "No vital organs were hit, and the bullet missed any bones."

As long as there was no more gunfire, they were both going to be okay.

Chance pivoted on his knee toward the hotel. He looked up at the rooftop bar and scoured the balcony for any sign of the sniper or Winter. He scanned for any sort of movement at all.

Light glinted, redirecting his gaze.

Then he saw him. The shooter.

Oh, no!

Then he spotted Winter, her gun leading her steps as she searched the rooftop. She wouldn't see the sniper. Not where he was positioned.

Whipping out his cell phone, Chance scrambled to his feet and took off running toward the hotel. He dialed her number as he bolted across the road. Her phone went straight to voicemail, and he cursed.

A blaze of red-and-blue flashing lights atop a line of cruisers zoomed down Main Street, but it would still take them a minute or two to reach the hotel. Time Winter didn't have.

She was in trouble.

WHERE ARE YOU?

Winter looked back over her shoulder. There was nothing by the pillars down the right side of the balcony. Turning around, she continued forward, sweeping left and right. Staying vigilant.

She spotted something up ahead, three pillars down, in the left corner. It was black and long and sleek. A golf bag on the ground tucked behind the column. Above it, draped on the railing, was a small navy blue bean bag, like one used to play cornhole.

The shooter must have used one to balance and steady his rifle. It was an excellent position to set up, take aim and pick people off one by one, easy prey.

But no sniper.

Another glance around full circle. Still no one. Where was he? Hiding?

Her heart thudded, body tingling. She'd been quiet, careful not to alert him to her presence. Winter thought back to when she had gotten off the elevator. Not a single gunshot since she reached the rooftop bar.

Had he abandoned his weapon and taken the stairs? Had she just missed him?

Don't doubt yourself, Stratton. Always listen to the inner voice. Training and experience had taught her that the hard way.

He's here. Somewhere.

She still couldn't see the back side of the pillar in the left corner from this angle.

Sirens grew louder. Maybe another two minutes before backup arrived at the hotel and then two more to reach the top floor, she estimated.

Weapon at the ready, she moved down the balcony, keeping the railing to her back. Gun trained in the vicinity of the golf bag. She eased farther down the balcony, still scanning the indoor portion of the bar through the glass walls. Another glance over her shoulder, checking her six.

Nothing stirred.

Winter drew closer to the black golf bag, creeping up to the stone column. She swung around to the other side of the pillar.

No one.

"All units be advised," said the dispatcher, voice low and crackly over a radio.

Behind her.

Winter whipped around at the same instant a man lowered himself from the eave—a wire from earbuds that had been connected to a radio on his hip hung loose. Holding onto the roof overhang, he swung forward, kicking her in the side.

Her breath left her lungs in a harsh rush. The blow was brutal, propelling her back into the pillar, arms flailing. Her head slammed against the stone. Pain roared through her skull, and the gun slipped from her grip.

The Glock landed on the tile floor, skidding away from her, as the shooter's feet touched down. A camo balaclava covered his face. He wore gloves and nondescript clothes, jeans and a long sleeve Henley.

Excruciating pain tore through her side when she struggled to catch her breath, her vision blurring. She couldn't be sure, but she guessed a few of her ribs might be broken.

The man grabbed the rifle slung over his shoulder. There was barely enough space between them for him to use it. She certainly wasn't about to give him any room to get a shot off at her.

Screaming in agony and white-hot anger, she closed the distance separating them and lunged at him.

"The shooter must've climbed up onto the roof overhang for some reason," Chance said to Logan over the phone in the hotel elevator, watching the numbers illuminate as the car ascended. "He was peering over the side. The sniper could see Winter, I'm sure of it, but I doubt she would've been able to see him." Or had any idea that she was being watched from the eaves.

"We'll be pulling up any second. Stay put!"

Everyone kept trying to tell him what to do as though they knew better. Chance was sick of it. Yeah, he wasn't a cop, but he'd worked on his fair share of hazardous cases. Understood the dangers of his actions as well as how to minimize the risks. All a part of the job. He even consulted for the BFPD on occasion after he'd caught a nasty perp who had eluded the authorities. He could trade battle stories and scars with the best of them.

"That's not an option. Just hurry up," Chance said and disconnected, shoving his phone back into his pocket.

Ding. The elevator opened.

Chance ran from the car and raced into the rooftop bar. His gaze flew to two individuals wrestling outside on the balcony, and his blood ran cold.

Winter was in the fight of her life with the shooter.

The masked sniper rammed the butt of his rifle into Winter's abdomen. She doubled over, grabbing her midsection.

Chance rushed through the bar. Bolting to the door on the left side, he burst outside.

Both Winter and the sniper caught sight of him. The assailant shoved her into a table, then ducked, grabbing something from the ground. A black golf bag.

Winter spun and punched the shooter in the face with the blunt part of her forearm. It was a hard hit thrown with so much momentum from her body that it sent the guy staggering back.

His pulse going into overdrive, Chance charged down the balcony toward them, desperately trying to reach her.

Winter swung another punch. But the shooter raised his knee and threw a powerful kick into her stomach. The impact of the blow propelled her backward with such violent force it pitched her over the side of the balcony.

No!

Chapter Four

Winter snatched hold of the balcony's railing, saving herself from a five-story drop to the ground, but a blinding pain sliced through her. Spots danced in her eyes for a second and faded, her vision clearing. She saw the sniper running into the indoor part of the bar. He was heading back into the hotel.

Her left hand slipped, and she hissed from the agony wrenching through her side. The grip of her other hand began to give out. She struggled to plant her feet on the brick wall and pull herself up when a strong, warm palm seized hold of her wrist.

"I've got you," Chance said, his face etched with worry.

"Has anyone ever told you that you have perfect timing?"

"As a matter of fact, yes."

Of course.

Chance hauled her up to the top of the glass balustrade. Wrapping an arm around her waist, he helped her climb over the side.

Wincing in pain, she put a hand to her side.

"Are you all right?"

She doubted it, but it wasn't anything that painkillers wouldn't ease. Meeting his gaze, she pressed her other hand to his chest and took a second to catch her breath. "Thank you," she said, not answering his question.

"Here to help whenever you need it."

She realized his arm was still wrapped around her, holding her a little too close. "Come on." She pulled away from him. "Let's go." Taking off after the sniper, Winter grabbed her radio. "This is DCI Agent Stratton. The suspect has fled the rooftop bar, carrying a sniper rifle and a black canvas golf bag. Be on the lookout for a white male. Between five ten and six two. Light-colored eyes, possibly green or blue." Everything had happened so fast. She couldn't be certain of his height or eye color. The best she could do was get them a range. "Dark wash jeans. Black long sleeve Henley. Steel-toe boots. Cover the elevator and stairs. Make sure the hotel is locked down. Be advised, he has a police scanner."

They reached the doors to the rooftop bar, and she headed for the stairs. Doubtful the perp had taken the elevator.

Chance caught her by the arm and turned her around. "I'll take the stairs. You take the elevator." Before she could protest, he added, "You're hurt." He flicked a glance down at her side. "No time to argue."

"If you find him, call it in." She handed him her radio. "Don't be a hero and try to take him on yourself."

"I'll leave the heroics to you." He winked and shoved through the stairwell door.

She hit the elevator call button, and the doors opened immediately. She rode down to the lobby, now swarming with cops.

Winter spied Logan pushing his way through the crowd while uniformed officers fanned out. He spotted her and made a beeline in her direction.

Logan put a hand on her shoulder. "You okay?"

"The shooter got away from me. Did you lock down the hotel?"

"We're in the process."

She heaved a sigh. The perp might've already slipped through their fingers.

"Where's Chance?" Logan asked. "I thought he'd be with you."

"He was." A good thing, too. Not once but twice today, he'd been there, looking out for her when she needed him. "He's taking the stairs." She headed toward the stairwell.

Logan walked alongside her. "I've got officers headed up to the top floor."

The door to the stairs opened. Chance came out and looked between them. "No sign of our guy. I didn't hear anyone running down. He might've gotten off on one of the floors and used a different staircase."

"Officers are positioning to cover all of them," Logan said.

Winter subtly pressed her arm to her side, not wanting to draw attention to her pain. "We need to get to the security office. Take a look at the playback on the surveillance footage. See where he went."

"The chief should be there now." Logan led the way.

"Hey," Chance said to her. "We can handle surveillance footage. You should let the EMTs check you out." His gaze dropped to the side she was favoring.

Guess she wasn't subtle enough. "They've got their hands full with people who have been shot. I'm fine."

"You're not."

"Did you get injured?" Logan asked, passing the front desk and turning down a corridor.

"Nothing serious." She flashed Chance a stern look. "It can wait, so drop it."

"Okay. I will," Chance said, much to her surprise. "Provided you agree to go to the hospital and get properly examined. Today."

There were always provisions of some kind with him. Lawyers.

"A trip to the emergency room is going to suck up hours of my time that would be better spent elsewhere." There was little the hospital would do for her if her ribs were broken. No issues with her breathing, so she didn't have a punctured lung. A doctor would only prescribe rest, ice and breathing exercises. Locating the shooter and bringing him to justice took priority.

Calls started coming in over the radio, all reporting the same. Officers had cleared their respective areas, and no one had seen the suspect.

They reached the security room that was abuzz with activity. Logan went inside, but Chance hurried around in front of Winter and put his arm up, blocking the doorway. "I can be an ally going in there. All you have to do is agree to get checked out before going home today. Or I can make things difficult."

"You're not law enforcement," she said. IPS provided security, investigative and intelligence solutions; that didn't make him a cop or qualified to be involved any further in this. "You shouldn't even be allowed to set foot inside that room." She gestured to the security office.

"I have a working relationship with the chief of police. We're on a first-name basis. You can't say the same." A sly grin tugged at his mouth that irked her more than she cared to admit. "From what I know of you, you're going to want this case to be yours," he said, lowering his voice, "not the BFPD's. But as a heads-up, the chief has a history of not playing well with the DOJ DCI. You won't get jurisdiction on this without his approval. That's something I can make happen for you."

The DCI major case section handled homicides and other felony violent crimes, if they crossed county lines. Which this incident did not. Or when the city, county or state requested DCI assistance.

"The shooter might be pinned down somewhere inside the hotel," she said, "which would make this discussion either premature or moot."

"I'm a gambling man, and I'm hedging my bet that it's neither. I think it's relevant. Presently."

There was no way she wasn't working on this and going after that shooter. "Logan will help me."

Chance shook his head. "Not when I tell him it'll get him in trouble with Summer. Don't think I won't bring her into this. I have no desire to worry or upset your sister, but I will if necessary."

Her little sister would call her nonstop and then show up at her house and push and pester until Winter took the time to take care of herself. One of the items on her to-do list when she moved here in the first place.

"I know you mean well," she said. His heart was in the right place, and nothing he had asked of her was unreasonable. "But I don't like your tactics, and I don't respond well to threats."

"I'm an acquired taste, too. You'll get used to it."

Winter didn't appreciate being backed into a corner. In Texas, there were two approaches to this kind of situation: survival or surrender. She was a survivor who had never been good at capitulation.

"I prefer us as allies instead of adversaries," Chance said. "Especially when I'm only trying to help you. You go to the hospital. Today. Do we have a deal?"

"We do." She decided this wasn't a concession since she intended to be seen by a doctor. Only his way, it'd be sooner rather than later. "But for future reference, I also don't like being told what to do."

"Well, that's something we have in common." He stepped aside, letting her enter the security room. "And commonalities build bridges. We've got to start somewhere. Right?"

She walked past him into the security office. The room was hot and stuffy, crowded with too many anxious bodies. She squeezed through the group and pressed in on those gathered around the security cameras, trying to get a peek at the screens.

"Ed," Chance said, clasping a hand on an older man's shoulder, "I'd like you to meet someone. This is DCI Agent Winter Stratton. She's the one who called in about the shooter."

The uniformed man turned, facing her. He was burly, barrel-chested, and his salt-and-pepper buzz cut contrasted with his ruddy complexion. "Edgar Macon, chief of police." He gave a curt nod in her direction. No handshake was offered.

"What's the status?" Winter asked. "Did we find him?"

"Afraid not." With a sigh, Logan shook his head. "The sniper left the stairwell on the third floor." He waved her and Chase over to look at the screen. "Play back the footage."

A security guard did as he requested. The monitor showed the shooter leaving the stairs, the rifle slung over one shoulder and the golf bag on the other.

The guard hit a button, toggling to different footage. Third floor hallway. The perp unzipped the golf bag, slid the rifle inside and pulled something else out. A garment. Quickly, he plugged the earbuds into the police scanner clipped on his waist. Then he turned and started putting on the garment.

"He positioned his back to the camera," she said. "He knew where they were located. What's he putting on? Coveralls?"

"Yeah." The guard seated at the control panel gave a nod. "The same kind the custodians wear."

After the shooter pushed the balaclava back off his head and down to his neck, he slipped on a ball cap and hustled along the hall to the service stairwell, keeping his head lowered. She caught a glimpse of his side profile. All she could make out was that he was clean-shaven.

"Where is he now?" she asked.

Logan looked up at her with a grim expression.

"He made his way to the basement," Chief Macon said, "walked by numerous hotel employees, including security, without being stopped. Got out through the service entrance before we could lock it down."

"Can we see his face at all from any of the cameras?" she asked.

"No, but we're going to go over the footage again slowly," Macon said.

"What about CCTV outside the hotel?" She glanced between the chief and Logan. "We should be able to track him."

"This isn't San Antonio," Logan said. "It's a small town. There's one tenth of the coverage here that you're used to. The camera coverage is so limited you can google to see where they're located. Not hard to avoid if you're trying. We'll go over any available footage from traffic cameras and surveillance systems in the area, but this guy looks like he knows what he's doing. If he wanted to steer clear of CCTV, it wouldn't be difficult to do. I wouldn't count on us getting much."

Defeat was a bitter taste in her mouth.

Chance had an *I told you so* expression. She couldn't look at him. At his handsome face when he made it so obvious he knew he was right.

Winter gritted her teeth. "This case should be mine." Better to get it sorted straight away. "I not only witnessed what he did, I tangled with him."

"I could partner up with her on this, Chief," Logan offered. She was grateful to have his immediate support.

"This case belongs to the BFPD, and there's no need for us to partner with another agency," Macon said, putting his fists on his hips. "As for you, Powell, you're already working a murder case. We've got one woman strangled. I don't want there to be a second. Griffin is bogged down with those robberies. I'll put Keneke on this."

She followed the gazes to a rail-thin guy in plain clothes standing in the corner, who perked up. He looked no older than twenty with one of those baby faces. Sweat beaded his forehead, and nerves etched across his smooth skin as he stared at them like a deer in headlights. She presumed he was Keneke.

Great.

Logan frowned and lowered his head.

"Ed." Chance put his hand on the older man's shoulder again. "Can Agent Stratton and I have a word with you in the hallway? It won't take long."

Wariness filled the chief's face, but Macon stepped out of the room. Winter and Chance trailed behind him and closed the door.

"Keneke? Your nephew?" Chance raised both eyebrows. "He's green as grass. When did he make detective? A week ago?"

"He hasn't officially made detective yet, but he's the best I've got available."

Chance kept his expression surprisingly neutral. "I think this one might be out of his depth."

Macon pursed his lips. "The kid has to cut his teeth on something. May as well be now."

"You need the DCI on this case," Chance said. "You need Agent Stratton."

"Really? Based on my experience, I'm better off not getting involved with DCI, and I know nothing about her," Macon said, gesturing in her direction with his head. He scrutinized her from head to toe like she couldn't hear or see him. "Give me one good reason I need the DCI. Or her."

Chance turned to her with a look that said *you're up*.

"I have fourteen years of experience, in CID, the army's

criminal investigation division and as a homicide detective with the San Antonio PD," she said, immediately wishing she hadn't given such a knee-jerk response. Starting with her résumé like she was on a job interview? This power dynamic was messing with her head. "Not to mention DCI resources. Forensics. Our lab is more robust and can process ballistics, prints and anything else we turn up, faster. What will take you days, possibly even weeks, will take us hours." That was if she pleaded and promised to owe the right person a favor or two.

"This is precisely one of the problems I have with the DCI. Flaunting your resources in our faces." Macon waved his hands around. "You saw the carnage out there firsthand. You should offer the use of your lab, no strings attached."

Her temper stirred, but getting defensive would accomplish nothing.

"We both know that's not how it works," Chance said. "Look, handing this off to Stratton saves you the hassle of dealing with the press. This mass shooting is going to get national coverage. National scrutiny. Every news channel in the country is going to descend like vultures, and it's only a matter of time before they learn about the strangler on the loose, too. You don't need nor do you want that kind of headache."

Chief Macon nodded, considering. "But if she takes over," he said, aiming a meaty finger at her, "I can't count on reliable updates. I need to be able to answer the mayor's questions about this case. Every time I've worked with DCI, my department has either been burned or buried. Happened to me one too many times for me to trust otherwise."

She had little patience for a game of jurisdictional tug-of-war. There was a mass shooter on the loose, who could very well strike again. Getting him before he had an opportunity to take more lives was all that truly mattered.

"Then don't trust DCI," Chance said, and she stared at him in surprise. "Trust me instead. I'll work with her on the case. As a consultant for the BFPD, seeing to your interests. You'll get daily updates from me personally, and you know that if you call my cell, I'll answer. Stratton and I will be attached at the hip."

Winter narrowed her eyes at Chance and mouthed, *What?*

"True, I can count on you. You've earned my trust in blood, and I won't soon forget it." Still, Macon deliberated as he rubbed his chin. "But the DCI will take all the credit."

She folded her arms and bit her tongue. A sniper just shot up Main Street, killing two people and wounding others, and the chief was worried about who was going to take credit for a collar. She kept her temper in check because it would serve no purpose to become angry. Cooperation was the goal, not contention, she reminded herself.

"That won't happen," Chance said. "When we catch this guy, the DCI will have done it with the assistance of a BFPD consultant. If for some reason we don't—"

"I don't fail." Cutting him off, Winter looked pointedly at both men.

"—the failure will fall on the DCI and Ironside Protection Services," he continued. "Not the Bitterroot Falls PD."

Chance didn't want anything for himself or his business and was willing to share the blame if the case turned cold.

"She won't agree to that," Macon scoffed.

"Why not?" Chance countered. "The woman just told us that she doesn't fail, which means she has nothing to worry about. Isn't that right, Agent Stratton?"

Winter did have to admit she liked this little superpower of Chance's when he wasn't using it against her. "That's right." She might not be well-versed in PR tactics, but even she understood how to extend an olive branch and establish a smooth working relationship. "We'll all share a win, DCI,

BFPD and IPS. On the other hand, if things go south, I'll own any failure." She offered her hand. "Only the DCI."

She didn't want any negative fallout to land on Chance or the IPS office.

Macon looked down at her palm, hesitating, but then he shook it. "I'll reach out to your boss, Isaacson, and make it official. I'm looking forward to his response once he finds out what you agreed to. You're about to find out you're fairly green yourself to the way the DCI operates, but I'm sure Isaacson will soon give you a fire-hose-style education." He turned to leave, but then reconsidered. "A bit of advice for you when it comes to the press, Agent Stratton. Less is more." Macon went back into the security office, leaving them in the hall.

Winter abhorred talking to reporters. When dealing with them, she turned brevity into an art form, but she would make any sacrifice if it meant this case was hers and she got to go after the shooter. Even if it meant taking the ire of her boss, Joe Isaacson.

"I'd say that went well," Chance said, looking entirely too pleased with himself. "Objective achieved. The case is yours. Or rather, ours."

"You were slick. Silver-tongued. Sly."

"I prefer smooth, persuasive, effective," he said, and she believed he was all of the above. "Minor adjustment in adjectives but significant impact in connotation, which is important as we move forward since we'll be working together as partners."

"We're not partners."

"Two people working so closely together they become a singular driving force with one goal." Chance stepped closer, oozing confidence that reeled her in. "Slap whatever label on it that makes you happy."

There was no denying he was witty. Charming. Smol-deringly good-looking and smart. Not simply book-smart but also street-smart, a hard-to-find combination. The entire Chance Reyes package was the problem. She'd been through hell and back when it came to clever, charismatic, smooth talkers. Her ex-husband was only the most recent disaster. Winter didn't want to box herself into having a type, but all the men she'd been attracted to in the past had distinct simi-larities that inevitably led to heartbreak.

The idea of repeating the same mistake with Chance, a man she couldn't easily escape, put her on the verge of break-ing out into hives.

"Associate. That label is acceptable," she said. Nothing scared her, except everything about Chance. Especially this arrangement, where they might be stuck working side by side for days or weeks. Downright terrifying. "I need to make one thing clear. If this ploy of yours impedes—"

"Settle down," he said, raising a palm, his voice soothing. "I don't hinder. I facilitate. You got what you wanted, even if the conditions aren't what you expected. Correct?"

"Well, yes."

"Because of me."

She took a deep breath and winced. Not only from the pain in her side but also because he was right. "Yes."

He lifted both brows and cocked his head to the side like he was waiting for something.

"Thank you," she said.

"You're welcome."

"What was Chief Macon referring to when he said you'd earned his trust in blood?"

"A case I worked. My first here. Old news." Chance waved a dismissive hand. "Listen, we both have skin in the game. Not only did the sniper nearly take my head off and hurt the people of a town I love, but the reputation of IPS is on the line here. Okay?"

They were both invested in getting this guy, which was what she needed to hear. "Okay."

"Now, let's get to work, Agent Stratton, and catch a killer."

Chapter Five

The clock on the dash of his truck read ten fifty by the time Chance reached Winter's house. He pulled into her driveway, lined with mature trees on each side. Approaching the cute farmhouse, he noticed the lights through the front bay window. The curtains were drawn, but it looked like she was awake.

Part of him knew he shouldn't be there. Probably better for him to simply go home. Where he belonged. It was late, he was beyond exhausted, his thoughts leaned far closer to inappropriate than professional, and Winter was going to be annoyed to see him after he'd wrangled his way onto her case. But he'd been thinking about her since late afternoon. They had separated, him to do legwork of interviewing witnesses at the hotel while she dropped off evidence at the DCI lab in Missoula and then went to the hospital to be examined.

Somehow on his way home, he'd convinced himself that this deviation from his normal route was a good idea.

Good mixed with bad.

Mostly bad.

Chance parked and strode up to her door, his gun still holstered at his hip since he'd been officially put on the case. Usually, the only weapon he had on him was his pocketknife. The one tool every rancher universally carried.

The exterior looked a little different from the last time he'd been there. She'd installed floodlights and freshened up her landscape, pruning the overgrown shrubs and adding the plants he'd recommended to brighten things up. Rocky Mountain columbine, bunchberry dogwood, clematis in bloom now with a second flush, fringed sage and bitterroot.

Through the door, he heard a television. The news. Winter's statement to reporters, one she'd kept tight and to the point, had already aired a couple of times. He rapped on the door and waited and waited.

She finally answered, opening the door, and his pulse spiked. He hadn't given any thought as to what to expect, other than irritation from her. It certainly wasn't for her to be half dressed.

"Do you always answer the door at night wearing hardly anything?" If so, he'd stop by unannounced more often.

Her hair was free from the usual ponytail, hanging in loose curls around her shoulders. She only wore a sports bra and a tiny pair of shorts that revealed plenty of tantalizing skin.

"It's not a big deal unless you make it one." She stood with half her body obscured by the door. "I wear the same thing when I work out if it's hot."

Hot was precisely how she looked. He frowned at her. "You didn't even bother to ask who it was."

"I knew it was you. You have a distinctive knock. Two raps hard, one light, all in quick succession. You never ring the bell."

A habit he'd change, but for her to determine who was at the door based solely on the type of knock struck him as odd for her. She was always so safety conscious.

"What are you doing here?" Her tone carried far more patience than he'd anticipated.

He stood at the threshold, hoping for an invitation inside.

"Came to see how you're feeling." He noticed her midsection wasn't bandaged. "Find out what the doctor had to say."

She searched his face. "You could've accomplished that with a phone call. Would've been easier. Faster, too."

Opting for fast and easy wasn't the way he was built. Maybe that was why he was drawn to Winter. She was neither. "If I had called, then I wouldn't have the pleasure of your company."

Shaking her head, she was visibly annoyed, but she stepped back, letting him in. Then she closed the door and faced him. The right side of her abdomen that had been shielded by the door was mottled purple.

"Oh my God." Clutching her arm, he took a closer look at her torso. Anger welled in his chest. He brushed her hair back from her face with his other hand. Grasping her chin between his fingers, he examined her cheek. A small cut below her eye, and a bruise was forming on the side of her face. By tomorrow, it would be black and blue. The sight of her injuries made him want to punch something.

"It looks worse than it feels."

He doubted that. "What did the doctor say?"

"My lower ribs are bruised." She clutched her side. "The doctor told me I'm lucky they weren't fractured. No other damage. No internal bleeding. Rest. Ice. Breathing exercises. And these." She lifted a medicine bottle she was holding and shook it, rattling the pills inside. "I was debating whether to take one when you knocked. I've decided to pour myself a drink instead." She hiked a thumb over her shoulder toward the kitchen, where a bottle of amber liquid sat on the granite countertop beside a glass tumbler and an ice pack. "Want one?"

His answer should be a firm *no*. He didn't need anything loosening his inhibitions tonight. Then he raked his gaze over her svelte body. Lean, toned muscles. Flat stomach. Mouth-watering curves that tempted him to abandon any professional objectives.

"What are you drinking?" he asked.

"Whiskey."

Winter, all that exposed golden brown skin, plus whiskey might be a recipe for disaster.

A beautiful, sexy disaster he'd never forget.

"You should replace your front door with one that has a peephole," he said, stroking her cheek, and realized he was still touching her.

She stepped back, breaking the contact. "A new door would be a pricey, unnecessary expense. I've already spent plenty on the move up here, buying the house and with constant repairs. Besides, I saw you pulling up the driveway through the curtains just fine," she said, and that sounded more like her. "Give me a minute, okay."

"Sure."

She headed toward the back of the house barefoot and ducked into the primary bedroom.

He glanced around her house.

Winter still didn't have any art or family photos up on the wall yet, but the place finally had furniture. Modestly decorated in a soothing color palette. There was something curated and reminiscent about it, as though she'd plucked things from a catalog. He doubted she had the patience to do all the shopping this cozy setup would require. When Chance and Logan had offloaded her moving container from Texas, there hadn't been a single piece of furniture. Only clothes and boxes of books and utilitarian stuff like cookware, kitchen appliances, and cleaning supplies. He'd figured she didn't want reminders of her old life contaminating the new.

Everyone deserved a fresh start. He was happy to do what he could for her, even though his thoughts about Winter then had been as indecent as they were right now. The only thing that had stopped him from acting on those feelings had been his apprehension over being a rebound.

And Logan had warned him to stay away from her. Vigorously. Frequently.

And Autumn had insisted Winter needed to heal from the breakup. As a forensic psychologist he'd managed to bring onto the IPS team, Autumn had a tendency to profile everyone, and he listened whenever she gave advice.

Though lately both sisters were prodding Winter to get back out there because she'd been alone too long. Summer was even planning a blind date for her with Logan's help.

But when Winter Stratton was ready to date, Chance wanted to be the guy she took a gamble on.

"Where did you get the furniture?" he asked.

"Malones in Missoula." The bedroom door opened, and she came back into the living room wearing an oversize pale blue sweatshirt that fell to her mid-thigh. There was nothing sexy about the giant cover-up besides the way she wore it. "It got too depressing living in an empty house. I finally caved and bought enough of their spring collection that was on sale."

Bingo. "I love being right," he said, and she drew her eyebrows together in response. "Never mind." He smiled. "You didn't need to cover up on my account." He gestured to the big sweatshirt that looked fluffy and warm.

"Yes, I did."

"You told me not to make what you were wearing, or lack thereof, a big deal. I didn't."

She tilted her head to the side. "Not with your words. It was the way you looked at me."

"And how was that?" He took a step toward her.

"Like you wanted to devour me."

He did. Slowly. Until they were both satisfied. But he

didn't want to give off that vibe tonight. Way too strong. Way too soon. "Apologies. Not my intention." Though it made him wonder. "Out of curiosity, did that look make you feel anything?"

She eased toward him this time, bringing her close enough for him to reach out and touch her. "As a matter of fact, it did."

He gripped her chin again and stroked her cheek. "Care to share that feeling?"

She lifted her hand and clasped his wrist, her fingers warm and soft against his pulse point. "Confidence." She held his gaze. "Unwavering confidence that this forced partnership is doomed to fail."

A collaboration had blossomed into a partnership, and they weren't even one day in. They were making headway, but she was still skittish around him. When was she going to trust him?

Chance caressed her jaw. "Strong words." He grazed her bottom lip with the pad of his thumb, and she shivered.

"Strong feeling." With a light tug, she removed his fingers from her face.

"Better me than sweaty Keneke."

She laughed but then grimaced, clutching her side.

"Seriously, I don't want you to feel forced to work with me." Never trap an anxious mare. Patience and persistence were key. He was done keeping his distance, but maybe this was a step too far, too fast. "I don't have to stay on this case. I can explain to Ed that you'd rather partner up with his guy."

"That would complicate things with Chief Macon. Besides, I prefer you over the alternative. I'll abide by the deal that I agreed to." She strode into the kitchen, moving a little stiffly. "You never told me whether you wanted a drink."

He trailed behind her, hating to see her in pain. "I'll have a small one."

Winter poured some whiskey in a tumbler. "Let me get you a glass." She set the bottle down and reached for the upper cabinet.

He hurried up behind her, opening it before she caused herself more pain. "Hey, I've got it."

She stilled, and then he realized their proximity. His chest was pressed against her back.

Putting a hand on her arm, Chance took a tumbler and shut the cabinet. He sidestepped around her. Poured a splash of whiskey in his glass.

She shifted, facing him.

They stared at each other. The air between them charged with electricity. He caught the look in her glittering hazel eyes. It was the same one he saw when they first met, and he'd seen it hundreds of times since. He knew when a woman was attracted to him, and this one was, without question, but she acted determined to deny it.

Lowering her head, she inched away from him.

Following her lead, he backed up as well. Not far but enough.

"My pal at the forensics lab agreed to fast-track things for us," she said, turning to business.

She kept holding back with him. Maintained this fake, frosty attitude for some reason.

"Any news so far?"

"No prints on anything." She leaned against the counter and sipped the whiskey. "He's rushing the ballistics. We should know something tomorrow."

"The sniper knew the position of the hotel cameras and how to slip out unseen. Using the golf bag with the GCSA happening was cunning."

"So was using a police scanner. He didn't go there to kill people and then die, and he doesn't want to be found."

"Well, we're going to disappoint him. We'll find him."
Easier said than done.

"I can't believe the most we got from CCTV in the surrounding area was that the shooter drives an old-model Chevy Blazer. He even thought to use a tinted plastic cover over his license plate, and it wasn't a coincidence it was smeared with mud."

They weren't able to read his tags at all. Based on the model, they'd narrowed it down to a K5, built from 1969 to 1994. More than ten thousand were registered in the state.

"Our guy planned this out methodically." He took a swallow of whiskey. "I've got the surveillance footage for the past two weeks. The hotel would only turn over coverage of the lobby, side entrance, the rooftop bar and the service entrance in the basement. I'll go through it tonight and see if he scoped out the place. Maybe we'll get a good shot of his face."

"With your luck, maybe we will."

What did she mean by that?

She nursed her drink. "In the morning, we should speak with the rest of the staff and the family of the two deceased."

"Lorelei Brewer and Abby Schultz."

"Did you know them?"

"Not personally. I was aware of who they were. I'd seen them around town, that sort of thing, but I was more familiar with Lorelei. I believe Keneke was going to notify their next of kin tonight. After we talk to the families, we can also follow up with the other two individuals who were injured," he said.

While Chance was tied up at the hotel, he had gotten one of his guys at IPS, Bo Lennox, to interview Ty Lee and Nora Santana. According to Bo, Ty and Nora had still been in shock when they were questioned and he had gotten few answers.

"With nothing substantial to go on, we have to dig into the

lives of the victims. Both women killed and the two survivors all came out of the fitness center," she said. "That can't be a coincidence."

"The sniper could've homed in on them because they were in a large group, standing around chatting."

"Possibly. Random sprees happen, but more than two thirds of mass shootings are linked to domestic violence, where the perpetrators either killed family or intimate partners. Or the shooter had a history of domestic violence."

"We've got to start somewhere. Victims' families it is. Oh yeah, trying to get a sketch of the perp from the employees who might've seen him didn't pan out."

She nodded, taking another healthy swallow of whiskey.

Silence fell between them. Growing uneasy. Brewing with something else that had him looking at her mouth and wondering what it would be like to kiss her.

"Chance." Her teeth caught her bottom lip. "Why did you really come here tonight?"

He wasn't so sure anymore, but he said, "I already told you, Winter." He didn't know which he enjoyed more—the feel of her name rolling off his tongue or the sound of his on hers.

"You did a lot for me today. Were you looking for a special thank-you?" she asked, the words hitting him like an accusation.

"I may be a lawyer, and I get that people might think that makes me a shark. An apex predator." In some ways, he was. The way he handled the situation with Ed Macon hadn't been entirely noble. Leveraging relationships was how the system worked, and he had manipulated things to his benefit. And hers since she wanted the case. But he wanted to get closer to her. To help her in a way no one else could. To show her who he was deep down. Still… "But I'm not that kind of guy."

"Prove it. Promise me while we're working on this case, you'll keep things between us strictly professional."

"No," he said unequivocally, no hesitation. "I don't make promises I can't or have no intention of keeping." They had chemistry. Raw and electric. He had zero interest in containment. "But I will promise to give you my all. To not let anything personal between us jeopardize the case."

She considered him. "I want that to be enough, but I'm not sure it will be." She sighed. "Rather than rely on you not to cross the line, I'll rely on myself." She gulped down her drink and set the glass on the counter with a hard *clink*. "I'll have to treat you like I would Logan. Or better yet, a brother."

That'd be worse than being in the friend zone. She was determined to keep him at arm's length.

He was just as determined not to let her. Chance eased closer, inch by inch, bringing them toe-to-toe. She tensed, gazing up at him and clutched the counter behind her. He leaned in, lowering his face to hers, until their lips were a hairbreadth apart.

She didn't move away. Didn't turn her face from his when she had every opportunity.

He looked at her for a long moment. Inhaled the scent of her, honey and chamomile and whiskey. "Good luck with that," he whispered, and he would've sworn she trembled again.

He reached around her, picked up the ice pack resting on the counter, handed it to her with a grin and took the bottle of liquor. Stepping to the other side of the small kitchen, he poured one last finger of whiskey.

She slipped the cold compress under her sweatshirt. Guilt hit him for making it inconvenient for her to ice her injury.

"What were you going to tell me earlier at the coffee shop?" she asked. "The whole reason for us to meet in the first place."

"Let's not get into it tonight."

"You're not going to tell me? You're going to make me wait?"

He wanted to tell her earlier at The Beanery, when they would've had a chance to talk about the news. It was something Winter would need to work through, and he wanted to be there for her, to listen to her concerns, to reassure her, but the sniper ruined his plan.

Now, whiskey instead of coffee was flowing freely, and he couldn't stop thinking about what she wore underneath that bulky sweatshirt and how badly he wanted to touch her.

Shrugging a shoulder, he finished his drink and set the glass down. "I'll tell you tomorrow. Promise. It's been a long day. I'll get out of your way."

"You're leaving? Now?" she said, sounding disappointed.

"I think that's best. I'll pick you up in the morning." He stroked her arm. "Ice your ribs and your face. I should go." He pushed off the counter and strode toward the door.

She was right behind him.

"Good night." He opened the door and hurried down the front steps.

"Chance." She came outside, not far behind him. "Please, wait."

He stopped near his truck and turned. "I need to leave."

"Why?"

His mind blanked. That only happened around Winter. The woman had the power to short-circuit his brain.

"You pop up at my house. Late at night. To see how I'm doing and talk about the case, which you could've done over the phone." She left the stoop and came over to him. "I ask you to share whatever news you had that brought us to Main Street where all hell broke loose, and suddenly you take off when I actually want you to stay. I don't get it." Something in her tone tugged at him, drawing his feet to move toward her. "Come back inside and tell me. I hate the suspense." She moved closer. "The not knowing."

It wouldn't be that simple. She'd need to talk it out over another drink, they'd get cozy on the sofa, drawing closer, like two magnets pulled together, and he'd touch her. His self-control would slip, he'd touch her, and he was sure she'd touch him back. But in the morning, she'd blame it on alcohol and push him away.

He wished he had kissed her, tasted her, held her, before they poured the whiskey. "I can't. Not to—"

A red laser dot slid along Winter's torso, moving toward her heart. His blood turned to ice, and Chance launched himself at her.

Chapter Six

A bullet missed Winter by a whisper, followed by another, shattering the bay window of her house. With Chance's arms banded tight around her, they hit the ground. Her chin slammed against his shoulder with a brain-rattling smack, her elbows banging on the asphalt.

Pain rocketed through her. Chance's sharp exhale rushed over her skin, and her heart lurched into her throat.

What the hell? What the hell? She lifted her head slightly.

Another suppressed pop. And another. Bits of pavement shot up from the driveway near their heads. Chance rolled, and she rotated along with him, adding to the momentum, moving them both out of the line of fire until they were shielded by his truck.

A flicker of relief trickled through her, then evaporated.

The sniper was using a silencer. Shooting at them.

At me! At my house!

He had tracked her to her home.

The realization ricocheted through her as Chance kept her tucked beneath him, covering her body with his.

They lay there, frozen for a second, stunned. His solid, heavy body pinned her to the pavement. A warm coppery taste hit her tongue, and the blistering sting of adrenaline flooded her veins. Pulse pounding, she blinked up at the sky, at the blackness sprinkled with stars. She clung to Chance, gasping and feeling as though she'd been body-slammed into a brick wall.

No more gunfire.

They kept still. She clenched her teeth against the pain ebbing and flowing through her, everywhere, like her entire body was a fresh wound. She forced herself to breathe. In and out. Over and over. Her mouth filled with blood. She'd bitten her tongue. Her head swam, skull throbbing, and her breath came fast as she pieced together their situation. A single thought blared in her mind.

"We have to move," she said. The sniper could still be in position, waiting for them to expose themselves. He could also be on the prowl, closing in on their position. Or, and she hoped the third option was the case, the shooter could be fleeing the scene. Regardless, they couldn't stay on the ground waiting to find out if he was continuing the hunt. "We have to get out of here."

Chance unfurled the strong arm he had wrapped around her head. "Are you hit?" he asked her.

She hurt all over, but there was no fiery bite of agony from a bullet. "No. You?"

"I'm all right."

Scanning their surroundings, he drew his gun from the holster on his hip and rolled off her into a crouched position. Grabbing her by the forearm, he moved her to the front of his truck and leaned her against the grille, keeping his head on a swivel. "I'll go around to the passenger side and open the rear door to give us some cover. When I tell you to move, do it. Okay?"

She nodded and clamped a hand on his arm. "But shoot out my floodlights first."

"Why?"

"To make it harder for him to see us, in case he's still in

position." Darkness was their ally. "Once you do it, you have to move fast. I mean like lightning. Just in case he switches to a nightscope." If the shooter did, he'd once again have the advantage.

Chance spun around and aimed at the bright lights that illuminated the front of the house and driveway. One by one, he shot them out, *pop, pop, pop, pop,* cloaking them in the dark.

Her fingers ached to be coiled around her gun, but it was inside the house on her nightstand. Having it in her hand always made her feel better. Brought instant reassurance and focus. Something she needed right now. Instead of this smothering sense of helplessness ballooning inside of her.

Chance put a hand on her shoulder. His touch comforted her, but it was fleeting. Then he was gone, ducking around the left side of his truck, and her chest constricted.

She scooted to the edge of his fender, braced herself against the sturdy frame and peeked around the side, watching him. Hoping he'd make it and be all right.

He opened the rear door, shielding himself, and next, the passenger door. "Winter."

Fear spurted through her at that moment, and she commanded herself to move. *Get up! Go! Now!* She darted around to him, staying low, and her brain clicked into gear.

He hopped into the truck and grabbed her hand, tugging her up into the cab as he climbed over into the driver seat.

"Keep your head down," Chance said, remaining low.

She was grateful for the dark tint on his windows. *Almost. Almost.* They were almost out of there.

He gave her an uneasy look as he fired up the engine. Threw the gear into Reverse. Zipped out of the driveway and cranked the wheel hard, tires screeching as he thrust the gear into Drive and sped off. His gaze darted to the rearview and side mirrors several times. At an intersection, he made a hard right turn, peeling around the bend, the truck fishtailing. He punched the gas. Checked the mirrors again. And again.

"I don't think we're being followed." He glanced at her. "Winter, you're bleeding," he said with a wince. "Your face."

Something wet trickled down her cheek. She touched her face, lightly, and her fingers came away with blood. A bullet hadn't grazed her, but something had. Maybe flying debris from the driveway. All those shots had landed so close. Only inches from both their heads. Not by accident. Not random stray bullets.

They could've been killed. She surely would've been if Chance hadn't acted as quickly as he had.

"You saved my life." Her voice was low and shaky and sounded foreign.

"I wasn't thinking." He shook his head. "Even if I had been thinking, I still would've done it. I mean, I just saw that red laser moving up your chest, and I reacted."

"Thank you." For coming over. For annoying her to the point that she had chased after him outside. If that sniper hadn't taken the shot tonight but had waited until morning when she was walking out alone, he would've put a bullet in her head or her heart.

Chance reached over, grabbed her hand and held it. Squeezed it tight in his. She didn't want him to let go. "We need to call the police," he said.

"What are they going to do?"

"The scene needs to be canvassed. To see if he left behind any evidence."

"The sniper is meticulous." She shook her head. "If we call it in, then Logan will know what happened and so will my sisters."

"It's possible he got sloppy. And even though he used a silencer, your neighbors would've heard my gunshots. Someone probably already reported it."

There was plenty of land between the houses, but surely the gunfire had woken neighbors. "Declan," she said, thinking out loud. "I can call him. Ask him to take care of it. Discreetly. The canvassing and ensuring the BFPD doesn't go out there." Declan was neck-deep in his own case, working long days, but he'd help her if he was available. Even if it meant he had to crawl out of bed. She was sure of it.

"All right," Chance said, nodding. "But you can't go back home. Not while that sniper is out there. It isn't safe."

The sudden reality crashed over her like a wave. Swept under the sensation that she was drowning, she clutched her stomach and tightened her grip on his hand, interlacing their fingers. "I've had angry suspects confront me. I've even had a guy I arrested once throw a bottle at me, and he ended up getting himself arrested again. But…" Her voice trailed off. "I've never been stalked before. Hunted." She reeled from what had just happened. To her. To Chance. "Why? How?"

"You're now the face of this case. All over the news. Maybe he didn't leave the area of the crime scene. Maybe he stuck around, watched us, watched the press conference. Then followed you."

"To the DCI lab and back to the hospital in Bitterroot Falls?"

"It's possible."

"Why? What would it accomplish? It wouldn't make the case go away."

"You're the only one who got close to him. Fought him. He did have a police scanner, probably anticipating a specific response time. You threw a wrench into his plan and maybe ticked him off." He shrugged. "I don't know, but now that you're a target, you can't go back home."

Winter thought about her sisters. She didn't want them to know how much danger she was in, much less endanger them by sleeping at their places.

"Stay with me," he said, as if reading her thoughts.

"I don't want to bring trouble to your doorstep, Chance."

"He shot at me, too. We're in this together. Partners."

CHANCE KNOCKED ON the guest room door.

Winter opened it, clad only in one of his T-shirts that fell to her thighs. She looked good wearing his clothes.

He handed her the leather overnight bag containing her things. "I'll wait for you in the living room."

She nodded and shut the door.

He trudged down the hall, his adrenaline finally dissipated. After he poured himself a drink, he set the first aid kit on the coffee table along with an extra glass and a bottle of bourbon—an exceptionally smooth sipper distilled in Montana.

Chance had gone back to her place and met Declan there. The agent found the nest the sniper had been perched in, atop a neighbor's garage across the street. Declan questioned the neighbor, who didn't know anything, collected and bagged what evidence he could find—there hadn't been much, not even casings left behind.

Fuming over the attack, Chance had gathered everything on the list Winter had given him. Clothes, makeup, painkillers, her badge and gun. He'd wanted her to rest back at his house, or at least try to, and get cleaned up and ice her bruises.

Many of his ranch hands lived in the bunkhouse, and they were all armed. He'd posted several of them around the perimeter of the main house, keeping guard as an extra precaution while he was gone. He was certain they hadn't been followed, but he wasn't going to make the mistake of underestimating the sniper. Not again.

Chance lit a fire in the hearth across from the sofa and waited for Winter while he sipped his drink.

The door down the hall opened, and she strode out, coming into the living room. She'd kept on his tee but had pulled on a pair of sweatpants. "I'm sorry you had to go through my underwear drawer." Averting her gaze, she sat beside him on the sofa.

This was the first time he'd ever seen her embarrassed. "No need to apologize." He wasn't sorry. She had a beautiful collection of frilly things, silk and lace. Not that he had taken much time to go through her stuff, but it was hard to miss. "It was my pleasure."

A hint of a smile tugged at the corner of her mouth. "Did you remind Declan not to say anything at the barbecue on Saturday? We'll all be there, and I don't want him to let it slip."

"I made him pinky promise."

She chuckled and then put a hand to her side.

Chance swallowed down his anger that she was hurt, more banged up than before. It gutted him to see her in pain. "Did you ice your ribs?"

"Yeah."

He pushed her hair back behind her ear and tipped up her chin, looking her over. A nick on her cheek, close to her eye. The bruise on her face had deepened in color. He took her arms and inspected them. Her elbows were scraped. His heart lurched. The sniper had nearly taken off her head.

"How are your legs?" he asked, opening the first aid kit.

"Not bad. I took the brunt of the fall with my elbows, and I bit my tongue. They hurt a little. The rest of my body hurts a lot." She looked at him, her gaze somber. She'd calmed down, her adrenaline undoubtedly drained like his, but she still appeared shaken.

Understandably so.

Winter picked up the bottle on the coffee table and poured herself a generous serving. Her hand trembled, and his gut clenched. She downed a swallow and winced, probably from the cut on her tongue. "You've got the good stuff."

"Thought you might like it."

"I do," she croaked.

He took out supplies from the first aid kit and treated her scrapes and nicks. Then he packed it away and picked up his glass.

Falling asleep was going to be tough for both of them, he wagered. For a few minutes he wanted to get her mind off the horror and close calls of the day. Far too many. But he drew a blank, staring at her over the rim of his glass.

She sipped again, and he noticed her hands still shook. "It's tomorrow."

"What?" he asked.

Winter gestured to the clock on the wall. One thirty in the morning. "It's past midnight and officially tomorrow." She brought her legs up onto the sofa, curling them beneath her and leaning closer. "You promised to tell me your news. I could really use a reset from everything else."

From the thought of almost dying.

He sipped his drink, letting the liquid coat his throat and belly in silky warmth, and then he slid an arm around her, resting it on the back of the sofa. Surprisingly, she didn't tense up. He stared at her, not wanting to miss the slightest nuance of her reaction when he told her. "Logan is going to propose to Summer. At the barbecue on Saturday."

Surprise. Shock. Joy. Fear. Concern. Everything he'd expected and so much more.

Summer was twenty-eight, the baby of her family, the one the sisters sought to protect the most. Logan was thirty-one. Neither of them were too young for marriage, but this was the first serious relationship for both.

Chance had established roots in Big Sky to open an IPS office long before the others moved there. A murder investigation of someone close to Summer and Logan had brought the two to Bitterroot Falls. They had fallen for each other quickly—*lightning in a bottle*—and had decided to make the town their home.

The two of them demolishing their old lives to build a new one here didn't surprise him. Montana had a way of capturing the imagination and stealing hearts. Opened you to different possibilities. But then they purchased a house after only being a couple for a matter of weeks. Even Chance thought things had been moving too fast, making him concerned.

Summer and Logan had been together for less than a year now. Surely Winter looked at the lovebirds through the wary lens of her own divorce.

Then again, they each had a lens coloring the way they saw things. For Chance, he knew all about Logan's past, had witnessed his heartbreak; an old situation with present-day relevance that Chance needed to disclose to Winter before it was exposed. Early on, Chance had questioned whether Summer was a rebound romance, but he'd come to believe Logan was truly, deeply in love.

The news of their engagement was not something to spring on Winter. At a family function. In front of her sister when she needed to rally and muster all her support. Winter was going to need time, even if he could only give her a couple of days. Even less now.

Emotions tangled, flitting across her face, radiating in her eyes. She was so beautiful it made him ache with a longing he'd never known. No woman had ever affected him like this. He wanted to touch her, all of her, body and soul.

Winter gulped down her drink. "I think I'm going to need another."

He poured her a refill, set the bottle down and raised his glass. "Here's to building bridges."

She hesitated, thinking, and then clinked their tumblers.

"A bridge is one thing. A substantial one takes two to three years of hard work. I figured this would eventually happen, Summer and Logan taking things to the next level. *Eventually*, after they'd gotten to know each other better. What's the rush?" She looked up at him. "Is she pregnant?"

A shotgun wedding? "As far as I know, she isn't."

Winter shook her head. "The fact I even need to ask *you* that question says it all."

"No offense taken." Well, maybe a little.

"I'm sorry, it's just Summer used to share everything with me. She was an open book, and that's changed since…" She lowered her head like she was thinking. Her eyes flashed up at him. "Does Logan have a terminal illness?"

"No." An unexpected dark turn.

A relieved look washed over her face. "That's good." She chewed on her bottom lip, and concern returned to her expression. "Summer never rushed into anything until Logan. Now everything with him moves at warp speed. This is nothing like building a bridge. It's different."

"Is it?" He eyed her.

"Yes."

"Marriage connects two people. Families. Not all consequential bridges take years to build. The RED HORSE Squadron can construct one in months. Weeks if necessary." He'd recruited the majority of his IPS team—Bo, Tak and Eli—from the specialized military unit out at Malmstrom Air Force Base in Cascade County. The Rapid Engineer Deployable Heavy Operational Repair Squadron Engineers personnel possessed cradle-to-grave design build capability. Always wartime ready, they provided combat engineering anywhere in the world, executing remarkable feats under extreme pressure.

What Summer and Logan had faced together, the connection they found, had been equally remarkable.

Winter squinted at Chance. A lock of brown hair hung over her eyes, and he tucked it behind her ear. "I'm not talking about your motley crew," she said. "Or some highly trained military unit. I'm talking about my baby sister."

"She's not a baby. Not anymore." Yet Winter and Autumn had both hurried to move to Bitterroot Falls like they worried Logan was taking advantage of their sister. "She's a grown woman. A successful lawyer. You should trust her judgment."

Chance had been guilty of questioning Logan's judgment. This was familiar territory for him.

"You can be great at your job and suck at your personal life," Winter said, sounding like she was talking more about herself than her sister. "My baby..." She shook her head. "My younger sister has led a sheltered life."

"There was nothing sheltered about what Summer and Logan endured." He'd witnessed most of it, and the couple had shared the story with Winter and Autumn. "Their courage, what they accomplished together as a team wasn't a fluke, and it wasn't luck." He now believed they were capable of weathering any storm.

She shrugged. "I guess so. Why are you always right? Has anyone ever told you how annoying it is?"

"Yes, my sister. It gets under her skin all the time." Speaking of which. "There's one more thing you should know." He took a breath and spit it out. "Logan used to be in love with my sister, Amber. For a long time." A decade. "But she never reciprocated his feelings. Amber is now married to Monty, Logan's eldest brother." That was the condensed version. "I wanted you to know in case someone said something at the wedding or the reception." When drinks were flowing freely and one of Logan's four brothers tried to make an inappropriate joke that wasn't funny.

Winter's eyelids grew heavy. "Is she, I mean, is he, is Logan still in love with her?"

Chance had had a similar concern but not anymore. "No." He shook his head. "No. He'll always love Amber, care about her." And it was that loyalty and concern for his sister, the way Logan had protected her, that had made the two men grow so close. "But he's not *in love* with her. Trust me, Summer has his whole heart. She's everything he could've wanted and more."

"Good." Winter gave him a drowsy nod. "That's good. Does Summer know about the Amber thing?"

"Yes." He took the glass from Winter's hand, set it down and thought about everything that he'd packed for her. "Did you take a painkiller?"

"Mmm, yeah." She put her head on his chest and nuzzled against him. "I can feel it working magic."

He pulled her in close, tight against him, wanting to protect her from anything that might hurt or upset her. "You're not supposed to drink when taking those," he said low, and she nodded. "Let's get you to bed."

Chance swept his arm under her legs and picked her up, and she draped an arm around his neck. With her tucked close, he carried her to the guest room. He set her on the bed, peeled back the covers and got her settled.

Her eyelids lifted, and she stared at him, a dreamy, peaceful look on her face.

He pulled the blanket up over her, leaned down and kissed her forehead. "Get some sleep."

She reached for him, pressing a palm to his cheek. "You're the best. Amazing. And you always smell so good."

He grinned. "I think that's the mix of painkillers and alcohol talking."

She stroked her thumb over the stubble on his jaw, a back-and-forth caress that set off sparks inside him. Heat flared in her eyes.

"Winter, don't—"

She brought his head down as she raised up on an elbow and kissed him, settling her mouth on his.

Warm contentment washed over him as he kissed her back, sliding his tongue between her lips. She tasted new and familiar and sweeter than he imagined. He stroked her hair, savoring the moment he'd long waited for. A groan rumbled up his throat, and the sound brought him back to his senses.

He pulled back. "I'm sorry."

"For what?"

"Kissing you."

She smiled. "You didn't. I kissed you," she said dreamily, and his gut churned with regret. "And I want to do it again." She reached for him.

He caught her hand and gave it a gentle squeeze. "I shouldn't be taking advantage." He finally got her to trust him, to let down her guard, and he was going to wreck it all.

"No, you're not," she said.

She was right because he wasn't going any further. "Good night, Winter." He set her hand down on the bed. "I'll see you in the morning." He switched off the lamp on the nightstand, left the room without looking back and closed the door behind him.

He might be an apex predator, but he was also capable of being a gentleman.

Chapter Seven

Looking out at the property in the daylight, Winter marveled at Chance's compound. She stood at a window in the front sitting room with a view of the bunkhouse, barn, stable and the wrought-iron gate they'd driven through last night.

Friday morning had come faster than expected. She didn't crawl out of bed until nearly eight. She'd showered, dressed and now waited for Chance to return to the house. He'd left her a note in the kitchen saying that he'd gone to get breakfast.

A couple of sturdy-looking cowboys were out front, holding shotguns, standing guard under the porte cochere that was large enough to fit four pickups. The house had been stunning at night, illuminated with exterior lighting. In the daylight, everything about the place was jaw-dropping. The single-story lodge was made of rugged logs and stone and had a limestone chimney. With its dark hardwood floors, soaring ceiling with wood beams, huge picture windows and stone features in the kitchen, it could've been featured in an architectural digest, yet the place was inviting and warm.

For several hours, she'd slept soundly until a nightmare woke her. Every time she tried to doze back off, she replayed both shootings. How close she and Chance had come to dying. The longer a case went unsolved, the edgier she grew. Though it had been less than twenty-four hours since this one had kicked off, she needed something to break soon.

Chance pulled up in front of his house. She grabbed her things and hurried through the door before he shut off the engine. Outside, she nodded hello to the armed ranch hands.

Sitting behind the wheel, Chance wore a smile and a cowboy hat, charcoal gray. One she had never seen on him. Regardless of the color, they all added to his appeal.

He rolled down his window. "Thanks, guys," he said to the two men. "I dropped the food at the bunkhouse."

One waved, and the other gave him a two-finger salute.

Winter hopped into his pickup. The cab smelled like him. A scent she always found sexy.

Suddenly, she remembered how close Chance had gotten to her in the kitchen last night, with that heated look in his eyes. They'd chatted on the sofa at his place about Summer and Logan.

Whether or not a hasty engagement was a mistake, it was her sister's to make. Logan was the only man Summer had ever been with sexually or seriously. Winter assumed her sister would want to experience more before settling down. Not that Logan wasn't a fantastic guy, he was, and things seemed great between them, but things often did in the beginning.

Chance had been sweet and understanding as they got closer on the sofa. So close she'd wanted to kiss him.

Then she drew a blank. Had she fallen asleep on the couch? She didn't recall climbing into bed.

There was a big black hole until the nightmare.

"I should pick up my car. Probably better if we drove separately," she said, reconsidering them working together. "We might need to divide and conquer."

"Good morning to you, too." He pulled out of the driveway and handed her a takeaway cup. "I went to the café down the road. Got you a latte with soy milk, light foam and one sugar."

She took the warm cup. "Thank you."

As they headed down the long driveway, she noticed armed men with dogs patrolling near the fence line. Chance waved to the guys and took the road that led toward town, away from her house.

"Your face doesn't look as bad as I expected."

"Makeup." An unfortunate necessity this morning with her bruises.

"How are you feeling, besides grumpy?"

She opened her mouth to refute it, but he was right. "I woke up around four. Tossed and turned." Then she overslept. The clock read five minutes past nine. A late start when she'd wanted an early one. "I am grumpy. Not your fault. Sorry." Winter sipped the coffee and tamped back a moan of delight.

"Did the pain wake you up? Or something else? I've heard you mention restless nights before to your sisters." Chance was far too observant.

"I have nightmares. On occasion. Always work related. My brain's way of processing everything, and there's a lot with this shooting." She took another swig of coffee. "Where are we headed first?"

"To see Lorelei Brewer's mother. They lived together."

"How old was Lorelei?"

"Twenty-four."

So young. Too young to have her life cut short. "How did you sleep last night?" she asked.

"After I tucked you into bed, I got a little work done."

"You tucked me in?"

"You don't remember?" His tone was skeptical.

"No. Why?"

Chance narrowed his eyes at her. "Honestly?"

"Is there something to remember?" Tension tightened through her shoulders. Besides her nightmare, she'd had a sweet, wonderful dream. They'd kissed, and then he was naked in bed with her. It had been a dream, right? "Did I say something wrong last night? Do something? Did we?"

Something shifted in his posture, a slight bunching of his shoulder muscles. "You didn't do anything wrong. After I put you to bed, I reviewed some of the surveillance footage."

"Good. I'm glad that's all." She exhaled a breath of relief. "Thanks for everything. I will not mix pain meds and alcohol ever again." A dangerous combination. Her head was fuzzy, felt like sludge. "Any luck with the footage?"

"I only got through four days before I fell asleep. The perp didn't check out the place, at least not during that period. I'll get one of the guys to finish reviewing the rest, but when I went back over yesterday's footage, I noticed the coveralls the shooter put on weren't hotel issued."

"How can you be sure?"

"The ones the custodians wore had the name of the hotel embroidered on the upper left-hand side. His were plain, and no one noticed."

"He could've purchased a pair of navy coveralls from a local store?"

"My guess, too. I called Bo this morning. Asked him to look into it, even though it's a long shot."

"Enlisting your motley crew to help?"

"The reputation of IPS is on the line. I'm going to use my resources to the fullest. I also passed him the list of hotel employees that we didn't get a chance to interview yesterday. Bo and Tak are going to question them, beginning with the custodians. Since the coveralls weren't hotel issued, I doubt the perp was an employee, but there might be some connection between the shooter and the hotel."

"I agree." Every person on Chance's team was sharp: Bo Lennox, Tak Yazzie, Eli Easton and her sister, Autumn. If there was a link, one of them would find it. Winter yawned and clutched her side.

"Did you take something for the pain?"

"I need to be clearheaded."

"I never told you, but you made the right call to pursue the sniper without waiting for backup. It's because of you he stopped shooting. He must've heard you were on your way up over the police scanner."

The timing would've made sense. "Yeah, I guess so." She took a deep breath and winced from the sharp slice of pain.

He slid a worried glance her way, the same concerned look from yesterday that still put an ache in the pit of her stomach. "You should eat and take a painkiller." He picked up the bag on the console between them and dumped it in her lap. "A sausage and egg wrap."

She opened the bag, and the smell made her stomach growl. "You're the absolute best." The words slipped out of her mouth without thinking.

"You really do mean it." He flashed a bright smile. "Glad you're finally catching on."

Winter had no clue why the compliment made him so happy, but he deserved it. She sipped her coffee. *Heaven.* "This is delicious." She took the breakfast wrap out of the bag. "Come on, tell me how you know this is what I drink?"

"You admit you love it?"

She bit into the food and chewed, stalling. "Yes. Satisfied?"

"Not even close." He grinned. "I'll answer one of your questions if you answer mine. Quid pro quo."

Always the lawyer. "Answer mine first."

"I've peeked in your fridge. Seen soy milk. But I've also noticed you're not a diva about it and will take your coffee with regular milk without complaint at family brunch. You always add a teaspoon of sugar to coffee and tea. As for the light foam, I guessed. You strike me as a no-fluff kind of woman."

Maybe he was a good investigator. "Not bad."

"My turn. Why did you get divorced?"

She groaned. "Not a fair question."

"All's fair in love and war. You have to tell me."

The weight between their answers was unbalanced, heavily in his favor, but she did agree. "My ex, Manny, was a detective with the San Antonio PD. He worked vice and came on strong. I was reluctant to get involved."

"Why?"

"Relationships with a cop in the same precinct can be bad. For a multitude of reasons."

"Such as?"

"Well, I didn't want to become the subject of locker room gossip if the relationship didn't go anywhere. Also, police work spills over into our personal lives. We emotionally compartmentalize. Finally, cops have a reputation for not being faithful. A lot of badge bunnies out there, you know, ladies who pursue cops."

"Like buckle bunnies. They hang out at rodeos chasing cowboys."

"Manny wore me down with his smooth talk and charm. When we spent time together, which wasn't a lot with work, it was easy. No arguments. Good sex. No complaints. Looking back, I realized it was because we never talked about anything real. Just circular conversations where we never delved into anything uncomfortable." They never knew each other. Didn't fit together. "I got pregnant or thought I did. He proposed. I said yes. We married quickly in Vegas." Her gut clenched.

Was she dragging her baggage into Summer's relationship? Autumn would have a field day psychoanalyzing her. Maybe fast didn't always mean bad. There were couples who fell in love at first sight, married and made it work. Few and far between, but they existed.

"It turned out to be a false positive on a home test," she said. "Things snowballed afterward."

"I take it he cheated."

She nodded. "I later found out he cheated the entire time. For Manny it wasn't just a hobby, he made it a vocation. All the guys on vice knew."

"Is that how you found out? Someone told you?"

"No, that would've required guts and decency. One of his mistresses showed up at the station. With their two-year-old son. Made a big scene. Then everyone knew. I filed for divorce. They got married. I moved here. He's her problem now. End of story."

Rehashing it didn't sting, no fresh wave of anger. Though the shame lingered. For not making better choices.

"How long were you married?" Chance asked.

"Three years."

"I'm sorry he was a scumbag. You didn't deserve to be hurt and humiliated, and then you had to grieve the loss of your marriage."

"I don't regret the divorce."

"Still, it lasted three years. Had to hurt." He picked up her hand and squeezed it.

A pang of yearning went through her for something she wanted, someone she wanted and couldn't have. "Have you ever been in a relationship that long?" she wondered, letting his hand linger on hers.

"No, I've never lasted more than a few months."

"Ever been in love?"

"I've been infatuated and in lust."

One red flag after another. "Never even said it as a knee-jerk reaction?"

"Nope."

"Only temporary romances?"

"Only temporary until I find the right person to build something permanent."

She glanced down at her hand in his. She liked it, his warm, strong fingers wrapped around hers. Liked it way too much. "Chance." She hesitated, but it was better to deal with it and move on to business. "You're my type."

He beamed. "I knew it."

She freed her hand from his. "My type is bad for my health. Mental, physical, emotional. I need someone different." To break old patterns. To stop repeating the same mistakes.

The grin fell from his face. He put on the turn signal and made a right. Signs advertising condominiums and touting luxury estates and a private airport coming soon lined the road.

Silence continued.

"Did you hear me?" she asked.

"I did. My takeaway is you're attracted to me. Is that why you try so hard to pretend not to like me when it's obvious you do?"

"Oh please." She struggled not to squirm in her seat. "You're either overly optimistic or delusional."

"I'm neither. Attraction doesn't mean I'm the same type of guy you've been with. Ask around, I'm not a cheater."

"They weren't all cheaters." She pushed her hair back and showed him the scar near her hairline. "One ex liked to hit. But I hit back. It didn't end well." All those guys had been wrong for her. Wreaking havoc. Destroying pieces of her life.

"Maybe you haven't gotten to know me well enough. If you did, maybe I'd surprise you. Pleasantly."

"Maybe, but it doesn't matter."

"Why is that?"

"I can't take the risk of a hot, wild fling with you blowing up like a lit powder keg in my face. This is literally too close to home." Once Summer and Logan got married, Chance would be locked in as family. "Things could get messy." She wasn't uprooting her life and moving halfway across the country to get away from a man again. Bitterroot Falls was where she wanted to stay, close to her sisters. "This can't happen."

Chance Reyes was a difficult man to resist. But she would. She'd have to find a way.

His expression registered the change in tone as his jaw clenched. "We're here." He parked in the lot in front of a small apartment building and cut the engine. "The mother, Sadie, is in apartment 3K."

Tension hung in the air, exactly what she didn't want. "Are we good?"

"We are," he said easily and hopped out.

She climbed down from the truck and hurried alongside him as they crossed the lot. It wasn't like Chance to simply give up. He wasn't a quitter. They strode along the open breezeway and hiked up the stairs.

"Why does it feel like we aren't?" she asked.

He shrugged. "I don't know."

"Why haven't you responded with some kind of witty retort or persuasive appeal?"

"What's there to say?"

He always had a rebuttal. A closing argument. "Something. Anything." Getting zilch from him niggled at her.

On the third floor, they headed to the right.

"What's going through your head?"

"You don't want to know," he said, his tone taunting.

They came to apartment K.

She tugged on his arm, stopping him. "Try me."

"You haven't done your research when it comes to me. Instead, you're making premature judgments because you're scared." He turned toward her. Their gazes locked, and a rush of physical awareness swept through her. "I get it, I do, but last night in your driveway, I've never felt fear like that. When I saw a red laser on you, my heart stopped, Winter. I couldn't breathe." He caressed her jaw, and her nerves flitted at his touch.

Time slowed as he eased closer and closer, and she backed into the wall beside the apartment door. His hand slid from her cheek and cupped the back of her head.

She read the look on his face, the intensity in his eyes. Her stomach dropped, and her breath caught in her throat, and then his mouth was on hers.

Every inch of her body went into shock.

His lips were warm and firm, his tongue tangling with hers. The hardness of his chest pressed to her. His other hand curled on her hip, pulling her closer, holding her steady. The rapid pounding of her heart, or was it his?

Chance Reyes was kissing her. She'd wondered what it'd be like since she first met him. First shook his hand. Always had a burning curiosity that flared in his presence. Now it was happening.

She found herself letting him in. Sliding her hands up over his shoulders and curling her fingers into his hair. The world fell away, and she was the one holding onto him, clinging to him. She made a small needy sound in her throat, and he abruptly backed away.

A chill crept over her as a tug of disappointment twisted in her chest.

"If a powder keg exploded, there'd be damage for us *both*," he said. "But it'd kill me if I ever hurt you." He pivoted toward the apartment door and knocked. Two quick raps, and he stopped like he caught himself, then rang the bell.

She straightened her jacket with trembling hands and moved up to the door beside him.

Without looking at her, he put a hand on her arm. "It's

okay." His tone was gentle as he squeezed her shoulder softly. "No matter whatever happens between us. You and I will always be good. Promise."

The door swung open. He dropped his hand from her arm, leaving her rattled.

On the other side of the threshold stood an older woman with no resemblance to the deceased. It could have been due to age. She was in her late fifties, possibly early sixties. Mousy brown hair cut in a bob, bloodshot eyes and cheeks flushed from crying.

Struggling to collect her thoughts, Winter flashed her badge. "Sadie Brewer, I'm DCI Agent Stratton, and this is—"

"Chance Reyes. I know who you are. Why are you two here?" Mrs. Brewer asked. "I spoke with the police late last night."

"We had a few questions," Winter said. "May we come in?"

Mrs. Brewer let them inside. They stepped into the small living room. The older woman plopped down in a worn armchair.

Winter and Chance took the sofa. She clasped her hands, trying to get them to stop shaking.

My heart stopped, Winter. I couldn't breathe.

"We're sorry for your loss," Chance said. "To lose a daughter like that."

"Thank you. Lorelei was my stepdaughter. I married her dad when she was twelve, and she needed a mama."

"We have you listed as her emergency contact," Chance said. "Are you her next of kin?"

"The closest she has around here. Her uncle moved to Boston not too long ago. He's technically her next of kin. Her dad died four years ago."

Winter snapped herself out of the sucker-punch haze and back into work mode. "Has Lorelei always lived with you?"

"Yes, she has. Or did. We were very close. It was cheaper

for her while she was working and getting her degree. In business. At the state university. She had such big dreams. Once she finished school, I needed financial help. Social security isn't much. Lorelei wanted to take care of me. She also helped her uncle George with some money so he could move to Massachusetts even though they weren't close. He's elderly and sick and wanted to live with his son, but the cost of relocating was expensive. Lorelei was that generous and kind. She was such a sweet girl. I never got around to adopting her when she was little. I wish I had. But she was still my girl."

"You mentioned Lorelei had big dreams," Chance said. "Did she ever share those with you?"

"Not the details. Lorelei was tight-lipped. Even as a child she was secretive. But she was so smart. Could've accomplished anything." Mrs. Brewer plucked a tissue from a box of Kleenex on the side table. "Her murderer deserves to pay for what he did. Has he been arrested yet?"

"The shooter," Winter said. "We're trying to figure out who he is and a possible motive."

Confusion riddled Mrs. Brewer's brow as she scooted to the edge of her seat. "But I already told the other officer everything he needed to know last night to make an arrest."

Chance and Winter exchanged a glance.

"What officer and what exactly did you tell him?" Winter asked.

"Officer Keneke. He came by to notify me about what happened to Lorelei. I told him all about how she was harassed. Stalked. Threatened. How that son of a…" She swallowed the word and took a breath. "How he said he'd kill her."

Winter stiffened. "Who?"

"Neil Reynolds."

Chance reeled back, his gaze falling as though he recognized the name.

Chapter Eight

Neil?

Chance refused to believe it. Neil was a friend. No, more than that. He had known the kid for nearly five years. Looked out for him. Employed him.

"What was his relationship to Lorelei?" Winter asked, taking a small spiral pad from her jacket pocket, and Chance noticed her hands shaking. "Was he her boyfriend?"

"They dated for a while," the stepmother said. "It was on and off again until Lorelei walked away from him for good."

Winter opened the notepad and pulled out a pen. "Did she give a reason why she broke things off with him?"

"He was a weird guy." Mrs. Brewer rubbed her arms like she was cold. "A real freak."

Chance clenched his jaw, hating when ignorant people spoke about Neil that way. "Can you be more specific?" he asked.

"You'd have to be around him to get it." Sadie Brewer shrugged. "Lorelei tried to make it work with him. He seemed so nice at first and was interested in her as a person. Not just because of her looks, like he only wanted to sleep with her," she said. "A lot of guys were like that because she was so pretty. But not him. I don't know why, but they started fighting all the time. Young people being young, I guess. But it reached a point where enough was enough."

Neil did his best to get along with everyone. When he thought someone was upset with him, he did what he could to make things right. Not let it fester. If there was a problem, he was driven to fix it.

"After the breakup, were they friends at all, at least friendly?" Chance asked, and the woman nodded. "Did something happen between them?"

"Neil became controlling. He tried to tell her what she should and shouldn't be doing with her life. She didn't want to listen to him," Sadie said, and Chance studied her as she spoke, looking for any telltale signs of lying or holding back. "Anyway, they broke up. Lorelei was the one who ended things, and Neil couldn't handle it." With a look of disgust, Sadie shook her head. "Wouldn't accept the fact that they weren't together anymore. He was in love with her. Obsessed with her." She raked a shaky hand through her hair. "Neil began stalking her. He would show up here at all hours, banging on the door, screaming for her to answer. It got scary. Finally, Lorelei couldn't take it and got a restraining order against him."

This was the first Chance was hearing of it. "When was this?"

"Three months ago. He was ordered to stay at least one hundred yards away from her. But that didn't stop him. Neil started harassing her online. Popping up in her DMs on Instagram. Sending threatening messages to her on Snapchat, Spotify, Facebook. Everywhere she had an online profile."

Winter jotted down notes. "What kind of threats?"

"That if she didn't listen to him and do what he said, she was going to die." Tears welled in her eyes, and she dabbed at them with the tissue. "He's big into shooting. Joined a marksmanship program. He's so good he competes. Wins at a championship level."

"Is there anyone else who might've wanted to hurt your stepdaughter?" Chance asked. "Anyone with a grudge?"

"No, of course not. She was a social butterfly. Everyone loved her, and Neil couldn't handle not having her anymore. Plain and simple. Something isn't right about him. He's *off* in some way. But he wanted to punish Lorelei for leaving him, I just know it. Neil Reynolds did this. He killed her."

That didn't sound like the Neil that Chance knew. The kid would never hurt anyone. "There's nothing to indicate your stepdaughter was specifically targeted." Chance clasped his hands. "Others were shot yesterday, too. Another woman killed. What makes you so sure that Neil was the sniper?"

"The officer, Keneke, told me the only other people who were shot had been with Lorelei. That they all left the gym together. Neil went after her and killed her." Sadie blew her nose and grabbed a fresh tissue. "Probably wanted to take out her friends right along with her. Oh goodness. Phoebe. Poor Phoebe could've been killed, too."

"Who's Phoebe?" Chance asked.

"Phoebe O'Shea. Her best friend. They usually work out together. Do almost everything together. In fact, when Phoebe bought one of those fancy new condos, Lorelei would stay over with her. It even had a water view of Bitterroot Lake. Lorelei would sleep there about four nights a week. Phoebe called me yesterday after she heard about the shooting. Asked me if Lorelei was all right because she'd been calling her and Lorelei's phone kept going straight to voicemail." Sadie sobbed. "I had to tell her. That Lorelei was dead."

"Did Lorelei go to Big Sky Fitness regularly?" Winter asked.

Sadie nodded. "She and Phoebe did. Like clockwork. Every Monday, Tuesday, Thursday and Friday morning. Lorelei usually spent the night at Phoebe's the night before, and they would go to spin class together."

Winter looked up from her notepad. "That's a lot of spinning."

"Yeah, well, it's important for the girls to stay fit. To look good for their jobs. The pretty ones got better tips is what they told me."

Putting her forearms on her thighs, Winter leaned forward. "Lorelei and Phoebe worked together?" she asked, and Sadie nodded. "Where and doing what?"

Mrs. Brewer took a breath and stared down at her bare feet. "Waitresses. At the Buckthorn Club."

Most people who worked there were proud of it. Hard place to get into, as a member and as an employee. Either Sadie was embarrassed for some reason or hiding something.

"Phoebe wasn't at the gym yesterday morning at the time of the shooting," Chance said. "Any reason that you know of why she might not have gone to class yesterday? Did Lorelei spend the night prior with Phoebe?"

"No, Lorelei didn't sleep over there." Mrs. Brewer waited a beat. "I think she said something Phoebe ate made her sick." She thought for a moment. "Bad sushi. The girls had Japanese food the night before last. Lorelei wanted her friend to rest and came back here."

"Do you happen to have Phoebe's phone number and address?" Chance asked. Getting the contact information would save them time looking it up.

"Of course, I do." Sadie picked up her cell phone from the side table and passed along the contact information. "Lorelei and Phoebe were two peas in a pod. Always together. They had big plans of making something of themselves. I'm glad at least Phoebe wasn't there. If she'd gone to that class yesterday, she'd probably be dead, too." Sadie pressed a palm to her chest. "I'm telling you it was Neil. He did this. He stalked

Lorelei. Threatened her. And now she's dead. Why are you sitting here talking to me instead of putting that monster behind bars where he belongs?"

Winter stopped taking notes and gave the older woman her full attention. "We have to do a thorough investigation before making an arrest. Doing so prematurely only hurts the case and won't bring justice any faster."

"Then go do your job and investigate! Find the evidence that proves Neil Reynolds is a murderer!" Sadie leaped up from the armchair and marched into the dining room.

Looking at each other, Winter and Chance stood.

The older woman snatched a stack of papers from the table, stormed back up to Winter and thrust them at her. "Here. Printouts of the messages that Neil sent to Lorelei. I've been up all night compiling them. And it should be easy enough for you to verify the restraining order."

Winter took the printouts and glanced at the thick stack. "Did the order prohibit all contact? Direct and indirect?"

"Yes," Sadie said. "He wasn't supposed to email, text, call. Nothing."

"Did she report this to police? Have him arrested?"

Sadie pursed her lips. "No. She didn't. Lorelei was too forgiving for her own good." Fresh tears fell from the woman's eyes. "Now, if you'll excuse me. I need to go to the morgue and see my girl's body. Make funeral arrangements for her."

"Thank you for your time." Winter handed her a business card. "We'll let you know if we have any other questions."

They left, and Sadie slammed the door behind them. They strode down the breezeway toward the staircase.

Winter turned to Chance. "Have you ever heard of the Buckthorn Club?"

"Yeah, it's exclusive. Private."

"How exclusive?" she asked.

"Very," he said. "You have to be recommended by a current member and pay a fee."

"How much?"

"Twenty thousand."

Fanning herself, she whistled. "Please don't tell me you're a member."

They hit the stairs.

"Okay, I won't tell you," he said. "Being a member is good for networking. Information and connections mean everything in my business."

"Sure," Winter said, like she wasn't sure if she believed him. "I got the sense we weren't getting the whole story about the club from the stepmother. So, were Lorelei and Phoebe only waitstaff at the club or possibly escorts, too?"

Chance shot her a warning look. "It's not that kind of club, and if it was, I wouldn't be a member." She must really have a low opinion of him. "I get that the type of men you're used to associating with haven't been the best sort, but that's not who I am. I'm not a cheater. I don't show up at night on a woman's doorstep looking for a special thank-you, especially if she's been injured, and I don't frequent places with hookers."

Winter raised a palm. "Listen, Chance, I don't think you're a bad guy."

"You only think I'm bad for you based solely on the fact you're attracted to me. So attracted you know deep down we'd be hot and wild together."

She held his gaze. "A lot of bad things burn hot and wild and *out of control*. Take human-sparked wildfires. They spread faster, burn hotter, kill more trees and can cause incalculable damage, but thankfully they don't last. Hot and wild isn't sustainable." She cut her eyes away from him and glanced down at the printouts. "When Sadie Brewer mentioned Neil Reynolds, I got the impression you might know him. Do you?"

"Am I being interrogated now?" Certainly felt like it.

"Do you know him?" she repeated.

"I handled a case for his grandmother when I was first getting the IPS office up and running about five years ago. He lives with her. She was a victim of fraud."

"Then you've met him."

Chance sighed. "More than that. Neil works for me."

Looking up at him, she didn't hide her surprise as her eyebrows hitched up. "Care to explain?"

"Neil finished his degree last year in business administration and accounting. He had difficulty getting hired. I brought him on to handle the business side of my ranch. This summer, he took an interest in the investigative field. He asked if he could learn more about IPS. I didn't see any reason not to let him. He works in the office several hours a week, as an intern."

They crossed the lot, headed to his truck.

"He started interning at IPS a few months back? Can you be more specific about when?"

"I don't know. He talked to me in, I guess, late June, I think, and started after the Fourth of July weekend."

"As in three months ago? Neil gets hit with a restraining order and then becomes your intern at IPS, where he can learn how to investigate and stalk someone?"

Chance's gut knotted. How had he missed that connection? He scrubbed his hand over his jaw.

"What did Mrs. Brewer mean when she said there was something off about him?" Winter asked.

"He has high-functioning autism. Really good with numbers. But he needs things to be a certain way. For example, the kid hates electrical outlets and can't sit where they're visible. He doesn't like the feeling of the wind blowing his hair, so he always wears a hat outdoors. He doesn't process humor the same way. But there's nothing wrong with him. It is true he's big into guns and hunting, but so is half the state."

"Is he really a competitive-level marksman?"

"A crack shot." As soon as the words left his mouth, he heard how it sounded. "But Neil is a good kid."

"If I had a dollar invested for every time I'd heard a bad guy called good—a good son, a good worker, a good soldier, a good cop—I'd be set for life financially."

"This is different. Neil really is a good person."

"Everyone is good until they aren't," she countered, turning back to the printouts. "Courts don't award an order of protection based on nothing. He did send her troubling messages, lots of them, and they were recent, which means he did so after the restraining order was issued. Each message is a violation. These are big red flags."

Chance didn't need her to spell it out in capital letters that this was a problem. "I can't explain that, but he didn't outright threaten to kill her, did he?"

"Doesn't look like it. Not so far, anyway, but there's lots of messages." She passed some to Chance. "Neil talked about watching her. Warned her to do the right thing before it was too late. I have to admit, it does sound creepy."

Chance glanced at the printouts. "Neil isn't a cold-blooded killer who would open fire on the crowded streets of downtown. He certainly didn't track you to your house, set up a sniper's nest and shoot at us. What happened yesterday on Main Street wasn't a crime of passion."

"I won't argue on that point. The shooter was calculated, controlled. Thorough. No casings left behind. Not a single stray hair. No fingerprints. He wasn't acting out of rage, but maybe he was so controlled, so skilled the only person he'd intended to kill *was* Lorelei."

They climbed into his pickup, and he pulled out of the parking lot. "Then why shoot the others?" Chance asked.

"Not sure. What if he didn't want to draw attention to Lorelei's murder? Hit a few others to make it look like a shooting spree?"

"If that's the case," Chance said, "why kill Abby Schultz?"

"To muddy the waters? I'm not sure." Winter mulled it over. "He took out Lorelei with a single shot to the head. Schultz was standing very close to her. Maybe he hit her by accident."

"He shot one in the head and the other in the heart. Execution style. That's not an accident."

"One shot, one kill. A sniper's motto. If our guy is a sharpshooter, then he could have easily killed Lee and Santana instead of injuring them."

"He only hit Ty in the arm and leg. Same with Nora Santana. A clean shot that passed through her shoulder. Didn't even hit the bone. Like he didn't want to inflict any serious damage to them. What are we dealing with, a killer with a conscience? Someone who only wanted to take out one or two people but not the rest?"

"I don't know, but let's go to the BFPD," she said. "We need to talk to Keneke and find out why he didn't share what he learned from Mrs. Brewer, and then bring Neil in for questioning. I'll call Phoebe O'Shea." She opened her notepad and took out her phone. "Maybe she can meet us there. Give us her perspective on the situation with Neil." Winter dialed the number and put the call on speaker.

Two rings. "Hello," a female voice cracked.

"Phoebe O'Shea?"

"Um, yes." She sounded like she was crying.

"This is DCI Agent Winter Stratton. I'm calling in regard to the murder of Lorelei Brewer."

A sob broke out. "Yes, how can I help you?"

"Would you mind coming in to answer a few questions for us?"

The DCI had a few small satellite offices. The one closest to Bitterroot Falls was a thirty-minute drive. The only staff were Declan Hart, Winter and an office manager, Heather Sturgess.

"I haven't left my apartment," Phoebe said. "Not since I got back from dinner with Lorelei. I was so sick. Throwing up all night. By the time I was feeling better, I crashed and slept. When I woke up, I saw the news about the shooting, and I tried calling her." Phoebe's voice cracked again. "Found out she was dead. This can't be happening."

"We can come to you if that would be easier."

"No, that's okay. I need to shower. Pull myself together. Leave my apartment. Get some fresh air. I'll come to the police station."

Chance mouthed, *the IPS office.* A shorter drive than to DCI, and if the BFPD wasn't sharing information with them, he didn't want to question Phoebe at the police station.

"Actually, we'll see you at the Ironside Protection Services office. I'm working with Chance Reyes, an IPS investigator on this." Winter gave her the address. "We'll see you there at noon."

"Can we make it three?" The woman sobbed. "I think I might need a little longer to get myself together, if that's all right."

That would give them time to swing by the hotel. Check in with Bo and Tak. Get an update on the interviews of the hotel staff. He nodded to Winter when she glanced at him.

"Sure. See you at three." Winter hung up.

"Hopefully, Phoebe can shed more light on all this for us." Chance's phone rang. Bluetooth brought the caller ID up on the dash. The Bitterroot Falls PD. He tapped the green icon. "Hello."

"Uh, Mr. Reyes, this is Neil Reynolds," the shaky voice said, and Winter looked over at Chance. "I've been arrested.

The police think that I was the shooter yesterday. I wasn't. I didn't do anything. I promise. You're my one phone call since you're the only lawyer I know. Can you help me?"

"I'm actually on my way there now with a DCI agent," Chance said. "We're investigating the case together. Don't say anything until we arrive."

"I already told them that I didn't do it, but okay, I won't say anything else. Please, hurry."

"Be there in twenty minutes." Chance disconnected the call.

"You can't represent him," Winter said. "It would be a conflict of interest if you work this case with me."

"I'm not going to represent him, and I'll make that clear when we get there. But I can get a court-appointed lawyer to show up quicker than the police department." He scrolled through his phone while he drove.

"Safety first." She took the cell from his hand. "Whose number are you looking for?"

"Gretchen Price," he said. "She's a great public defender. Has a heart of gold."

"High praise. Are you sure she's going to drop whatever she's doing right this second and race over to the police station?"

"For me, she will." He and Gretchen had a bit of history. She was the last woman he dated. Pretty, smart, sweet. The relationship had been going along fine, even though he felt like something was missing. Then he met Winter and realized what he didn't have with Gretchen.

A spark.

A sense of excitement being near her.

Anticipation to see her again.

Chance experienced more heat bantering with Winter than he did making love with Gretchen. That told him everything he needed to know. He wanted to kindle the spark with Winter and fan those flames. Gretchen deserved a guy who felt that way about her. So, he did the honorable thing, was honest and broke up with her. Something he'd never done before—end a relationship with one woman in the hopes of being with another. They had parted as friends and still met up to play pickleball, and she moved on to dating city council member Bill Nesbitt.

Grabbing her coffee, Winter shifted in her seat and looked at him. "How is it that you have everyone from the chief of police to the public defender with a heart of gold wrapped around your little finger? Or are you capitalizing off this apparent celebrity status where everyone knows who you are? What's the deal with that anyway? Is it a rich guy thing?"

This was all new to her since they had never spent time together in public before. He guessed neither sister had shared his history with her, which he preferred. Chance wanted Winter to get to know him one-on-one, not secondhand through someone else's lens.

"I'm not rich. I made smart investment choices. I'm well-off."

"Says the guy who drops twenty grand a year on a club membership without batting a lash. That's the cost of a car. Some people's annual salary."

"I'm a social person. It's important to put myself out there to grow the IPS business. Gretchen will come once I tell her about Neil," Chance said, matter-of-fact because that was also true. "He's innocent. I'm sure of it. I want him to talk while I'm there along with his attorney. Let him provide an alibi and explain his side of things."

"*If* he has an alibi."

Chance hoped like hell that Neil did. "He was somewhere doing something yesterday morning, and it wasn't on the rooftop bar of the hotel picking people off on a crowded street." Chance would bet everything he had on it.

Winter clutched his forearm. "I couldn't imagine anyone I knew well, an employee, an intern I had taken under my wing and trusted, killing people and deliberately wounding several others. I think I would immediately defend the person, too, then find out the specifics of what happened and why. I can't blame you for your loyalty, Chance. In fact, I like that about you. Admirable trait to stick by your friends, even when it isn't easy." She dropped her hand. "I guess we'll see if you're right." She hit the call icon, dialing the number for the public defender.

"Let me do all the talking with Gretchen."

Chapter Nine

Talking to Keneke was a waste of time. His answers were all the same and getting them nowhere.

"The chief gave me the go-ahead," Officer Keneke said. "To get both an arrest and a search warrant and to bring in Neil Reynolds first thing this morning."

This had been set in motion the night before, with the request for the warrants, and executed today. More than enough time for the BFPD to have apprised them of the situation.

"Why didn't you call us?" Winter asked. "So that we weren't hit with any surprises. We're the leads on this case. You should've made it a point of keeping us in the loop. It's called professional courtesy."

"The chief didn't give me any instructions to—"

"Okay." Chance patted him on the shoulder. "We get the picture. Where's Ed?"

"Over at the hotel. You just missed him. He heard some IPS fellas were conducting interviews with the entire staff. He wanted to sit in. Funny how upset you two are about us not calling you. Where was the professional courtesy when it came to the interviews?"

Was she living in an alternate version of reality? "Chief Macon agreed the BFPD would take a hands-off approach to this case. Notifying Lorelei Brewer's family about her death was one thing. Sitting in on interviews of the hotel staff, getting an arrest warrant based on circumstantial evidence and hauling in a suspect without giving us a heads-up is entirely different."

"The chief felt the evidence we had was strong enough to bring Reynolds in. The suspect's level of marksmanship, his repeated threats and harassment of Miss Brewer, along with the restraining order." He handed them a copy.

Winter and Chance looked over the order of protection. The respondent was not to harass or contact the petitioner and was to stay away from her, her residence and place of employment for two years. No direct or indirect contact, just like Sadie had told them.

Fairly standard issue, though the length of time was the maximum. The duration was strong considering this was the first one and Lorelei had cited stalking as the reason for the order, with no assault, aggravated or otherwise.

Winter would rather have a straightforward domestic violence case or gang attack instead of this. At first, the shooting appeared random, senseless, and it still might be, but Sadie Brewer's accusation had changed the focus to a possible targeted hit.

"Neil Reynolds is clean," Chance said, "except for this, right?"

Keneke hesitated. "He is. Doesn't have a record. But there's a ton of evidence that he continued to harass and stalk Lorelei Brewer online. Emails and direct messages. Over a hundred of them since July."

Nearly one message a day. Quite a lot. Neil was persistent if nothing else.

Winter handed the document back. "Did she ever report any violations of the order of protection to the BFPD?"

The soon-to-be detective blanched. "Well, um, no. No, she never did."

According to the stepmother and the printouts Winter was holding, there had been plenty of opportunities. Why didn't Lorelei have Neil arrested when she could've done so a hundred times?

"But that's beside the point," Keneke added. "Two women are dead, and two others injured because Reynolds might have snapped and gone into a rampage."

She wanted to catch the person responsible as much as anyone, but it had to be the right guy. "A rampage suggests an uncontrolled burst of violence. That's not what yesterday's shooting was."

"The chief said—"

"I think we understand," Chance interrupted him. "We'll take this up with Ed."

"Fine by me," Keneke said.

Something caught Chance's eye as he turned. Winter followed his line of sight to a cute, leggy blonde who strode into the police station. She was pretty, slim and tall enough—easily five ten—to be a fashion model. The only things setting her apart from those gracing a runway were the dark suit she wore, the messenger-style briefcase she carried, her hair pulled back in a low, sleek bun and chic glasses.

"There's Gretchen." Chance waved to her, and she lit up, acknowledging him with a head nod before turning to the officer at the front desk. "Neil Reynolds's lawyer is here," he said to Keneke. "We're ready to talk to him."

"Without you," Winter said, also looking at Keneke. "You've already had your time with Reynolds, but you're more than welcome to listen in."

Keneke folded his arms. "The chief won't like this. He hasn't had a chance to interrogate him yet."

"Let us worry about Chief Macon," Chance said. "Which interview room is Neil in?"

"Two. I'll be in the observation room, watching and listening, and I'm going to call the chief."

"Excellent," Chance said. "Because we'd love to have a word with him. Face to face."

Taking out his cell phone, Keneke walked away.

The public defender cut through the bullpen and hurried over to Chance. She wrapped her arms around his neck, hauling him into a big hug. "Thank goodness, you're all right."

Their embrace took Winter by surprise. Chance had neglected to mention they were such close friends, but it would make sense if he was certain he could count on her to show up at a moment's notice.

Gretchen pulled his Stetson from his head and looked him over. "I can't believe you were caught in the crossfire. Everything that's been reported sounds terrifying." She pressed her palm to Chance's cheek. "You almost died yesterday."

Winter's fingers tingled, and her neck heated. What was wrong with her? Was she jealous?

No. That would be ridiculous.

Yet, she didn't like the interaction between Gretchen and Chance. They were more than friends. Winter felt as though she was intruding on an intimate moment.

"I got lucky." Chance removed her hand from his face and stepped back from her. "I can't say the same about some others."

"It's been all over the news. The names were finally released this morning. Poor Lorelei Brewer and Abby Schultz. At least Ty Lee and Nora Santana are going to be all right. Our town hasn't been rocked by something like this since the slaughterhouse murders." She gave him another tight hug as she curled her manicured fingers in his hair. "I'm glad we didn't lose you." Her face filled with relief and deep affection.

Tightening her grip on the printouts in her hand, Winter

gritted her teeth against another surge of jealousy that both surprised and embarrassed her.

She gave a little cough to get their attention.

Chance took his hat from the public defender. "Gretchen Price, this is the DCI agent I'm working with on the case, Winter Stratton."

Gretchen's blue eyes widened. "Ah." She gripped her bag with both hands, her demeanor changing in a snap to reserved. "One of the *season* sisters."

"Excuse me?" Winter stiffened. "Is that what people around town are calling us?"

Gretchen turned to Chance and stared at him.

He cleared his throat. "I'm the one who started calling you three that. Before I met all of you."

Winter narrowed her eyes at him. "The season sisters?" She expected something as juvenile as that in middle school and had been called worse. Her parents had their reasons for their choices in naming them, not that it meant she had to agree with it.

He shrugged. "No insult was intended."

"Is it her?" Gretchen asked casually, coolly. "Or the psychologist who works for you, Autumn?"

"What are we talking about?" Winter glanced between them, disliking how she was clearly missing something important.

Chance plastered on one of his perfect smiles, an ideal weapon to disarm a person. "Gretch, how about we discuss this later?" His tone was soft as cotton. "Over lunch?"

"I rushed out of a meeting with my boss to do you this favor," Gretchen said, her voice like cotton candy—airy, light and spun with sticky sweetness. "I'd like an answer now. Not later." Rather than being disarmed, the lawyer flashed her own weapon—a polite smile, a single deep dimple punctured her cheek. The asymmetry of it shouldn't have been beautiful, but it was. Like a collapsing star.

"I appreciate the favor," Chance said, "and I'll return it in kind. I'm good for it."

"Of course you are, but that's not the current topic of discussion. Don't get me wrong, what happened between us was for the best because Bill is fantastic. I'm relieved you weren't hurt yesterday and more than happy to help you and Neil Reynolds. I'm asking for very little. I think I deserve to know. Don't you?"

A twinge of irritation prickled Winter. "Know what exactly regarding me and my sister?"

Gretchen pivoted toward her. "Is it you or Autumn who's dating him?"

Winter raised both eyebrows. "Dating Chance?" She was so caught off guard, she had to repeat the question to be sure she'd heard correctly. "Neither of us." Autumn was already in a relationship.

"Really?" Gretchen tilted her head and glared at him—all pretense of niceness evaporated. "Why did you lie to me?" Her tone was low but razor-sharp. "You didn't need to make up an excuse. We're both adults."

Chance lowered his head, his usual casual confidence deflating like a balloon. "I didn't lie." He lifted his eyes. "I was trying to do the right thing by being honest."

Winter's phone buzzed with an incoming call, and she took the cell from her pocket. It was Summer.

"You should take that," Chance suggested quickly. "We'll meet you by the interrogation room." He put a hand to the small of Gretchen's back and led her down a corridor away from the bullpen and out of earshot.

Winter cursed the timing of the call. "Hey, I can't talk right now."

"Are you okay? Logan got in late last night. He didn't mention you might've gotten hurt yesterday until this morning."

"I'm fine. A few bruised ribs."

Summer gasped. "Oh, my God. You should be resting. Please tell me you're going to take off a few days."

"I'm working."

Her sister sighed. "You promised me you were going to do things differently once you moved here. Slow down. Enjoy life. Take care of yourself."

Summer was the beating heart of their family, nurturing, always taking care of everybody. Autumn was the head, their light in the darkness, leading the way, and Winter, she was the backbone.

"I will," Winter said. "I promise. After this case is wrapped up."

Her sister made an exasperated sound. "You're hopeless."

"That's me, the lost-cause sister." One thing in her life she got right, did well without exception, was being a cop.

"Is it true you're working this case with Chance?" Summer asked.

"Yep." She looked down the corridor at Gretchen and Chance. They were still talking, and the supermodel/lawyer kept glancing at her. "I am."

"How did that happen?"

"Long story. I can't get into it right now," Winter said. "I really have to go."

"Okay, fine." The disappointment in Summer's tone was clear. "Two quick things. First, keep your distance from Chance."

"He's been helpful." In more ways than one. "An unexpected facilitator." A protector.

"That's not what I mean. I love Chance, he's a great investigator, a fantastic guy. But," Summer said, drawing out the word, "I've seen the way you look at him. He isn't the marrying type. He's a playboy. That's not what you need, but I may have found the perfect guy for you."

Winter didn't like the sound of that. She didn't need her sister to play matchmaker.

She glanced at the hallway again. A smug expression hung on the blonde's face as she smoothed down the front of her jacket. Then she disappeared inside the interrogation room.

Chance leaned against the wall and tipped his head back.

"What I need is to solve this case, not be set up on a date with anyone," Winter said, and Summer grumbled her annoyance. "The second thing?"

"Logan wants to make sure everyone shows up this time for the barbecue, so we can have a proper family meal together."

Where he can propose. Her baby sister deserved every happiness in the world. She was special, full of hope, with a dauntless belief in the magic of soulmates.

They weren't built the same. If Logan ever hurt her sister, if the marriage didn't work out for some reason, it would devastate Summer and forever shatter her fairy-tale ideas about love. One jaded sister among them was enough, and Winter filled the position.

She started down the hallway. Chance was right, her sister wasn't a baby anymore. "I like Logan. You two are good together," she said, meaning every word. She'd never seen her sister so settled and satisfied in a relationship. "It's great that he cares so much about family. Don't worry, I'll be there." Nothing was going to stop her from showing up for her sister.

"Get some rest and take care of yourself for once. Prioritize your health," Summer said. "You're not the only person who can solve this case, you know."

For Winter, this became personal the moment the sniper had nearly shot her and Chance. Nobody messed with her family. "Love you. Bye."

"Love you, too. See you tomorrow night."

They hung up. Summer had two valid points. Winter needed to keep her distance from Chance—which would be impossible while staying with him at his house—as well as make more time for her sisters and all the other things on her to-do list.

Winter met up with Chance outside interrogation room two.

"Gretchen went in to talk with Neil," he said. "I had Keneke turn off the audio in the observation room while they're speaking."

"Chance." Winter eased closer to him.

"I didn't expect the conversation to take that kind of turn." He scrubbed a hand through his hair, ruffling his thick curls. "I'm sorry if it made you uncomfortable. Now's not the time to discuss it, but if you need details, ask me some other time. After we get through this." He crossed his arms over his chest.

She was curious why Gretchen had the impression either Winter or Autumn was dating Chance, but she agreed with him. This wasn't the time or the place.

There was something far more pressing, and he was going to hate hearing it, but it had to be said. "I don't think you should come in with me. It'd be better for you to wait in the observation room."

"What?" He pushed off the wall and straightened. "Why?"

Chapter Ten

Wait in the observation room.

The words hit Chance like a betrayal. "I should be the one interviewing him. Neil trusts me to help him through this. Not only is he expecting me to be in there, but I can also get the answers out of him that we need."

Trust and loyalty meant everything to Chance. At twenty-three, Neil had already experienced too many difficulties. Chance had witnessed firsthand how the young man had been unfairly judged and mislabeled by those who didn't know he was autistic or understand his ASD. How hard it was for him to make friends, to find a job, to fit in. Sadie Brewer's assessment and vilification of Neil only reaffirmed Chance's worst fears. He couldn't let the kid down now. Not when he needed support more than ever.

"You're his friend and employer," Winter said, "and you provided him with resources that he possibly used to stalk and harass Lorelei Brewer. I can't have you tainting the interview."

He rocked back on his heels. "I would never. My goal is to find the shooter and bring him to justice, whoever it is. Even if it turns out to be Neil." But Chance was still certain the young man wasn't the perp they were after.

"I'm not questioning your ethics or your character on this.

Please believe me." She put a hand to his chest, her touch and her tone calming. "I'm asking you to zoom out. Big picture. Think about how your direct involvement in his interrogation will be perceived by Chief Macon, a prosecutor, a judge. If you want to clear his name and protect him, then someone objective should talk to him. It can't be you, Chance. You're too close to Neil."

"Fine. I don't have to ask a single question. I'll just sit there. Quietly. Reassuring him simply by being there."

"Your presence in that room won't help him. In fact, it might hurt him. As a cop, I'd prefer to have you in there, making Neil comfortable, getting him to open up and spill his guts. But as *your* friend, as someone who cares about you, I don't want you to regret walking through that door and having your good intentions backfire. Trust Gretchen and me to both do our jobs." She moved her hand to his arm. "Wait with Keneke. Okay."

Chance hesitated, deliberating. He trusted Gretchen to watch out for Neil and ensure he wasn't railroaded by anyone. Not that he thought Winter would ever do such a thing. She was tough, and as a cop she had to be, but she was tender and fiercely protective, too. A sort of mama bear with no cubs. She fought for the weak and defenseless as hard as she fought against the bad guys. He trusted Winter to have an open mind, to look at the facts, to use her experience and instincts to get to the truth.

"All right," he said with a reluctant nod.

They separated, each going inside the adjoining rooms.

"You can start recording again," Chance said to Keneke.

The officer flipped a switch, and a light on the wall turned from red to green. "Chief Macon is on his way."

Chance cut his eyes from the officer to the interrogation room.

Winter stepped behind the table across from Gretchen and

Neil. His sandy brown hair peeked out from a beanie hat he wore, and he chewed on his thumbnail.

Nail biting, drumming fingers, cracking knuckles, rocking were all forms of stimming. Self-stimulating behavior, Chance had learned, occurred whether someone was autistic or not, but with ASD, the behaviors tended to be repetitive.

Neil looked up at Winter and then at the door, his brow furrowing. "Where's Mr. Reyes?"

"I'm DCI Agent Winter Stratton." She showed him her ID. "Chance Reyes won't be sitting in."

Neil's shoulders hunched. "Why isn't he coming in?"

Winter remained standing for some reason. "I wanted to ask you questions without him being in the room because you two are not only friends, but he's also your employer. It's better for the investigation and for you if he's not present, but he's watching and listening." She pointed to the two-way mirror over her shoulder. "Right in the next room. When we're done, you can see him."

Chewing on his nail again, Neil nodded.

Chance hoped he was doing the right thing by not being in the room. He thought about Mrs. Reynolds and how heartbroken she would be, how this could ruin Neil's future, if this interview didn't go well. Prosecutors made cases all the time based on circumstantial evidence and got convictions. Evidence, such as the restraining order along with recurring violations, witness testimony—Sadie Brewer would be compelling on the stand—and everything when considered together could point to a defendant's guilt.

"Would you mind standing for me for a moment?" Winter asked. "And turn slowly in a full circle."

Neil looked at his attorney, uncertainty furrowing his brow. Gretchen gestured that it was all right, and he did as Winter asked.

She had gotten the closest to the shooter, had the best look at them. Winter was probably trying to determine whether Neil fit the physical profile.

Lean. Athletic frame. Broad shoulders. The right height, between five ten and six two. He had pale green eyes. Over the radio, she had only stated that they were light in color, which meant she wasn't sure if the sniper's eyes were green or blue.

Unfortunately, Winter wouldn't be able to rule Neil out based on his physical build.

"Thank you." Winter sat and gestured for him to do the same.

"Is it true?" Neil asked. "Is Lorelei really dead?" He must've been arrested before her name had been released to the press.

"Yes." Winter nodded. "It's true."

His face tightened, and he shook his head. "No. Goodness, no." He looked up at the ceiling and breathed deeply. "I knew this would happen. I tried to tell her." He tilted his neck. "Warned her that she was being reckless. I just—oh, Lorelei." Neil squeezed his eyes shut. "I can't believe she's gone."

His tone was full of anger and accusation and grief. One second, he sounded bereaved and the next, furious. Chance could only assume how Winter or Keneke or Ed watching this later might interpret Neil's intense emotions. The way he flipped a switch so fast, so easily wasn't a good sign.

"Where were you yesterday morning?" Winter asked.

Neil tensed. "What? I don't believe this!" Sitting up straight, he slapped the metal table. "She told me you're working with Chance," he said, pointing at Gretchen. "That you two are friends. Did you come here to accuse me, too?" Sorrow swung like a volatile pendulum into hot anger.

Keneke turned to Chance in the observation room. "He's unstable."

"He's not," Chance snapped back at him.

The door opened, and Ed dipped inside, shutting it behind him.

"You should have told us about the warrant and hauling in Neil Reynolds," Chance said.

"Told you our prime suspect is one of your employees?" Ed scoffed. "So you can go into damage control and launch a campaign to save him? I think not. I've seen how you rally to protect your own."

Chance didn't bother to argue. What counterpoint could he offer? He took care of his family and friends, and he wouldn't apologize for it, but he also wouldn't defend a cold-blooded murderer.

"How did you find out so fast that we have him?" Ed asked.

"I was his one phone call."

Ed shook his head. "Of course you were."

"Calm down," Gretchen said to Neil, folding her hands on the table in the interrogation room. "These are routine questions. She has to ask them. I need you to answer, but keep your responses short."

"I'm sorry." Neil shook his head and drummed his fingers on the table. "I just—I called Chance for help. I thought you were coming here to do that. To get me out of this place."

"I'm here to get to the truth about what happened," Winter said. "If you're innocent, then this process will help you."

"Why does everyone think I'm the shooter, huh?" Neil lowered his head. "That I would ever hurt Lorelei?"

"You used to be in a romantic relationship with Lorelei. After you broke up, she got an order of protection against you because you were harassing her. Stalking her." Winter set the printouts down and pushed them across to the other side of the table. "Then you sent her threatening messages."

"That's all being taken out of context, and I—"

"Neil," Gretchen said, interrupting him. "Agent Stratton didn't ask a question that time. Let's stick to only answering her questions. Where were you yesterday morning and what were you doing?"

"It doesn't have anything to do with Lorelei."

"Your whereabouts could establish an alibi," Winter said.

"When yesterday?" Neil asked through gritted teeth, tapping his fingers. "What time?"

The shooting happened at nine fifteen. They needed to establish a decent window before and after that time. At least thirty minutes on either side.

"Let's start at eight thirty," Winter said, "and work your way forward to ten."

A forty-five-minute window was even better.

"I made breakfast for my grandmother," Neil said. "Oatmeal. She has high blood pressure and cholesterol. The doctor recommended it. Skim milk sweetened with honey."

Ed grunted. "A close family member as an alibi is the worst. In my experience, they tend to be unreliable. Loved ones sometimes try to protect their family by stretching the truth, sometimes with outright lies," he said.

"Then what did you do next?" Winter asked.

"I finished fixing the front porch. We had some loose boards, and I replaced the blown lightbulbs out front. I dropped off a quilt my grandmother made for Ms. Phyllis."

"Phyllis who?" Winter scribbled everything down in her notepad.

"Tenney."

"Did you speak with her?" she asked.

"No, she wasn't home. I guess she had already left for work. Ms. Phyllis teaches painting at the senior center. I set the wrapped quilt by her front door. Then I went to work at Mr. Reyes's ranch. I got there at ten thirty."

"See." Ed gestured to Neil through the glass. "A big gap

of time where no one can confirm his whereabouts besides his grandmother. A flimsy alibi at best."

"Kind of late for work," Winter said, "isn't it?"

Chance afforded him a lot of latitude. Neil was a hard worker, did an outstanding job at balancing the ranch's books and cutting costs to save him money. The kid was salaried and could work whatever hours he wanted.

"I need to go to the ranch most days to do my job," Neil said. "I can work from my house on my computer, but Mr. Reyes wants me to work out of his home office. He says it's good for me to be around the other folks on the ranch. To socialize."

Expanding his circle of friends, getting exposure to more than his grandmother now that he wasn't in college anymore was good for him.

"Neil." Winter set her pen down. "When was the last time you saw Lorelei?"

"Last Friday night. I followed her, waited for her to finish a hair appointment at the salon, Pizzazz, and we talked in my car."

The admission struck Chance hard in the gut.

"Unreal," Ed said. "He's hanging himself."

Gretchen leaned over and whispered in Neil's ear. He shook his head in response.

"You followed her and spoke to her," Winter said, "when there's an order of protection stating you are not allowed within one hundred yards of Lorelei?"

Gretchen leaned over again.

But he pulled away. "I didn't do anything wrong."

"Yes. You did." Winter kept a patient tone. Not too firm. "You got within one hundred yards of her."

Neil wrapped his arms around himself and stared down at the table. "No, I didn't. Lorelei walked over to *me* and hopped inside *my* car."

Chance believed him, but why would Lorelei do that if she was terrified of Neil?

"But you weren't supposed to be anywhere near her," Winter said. "Yet you just admitted to following her."

"You don't understand."

"Neil." Winter stayed silent until he looked up at her. "Explain it to me."

He went back to chewing on his nail, keeping one arm tucked around his midsection, not saying anything for almost a minute.

Too long.

Surely, Winter and Ed were wondering if he was trying to come up with a story. Fabricate a lie. Neil was holding back, deciding what to say. Only Chance couldn't understand why.

"Relationships can be complicated," Winter said. "Why don't you start at the beginning?"

"Lorelei and I met in college," Neil said. "We were both working on our business degrees at the same time. We liked the same movies and music, and she said she could be herself with me. Didn't have to pretend the way she did with other guys. We broke up last winter because we were fighting a lot."

"Fighting about what?"

"She and Phoebe started working for this bad guy, Dallas, at a club."

"Phoebe O'Shea."

He nodded. "This guy is trouble."

"Is Dallas his first name? Surname?"

"No, it's just what people called him. A nickname."

Winter glanced at her notes. "So Lorelei and Phoebe started working at the Buckthorn Club, and you fought about it."

"What? No," Neil said, shaking his head. "They used to work as much as possible at the Buckthorn as waitresses. For two or three years. I didn't care. That's how Lorelei paid her way through college, but then she and Phoebe got tangled up with Dallas. They cut back on their hours at the Buckthorn Club and started working for Dallas instead. But the guy is into drugs. All sorts of illegal things. Maybe even sex trafficking. Lorelei thought I was acting controlling, trying to tell her how to live her life. But I was only worried about her. When we broke up, we parted as friends. Ask anyone."

"Lorelei's stepmother, Sadie, told us that you couldn't handle the breakup and became angry, possessive, scary."

"Mrs. Brewer never liked me," he said. "A lot of NT girls hate my guts. It's easier for me to make friends with guys, like the ones on the Reyes ranch."

"NT?" Winter asked.

"Neurotypical. Mrs. Brewer thinks I have weird vibes. Says my face is always too judgy. She never wanted Lorelei to go out with me. Tried to get her to break things off with me from the beginning," he said, drumming his fingers. The motion calmed him. "After Lorelei and I broke up and just became friends, I couldn't stop worrying about her. Then in June, I confronted her and warned her about Dallas. We got into a really bad argument. Phoebe was there and screamed at me that I was going to ruin everything. Tick off the wrong people. That's when Lorelei got the order of protection against me."

Chance folded his arms, unease sliding through him.

"Because you threatened her?" Winter asked.

His gaze flew up to hers. "No! Never."

"Then why was she so scared of you that she needed an order of protection?"

Neil clenched his hands into fists and went back to staring at the table. "She wasn't scared of me. She was scared *for* me. Lorelei got the restraining order to protect me."

"Protect *you*?" The same surprise that jolted through Chance rang in Winter's voice. "From what?" she asked.

"From myself. That's what she told me. From finding out too much about what she was doing with Dallas. She still cared about me, the way I cared about her. I warned her Dallas was going to get her hurt." His face reddened as his voice grew low. "That if she wasn't careful, he might get her killed with the sorts of things he's involved in. I know it sounds awful, but I needed her to see that when she messed around with bad people, there were bad consequences. Whatever she and her best friend were doing, it wasn't worth all the extra money."

Extra money. Lorelei and Phoebe had big dreams, according to the stepmother. Big plans to make something of themselves. What had they gotten themselves mixed up in?

"Last Friday," Winter said, "why did you go see Lorelei? What did you say to her?"

Neil chewed on his nail, looking down at his lap. "That night, I told her that I had been investigating Dallas. I found out his real name is Devon Groban. He's from Dallas, Texas. Has an arrest record."

"Do you know where we can find him? Groban?"

"I never found an address for him, and every time I tried to tail him, he spotted me, but…" Neil's voice trailed.

"But what?" Winter prodded.

"Lorelei and Phoebe called whatever they were doing a 'club,' but I followed them to the Bitterroot Mountain Hotel. That's where they were working. With Dallas. Out of the presidential suite."

"Do you know how often they worked out of the suite?"

Neil shrugged. "I could interpolate a number."

"Interpolate? Not extrapolate?"

"Extrapolation is estimating a value that's outside the data set. You use it to forecast. That's what I did to figure out when the next club nights would be. With interpolation, you read the values between two points in a data set. I could use it to identify missing past values."

"How did you collect your data?" Winter asked.

Gretchen whispered in Neil's ear.

"I didn't kill Lorelei," he said to his lawyer. "Telling Agent Stratton everything might help them figure out who did. I don't care if it gets me in trouble." Neil chewed on his nail. "I followed Lorelei and Phoebe nine times. It was never the exact same nights. So, I looked for a pattern. I helped Lorelei do that once when she asked me how to create a pattern for something where it wouldn't appear as though one existed even though it did."

"Pseudorandomness," Winter said.

He nodded. "I figured out her pattern was based on the lunar calendar. Every full moon, first quarter, last quarter and new moon she had a 'club' night in the presidential suite, where others would show up. Mostly men."

"Did you recognize any of those men?"

"I didn't see everyone, and I didn't know how to set up proper surveillance to monitor the people who came in and left."

"What kind of clientele did you observe going to the presidential suite on those nights? Were they poorly dressed? Scary or rough looking? Did they blend in with everyone else?"

"They didn't blend in. A couple of the ladies, both older, looked fancy. Pearls. Diamonds. High heel shoes. Some of the men wore suits. The ones who didn't were dressed like Mr. Reyes."

"What do you mean?" Winter asked.

"The guys at the ranch would describe it as classy. Sophisticated. Without being stuffy. Nice boots. Expensive jeans. Stetsons in pristine condition."

The clientele had money and dressed like it.

Keneke turned to Chance and Ed. "If that's true, how did a drug dealer and two girls manage to get a bunch of rich people to go to their exclusive club in the presidential suite?"

Exclusive club. "By networking," Chance said. "While they worked at the Buckthorn." The Bitterroot Mountain Hotel only kept surveillance video for up to thirty days before the system was overridden. "We'll have to get the security footage for the past month that covers the presidential suite," Chance said. "See exactly who was attending those *club* nights."

Ed looked at him. "You'll need a warrant. Who knows what was going on in that suite? After the shooting, the hotel has battened down the hatches. They're in self-preservation mode. Investors of the place are nervous. If there were drugs involved or some kind of kinky sex ring going on in that suite, it would open up the hotel to serious liability. They won't comply unless they're forced to cooperate. I guarantee it."

"From here on out, Ed," Chance said, "information is a two-way street, and we work in tandem. No more stunts like today."

The chief didn't say anything, but he nodded. Chance would have to take that.

"When I told Lorelei what I learned," Neil said, "it seemed to really scare her that I knew so much about Dallas and what she was doing. I threatened to keep digging, to find out everything I could about his business, to take pictures of the people attending the club nights and turn it over to the police. Lorelei told me that if I truly cared about her that I would stop and leave it alone. She yelled at me about going to the police. Said I had to forget about everything. That I didn't know who I was messing with by snooping. She didn't want to have me arrested, but she told me that she would, to save me from myself. Because if I didn't back off, stay out of *her business* and stop meddling in things that were none of my concern, I would be the one who ended up dead."

Chapter Eleven

Pacing back and forth inside Chance's office at IPS, Winter couldn't shake the sense that something was off about this case. "I can't believe the judge didn't grant us the warrant."

"Judge Hyllested didn't deny it, either," Chance said. "He wants time to review everything."

"We presented the affidavit with a clear probable cause. What more does he need?" She thought Chance would be more upset about this. "Lorelei Brewer's death could be related to whatever was going on inside that hotel room four times a month. It could lead us to the real killer and get Neil out of a holding cell." Where the kid was going to sit for the next seventy-two hours. Possibly longer, if the office of the district attorney decided to file formal charges. Neil did admit to breaking the law, on numerous occasions, when he violated the order of protection.

"I'm not letting Neil stay in a cell any longer than necessary. We should release details to the public like the description of the sniper's vehicle, and I'm going to offer a reward for any information about the shooting. Twenty-five grand if it leads anywhere."

"A lot of money for a tip. Who's paying for it?" No way Director Isaacson would authorize it.

"Worth it for the right tip. I'll forego next year's Buckthorn membership."

Generous of him.

"The only thing is," he said, "since I've got the entire team working on this case, I'll need someone to handle the influx of tips. Do you think your office manager Heather can do it?"

"I'll text her. You send her an email with the details, and she'll get the hotline set up."

They both got on their phones and contacted Heather. The office manager had delayed retiring for the last two years because she enjoyed working, always eager to take on extra tasks. Now that Winter finally had something for her, she was certain Heather wouldn't give them any pushback.

"You know the judge's questions can't be ignored." Chance stretched his neck and sat on the edge of his desk. "We need to dig into Abby Schultz. Take a look at Ty Lee and Nora Santana beyond their preliminary statements. The shooter could've been targeting any one of them. Or none of them. This could still be a senseless, random act of violence."

"You don't buy that it was random any more than I do." Winter sighed in frustration. "How well do you know Hyllested?"

"What do you mean?"

"In the affidavit, it was clear the clientele who frequented those club nights were wealthy. At least the ones Neil spotted. It's also possible they're influential members of the community."

"I think Lorelei and Phoebe found their clients among the members of the Buckthorn."

"Adds up." She nodded. "Is it possible Judge Hyllested got the same impression and might be deliberately delaying approval of the warrant because he doesn't want us taking down the wrong people in his opinion? This mass shooting could turn into a massive scandal."

Chance strode closer to her, radiating confidence that bordered on arrogance. "The one thing small towns and enclaves of wealth and privilege have in common is they avoid scandals. At all costs."

He'd know. Chance and Logan grew up in both. Though neither man acted spoiled. Her soon-to-be brother-in-law made it clear his family's money belonged to his parents, and he had to live off a civil servant's salary.

With Chance, she still hadn't figured him out. He was thirty-five and self-made. Logan had once mentioned Chance's sister received the entire Reyes inheritance after their parents passed away. Everything about Chance screamed wealth: the pedigree, the Ivy League education, the clothes, the ranch he could afford to not manage himself, the splurge of the Buckthorn membership.

Yet, he worked as a private investigator—raking in far more than her but not rolling in big bucks the way he would as a partner in a top firm. Didn't drive something with souped-up hydraulics or flashy like a Hummer. His Ford F-150 was one of countless other pickups in big sky country, though he'd chosen the King Ranch model—not a no-frills, bare-bones package but not top of the line, either. He not only wrote checks to charity but donated his time. Made food runs to bring his employees a hot breakfast. Rallied behind friends when they needed him most. Loyal to a fault.

Fearless when jumping into the fray, willing to risk his life to protect hers.

Chance Reyes was impressive.

"So, yes," he said, "it's possible the judge is trying to avert a scandal, but a delay in issuing a warrant isn't an outright denial. We can't jump the gun with assumptions."

His tone was cool and businesslike, but there was nothing professional about the way he was staring at her. The simmering look in his eyes sent a flutter through her belly.

His attention dropped to her mouth. She found herself thinking about kissing him. Again. About how much she wanted to feel his mouth and his hands and his body pressed up against hers.

Winter turned to move away from him, too quickly. An ache sliced through her side. She groaned and resisted the urge to pop one of her painkillers. She needed all her faculties sharp, not dulled by medicine. Maybe she'd take one later tonight to help her sleep. Winter grabbed a bottle of water from the table beside her and guzzled some.

Coming up alongside her, Chase grazed her jaw with his knuckles and grasped her chin gently, tipping her face back up to his. "Hurting again?" Concern was heavy in his eyes, along with that electric heat.

Her mouth went dry, and she nodded. "I'm okay. It's manageable."

"We should get something to eat, so you can have a painkiller with food. I don't want you taking them on an empty stomach." The protective, almost intimate tone of his voice unsettled her.

It was as though they'd crossed a line, entering a new zone, something deeper and more familiar. Had it happened when the bullets were flying? Or afterward in his truck, when she was holding his hand like a lifeline? Or when he kissed her outside Mrs. Brewer's apartment?

"Winter." His voice was husky with an edge of gravelly heat as he cupped her cheek. He stared at her, his palm pressed to her skin, and to her dismay a warm tingle slid through her body.

She fought against it, but her thoughts careened down a road she had no intention of traveling. Even though she was tempted.

"You're almost as bad as Summer with your worrying." She brushed his hand away and looked through the glass wall of his office across the hall. In the conference room, Autumn was working with Eli Easton to find Devon Groban, aka Dallas. Thankfully, the two hadn't noticed their contact. "Does Autumn know?" She wandered to the other side of the room, needing space to think, to breathe without inhaling the scent of him. "About the engagement."

"No. You're the only person I've told."

Surprising. "Why is that?"

He flattened his mouth into a thin line and closed the distance between them as though he didn't want her beyond his reach. "Can we be completely honest with each other without you getting upset with me or defensive?"

The answer didn't come to her straight away. She rubbed the back of her neck, thinking it over. "Yes. Complete honesty."

"The engagement is supposed to be a surprise. After Logan showed me the ring and told me his plan, I thought of you. That you'd need time to adjust to the idea, and it'd be better for Summer if your happiness for her at the proposal was genuine. Rather than forced. If you're apprehensive or worried, your sisters will see it. I didn't think you'd want to spoil her big day."

A lump formed in Winter's throat at his thoughtfulness. At the fact that he was right. At how he knew her so well. The last thing she'd ever want was to diminish Summer's joy. Tears stung her eyes. Turning her back to him, Winter didn't want him to read anything else on her face. To see the emotion gathering that she had to tamp back down.

"Thank you. For telling me." She was grateful beyond words. All she wanted was for both of her sisters to be safe and happy.

"Sure. It was nothing," he said, but to her it was a lot, it was everything. "You know it would be ideal to have footage of the fourth floor of the hotel to see exactly who was entering and leaving the presidential suite on those nights, but maybe we can still figure out who attended."

She glanced over her shoulder at him. "How?"

He took out his cell phone and scrolled. "We do have the last couple of weeks of surveillance footage of the lobby as well as the side and service entrances. During that time, according to the lunar calendar, there was a full moon on the ninth and a last quarter moon on the eighteenth. They would be scheduled to have a club night this evening, too. There's a new moon."

"We have security footage of the nights they had their last two meetings." She looked up at the clock on the wall. Four thirty. "I believe Phoebe O'Shea is officially a no-show."

"I could try her again, but we've already left three messages."

None of them returned.

"Don't bother." Finding her composure, she pivoted, facing him, and folded her arms. "We should go to her place and knock on her door."

"If she doesn't want to be found, then she won't be there." He leaned against the wall and put his hands behind his head. "Maybe she pushed back the time of the interview to give herself a bigger head start at running."

Running from what? The shooter? From answering questions about the club nights in the presidential suite? Winter hadn't even brought that part up yet.

"It's possible, but she really sounded like she was grieving." Heartbroken. "I believed her when she told us that she needed extra time to get herself together. I say it doesn't hurt to try."

"Okay." He strode across the room and picked up his jacket and hat. "Let's go. I'll get the others to comb through the security footage."

Winter put on her sunglasses to conceal from her sister

what makeup didn't on her face. Not only the bruise starting to poke through her foundation but also the mushy emotions for Chance that were brewing. She hoped she'd look and feel better by the barbecue tomorrow.

On their way out of the office, they swung by the conference room.

"How is it going?" Chance asked. "Make any headway locating Dallas?"

Autumn shook her head. "Unfortunately, we haven't."

"He must be living here under a different alias," Eli said. "Good at covering his tracks."

"There might be a different way to find him." Autumn leaned back in her chair, playing with a pen between her fingers. Something she often did when she was thinking. "He has a history of being a dealer in Texas, and Neil Reynolds thought he was doing the same here. We should assume that's correct. If we can't find Dallas, there's a subset of people who can. Drug addicts. They always know how to locate a dealer."

Eli snapped his fingers. "I know exactly where to start."

"Do I even want to know how?" Winter asked. She rested her shoulder against the door jamb and hid a wince to keep from drawing Autumn's attention. Still, her sister narrowed her eyes at her like she'd spotted it.

"It's not like that," Eli said with a smirk. "Narcotics Anonymous. They have meetings over at the auxiliary building of the church on West Street. They rotate between AA and NA. We should start there."

"I'll go with you," Autumn said.

"Not so fast." Chance raised a palm. "I need one of you to review the surveillance footage of the hotel for the evenings of the ninth and eighteenth."

"What are we looking for?" Autumn asked.

"We need to ID the clientele who attended the club nights

at the presidential suite," Chance said. "Pick out wealthy individuals, possibly powerful people in the community, who came in and left on those nights. That's why I'd rather have Eli do it. You know who's who around here better than Autumn."

"I don't mind going to the church by myself." Standing, Autumn grabbed her purse. "I'm good at getting people to talk."

"I mind," Eli said. "You're still learning the hang of things. Tracking a drug dealer could get dicey, and we don't know if he's involved in the shooting. The odds are we'll have to sit around at the church and wait to chat with someone who's willing to talk to us anyway." Eli closed his laptop. "I can review the footage during the downtime. We'll go together."

It was reassuring how the team was looking out for her sister and keeping her safe while teaching her everything she needed to know about being an investigator.

"One more thing," Chance said. "I only had an opportunity to review the past four days to see if our shooter scoped out the hotel. Finish going through the footage and flag anyone that looks suspicious for us to dig into further."

Eli gave a curt nod. "Got it."

Autumn strode around the desk and came up to Winter as they all headed out. "Hey, are you okay?" Autumn asked. "You looked like you were in a bit of pain."

"Bruised ribs. No big deal."

"It's a very big deal," Chance said. "She's in pain right now and can't even laugh without it hurting."

Winter gave him a scathing look.

"What?" He shrugged a shoulder. "She's going to find out from Summer tomorrow night at the barbecue anyway."

True, but it was up to Winter to decide when and how much to tell her sisters.

"What happened?" Autumn asked.

"Altercation with our shooter. I'm fine." Winter didn't want to worry her. "No serious damage done." They stepped outside. "Stay safe."

"I should be saying that to you. Don't worry about me. None of the guys at IPS would let anything happen to me."

Good to hear. Autumn looked fulfilled, excited, as though she was enjoying the work at Ironside. Being a forensic psychologist/investigator suited her.

Winter and Chance climbed into his truck. He cranked the engine, and they sped off, leaving the lot at the same time as Autumn and Eli.

"I could've said more to Autumn about what you've been through." Chance glanced at her. "Instead, I'm keeping your secrets."

"Don't say it like you're doing me a favor. Deep down, I think you enjoy it, having this clandestine pact between the two of us that gets me under your roof." And potentially closer to his bed. "Rather than under one of my sisters'."

A Cheshire cat grin curled on his mouth, and he didn't bother to deny it. Then he had the nerve to wink at her. Insufferable and incorrigible and…so darn irresistible.

Even more annoying was that she preferred Chance's company to working a case alone, which was how they handled things at DCI with a small staff. It wasn't about loneliness, though. She was beginning to crave his company.

A worrisome sign.

Winter took out her notepad to get the address for Phoebe O'Shea.

"I know where the new condos are," he said, like a mind reader. "They're on the opposite side of the lake from Logan and Summer."

She figured it'd take twenty minutes to get there.

"Do you want to grab a bite on the way?" He turned on

to Lake Shore Drive, the road that would take them straight there.

"Afterward. Unless you're starving."

"I can wait."

In the middle of Lake Shore, a uniformed officer was directing traffic. On the other side of the road, traffic cones had been set up.

When they came up to the cop, Chance stopped and rolled down his window. "Officer, what's going on?"

"Vehicle accident." The cop kept waving at traffic, not really paying them much attention. "Please move it along."

"Everyone okay?" Chance asked.

"You're holding up traffic, sir. If you could—" The officer finally looked at them. "Oh, Mr. Reyes. I didn't realize it was you. The driver didn't make it. The car ran off the road. Looks like a tire blew. Went down the side of the embankment toward the lake and smashed into a tree," he said. "The vehicle was totaled, and they're going to have to cut the body out of the car."

Chance and Winter exchanged a glance, and a queasy sensation slid through her. She hoped it wasn't Phoebe O'Shea.

"Man or woman?" Chance asked.

"Woman. She was killed on impact."

Winter leaned over, made eye contact with the officer and flashed her badge. "Has a positive ID been made yet?"

The officer shrugged. "I'm in charge of the traffic. I don't know. I believe Officer Keneke is handling that part."

"Thanks." Chance rolled up the window and looked around like he was thinking of trying to make a U-turn. But this Montana highway was only a single lane in either direction. Both were packed with slow-moving cars due to the accident. He kept going. "We'll check the apartment first," he said, like he desperately didn't want it to be the young woman, either. "We're not far."

The rest of the drive along the lake was gorgeous, one of the reasons she loved this scenic road so much, but she couldn't enjoy it. Every minute it took them to reach the condos grated on her nerves.

Chance pulled into the connected two-level parking garage and turned into one of the first available spots. Winter climbed out and met up with him at the rear of the truck.

"What apartment number?" he asked.

"Four twenty-three."

"My gut tells me that she's not home."

Hers did, too. The only thing neither of them said was that they believed Phoebe O'Shea might be the woman dead on the side of the road. A defeat, a setback, another person dead, wasn't what they wanted.

They walked through the long parking garage. The spaces weren't numbered, so not assigned to units. Sometimes residents had to pay for reserved parking, but the garage looked large enough to easily accommodate all condo owners as well as guests. Dinnertime on a weeknight, and the garage was only half full. "Do you know if all the units are sold out?"

"I don't think so. Why? Are you looking to buy?"

"After last night, maybe," she said, half-heartedly.

She wasn't really interested in selling her farmhouse and buying a new place. Not that she was in love with the quaint, old house that constantly needed something repaired or updated. Since her purchase of the home had been less than a year ago, she would lose money if she tried to offload it now, especially this close to winter.

"No need to sink more money into a different place. You're welcome to stay with me for as long as you want." Chance took her hand in his, and her heart skittered. He was actually holding her hand like it was as natural as breathing, like they did this all the time.

She glanced down at their joined hands. "What are you doing?"

"Living in the moment." Interlacing his fingers with hers, he stopped walking. "We need to be in the moment, every moment, and not let a single opportunity to grab joy or appreciate something special, *someone special* standing right in front of us pass us by because it can all be gone in a blink." He pulled her sunglasses up, propping them on her head and caressing her face.

A jolt of heat rushed through her, and she wanted to avert her gaze, but she couldn't bring herself to look anywhere except at those sparkling brown eyes. He was challenging her, and she didn't want to show fear.

"After we almost died last night," he said, "when we were in my truck, you held my hand. Without thinking about it, because you wanted to, and later when I tucked you into bed, you kissed me."

Her jaw dropped slightly, and she rocked back on her heels, but he didn't let her move another inch away from him.

"I kissed you?" It hadn't been a dream.

"I stopped it and left, but those moments between us were real. Honest. I just don't want them with anything clouding your judgment. Not when you're coming down from an adrenaline rush. Not when you're feeling loopy from pain meds or alcohol." He stroked her bottom lip with his thumb, and the warm tingle that flared in her stomach slid to her thighs. "You feel this connection the same as I do, only I'm not running from it, I'm running toward it. To you." Lifting their joined hands to his chest, he pressed the back of hers to his sternum. "You're so fixated on this thing between us turning into a disaster, but you never struck me as the type to give into fear without a fight." He took a breath. "What if this turns into something beautiful and lasting? Wouldn't it be worth the risk?"

Her throat tightened as she tried to scrape together some argument. The truth was his intensity appealed to her. Every single thing about him appealed to her. Except for his familial ties to Logan.

He lowered his head and kissed her, and she let him, opening for him—no resistance, no hesitation. The first touch of his tongue sent a bolt of heat rippling through her.

Her mind emptied, and she sank into him. She loved the way he kissed, confident, unyielding, and she suspected he'd make love to her the same way.

After telling herself so many times that she was going to steer clear of him, to protect herself from any more heartache that would inevitably follow another bad choice, this didn't feel wrong or bad. It felt incredibly good.

He tilted her head for a better angle, caressing her, holding her. The sweep of his tongue brought another surge of heat as he cupped her hips, bringing her pelvis to his. She clutched his neck and gripped his jacket and kissed him back hard. A part of her wished she didn't want what he was offering, wishing she didn't need his mouth on hers, his touch, his affection.

But if she was honest with herself, she did. She wanted it. Wanted him.

The soft purr of a car engine had them easing apart.

An SUV pulled out of a parking spot and rolled down the aisle in their direction. It wasn't an old-model Chevy Blazer like the one that belonged to the sharpshooter. A dark Tahoe drew closer.

Nothing unusual about the vehicle. Could've been a resident or guest leaving or a maintenance worker behind the wheel. She saw him clearly through the windshield. The driver was an older man, heavyset, wearing sunglasses. The car's sun visor partially obscured his face, but she didn't get the feeling that he was trying to hide. The man cruised down the aisle, turning his head left and right, like he was looking for someone or a particular car.

Yet, the fine hairs on Winter's arms rose. If she hadn't been attacked less than twenty-fours ago outside her house, she probably wouldn't have paid the vehicle more than cursory attention. Something deep inside of her was still furious and frightened over the fact the sanctuary of her home had been violated by someone making an attempt on her life.

Chance edged them over, more to the side, giving the vehicle plenty of room to pass, as though he sensed it, too.

Wanting to shake it off as paranoia, she gripped his arm, and they started walking again.

The SUV drew closer and closer. Then the man gunned the engine, heading straight for them.

Chapter Twelve

The black SUV was going too fast. The vehicle rocketed at them, bearing down.

Chance turned and drove his shoulder into Winter, knocking her sideways into the space between two parked cars—a Subaru and a GMC—and she kept a tight grip on him, hauling her with him.

They both hit the pavement on their sides. His left knee banged against the concrete.

The SUV crashed into one of the cars beside them, and the Subaru rocked wildly on its suspension as it was hit. The rear end of the Subaru skidded around toward them while the front end of the vehicle crashed into another car on the other side and bounced back. His head rapped against the side of the moving car, which came to a stop with the rear tire only an inch from Winter's face.

His gut twisted at how close it had gotten.

The big black Tahoe scraped along the car, metal screamed as it tore and bent. Shots fired, pinging off the Subaru, over their heads, and then the SUV peeled off.

Tires squealed in the parking lot. Someone screamed.

Winter jumped up from the ground, with her Glock drawn. She practically vaulted over the back end of the Subaru and slid to the other side. Planting her feet in a wide stance, she took aim and opened fire.

Glass shattered.

Chance was slower to rise but was up on his feet, his weapon at the ready. His vision blurred and then cleared.

On the move, Winter hurried forward as she tracked the vehicle with her gun, continuing to shoot at it. The back windshield burst. A tire blew. Two more shots from her. The Tahoe jerked to the side, sped forward and plowed into a pillar. The horn blared.

Winter took off running toward it. Chance was right behind her with a slight limp. His knee throbbed from the fall, and the sharp ache slowed him down, but he hustled along.

The license plate had been removed from the rear of the vehicle. Safe bet that it was the same on the front.

Training their guns at the driver, they came around to the side of the Tahoe. The man was slumped forward, his head on the horn.

Winter positioned herself near the front of the SUV, taking aim through the windshield. Chance grabbed the driver side door handle and wrenched it open. Keeping his weapon up, he stepped closer and tipped the man's head back onto the seat. His eyes open and lifeless. Still, Chance checked for a pulse to be certain and found none.

The man was dead. Snow-white hair covered his head. Stocky with a barrel chest. Sweeping walrus-style mustache that was equally white. Open pale green eyes lined with wrinkles. Looked like a Montana good old boy.

But familiar somehow.

It took him a moment to place the man, and Chance hated the sinking sensation in his gut once he did.

"I know him," he said, a bitter taste filling his mouth.

She stared at him, and when he didn't meet her eyes, she put a hand on his shoulder. "From where?"

"That's Vern Tofteland. He resigned as sheriff over in the next county."

"Why would a former police officer try to run us down and shoot at us?" she asked, holstering her weapon.

He shook his head at a loss for words, but he had the same question and feared the answer was only going to complicate this case even further. "Do you remember the murder investigation that Summer and Logan told you about, the one they worked on?"

"The death of Logan's cousin. Dani Granger. Of course, it's what brought the two of them together. Why? What does that have to do with any of this?"

"I don't know. Maybe absolutely nothing. But this is the sheriff who harassed Summer. Colluded with the old medical examiner not to have an autopsy of Dani's body. He was long suspected of being a dirty cop. During Logan and Summer's investigation, incriminating information came out about him. Rather than face the scrutiny that would surely come with an election, he resigned."

"What has he been doing since leaving the sheriff's office?" she asked.

"We need to find out." Chance was sure it was a critical piece of the puzzle. With it, things might come into focus.

Winter called it in. Within less than fifteen minutes, the parking lot was swarming with emergency personnel, both the paramedics who had been at the mass shooting scene on Main Street, two patrol cars, as well as Keneke and Logan.

Chance sat in the back of an ambulance, getting examined by one of the EMTs after they made sure Winter was all right. The paramedic flashed a light in Chance's eyes and held up fingers for him to count.

"I heard you two were involved in an incident." Logan came over to them and put a hand on Winter's shoulder. "I was nearby in the area and stopped to see if you were both okay."

"I'm fine," she said, "but I'm worried about Chance. He's got blurred vision, a headache, and a limp."

"I did hit my head and bang up my knee. It's not like I have bruised ribs that'll take weeks to heal."

Winter narrowed her eyes at him. "Now isn't the time to crack jokes."

"It's the perfect time if you ask me. A little levity should be prescribed whenever someone tries to kill you and doesn't succeed." A wave of nausea swept over him, and he doubled over, clutching his thighs.

"Mr. Reyes, you have a mild concussion," the paramedic said. "Right now, your symptoms are headache, blurred vision and nausea. Be on the lookout for ringing in your ears, vomiting, fatigue, drowsiness, numbness and slurred speech. Exposure to bright lights, loud sounds and movement could make your symptoms worse. Try to avoid those. Get plenty of rest for the next forty-eight hours and someone should check on you every three hours while you sleep. If you're not feeling better in two days, you should come into the hospital. As for your knee, it's swollen and bruised. Elevate it and ice. If that doesn't improve within the same amount of time, you'll probably need to get an X-ray."

"All that being said, how would you rate me? Better or worse off than someone with several severely bruised ribs?"

"Definitely better," the EMT said.

Shaking her head at him, Winter motioned for him to get out of the ambulance.

Chance got up, putting pressure on his knee, and gasped from the sudden throbbing in the joint.

Logan and Winter both offered a hand to help him climb down. Chance wanted to wave his best friend away, but he took assistance from both and eased down from the ambulance.

"I heard about your tip hotline," Logan said. "Along with the entire town. Every crackpot and individual looking for a payday is going to call."

"It's a small town." Chance curled his hand around Winter's shoulder, pretending to lean on her but making sure he didn't put too much weight on her. "Someone has seen something. Heather Sturgess will screen them and find one we can use, if it exists." They walked toward the crashed Tahoe. He limped along, not needing Winter for support, but he kept his arm around her nonetheless. "Any idea what your old pal," Chance said to Logan, sarcastically, "Vern Tofteland has been up to since he resigned as sheriff?"

"No idea, but I can find out."

Chance shook his head. "We can handle it. You've got your own investigation to worry about."

"You need to rest," Winter said to him. "Logan can drop you off at home, and I can take your truck." She held out her hand, waiting for the car keys.

Chance frowned at her. "*We* need to rest, Ms. Bruised Ribs. Once you're ready to, so will I."

"Give me the keys, Mr. Concussion. Even if you insist on working, I need to drive."

He pulled the fob from his pocket and dropped it in her palm. "*Mild* concussion."

"Hey." Keneke slunk over to them. "I was out at a crash site down the road. We identified the woman killed. Phoebe O'Shea."

The air drained out of Chance, and Winter's shoulders sagged. He let his hand slide from her shoulder to the small of her back and gave her a comforting pat. She leaned against the side of him. Neither of them wanted to see another young life lost in whatever this was.

"We've got to get him," she said, her voice low. "Somehow. We're going to make that… We're going to make him pay for all of this."

"We will," Chance promised, thinking of that red laser on her chest.

Logan's gaze dropped to the point of contact between them, and Chance lowered his hand. Convincing Winter they should take a shot at a relationship was challenging enough, though she was warming to the prospect. He didn't need to contend with disapproval from his best friend and pressure from Summer, too.

"I called it in to the chief since Neil Reynolds mentioned the name in his interview," Keneke said. "Chief Macon wanted me to let you two know. He said something about a two-way street."

Chance was relieved that their chat in the observation room was bearing fruit.

"Any evidence of foul play?" Winter asked.

"Looks like she blew a tire, lost control of the vehicle and plowed into a tree. Probably killed on impact." He took a cell phone from his pocket. "I took pictures of the accident." Keneke held out the phone in front of her.

Winter took it, holding it so that Chance could also see, and swiped through them. Several captured the car at different angles.

"Did you check the tires for bullets?" Chance asked.

"No, why would I?"

"O'Shea's tire might not have blown but been blown out. A precise shot to her tire from a high-powered rifle while she was traveling fifty miles per hour could've caused her to crash," Winter said, finishing Chance's thought. "Didn't you find it odd that the two women who were running this mystery club are both dead within thirty-six hours of each other?"

Keneke grimaced. "Of course, that's why I'm here talking to you and showing you pictures of the scene."

"Is this your personal phone?" Winter asked.

"Yeah."

"It can be subject to seizure as evidence. Next time, use a work phone." Winter took a breath and kept scrolling until she got to a photo of Phoebe O'Shea laid out on the ground before they put her in a body bag. "I don't believe it. Are you seeing what I am? Who does she look like?"

Chance stared at the photo. At the dead woman's lean figure. The fair skin. Her black hair pulled back in a long braid. The resemblance was uncanny. "Abby Schultz." The two could've passed for sisters. With her back turned to the shooter, they could've been twins. Easy to mistake one for the other. "The shooter killed Schultz thinking it was O'Shea."

"I better let the chief know." Keneke grabbed his phone back and started dialing as he walked away.

"We should get to the scene of the crash and take a look at it before her car is towed," Winter said. "I'll grab the truck and bring it around."

"No, I can walk. I'll feel better going with you."

"She'll be fine," Logan said. "She's trained, armed, and the garage is full of cops. Besides, I need a minute with you. Alone."

Chance didn't care for Logan's tone and could tell this wasn't a conversation that either one of them wanted to have.

Winter nodded and went to go get his truck.

Once she was out of earshot, Logan turned on him. "What's going on between you two?" he asked, pointedly.

"What do you mean?"

"Don't play ignorant with me. You know damn well what I mean."

"We're bonding. It happens when two people work closely together."

A wary look crossed Logan's face as he pointed at him. "Winter is off-limits. Am I clear? Off. Limits."

"Yeah. I heard you."

"You hear me, but you're clearly not *listening* to me. I saw the way you touched her. You're just doing whatever the hell you please. Typical Chance. Listen, if you make my soon-to-be wife's sister your next flavor of the month and hurt her, Summer won't just kill you, she'll kill me, too."

All three season sisters would be after Chance, ready to gut him like a fish. That was not a scenario he was interested in. Why was everyone expecting the worst outcome?

"Aren't you jumping a step from girlfriend to wife?" Chance said. "Fiancée should be in the middle, and you haven't even proposed yet."

"I'm. Serious," Logan said, punctuating each word by stabbing Chance's chest with a finger.

"So am I."

Logan heaved a breath. "Don't date where you eat, man."

"I believe you got the wording of that phrase wrong," Chance said, and Logan's shoulders bunched in frustration, his cheeks turning red. "Calm down."

"I don't want the thirty-five-year-old playboy who is chasing after someone I care about, my *soon-to-be wife's* sister, to tell me to calm down."

"I'm not a playboy." He was never with more than one person at a time. "I don't understand why I'm portrayed as a bad guy. I should be commended for not stringing women along. If I know it's not going anywhere or I'm not falling for them, I do the decent thing and let them know. Don't you think I want to settle down someday?"

This merry-go-round of dating was exhausting. He'd started to believe what he wanted didn't exist. That mix of a connection and a spark. Until he met Winter. He was tired of starting over with someone new only for it to fizzle out and was ready to build a life, a future with someone.

The right someone.

"Winter can't be one of many in your never-ending line of women. Put an end to it," Logan demanded, "before it goes any further."

Chance hated when people told him what to do, especially since it never worked. "I've got this."

"Got what exactly? I don't even want to know what you're thinking when you say *this*."

Winter pulled up in his truck and stopped beside them.

"Trust me. I've got it all under control." Chance patted his best friend, the man he loved like a brother, on the shoulder. "Don't worry."

Chapter Thirteen

Seated behind the steering wheel of Chance's truck, Winter drove to the Wolverine Lodge so they could grab dinner. Located on Bitterroot Lake, it was one of the best restaurants in the area and was a quick drive along the road from where Phoebe O'Shea had crashed.

They had invited Logan to join them, but they needed to check the crash site first. Logan had one more suspect to question for his own investigation before he could wrap up for the day and have dinner with Summer.

On the way to the Wolverine, they stopped and inspected O'Shea's car before it was towed. It looked like the sniper might've shot head-on at the treads, making quick work of the tire. A full metal jacket bullet had made a clean entrance through the front of the tire, possibly completely through both sides of the circular rim to the rear tire. Or he used two bullets. The entry hole was smaller than the exit. The back of both tires had large exit holes where the bullet took out a good size chunk of the tread.

They weren't sure where the sniper had set up his nest to wait for Phoebe O'Shea to leave her apartment. The only possible positions were eight hundred to a thousand yards out. An incredible shot that could only be made by someone with highly specialized training.

Only forensics would tell them if the bullet used on O'Shea's car was the same as the ones fired during the mass shooting.

Winter pulled into the parking lot and luckily found a spot close to the door so Chance didn't have far to walk.

Her cell buzzed with a call. She whipped it out. "It's the DCI lab."

"Speaker?"

"Yeah, sure." It only made sense since she would relay everything to him anyway. "Stratton," she answered.

"Hey there. No prints or fibers on the bean bag," Paul Parker said on the other end of the line.

Declan Hart had introduced her to Paul when she first started working at DCI, going out of his way to help her make a seamless transition from the San Antonio PD to the DOJ criminal division. Declan was like a walking encyclopedia combined with a *Who's Who* of folks at the agency. The right introductions had been essential to her success early on. She appreciated his friendship as much as his insight.

"Not what I wanted to hear. Paul, just so you know, I've got you on speaker with Chance Reyes. He's an investigator with Ironside Protection Services, consulting on behalf of the BFPD."

"I heard about the little deal you made. Director Isaacson isn't too happy about it."

"I'm well aware." Her boss had chewed her out over the phone while she was in the emergency room waiting to be seen by a doctor. There was bad blood between Macon and Isaacson, and she had stepped right in the middle of it. "Have you got anything else for me?"

"Bright and early this morning, Declan dropped off the bullets from the scene at your house. They match the ones of the first shooting. Ballistics came back on those," Paul said. "I've got a good-news-bad-news sandwich."

"Start with the good," she said, needing some. Hopefully the bad would be minimal, layered between positive news, rather than the reverse.

"We got a match on the weapon. An Mk 12 SPR."

"Military?"

"You've got it."

That wasn't what she wanted to hear. "What's the bad news?" she asked, as though the weapon being military issue wasn't bad enough.

"The Mk 12 is special. Used throughout the wars in Iraq and Afghanistan by Navy SEALs, Army Rangers, Army Special Forces and marksmen in the Marine Corps. The magazine holds twenty to thirty rounds, and the weapon allows for rapid follow-up shots at ranges out to seven hundred meters. It was only in service between 2002 and 2017, when it was deactivated."

She sighed. "The deactivation might make it easier to find the shooter. But a fifteen-year time span is pretty big. Paul, what does the military do with deactivated weapons?"

"They store them. Sell them. Lose them."

"Lose them?" Chance asked.

"Yeah. The DOD is the only government department that's failed every audit for the last twenty-five years. They lost track of a billion dollars' worth of weapons in Iraq and Kuwait alone."

She hung her head in frustration as Chance expelled a long-suffering sigh.

"To complicate matters," Paul said, as if they needed more complications with this case, "clones were produced after its phaseout by Centurion Arms and Troy Industries in 2017. Oberland Arms in 2019 and Palmetto State Armory as late as 2023."

Winter swore. "Please tell me the final layer of this sandwich isn't bad."

"Here's the other piece of *good* news that should help you narrow it down. The Mk 12 SPR doesn't use standard-issue ammo. There were limits in terminal performance and accuracy with the M855. So the Mk 22 open tip match round was developed by Black Hills Ammunition for the SPR. Fast forward several iterations to a Sierra MatchKing 77-grain hollow point boat tail bullet dubbed the Mk 262 Mod 1. But in late 2014, they started using a tipped version of the bullet, which added a polymer tip to improve ballistics, but it was only distributed to the military. The clones used different bullets."

She perked in her seat. "The ammo in our shooting has the tipped version?"

"You've got it. Sierra part number 7177 for the bullet."

That did narrow it down. They couldn't necessarily track the weapon, but they might be able to track the sharpshooter because of the ammo. "We're most likely looking for someone who was trained as spec ops," she said, a chill running through her at the thought, "still on active duty between 2014 and 2017 when he had access to the Mk 12 SPR and Sierra MatchKing tipped bullets."

"I'd say so," Paul said. "Best place to start."

Thinking about her next step, she gritted her teeth. "I'll need Director Isaacson to tap his contacts at the DOD to get us a list of names."

"Good luck with that. You're on his naughty list."

"Can you make sure he gets a copy of your report ASAP? And I'll call him. His assistance shouldn't be about helping me or not wanting to help the BFPD. This is about stopping a killer. Getting justice for those murdered."

"I'll see to it that he has it within the hour," Paul said.

"Once we get a list from the DOD," Chance said, "we can cross-reference any individuals we find with veterans affairs'

records of vets living within a twenty-five-to-fifty-mile radius of where the shooting took place."

"The list has to be short." Winter nodded to Chance.
"Thanks, Paul. If I could hug you right now, I would. I have
to go. I owe you a steak dinner. You earned it for getting that
back so quickly."

"No problem. Happy to work without sleep for food."

"Thank you." She disconnected.

Chance reached over and took her hand. "This changes
everything," he said, his face somber.

She had no idea what he was talking about. "Changes
what?"

"The man you fought on the rooftop bar, the one who
tracked you home and is now targeting you, is highly trained.
Special Forces."

The man who was two steps ahead and besting them over
and over. "I know." She'd never faced off against a tier one
operator before and was in no hurry to do so again, but she
was not backing down from this. No matter how dangerous
the task. No matter how deadly the perp.

"He isn't like anyone that either of us have gone up against
before." Chance tightened his grip on her fingers. "It changes
things."

"Knowing changes nothing. We still have a job to do, and
we're going to do it while taking every precaution possible."
She wanted to cling to the feeling of getting good news, no
matter how small. Her appetite was starting to return, and she
didn't want him spoiling it. "Come on. Let's eat. I'm starving."

They got out, and she hurried around to his side. She
wrapped one of her arms around his waist and put his arm
over her shoulder and held him close.

"It's just a bit sore," he said. "I can do it on my own."

"You can, but you don't have to. I'm here. Lean on me and
live in the moment."

He smiled at her, and she ached. Not with pain, but with the desire to kiss him.

They left the parking lot, heading to the curb. Although he allowed her to help him, he didn't put any real weight on her, otherwise her ribs would've felt it. Even when he was hurting and could've used physical support, he was looking out for her. The sensible part of her told her to end this farce and let him walk on his own, but the other part liked the excuse to be close to him.

"I'll call Isaacson and grovel while we wait for our food to come."

"I'll let Gretchen and Ed know what we learned from the DCI lab. It should be enough to get Neil released. Also, I have a contact at the local VA office who can start compiling a list of guys who served during the time frame we're interested in."

"You have latitude as an investigator, but as a cop, I have to do this by the book."

"She can hold the list until you get the warrant. Make it official. It'll be faster for her to work on it now, so that when we receive the spec ops names, we're ready to cross-reference and whittle it down based on the VA list of locals."

She nodded. "It doesn't hurt to get the ball rolling."

They made their way slowly to the steps. When they reached them, Chance pulled her to a stop. "Hey."

His eyes were deep and electric, and the intensity in them set a flutter loose inside her. That intensity was a huge turn-on. It also scared her senseless. She now understood he applied it to everything in his life, his work as well as his relationships. His nonchalant demeanor was a facade. No, a camouflage, an outer layer most people didn't see beyond. He only acted and sounded nonchalant, but in actuality he was always laser-focused on getting exactly what he wanted.

Deciding to lean into the fear rather than pull away, she

rose on the balls of her feet and kissed him. Quick and soft. "Hey."

He slid his arm around her and pulled her against him.

Her cell chimed. "Text message." She eased away from him and dug her phone back out. "It's from Autumn."

We have a phone number for Dallas. Can use it to set up a meet for a drug deal.

Sting operation tonight.

"Sting operation," she said, "to corner Dallas. Tonight."

"No rest for the wicked." He sounded lighthearted but looked weary.

ANOTHER CHIME. THIS time it was from Chance's phone. He pulled his cell from his pocket. "It's Eli." Chance read the message and swore.

"What's wrong?" she asked.

With a scowl, he showed her the screen and she read it for herself.

A lot of heavy hitters entered the hotel on the two dates in question.

The biggest one used the service entrance. You'll never guess who.

Spoiler alert: Governor Arlo Forrester.

Chapter Fourteen

They were all set for the sting operation. Dallas had picked a location on the outskirts of the west side of town for the meeting. Nine o'clock in the parking lot of the Wobbly Caboose, a diner near the interstate that was popular with truck drivers. Autumn was the lure.

Following Dallas's instructions, Autumn waited in the alley behind the diner near the dumpster. Bo was behind the large blue trash receptacle, hidden from sight.

At one end of the alley, Tak was in a van that they used for surveillance. Near the other end, parked with headlights off and engine idling, Chance sat in his truck with Winter in the driver seat and Eli in the back.

"Here you go." Eli handed them his laptop. "It's keyed up to the exact moment."

Chance set the laptop on the dash where Winter could also see it. The screen was paused on footage of the service entrance of the Bitterroot Mountain Hotel for the night of the eighteenth at 11:00 p.m.

He hit Play.

A black SUV pulled up, a Cadillac Escalade. Someone hopped out of the front passenger seat, looked around and checked the corridor inside the hotel.

Vern Tofteland. He hurried back over to the Escalade and opened the back door.

The governor stepped out. Arlo Forrester.

Chance and Winter exchanged a knowing glance. They had answers to two of their earlier questions.

"Judge Hyllested is protecting the governor," Winter said.

"Actually," Eli said from the back seat, "he's protecting the governor and himself. I spotted the judge using the side entrance. He showed up at nine with a woman who wasn't his wife. They had drinks on the rooftop bar for an hour. Then they got in the elevator. I don't have any footage of the two of them leaving until two in the morning."

"They could be having an affair," Chance said.

Eli tipped his head back and forth. A clear sign he thought his boss was wrong and didn't want to come right out and say it. "The only other time I saw Hyllested on the surveillance footage over the last two weeks was again on the evening of the ninth. Same routine. Same woman."

"The judge tipped the governor off to our request for a warrant," Winter said. "Whatever was going on in that presidential suite was illegal, and the governor didn't want it tarnishing his reputation or sending him to prison."

Chance snapped the laptop closed. "So he sends former disgraced sheriff Tofteland to do his dirty work and take care of us, and the matter of a warrant is done."

"Look alive," Tak said over the comms. "We got movement on my end of the alley."

Autumn perked up, rubbing her hands like she was cold. Although she wore a jacket, it was chilly out tonight. "I'm ready," she said.

This was her first time participating in the kind of operation that required her to wear an earpiece. She had fully embraced the investigative side of the business, as Chance had hoped that she would.

"Are you sure she can handle this?" Winter asked. "She's used to working out of an office, not out in the field. I don't want her getting hurt."

"We're all here with her to make sure nothing happens." Chance covered Winter's hand with his. "She's also an investigator now. If she's comfortable doing this sort of thing, I'm going to support it," he said, but he could still see concern on Winter's face.

Headlights turned into the alley from the north side. A silver sedan headed slowly down the back lane and stopped at the dumpster.

The driver's window rolled down while the car kept running. "Hey, honey, what are you looking for?"

"Are you a cop?" she asked.

"No way, sweetie. What do you want? You looking to party or relax?"

"Something to take the edge off, wind down," Autumn said. "But first, I need to make sure you're Dallas."

"You called me, honey, remember."

"My friend told me to be sure I only bought from Dallas. Not some lackey who might lace the product with something dangerous that could kill me. Like fentanyl. She said Dallas has a tattoo on his forearm. An ankh. Let me see it."

Winter glanced over her shoulder at Eli. "My sister is a little too good at this. Did you guys coach her?"

"Not really," Eli said. "I just reminded her to put him at ease that she wasn't a cop and that we needed to know for certain it was really him before we could move in."

The guy in the sedan pulled up the sleeve of his jacket, stuck his arm out the window and turned his wrist up for her to see. "Okay? We good?"

"Now that I know you're Dallas," Autumn said, nodding, "yeah, we're good."

"Move in," Bo said over comms. He popped up and darted

out from behind the dumpster, pointing a gun at the driver while Autumn backed away, moving toward the van.

At the same time, both Tak and Winter hit the accelerator and sped into place, blocking off the alley, preventing Dallas from going anywhere.

"We just want to talk," Bo said. "Be cool, Dallas, and keep your hands on the steering wheel where I can see them."

Winter drew her gun and hopped out of the truck along with Eli, who was also armed.

With his knee throbbing, Chance stayed put in the cab of his Ford. The situation looked well in hand, and Winter had far more experience with this sort of thing than his whole team combined.

Gun leveled at the driver's face, Winter swept over to his side of the car. "I'm DCI Agent Stratton. We have some questions for you."

"Yo, you can't bust me!" Dallas said. "This is entrapment!"

"Hands on the back of your head. We're going to have a little chat," Winter said. "I'm not here to bust you for dealing drugs."

Raising his hands slowly from the steering wheel and sliding them behind his head, Dallas complied.

Bo opened the door and waved at the guy with his gun. Dallas stepped out. He was a big guy. Beefy and tall, easily six three and two hundred forty pounds.

"Pat him down," Winter instructed.

Bo checked the guy's arms, the front and back of his torso as well as his legs. "He's good. No weapons."

"Get in the back seat of the pickup." Winter gave him a hard nudge forward, jostling him.

"Great job, Autumn," Chance said over comms.

"Thanks," she replied. "That was actually kind of fun."

After Dallas climbed in, Winter and Eli got in on either side of him and shut the doors.

Chance shifted in his seat and took in the guy. Goatee. Greasy, stringy hair that fell below his collar. "The quicker you answer our questions, the quicker you might get to leave. Got it?"

"How do I know you're not going to arrest me if my answers to your questions are incriminating?" Dallas asked.

"Depends on the crime," Winter said. "As a general rule, though, I don't arrest my confidential informants. I thank them."

Dallas sighed. "What do you want to know?"

Keeping the gun pointed at his midsection, Winter asked, "What kind of illicit enterprise did you have Lorelei Brewer and Phoebe O'Shea caught up in that was operating out of the presidential suite of the Bitterroot Mountain Hotel?"

"Me? Nothing." Dallas shook his head. "Those two hired me to be muscle, security, for *their* business."

Winter slid a surprised glance at Chance.

"Tell us the nature of that business," he said. "Was it drugs? Prostitution? Sex trafficking?"

Dallas frowned. "Nah, nothing like that. Lorelei and Phoebe had a high-stakes gambling club. They had regular clientele, but also had to bring in fresh meat every week. They had a classy thing going. Premium booze. Catered food. Cuban cigars. Any specialty items requested, they had available. They made sure the players were well taken care of and hired a skillful dealer. The girls had a sweet rake."

"A rake?" Winter asked.

"A percentage of the pot. The girls got to keep ten percent. That was on top of charging the new people, the fresh meat, a buy-in each week or an entry fee of five grand just to play. Plus, they made impressive tips, too. Tens of thousands moved through the room on a single night. I made sure no one got stupid and everyone stayed in line, and if someone wanted a hit of something extra from me, you know a little coke, then I conducted my business on the side. Lorelei and Phoebe made a lot of money catering to the filthy rich who had a lust for more money. They were smart. Until it got Lorelei killed."

Dallas didn't know about Phoebe yet.

"A high-stakes gambling game is illegal, sure," Eli said, "but the penalty isn't that bad. Brewer and O'Shea were probably the only ones who would have faced any serious jail time. The players probably would've gotten a slap on the wrist."

"For gambling, yeah." Winter nodded. "Not for tax evasion of all those winnings. We're talking a flat twenty-four percent not going to the IRS and also there's the crime of money laundering. Time in prison can add up to a lot of years, really fast, for those kinds of charges." She looked back at Dallas. "Do you know anything about Lorelei's death? Who would've wanted her dead?"

He shook his head. "I don't know. People like coming to the games. The girls were talking to some of their bigwig clients about expanding, setting up more gambling rings."

"Is there anyone who might have a grudge against her or Phoebe?" Winter asked. "Anyone who might want to hurt them?"

Dallas sighed. "Some players tended to win more often than others, if you know what I mean. I can't say for certain if any of it was rigged. Only who consistently won a lot of money on a regular basis. Looked fixed sometimes to me."

"Give us a name," Chance said, "and then you're free to go."

Dallas looked around at all of them. "Whatever I tell you is confidential? My life could be on the line here."

Winter nodded. "A name."

"Forrester," Dallas said. "Arlo Forrester. He walked away

with huge pots of money every month. A few times, it was six figures."

"We need one more name," Chance said. "Who was the dealer?" They needed to confirm the games were rigged.

"Harper Jones."

Winter stared at Dallas. "Any idea where we can find her?"

"She lives in the same condo building as Phoebe. Apartment 206."

Chance slid Winter a questioning look. *Are you good with us releasing him?*

She answered with a subtle nod.

"Okay," Chance said to Eli. "Let him go."

Opening the door, Eli hopped out and gave the man plenty of room to leave.

"Thank you," Winter said to him before Dallas exited the truck.

Eli jumped back in, slamming the door, and Winter returned to the driver seat. They were all silent for a moment. Processing.

"Why would anyone want to kill Lorelei Brewer and Phoebe O'Shea over hosting a card game?" Eli's brow furrowed. "I get it was high stakes, but still. Especially the governor? That's a huge risk, and for what?"

"Maybe they were blackmailing him," Chance said. "The only thing we know for sure is that Forrester sent his goon, Vern Tofteland, after us, and he nearly killed me and Winter after we requested the warrant. The governor doesn't want anyone to know about his involvement in the games. So much so, he's willing to murder people to keep it quiet."

"We need to know why he'd want Lorelei and Phoebe dead," Winter said. "Figure out what they might've had on him. Best way to do that is to poke the bear in person and see if he bites."

Eli chuckled.

"Only problem is," Winter continued, "something tells me the governor is not going to agree to a sit-down for a single question or allow us into his office."

"Then we do it another way." Chance glanced at her. "One he can't simply dodge and evade our questions with his lawyer standing guard."

She angled toward him in her seat, and the pinched look on her face made it evident she was in pain again. As soon as they got back to his ranch, he was going to encourage her to take something for it. Heck, he could use a painkiller himself.

"What are you thinking?" she asked, putting a hand on his arm.

He repositioned her palm to his thigh, covering her hand with his. At the softness of her touch, his pulse quickened. "The Forrester Family Foundation's annual Diamond Ball at the Buckthorn tomorrow night. A black-tie gala hosted by the governor, and it's the last place he'd want a scene, where he's the focus. I had no plans to attend. It's such a bore to go solo," he said. "But now I have a date to keep things interesting."

A hint of a smile danced on her full lips, but when he met Winter's pretty hazel eyes, a sharp pang cut through him. He had an inkling of her response.

"This is business," she said. But her voice was throaty, sexy, like the potential existed for the evening to turn into more.

"You sure?" he asked. "I'm great at multitasking."

She nodded. "I'm sure."

Eli cleared his throat, as if to remind them he was still in the vehicle. Honestly, Chance had forgotten about him for a moment.

Pulling her hand away from his leg, Winter straightened behind the wheel and thrust the gear into Drive.

There was nothing wrong with mixing business with pleasure, but Chance was clear on his priority. He didn't want to poke the bear. He wanted to rattle his cage, putting so much unbearable pressure on Arlo Forrester that the governor never dared to come after him or Winter ever again.

Chapter Fifteen

Once the team dispersed from the Wobbly Caboose, Chance leaned over in his truck and kissed her. Light and sweet. The opposite of their other kisses, where she'd felt as though he wanted to consume her, body and soul.

"Let's go home."

Winter knew he meant *his* home, but something about his tone made her heart give a little kick.

They were mostly silent on the drive to Chance's ranch, but there was no awkward tension between them. When he held his hand out, she put hers in his and enjoyed the feel of the simple gesture, without thinking about the next step of the case. Without worrying about how wildly attracted she was to him and where things like hand-holding could lead.

He pulled up to the eight-foot wrought-iron gate, the name Lady Luck Ranch in scrollwork at the top. He used an app on his phone to open it.

They drove up the illuminated driveway. Ranch hands with dogs still patrolled. She guessed the high security would continue until they caught the shooter.

Chance parked under the porte cochere, grabbed a plastic bag from inside the console compartment and shoved it in his jacket pocket. At Winter's questioning look, he explained, "I stopped at the pharmacy while I was waiting for the breakfast order. Needed to restock some supplies."

They climbed out. There was a nip in the air. A portable fire pit had been placed under the overhang, and the two men keeping watch were warming their hands.

Winter rounded the front of his truck. Wrapping her arm around his waist, she encouraged him to lean on her, though she doubted he needed much assistance. He'd been so nice, so generous that she wanted to do what she could for him. Once again, he accepted the gesture of her support without putting any weight on her.

"Evening, Mr. Reyes," the taller of the two ranch hands said. "Are you all right? You need us to help you inside?"

"I'll be fine. I'm only letting her help me so I have an excuse to touch her."

The men smiled.

"What happened to your leg?" the other one asked.

"Banged it up in a car accident."

"Your truck looks fine." The taller one examined the pickup. "I don't see a scratch on it."

"Someone tried to run us down with a car," Winter said, "while we were walking through a parking garage."

The ranch hand tightened his grip on his shotgun. "Did you catch the guy?"

"She killed him." Chance gestured at her with his head. "Shot him."

"Figured you'd eventually pick a down-to-earth scrapper once you got tired of the prissy princesses and snooty lawyers," the shorter one said.

"I do have a thing for a woman who carries a gun and knows how to use it," Chance said. Winter smiled up at him.

The guys seconded the comment in unison, and she and Chance entered the house.

He pulled out his phone and brought up a security app.

"Enter a six-digit code. It'll be yours to access the gate and use on the front door. I'll download the app on your phone."

After she got her car, it'd be nice not to have to be buzzed in or knock. She picked a code and gave him her phone.

"Want to ice our injuries in front of the fire?" he suggested.

She shrugged. "I don't see why not. Let me freshen up and change."

"How about some tea?"

"Sure, but I'll make it."

"Okay, under one condition."

Always some stipulation. "What?"

"No big sweatshirt. I want you completely at ease, and I'll be on my best behavior. No *I want to devour you* looks."

She secretly loved that look. "Are you trying to get me out of my clothes?"

"I won't deny it, but from a purely practical standpoint, it'll be easier to ice."

After the day they'd had, being at ease was exactly what she needed. "All right."

In the living room, she left him to build the fire. She took a quick shower and rummaged through her bag. Sighing at the options, she slipped on a plunge bralette and mini shorts. Neither were acceptable gym attire, but he hadn't packed any of the dowdier stuff. This was *hanging with your boyfriend* lounge attire.

Maybe he didn't realize, and his male brain was repelled by the running shorts and high-neck sports bras. Not that she faulted him. He'd packed for her in a hurry during a stressful night. She had the oversize sweatshirt if she wanted to wear it, but it'd be easier to ice without it.

Leaving her hair loose, she left the room, head held high, feigning nonchalance.

She found him lying on the sofa with an ice pack on his knee over his jeans. His gaze dipped, sliding over her body.

The glance was brief, one of awareness and didn't leave her self-conscious. It also didn't give her tingles.

"Easier for you to ice with your pants off," she said, "but underwear stays on."

"If you insist." He stood and unbuckled his belt.

"Want help?"

He gave a devilish grin. "Yes, please."

Undressing him might be too much temptation to resist. "I believe you can handle it. Where can I find the tea?"

"Left cabinet beside the stove."

In the kitchen, she saw that he'd already done all the work. The electric kettle was filled with water. She only had to flip it on. An assortment of teas was lined up on the counter. Two mugs sat on a wooden tray, one with a tea bag inside, along with a sugar jar and porcelain creamer with cold milk.

She chose a Madagascar vanilla rooibos, filled the mugs with hot water and carried the tray to the living room. Grabbing a pillow, she stuffed it under his knee to elevate it.

He'd stripped down to a formfitting T-shirt and pair of boxer briefs. She gazed at the smooth, hard landscape of his sleek muscles on display. Chance was an avid runner, and Logan worked out with him all the time at the Lady Luck Ranch gym, but there was fit and then there was peak condition.

Chance was the latter.

Forcing herself not to ogle him, she turned to the tray on the coffee table. "Milk or sugar?"

"Neither for me. The sugar and milk are for you."

Her heart did a little dance at his thoughtfulness. Everything he did made her want to be closer to him. She'd never been with a man who'd put in effort to improve her life, to make her comfortable, to take care of her.

She handed him his mug, added sugar and milk to hers, grabbed the ice pack and sat back on the sofa.

There was too much space between them. She scooted closer, putting his calves on her lap. Cozy and warm and icing together.

He adjusted the ice pack on his knee. "Don't we make a delightful, banged-up pair?"

"Banged up is better than dead."

He clinked his mug against her cup. "I couldn't agree more."

This was nice, but she couldn't help thinking how much nicer it would be with even fewer clothes, getting as close as possible to him. Only skin to skin and heat.

THEY SPENT THE next hour perched close, chatting about anything other than work. It was so nice to be near her. Chance had felt more alive and awake during this downtime than he had in months, and without question it was because of Winter. She had this effect on him.

But if this was what it felt like just being next to her, how would he feel if he truly touched her? Made love to her? Got to appreciate every inch of her?

He looked at her, and she smiled. Her golden-brown skin gleamed in the firelight. Even though she looked sexy as hell and he wanted to have her in his bed, he enjoyed this, too. The closeness. The intimacy between them that had nothing to do with sex.

"There's something I've wondered about you," she said.

"What's that?"

"You grew up on a successful ranch, you're now the owner of another... Why aren't you a full-time rancher, overseeing the day-to-day operation? Or working as an attorney with a top firm? Or doing commercial ads for toothpaste with that perfect smile?"

He grinned. Simple questions. Complicated answers. "My dad wanted something different for me. Better, in his opinion. He didn't want me with dirt under my nails and calluses on my hands. With my blood soaked into the earth and my sweat covering every fence post."

"Why wouldn't he want to pass down that legacy?"

"He did. Only not to me. His dream for the ranch was big and bold. I think it corrupted something in him. My father would've done anything to ensure not only the ranch's survival but also its success. Tried to manipulate my sister, Amber, and Logan's eldest brother, Monty, into an arranged marriage. It backfired. Amber disappeared for years until our dad died. His antics continued in his will with rigid conditions. He only left me his rodeo buckles and this watch." He showed her the Timex on his wrist. "But he paid for my schooling. In the end, my father got what he wanted. Monty and Amber fell in love and married. Now, I've got a gorgeous nephew, and the Powell and Reyes ranches are joined as one." His dad's legacy cemented.

She put a palm on his shin, rubbed his leg, and her touch felt good. Soothing yet energizing at the same time. "So, you became a lawyer instead of a rancher."

"That's what my father demanded of me, the good son. After I passed the bar exam, he bought me four pairs of Lucchese boots. As a reminder of how proud he was I'd be working a fancy job."

Squinting at him, she shook her head. "Then why aren't you a bigwig at some high-profile firm?"

"I was. For a while."

"And what happened?"

He sighed. "That brings us to how I got this perfect smile."

She cocked her head to the side. "I don't understand."

No, she didn't, because Summer and Logan didn't discuss him with her. One of Summer's rules that Chance didn't understand.

"I was working in Chicago at one of the biggest powerhouse firms. One night, I was leaving the office late. My car was parked in the garage. Three guys were waiting for me. Two had baseball bats, one a crowbar. I held my own until security got there. I sent two to the hospital. But the third guy with the crowbar got me good. I spent a few weeks in ICU. This perfect smile is courtesy of veneers and dental implants."

Her eyes widened. "Oh my God. I had no idea." Her grip on his leg tightened. "Why did they attack you?"

"The ringleader was in the middle of a contentious divorce. He was going to lose way more than fifty percent of his assets. He was furious and believed his wife was sleeping with her handsome attorney. Decided to teach his wife's lawyer a lesson."

"That's madness," she said. "Hang on a second, I could've sworn Autumn told me you once worked in corporate law, not divorce."

"She's correct. Those men had the wrong attorney. They were looking for my colleague, Daniel Rios. Our assigned parking spaces were adjacent. We were about the same height. Both Latino. Both devilishly good-looking."

She grimaced. "I'm so sorry." She scooted closer, moving the pillow and using her lap to elevate his legs, took his hand and held it tight. "I can't imagine the pain and suffering you went through."

It was a story he rarely shared. He didn't want to be pitied. "Whatever doesn't kill you makes you stronger, right?"

"Not always."

He glanced down at her hand that was still in his and her other, which kept stroking his leg, soft and tender, and he smiled. "Those three guys went to prison, and I left Chicago. I'd invested well and took a break from everything. I knew the founder of IPS, Rip Lockwood, a veteran from my hometown. He recruited me for a job that required an attorney. After that, I opened an IPS office. I'm licensed here and in five other states where we have other offices. I do legal work for IPS when necessary, corporate, a little criminal, but I enjoy the investigative side of the business. I also love having a ranch, giving people who need a job honest work. This is the best of both worlds." He didn't have to honor someone else's legacy and had the life of his choosing.

"I admire you. Your strength. Your optimism after what you went through."

He ran his palm up her arm, slow and steady. "I'm a survivor. So are you. Like attracts like."

Silence settled over them as Chance watched her and caressed the side of her neck, stroked her jaw with his knuckles.

The air was suddenly charged between them. Her gaze fell to his legs, roamed over his body before she caught herself and looked away.

Winter cleared her throat. "It's getting late. It'll be a long day. Director Isaacson told me his DOD contact was going to get us a list of names who had access to the Mk 12 SPR. Isaacson thinks tomorrow afternoon at the latest. Also, the warrant for VA's list of veterans in the local area came in."

After two hours decompressing from work, she flipped back into business mode, like a defense mechanism.

"Excellent," he said, with no enthusiasm. "I'll pass the warrant along to my contact in the VA office. The list of all veterans in the area who served during the time period we're looking at is ready. Once we cross-reference that with the names from the DOD, we can question possible suspects."

"We still have to talk to the card dealer, Harper Jones, go to the barbecue for Summer and Logan and then confront the governor at a black-tie gala for which I have nothing to wear." She lifted his feet from her lap and rose from the sofa.

He slowly climbed to his feet and took her hand. "Don't worry about the Diamond Ball. Borrow a dress from Summer." The youngest Stratton was big into fashion and would have options. Winter was lucky to have sisters who were about the same size. Though Winter had a slightly more athletic physique, her muscles lithe and lean. "You'll look fantastic in anything."

They stood there, staring at each other, and the moment stretched between them, crackling with an undercurrent of electricity. He took her hand and pulled her to him. She put a palm to his chest, as if to keep some distance.

"Still skittish around me?"

She jutted her chin up. "No. Just being sensible around you."

"Sensible is overrated." He slid his hand into her hair and kissed her, holding her tight to him.

She tensed for maybe a heartbeat, and then her body loosened, and she let go. Her arms wrapped around his neck, her tongue plunging deep, tangling with his, and he tugged her hips to his pelvis and drank down the hot, sweet taste of her.

At last, she *finally* kissed him the way he'd imagined for months. He slid his hand over her bra, caressing those soft curves he'd ached to touch.

She moaned in his mouth, her fingers combing up into his hair, as she pressed closer. He couldn't believe they'd waited so long to do this. She tasted so good. Felt perfect in his arms. She rocked her hips against him, and the whimper deep in her chest gave him a rush of adrenaline.

The way she was kissing him told him maybe she did want hot and wild, and maybe she'd been yearning for this as much as he had.

Then Winter broke off the kiss like she had been burned and eased back.

He saw it in her eyes, second thoughts. She was going to run from him. "Don't." He pulled her back against him and kissed her, hard and possessive. "I know what you're going to say, but don't."

She dropped her forehead to his chest. "What is *this*? If it's one night to satisfy our mutual curiosity or a fling we burn out of our systems, I'm fine with that. I just need to know before we sleep together."

He put a knuckle under her chin and lifted her head. "I wouldn't be fine with that." One-night stands took the temporary edge off, but ultimately left him unsatisfied, and he wanted more than a fling with her. "I want this to be the start of…" He cupped her face in his hands and shrugged, unsure how much to say, not wanting to scare her off. "Something."

If he could walk away from her without feeling like he'd regret it for the rest of his life, he would. Then he wouldn't have to worry about Summer fretting and Logan harassing him and destroying their forged family unit. But she was worth the risk.

"I need to know where this might lead," he said, "but you set the pace. We don't have to sleep together tonight. We can wait."

She chuckled until she clutched her side. "Chance, you've been setting the pace the entire time."

"I'm sorry." She was right. "I'll stop."

"No, you won't." Running her hands up his chest, she kissed him. Licked her lips like she was savoring the taste of him. And kissed him again. "I'm not sorry. You got us to this place, where I'm half-naked in your arms and can't pretend any longer I'm not attracted to you. Where I can't stop thinking about making love with you."

He searched her face in the firelight for any hint she didn't want to do this. Even though she trembled, all he saw was desire in her eyes. "Why are you shaking?"

"Nerves, that you only wanted to scratch an itch with me."

He brushed hair from her face. Caressed her cheek. "Far from it."

"I don't want to wait." She pressed closer. "Take me to your room."

THEY KISSED ON their way down the hall to the opposite side of the house. He tasted like heat and oolong tea. The smell of him was divine, cedar, musk and all male.

He undressed her—peeling off her bra and shorts as they stumbled along.

Winter was sure that fighting this temptation was no longer a battle she wanted to win. She had no more qualms about giving herself to him.

Her body, not her heart. With guardrails up, when this burned out like his other relationships, no one would get hurt.

With their arms wrapped around each other, they tripped over the threshold into his room bathed in flickering amber light. The primary suite was massive, the size of two or three bedrooms combined, with a sitting area and stone fireplace.

"When did you light the fire in here?"

"While you were showering. I dropped off what I picked up at the pharmacy." He gestured to his nightstand, to a box of condoms.

Wow. "You were certain of yourself." Of her.

"Not certain." The sincerity in his voice touched her. "Only hopeful."

"I like a man who's prepared."

He gazed down at her, the raw intensity in his eyes making her legs weak. "You're so beautiful, so sexy."

No one had ever looked at her with such burning heat. Not the handful of lovers she'd had. Not even her ex-husband.

She kissed him, giddy from the compliment and wanted him even more.

He cupped her small breasts, flicking his thumbs over her

sensitive nipples and kissing her neck. She shuddered in response, rubbing against him, needing to be closer.

Gripping the waistband of his boxers, she pulled them down. As he stepped out of them, she grabbed his shirt, but he caught her wrists.

"I have scars," he said, with a nonchalant demeanor that she knew was a veneer.

"From the assault?"

He shook his head.

She tensed. "What happened?"

Smiling softly, he stroked her cheek with such tenderness. "I'll tell you but not tonight." He brushed his lips over hers, a featherlight caress. Then he pulled off his shirt.

In a ragged breath, she took in his sculpted shoulders, his broad chest, his ripped stomach…and the scars. Jagged lines across his chest. Not from an accident, like a car crash. Someone had deliberately done that to him.

Her heart squeezed. "Chance—"

He crushed his mouth against hers. The kiss was hungry and all-consuming, sending a bolt of desire straight to her core.

Steering them to his king-size bed, he sat down, taking her with him, his hands on her hips. She settled onto his lap, straddling him, slid her arms around his neck and kissed his jaw, loving the scratchy feel of his day-old stubble on her skin.

His warm palms caressed her thighs while he explored her body with his mouth, hot and greedy. Kissing, nibbling, sucking. He slid a hand between her legs, his fingers finding her core. He stroked and caressed, making her quiver and ache until she felt ready to combust. Raw sensation ignited, and she cried out, coming apart for him.

He grabbed the condoms. Ripped open a foil packet. Rolled one on. He lifted her hips and lowered her onto him.

Pain and pleasure speared through her, and she gasped, holding still, letting her body adjust to him. He kissed her, fingers tangling in her hair. Kissing him hard, she rocked her hips, taking him deeper.

Surging up, he flipped her onto her back, keeping them joined. Careful not to press his weight on her, he pushed himself up and drove into her with a fierceness, an insatiable hunger, like he needed more, needed all of her.

Tension coiled, and she lost herself in the heat. In the pressure and the sweet, hard friction. In the urgent sense of need. They were in sync in a heated rhythm, and everything inside of her tightened again, building and building.

"Winter—"

The next forceful thrust brought a dizzying burst of pleasure. Her control shattered. A guttural groan tore from him, and he shattered with her.

He rolled to her uninjured side, staying pressed against her, a solid arm around her.

Her mind reeled. For nearly six months, she'd kept her distance, resisted his charms. Now there were no thoughts of mistakes and consequences. This felt right.

She nuzzled beside him, putting a hand on his chest, feeling his heart pound, and the knot of loneliness buried deep inside her unraveled.

Chapter Sixteen

Winter awoke to an empty bed later than she'd intended. She had a hangover that had nothing to do with painkillers or alcohol and everything to do with Chance. She ran her palm across the cold empty space beside her and found a note.

Went to grab breakfast.

She should've expected as much. Squeezing her eyes shut, she pulled the covers up and smiled. She had no regrets about making love with him. Their chemistry, their connection, had been off the charts. Better than any of her dreams in every way. She'd never felt like this, that everything was in high definition. Too strong. Too intense. Yet, she was also light and happy.

Hopeful.

And cautious. She wasn't a fool and didn't expect Chance to change who he was for her. He didn't do serious. He didn't do commitment. He was the type that didn't fall in love.

Summer called him a respectable playboy, the kind who only slept with one woman at a time. Mr. Like 'em and Leave 'em.

So long as Winter knew from the outset what she was getting herself into, she could handle it. She didn't have on blinders. No fairy-tale expectations. They just needed to enjoy it for what it was, get their fill of each other, live in the moment. Then end it on a good note before things turned sour. Before she got her heart all tangled up in him.

Sitting up, she set her feet on the fluffy area rug and pulled back the covers. No pills for her today. She was done with them and done with having a fuzzy head. Instead, she would do her best to deal with the pain if she could.

No nightmares last night, and she'd gotten solid sleep thanks to Chance not waking her up when he should have. But she had been running on fumes and needed the rest.

In the light of day, his bedroom was even more impressive. Sleek dark furniture. Plush area rugs. Tasteful artwork. On the mantel above the fireplace were framed photos. She presumed family and friends since Logan was in a couple of them. Built-in bookcases in the sitting area framed a large screen TV.

Her underwear was folded on the bench at the foot of the bed. She collected her things, staggered down the hall to her room, hurried through a shower and got dressed.

In the front sitting room, she peeled back the curtain. More armed cowboys. Different sturdy-looking fellows from yesterday.

Waiting in the foyer, she checked her messages and emails. One from her boss. Director Isaacson expected to have the DOD list of Special Missions Unit operators who had access to the Mk 12 SPR from 2014 to 2017 no later than noon.

In three hours.

There were two messages in a group IPS text to which she had been added. One chain store sold the exact type of navy coveralls the sniper had worn—Murphy's. Bo was going to the closest store to check sales records for the past two weeks against their security footage. Tak and Autumn were going to handle getting the VA records from Chance's point of contact.

Chance's azure gray Ford F-150 sped up to the house.

Throwing on her wool blazer, Winter stepped outside. "Good morning," she said to the ranch hands who were standing guard to help keep her safe.

They acknowledged her with head nods and smiles.

Chance rolled down his window, spoke to his men and reached over, flipping open the passenger door. "Hello, beautiful."

She stilled, not expecting such a greeting. Then she realized he was going to keep testing boundaries and pushing them inch by inch until… She honestly didn't know.

One step at a time, that was how she had to take this.

What harm could it do to let someone compliment her?

Winter climbed in and shut the door. "Good morning, handsome," she said with a straight face, but it still made him beam. It also didn't hurt to give a compliment in return.

He took hold of her blazer, tugged her over to him and kissed her, long and hard. "Missed you."

The look in his eyes put a little lump in her throat. The truth was, she'd missed him, too. "We can't be like this around the others. Around my sisters."

"Be like what?" He pulled off. "Ourselves?"

Yes!

He must've seen the answer on her face because his expression hardened. "I won't hide how I feel about you."

"Feel?" She shook her head. "It was sex. They don't need to know I'm your latest lover," she said. When he opened his mouth, she held out her palm. "Stop. Whatever you were about to say, don't. Logan is going to propose to Summer tonight. I want that to be everyone's focus. Not us. Okay? You told me that I set the pace." She picked up her soy latte, her mouth watering in anticipation of the first sip. "Thanks." She held up the takeaway cup. "How's the knee?"

With a bright smile, he drove through the gate. "A lot better. The swelling is down and doesn't hurt nearly as much anymore."

"Happy to hear it." She sipped the coffee and moaned. "Are you sure you're okay to drive? Any blurred vision? Headaches? Nausea?"

"No, I'm feeling good all around."

"After we speak with Harper Jones, I'd like to stop by my house. Pick up my car."

The smile faded. "Are you trying to get rid of me?"

A pang of guilt hit her. "No," she said, and he looked wary. "Honestly. I'm just used to being independent. Having my things." Her roadside emergency kit and armored vest were in her trunk. "Besides, it'll look better if we show up at the barbecue in separate cars."

"Even though we're all working together and will head to the barbecue from the IPS office? Plus, we're going to the Diamond Ball together. Do you really think it's necessary?"

"Yes. Trust me." She opened the white paper bag on the console, took out both breakfast burritos and handed one to him.

"Fine." He nodded but didn't look happy about it. "How are your ribs?"

"Still sore," she admitted. "Will be for about six weeks. I've decided to grit through the pain. The meds make me oversleep and my head fuzzy."

"You could always take something over the counter if you really need it." He reached out and rubbed her forearm. His eyes met hers for a second. "Can I ask you something personal?"

The question surprised her. "Sure, what?" She bit into the burrito in case she needed time to think before answering.

"Why did your parents name you three after seasons?"

She chuckled, relieved by the no-pressure nature of his question. "Our family used to live in South Carolina before we moved to San Antonio when we were little. My grandparents named our mother April Rose. She was born on the fourth day of the fourth month and all the roses bloomed early that spring. Autumn came late during an uncharacteristically warm fall, and it struck my mom as special like when she was born." She shrugged. "With me, Mom endured forty hours of labor during a blizzard the newspapers referred to as snowmageddon. The biggest winter storm they've ever had. Summer as a quick and easy birth on an oddly temperate day in July, when my mom's garden never bloomed better." She sipped her coffee. "I guess our names are fitting since I'm not the easiest *season sister* to get close to."

He smirked. "You know what else is overrated besides 'sensible'?"

She shook her head.

"Easy and fast." He took her hand in his. "Explorers have faced snowy, unfriendly treacherous mountain passes and have said *challenge accepted*. Even though they knew it would be grueling. Lewis and Clark braved the Bitterroot Mountains. The most formidable part of their trek tested them, but the miracle wasn't making it through. It was the journey itself, where Lewis wrote that he had experienced inexpressible joy."

She didn't know he was into history. All these months, she'd done her best not to feed her curiosity about him by getting to know him while he had been paying attention to the smallest details about her.

Frowning, she tilted her head. "You think of me as an unfriendly, treacherous mountain pass?"

He smiled. "I look at you, and I think none of the men who have come before me have been able to hack it. They were not only fools but cowards, who'll miss the *inexpress-ible joy* of being with you."

Her heart squeezed with so much emotion she couldn't process the flood. Why did he have to say the sweetest things?

They pulled into the parking garage of the new condos. This time Chance parked as close to the entrance of the residential building as possible.

He pointed at a silver Nissan parked three cars down. "Harper Jones's car. I had my contact in the BFPD look up the make, model and plate number for us."

"You mean Logan?"

Chance gave a one-shoulder shrug. "I don't divulge my sources."

Smiling, Winter shook her head. On their way inside, she noticed that his limp had improved and was barely perceptible. They rode the elevator to the second floor.

Standing next to Chance, Winter rang the doorbell for apartment 206. They waited and waited and waited. She pounded a fist on the door.

Footsteps came from the other side.

The door cracked open, held by the security chain. Through the gap, she saw a woman with thick auburn hair, pale skin, and big blue eyes, scowling.

"You're Harper Jones, right?" Winter put a friendly tone into the words. "I'm DCI Agent Winter Stratton," she said, showing her badge, "and this is private investigator Chance Reyes."

"What do you want?" Harper's voice was heavy with sleep.

"We have a few questions for you regarding the deaths of Lorelei Brewer and Phoebe O'Shea. Can we come in?"

"Phoebe's dead, too?" Shock riddled her face. Harper looked at them for a couple of seconds before she put her hand on the door to push it closed.

Chance wedged his foot in the diminishing gap. "You don't want to do that."

"I don't want to talk to you."

"Either let us in and talk discreetly now or talk to us in an interrogation room down at the BFPD station, where someone will get word to the governor."

Harper slid the chain off and let them inside. After locking the door, she showed them into her living room that overlooked Bitterroot Lake.

"Stunning view," Winter said, glancing around the small condo. The larger units affording more space were on the higher floors.

"Yeah, thanks. I'd like to live long enough to truly enjoy it. What do you want from me?" Harper pointed to a two-person sofa. "Sit." She remained standing.

"Were you close with Phoebe and Lorelei?" Winter sat, and Chance stood behind the sofa.

"We were friendly." Harper grabbed a pack of cigarettes from the coffee table and lit one. "Not bosom buddies. It was a business arrangement."

"Were the card games ever fixed?" Winter decided it was best to cut straight to it. "Did you help Arlo Forrester rig any games?"

Harper blew out a stream of smoke. "Any information I give you, how is it going to be used? Is my name going to be in the paper? Will I be on a witness list? Have to sign some affidavit?"

Chance put a hand on Winter's shoulder. "The governor tried to have us killed. Yesterday. In your parking garage," he said, and Harper cringed as she took a long draw on the cigarette. "I want to use that information to protect us. To protect you."

Harper sneered. "Protect me? Like you care one whit about me."

"We witnessed Lorelei's murder," he said. "We care about

what happened to Phoebe. We don't want anything bad to happen to you. If we can protect you, we will."

Harper tapped the ash from her long, slender cigarette into a mug on the table. She debated and sighed. "Some of the games were fixed. My aunt is a dealer in Vegas. I know a few tricks. I didn't mind rigging a game here and there because I always got a ten percent cut of the pot. That was until Lorelei and Phoebe started bringing Russian mobsters as fresh meat to the games. Even I know you don't cheat the mafia. The governor threatened me. Told me to do what he said, or I would disappear. It scared me. So I took out insurance."

"Insurance?" Winter asked.

Harper nodded. "I recorded a few of our discussions, where he's threatening me and some of the games with the Russians. Where he won big pots with fixed hands and admits it." She left the room, going into the bedroom. Drawers opened and closed. A minute later she came back with a thumb drive and offered it. "I used my cell phone. Hid it in the room. I have multiple copies. Even sent one to my aunt in case I have a nasty accident."

"Thank you." Winter took the thumb drive and stood. "One last thing. Did the governor ever threaten Lorelei or Phoebe?"

"No, they all got along great. Very chummy. He seemed to really like them."

Winter looked for any signs that Harper was holding something back, but the woman came across as forthcoming. "Do you know of anyone who might've been angry at them, had a grudge for some reason? Maybe wanted to hurt them?"

"No, not really," Harper said, but her gaze dropped as she thought about it. "One time I came into the presidential suite early and overheard them arguing."

"When was this?" Chance asked. "And about what?"

"I don't know, maybe two months ago? Phoebe was terrified. She was saying that they needed to take the warning seriously. From some super scary guy. Phoebe kept calling him the commando," Harper said, and Winter and Chance exchanged a look. "It was weird because it made me think of that old Arnold Schwarzenegger movie with the same name, where he plays a Special Forces guy. Phoebe insisted that they needed to give it back and just let it go. But Lorelei was trying to reassure her that everything would be okay. Once they sold the land, they wouldn't have to worry about the commando anymore. The money would solve all their problems. They would be set and could disappear if they wanted. Phoebe seemed to calm down. After that, I never heard them talk about it again."

"What land?" Winter stepped closer. "Who warned them? Did they ever say a name?"

Harper shrugged. "I have no idea. I'm sorry. Those two played their cards close to their chests. They had a lot of secrets. In our business, asking questions could get you hurt. Or worse. So I was smart enough never to ask any."

Chapter Seventeen

"Twenty-two." Chance stared at the whiteboard where they had listed the names of all former Special Mission Unit personnel or tier one operators who had access to the Mk 12 between the specified three-year period and currently lived within a fifty-mile radius of Bitterroot Falls. "More than I expected," he said, pinching the bridge of his nose. He was at least hoping for single digits. Five or less would've been good. "I can't keep all of you working this." Turning around, he faced everyone seated in the conference room. "We have two other cases that need our attention."

Bo sat back in his chair. "How about you keep us on this until we get through interviewing the twenty-two on the list?"

They needed to narrow it down. "How many don't have physical addresses?" Chance asked.

"Seven," Tak said. "They have PO boxes."

It could take them a week to track them all down. "You have two days, guys," Chance said to the entire team. "That's how long this remains the office priority. Monday, I need you all focused on the work that pays the bills."

The clients were their bread and butter, but it wasn't just about keeping the lights on and ensuring his people got paid. They'd been hired to do jobs that were important to those clients. He'd never pull anyone from any kind of protective service or a security detail or anything time sensitive to help with this investigation. Still, he'd taken them away from what should be their primary focus long enough. "In the meantime, we'll give Chief Macon our list of names. Have the BFPD cross-reference it with the list of Chevy Blazer K5 owners. See if one is a match."

"Thank you for all the time and effort you've put in," Winter said.

Autumn stopped twirling her pen between her fingers and raised it. "I'm free to keep working on this, if you want to use me. I've been reviewing the case. Criminal profiling is basically reverse engineering a crime. I analyzed the victimology—the choice of the victims, the scene, the level of organization, pre-imposed event behavior, the choice of weapon, why the crime happened on Main Street during peak hours rather than a more isolated location. All those things can tell us the kind of person we're dealing with."

"What did you come up with?" Winter asked.

Autumn got up and went to the whiteboard. "We know our unsub is a white male. Former spec ops. Trained to kill. Used a police scanner and a prior military weapon that has been deactivated and can't be easily traced. He was after Lorelei Brewer and Phoebe O'Shea, but he killed Abby Schultz by accident because the two women resembled each other. His exit route was planned. He purchased coveralls rather than stealing a set from the hotel to limit his exposure to surveillance cameras. The same with us not getting any footage of him pre-incident inside the hotel doing reconnaissance."

Autumn grabbed a dry-erase marker and began writing things beside the list of names.

White male
Age: 40-50
Highly trained + highly intelligent

Emotional control = may have stable relationships
Patience
Psychological resilience
Served 15+ years
Might have medical discharge PTSD
Stalked the victims to learn habits
Used service weapon = joblike task = duty
Murder was possibly personal
Undetected pre-attack surveillance = hotel helper
No grudge against society
Main Street shooting = conceal targeted kills

"This is who we're looking for," Autumn said.

Chance nodded. "Good work. Let's whittle down our list of twenty-two even more based on the factors here on the board." He looked at Autumn. "How certain are you that someone at the hotel helped him?"

Autumn twirled her pen. "I know you only reviewed surveillance footage of the hotel for the past two weeks. You could go back the full month, and he won't be there."

"What makes you think so?" Chance asked.

"Because someone who works at the hotel told him that they only keep footage for thirty days. Someone told him what type of coveralls. A hotel employee might have even mapped out all the cameras for him to reduce his exposure. Either that or he worked there at some point and doesn't now, maybe as security and was fired or resigned."

Winter leaned forward, resting her forearms on the table. "Why do you think he might have PTSD?"

"The unsub would've served a full twenty years if available. Based on the level of training and experience displayed, he did at least fifteen," Autumn said. "Since he was physically fit and capable during your altercation, if he received a medical discharge, PTSD is the most likely condition. The average PTSD score for veterans who have been involved in the killing of civilians was 106. Compared to 80 for vets who had only reported seeing a civilian killed. More snipers suffer from the condition than infantrymen."

"This guy shot two additional people on Main Street," Bo said. "If Winter hadn't gone after him, he probably would've hurt a lot more. How come you listed no grudge against society?"

"The other two victims who were both shot, Lee and Santana, had clean wounds and no permanent damage. Our unsub took great care not to make the injuries worse than necessary. If he had a grudge against society, after he murdered Brewer and Schultz, he would've opened fire and had a free-for-all killing spree. He chose not to. I believe the only reason he decided to do it on Main Street was to obfuscate his true intention."

Eli folded his hands on his stomach, and the chair groaned when he rested back in it. "What do you mean by the murder might be personal?"

"Only that I don't think this was a murder-for-hire situation. There was nothing in the database that linked the use of this specific weapon to any other civilian crimes. Correct?"

"Yes." Winter nodded. "The DCI lab did confirm the ballistics found in O'Shea's car crash are a match, but we believe these two murders are linked."

"This guy was off the grid. He exposed himself only long enough to take out Brewer and O'Shea." Autumn's gaze swung to Winter, and for a second Chance wondered if the profiler was aware of what happened to her sister. "The only reason he would do that was because it was personal rather than a contract kill. Murder for hire, he's not going to use his military weapon, and he's going to remain a shadow."

"The stalking of the victims," Winter said to the room. "We know that he established their routine, specifically going to Big Sky Fitness every Monday, Tuesday, Thursday and Friday. According to Mrs. Brewer, Lorelei spent the night before every spin class at Phoebe's. We need to review traffic camera footage of their route from the condo to Main Street and look for a Chevy Blazer K5 around the time the ladies would've been leaving to go work out. We might get an unobstructed image of his tags. If we get his license plate, we have him."

"Another thing." Chance folded his arms. "Lorelei Brewer and Phoebe O'Shea purchased some kind of property. Someone gave them a warning in relation to it. A super scary guy that Phoebe supposedly referred to as the commando. We need to know everything we can about the sale."

Bo raised his hand. "I'll look into it."

"Let's get to work," Chance said. "We're burning daylight, and everyone is expected to be at the barbecue later. We've all got to eat anyway, and we can finish working afterward."

"Hey, I was able to get the seven with no physical addresses narrowed down to four," Tak said. "Based on ethnicity, age and time in service."

Chance folded his arms. "Those four go to the top of the list. What are the names?"

"Travis Johnson, Brandon Brown, David Rogers, Justin Miller. I'll finish scrubbing the rest of the list with the criteria Autumn gave us."

Chance put an asterisk next to those four. "We need to do everything we can to find those four as soon as possible." Every instinct he had screamed that one of those men was their shooter.

Winter looked up from the playback of the traffic camera footage on one of the IPS laptops, gave Summer's outfit a quick once-over and stifled another groan.

Today, of all days, her younger sister, a self-proclaimed fashionista, was wearing a Broncos T-shirt, jeans and sneakers with her long hair up in an intentionally messy bun. The hair was cute, but Winter doubted her sister would want that outfit memorialized in engagement photos.

"Who's the quarterback of the Broncos?" Winter asked.

Summer shrugged. "I have no idea, but this is how I show my support since it's Logan's team. Do you know who it is?"

Winter refocused on the footage. "Do you want the name of the current quarterback only or should I start with John Elway and work my way forward four decades?" Winter had started watching football with their father when she was little while her sisters were playing with dolls and makeup. Her knowledge of the game and about the NFL teams only grew after she joined the military.

Huffing a breath, Summer thrust a glass of red wine at her.

"Do you even watch the game?" Winter took the glass, though she doubted she'd have more than a few sips since she had work to do later. Right after the proposal, she and Chance were heading out to the Diamond Ball. She still needed to borrow a dress.

"This is the extent of my support, and I have no shame about that."

"I have to agree with Winter," Autumn said, looking casual chic in a cashmere skirt and matching sweater. She had the same lustrous almond brown skin as their mom, and she wore her hair in loose corkscrew curls that framed her face and fell to her shoulders. "I think the last time I saw you wearing sneakers was when you were in high school."

Autumn helped their little sister set out bowls of side dishes on the counter, baked beans, potatoes, corn, green beans, salad and mashed potatoes while Winter tried to multitask.

The commando followed Lorelei and Phoebe for several days. His license plate always had the tinted cover over it smudged with mud. After their spin class, the ladies headed back toward the new condo, Main Street to Lake Shore Drive, but the Chevy Blazer went a different way. Each time he'd turned down Briar Woods Road instead of following them to the condos. There were no other traffic cameras to track him.

Where were you going?

"I'm experimenting with something new." Summer pulled bottles of beer from the fridge and set them in a galvanized washtub filled with ice and cans of soda. "Tomorrow I'll be back to my usual stylish self, okay? Sheesh, what's with the scrutiny today? Logan said something, too. He was so surprised I was wearing this that he asked me five times if I wanted to change. I thought he'd be thrilled I was toning it down and showing pregame spirit."

Her baby sister was going to look back on her engagement photos and video and hate that T-shirt. Even Logan knew it.

Winter closed the laptop. "I think he just wants you to be you."

Out of her sisters, she was the tough one, capable of handling anything. Even a perp who was twice her size—unless he was Special Forces. At times, fleeting moments really, she envied her sisters. Summer was effortlessly feminine and beautiful. Autumn had a quiet, enigmatic allure. A super-soft way of being that men gravitated to and other women found comforting.

Winter had never known how to be soft and had no real desire to be. Soft and vulnerable had only gotten her hurt. Though Chance didn't seem to mind that she wasn't hyper-feminine and dainty.

Snowy, unfriendly, treacherous.

Grinning, Winter looked through the open patio doors that led to the backyard, where the guys were chatting while Logan grilled steaks and burgers. She looked past the IPS team and Bo working on a laptop, and Logan's brother, Jackson, who lived in Missoula, and Autumn's boyfriend, Erik, and her gaze zeroed in on Chance—handsome, sexy, confident—and she couldn't help but smile brighter.

Summer elbowed her. "Please don't tell me you're interested in Mr. Like 'em and Leave 'em. I told Logan that you two working together is only trouble waiting to happen. Trust me. Chance is a serial monogamist. You're better off staying away."

"At least he believes in monogamy." Winter grinned at her sister. "I consider that an upgrade."

Pursing her lips, Summer shook her head. "You shouldn't consider him at all."

"Why shouldn't she?" Autumn refilled her wineglass. "He's the town's most eligible bachelor."

Summer scoffed. "More like elusive."

"What kind of dirt does Logan have on Chance?" Winter wondered. "Does he have a checkered past with women?"

"No. No dirt. No checkered past."

"I heard that he's friends with all of his exes," Autumn said.

A chill skated over Winter, thinking back to his interaction with Gretchen.

Autumn sipped her wine. "He has a remarkable ability apparently not to leave any drama in his wake."

"When you say friends, do you mean the kind with benefits?" Winter asked. Gretchen had been quite handsy, as though they might still be intimate.

"No." Summer shook her head. "As far as I know, when Chance closes the book with a woman, it stays closed, and he has plenty of closed books lining his shelves, if you know what I mean."

Winter tilted her head to the side, perplexed. "You act as though you like him."

"I do. When I first met him, his overwhelming, overbearing approach wasn't my cup of tea. But I've grown to love him. He's family, but so are you. I don't want any drama."

"Didn't we just establish that Chance is anti-drama?" Autumn said.

"No drama with women he doesn't have to see and socialize with on a regular basis." Summer huffed. "This is good. Isn't it nice, all of us together having fun? I want to keep my entire family intact. No broken hearts. I told Logan he needs to make it clear to his bestie that you are off-limits."

Chance was his own man, and he was going to do as he pleased, as Winter well learned last night in his bed. She turned to Autumn. "How is it working for him?"

"Chance is a great guy, once you get to know him. It was actually his personal story about his first case here that convinced me to work for IPS."

"Not another word. Traitor." Summer wagged a finger at their eldest sister. "You promised not to tell her that story."

"Why not?" Winter asked, looking between them.

Summer heaved a breath. "I can already see you're intrigued and attracted to him. Once you hear it, you'll only find him more compelling. I daresay even irresistible to someone like you."

"Like me?" What was that supposed to mean?

"You're drawn to tragedy," Summer said. "The more wounded the better. Give you a tragic, wounded hero, and you're a goner. That's why I didn't want Autumn or Logan to tell you. I don't want you to become a notch on Chance's belt."

Unease slithered through Winter.

Autumn shrugged. "I actually think you two have great chemistry and would make a good match."

"I have to know the story." Winter propped a fist on her hip. "One of you spill it."

"Go ahead and tell her," Summer said, waving a hand in Autumn's direction. "But make it the bargain-basement

CliffsNotes version, and as for you…" She pointed at Winter. "Don't say I didn't warn you."

Smiling, Autumn leaned closer like she had a juicy secret to share. "He cracked the slaughterhouse murders case. The Beast of Bitterroot County. A sick guy had killed more than a half dozen people in slaughterhouses around here."

"So Chance was responsible for taking the killer down?" Winter asked.

"In part." Autumn nodded. "Working with the BFPD and the sheriff's department. What wasn't widely reported was that Chance made himself bait, the Beast took him captive and tortured him. Afterward he was hospitalized for over a week. Not only did he help catch the killer, but it was because of him they were able to find where other bodies were buried. He helped several families find closure."

"He still has scars on his chest," Summer said.

Winter's heart twisted at the thought of what he must've gone through, the pain and suffering.

"Chance made a convincing argument to have a profiler on his team. I agreed to give it a year," Autumn said, "but I'm loving it, and he's a great boss."

He was a protector and a fighter. A survivor. How did someone endure everything that he'd suffered, stare evil in the face and remain so full of light and love? Being a survivor wasn't even the most impressive thing about him. It was that he knew how to live without apology or fear.

Winter glanced across the yard and stared at him. He turned around, as though he sensed her looking at him. His gaze locked on hers, and something inside her chest melted. She smiled at him, wishing she could hug him, kiss him, simply hold him.

"Ugh." Summer made an exasperated sound. "There you go softening. I can hear your heart going pitter-patter. I knew it. Why did you have to tell her?" She glared at Autumn, who ignored her. "If those two hook up and break up and then mess up this family unity, I'm holding you responsible."

Tearing her gaze from Chance, Winter refocused on the big event that was going to happen as soon as the guys brought the food inside. She eased closer to her sister and pretended to stumble, splashing wine on her. "Oh no."

Summer stared down at her ruined outfit with wide eyes. "When did you start tripping over your own feet?"

Winter grabbed napkins and dabbed at the spots of wine. "You should change." She set the glass down and put a hand on her sister's back, steering her out of the kitchen. "Come on. We'll help you, and while we're in your closet, can I borrow a dress for the governor's Diamond Ball? And shoes?"

Her little sister grumbled something, but Winter took it as a *yes*.

In the bedroom, Summer went to her closet. She fingered through a rack of dresses. One minute later, she had pulled out three choices and tossed them on the bed. "Try those. They should fit. Wear whichever one you like best." She set down a pair of shoes for each option.

Winter pointed to the magenta dress. "That'll work."

Summer grimaced. "You didn't even try it on."

"I don't need to." Straps crisscrossing over the fitted bodice would bare her shoulders and arms, and the dress had a long loose skirt. "It's the only one that gives me full mobility. The others would either restrict my arms or legs. With the flowing skirt, I can easily conceal a gun. I'm working tonight and need to be prepared for anything, even a fight."

"We should do your hair and makeup," Autumn said.

"It's not a date." Winter shook her head. "This is work."

Autumn frowned at her. "Yes, but you still need to blend in. It'll be fun."

Winter wasn't so sure about the fun part, but blending in was important. "We can do it after we eat." She didn't want to get glammed up and take any attention away from the proposal.

"A smoky eye and neutral lip," Summer said, "with curls falling over your shoulder." She turned back to her closet and sighed.

"Don't worry about toning it down." Winter chose her words carefully so as not to spoil the surprise. "Just pick out something that makes you happy when you put it on."

Her sister immediately grabbed a short floral kaftan dress that would fall above the knee and went to the bathroom to change.

"Hey." Autumn elbowed her. "I know what's going on."

"Chance told you about the engagement?"

Autumn's eyes flared wide, and her jaw dropped. "Logan's proposing?" she whispered.

"Oops." Obviously, her sister didn't know about it. "What are you talking about?"

"You and Chance."

Stiffening, Winter decided to play it cool. "What do you think you know?"

"I saw you two at IPS yesterday when you were in his office. The way he looked at you. The way he touched you."

Winter cringed. She didn't think anyone had seen them.

"Anyway, I swung by your house last night to ask you about it in person because you simply would've blown me off over the phone. Lo and behold, what did I find? Your front window covered in plywood, your floodlights shot out, and your car parked in your driveway, but you weren't home. I checked the family locator app and saw that you were at the Lady Luck Ranch. If Logan knew anything about your house or your whereabouts, then Summer would know, and so would I. So I called Declan."

Sighing, Winter tipped her head back. "Of course, he told you everything because he's sweet on you." Or the man simply had loose lips and was telling anyone who would ask him all of her business. She still didn't know the identity of Chance's informant who had snitched that she hadn't been working on an active case.

"He isn't sweet on me. He's just nice."

Winter was confident the only reason Declan hadn't made a move on Autumn was because she had a boyfriend, but Winter doubted the relationship would last much longer. "Don't say anything to Summer."

"Have you slept with him yet?" Autumn asked like it was a foregone conclusion.

Lowering her head, Winter refused to answer.

"Oh my, you have." Autumn wrapped an arm around her. "He moves fast, but good for you, getting back in the saddle."

"We've known each other for six months." Winter peered over at her sister. "It's not that fast. Is it?"

"No judgment. You two flirt whenever you're in the same room together." Autumn rubbed her back. "Whatever feels right. I say trust your instincts and go with it."

Summer came out of the bathroom looking like a vision. Like herself. Effortlessly beautiful. She didn't even bother to put on shoes since they were going to eat inside the house.

They went back out into the main living area, where the kitchen, dining room and living room were all one open space. The guys had come inside. A platter of steaks and burgers was on the counter. Autumn's boyfriend, Erik, and Declan were deep in conversation. Winter wondered what on earth those two were talking about.

When Logan spotted Summer, he lit up like a football stadium on game night. "Sweetheart." He motioned for her to join him. "I want to make a toast before we eat."

"Let me grab a drink, babe," Summer said.

It was happening. Winter shimmied her way through the bodies gathered around chatting, scooting past Bo and Tak, to get a prime spot for taking pictures, which just so happened to be next to Chance.

He leaned in, bringing his mouth close to her ear. "Bo didn't find any properties purchased by Brewer or O'Shea," he whispered, his breath warm against her neck. "So, he dug deeper to see if they tried to anonymize a sale. Sure enough. They created an LLC. Pocket Queens purchased thirty acres of land."

She looked at him. "From who?"

"George Brewer."

"Her elderly uncle?"

Chance nodded. "I called Sadie Brewer. She didn't know anything about the sale. She thought Lorelei had simply given her uncle the money. Sadie gave me a house number since he doesn't have a cell. He's at an ice hockey game, Bruins versus Avalanche, with his son and grandkids according to his daughter-in-law, who answered. We have to wait for Brewer to call us back later."

Summer went to stand beside Logan, and he started thanking everyone for coming.

"Nothing solid turned up on the traffic cam footage," Winter said, keeping her voice low, "but when our guy was done following Brewer and O'Shea every day, he always took Main Street to Lake Shore and disappeared on Briar Woods Road."

Logan took Summer's hand and then looked out at the group gathered.

"Record it. Take a video," Winter whispered while she whipped out her phone. As discreetly as possible, she got ready to snap photos fast and furious in the hopes that one would be the perfect shot that her sister would cherish.

Chance subtly held up his phone and started recording.

"Summer, we first met at a funeral," Logan said. "I was immediately taken by you. You were so beautiful and sweet and compassionate and giving. I saw right away that you were special. Then we had that moment out on the porch together, just the two of us as we watched the sun set, and even though we barely knew each other, I knew that I didn't want to let you go. But like a fool, I did."

Everyone chuckled.

"Then another tragedy brought us together again. Looking back on it, I realized it was destiny, bringing the woman I was meant to love forever back to me, for a do-over to get it right." Logan set his beer bottle on the table, took out a ring box from his pocket and got down on one knee.

Gasping, Summer put a hand up to her mouth, and her eyes shimmered, turning glassy with tears.

"Summer Stratton, will you do me the honor of filling the rest of my days with happiness by marrying me?"

"Yes!" Summer bounced up and down, nearly spilling her wine. "Yes, Logan, I'll marry you." As he got up from the floor, she threw her arms around his neck without even bothering to look at the ring. The two kissed.

Winter got choked up watching them. She finished taking photos and slipped her phone into her back pocket. A warm hand brushed hers, one of Chance's fingers wrapping around two of hers, and a frisson of heat slid down her spine. She glanced at him.

Dangerous emotion sparkled in his eyes, and he looked like he wanted to kiss her or devour her or both. Her chest tightened, but her thighs tingled.

If she wasn't careful, she was going to get her heart pulverized.

Chapter Eighteen

With Winter on his arm, both dressed to the nines as they strode into the Diamond Ball, it was the first time in Chance's life that he felt like a million bucks. Winter wore a stunning dress in vibrant purple and four-inch heels that almost brought them eye level. Her dark brown hair was in loose curls pinned to fall over one bare shoulder. She was absolutely breathtaking.

They entered the ballroom of the Buckthorn Club, and a few heads turned their way. He plastered on a polite smile and scanned the room, getting his bearings.

The event started two hours ago. They'd missed the flurry of photographers snapping pictures of attendees in front of the gala's official backdrop, and the sit-down dinner portion was already done. The delay in their arrival was unavoidable since they had to stay at the family barbecue to celebrate Logan and Summer's engagement.

Unless they had been seated at the governor's table, which was highly doubtful, missing the meal over forced pleasantries wasn't a loss.

Winter began to fidget. "Is the makeup too much?"

Not her usual minimal style. Her sisters made her look like a model ready for a cover shoot. "It's perfect for this evening, but for the record, I think you're prettier without any."

She smiled, and her nerves appeared to settle.

"There he is." Chance gestured with a nod to the center of the ballroom, where the governor danced with his wife.

The dignified, graying man with sharp features clearly loved being the center of attention. His wife was a petite woman half his age, wearing a sequined silver gown and a diamond necklace—the cost of which could've been given to the charity the gala was supposedly raising money for. After everything Chance had learned, he wondered how much of the donations would go to do good and how much would fund the governor's retirement.

"We can't stand here not mingling and looking out of place," he said. "Shall we?"

"I have to warn you. I'm not the best dancer."

"No worries. All you have to do is follow my lead." He was already moving with her arm linked in his, headed for the dance floor.

There were plenty of familiar faces at the ball tonight. Over to his right, he glimpsed Gretchen and Bill Nesbitt dancing.

He steered Winter to the opposite side of the room. Picking a spot where they could keep an eye on the governor, he placed his hand on her hip, slowly lifted her palm and placed it on his chest right over his heart. He pulled her close, keeping the moves simple, and her lithe body pressed against him in all the right places.

"Sly move by you," he said, "spilling wine on Summer."

"You caught that."

"I did. Thoughtful of you. Logan was going to postpone the proposal. He didn't want her to look back and have a single regret."

"Logan is the thoughtful one."

She deserved credit for helping save the day.

"After the surprise wore off," he said, "and Summer realized you'd deliberately ruined her outfit, she was so happy you made her change." The evening had been entertaining and heartwarming to watch.

"Thank you again for giving me a much-needed heads-up about the engagement and for taking a video while I took pictures of the proposal. Summer will want both." Her gaze lifted to his, and the corners of her mouth curled in a smile that arrowed straight to his heart.

"It was my pleasure," he said as they swayed to the music. He fought to focus on their surroundings, on the governor, on the plan instead of the feel of her in his arms and how beautiful she looked and how badly he wanted to rip that dress off her.

Winter glanced around, and her gaze fixed to the right. No doubt she'd spotted Gretchen as well. She turned back to him. "Can I ask you something?"

"Sure."

"You and Gretchen Price once dated?"

He stiffened. "We did."

"Why did you break up? She seems perfect for you. Like your type of woman."

"If you think that, then you haven't been listening."

"I have." She pressed her palm to his cheek. "I'm trying to figure out why you haven't settled down."

"I suppose I hadn't met the right person. Gretchen and I weren't meant to last."

"How do you know if you didn't try?"

"Because I did. Then I met you and realized she wasn't what I wanted. I told her I had feelings for someone else. She deduced it was one of the season sisters since I'd been spending a lot of time around you both, but Gretchen didn't know which one."

"The questions in the police station."

He nodded. "I apologize for putting you in that position.

The bottom line is that for me, Gretchen was like an easy Sunday morning. When what I really want is—"

"A treacherous mountain pass?" Winter smirked.

Grinning, he held her gaze. "I guess you are listening."

She looked away. "The governor is leaving the dance floor."

Chance twirled her, brought her back in close and turned, watching Forrester strut over to the silent auction tables. "Let's go. This is our opening."

"Have you ever met?"

"Nope. It'll be the first time for both of us."

Hand in hand, they cut across the dance floor, wove in between several dinner tables and made their way to the designated silent auction area.

Chance's cell chirped, and Winter's buzzed in her purse as well. They both took out their phones and glanced at the text from Heather Sturgess.

A nurse says her neighbor's boyfriend drives a Blazer matching the description, but she hasn't seen it at the house in a couple of days. Wants the money before giving any information.

People always wanted the money upfront. Chance was used to such demands. He'd found that giving them anywhere between a hundred and a thousand was enough to get them talking with the promise of receiving the rest provided the information panned out. He fired off a text back.

I'll meet her tomorrow.

In the silent auction area, several tables were covered with black tablecloths with a digital tablet on each. Various items were up for bidding: sponsored gift cards, baskets of local goods, travel packages, spa services, memorabilia and a one-year membership to the Buckthorn Club.

Arlo Forrester stood with his wife, considering a bid on a travel package to Turks and Caicos.

"Good evening, Governor," Chance said, and Forrester smiled, nodding hello. "May we have a moment of your time, alone?"

"Alone?" The sixty-seven-year-old man's grin widened. "My, that sounds ominous. Anything you have to say can be said in front of my wife." He wrapped an arm around his wife's slender waist.

"I'm Chance Reyes, and this is DCI Agent Winter Stratton."

The smile fell from Arlo Forrester's face. Either from the mention of Winter's professional title, or he recognized their names from the warrant they'd requested, which had drawn his attention. "What do you want?"

"To speak in private," Chance repeated. "For your discretion, not ours."

"Darling, go ahead and make a bid, whatever you think is reasonable, and get me a scotch. Neat." Forrester looked between Chance and Winter. "Why don't we speak in the library upstairs?"

It was for members only and away from the crowd. "I'm familiar with it," Chance said.

They proceeded up the grand stairs, followed by the governor's security. One of his bodyguards cleared the library first, then gave the okay for them to enter and closed the doors, standing watch inside the room.

The governor led them to the other side of the room near a lit fireplace. "Let's make this quick. I am the host tonight."

"You sent your guy, Vern Tofteland, to kill us," Winter said, jumping right in, "after we requested a warrant for security footage of the presidential suite at the Bitterroot

Mountain Hotel that would've shown you entering for an illegal card game."

Forrester laughed. "I've been on the receiving end of many
a wild accusation in my day, but I must say that is the most
outlandish. Vern Tofteland used to be my employee, but he
was let go."

"When was that?" Chance asked. "Before or after he tried
to kill us, and she shot him dead?"

"I am not responsible for the actions of any misguided,
disturbed, *former* employees." The governor grinned. "Is
that all?"

Hardly. "We have video footage of you gambling inside
the suite. With the Russian mafia. Acknowledging that the
game was rigged in your favor," Chance said, and Forrester's
mouth tightened in grim line. "A copy of the footage could
make its way into the right hands. The media for starters
and then the mob."

The older man narrowed his eyes. "How do I know such
a video exists?"

Chance pulled out his phone, pressed Play on a copy of a
clip he'd downloaded and showed it to the man.

"What do you want?" the governor asked.

"Lorelei Brewer and Phoebe O'Shea are both dead," Winter said, and a flicker of surprise crossed the older man's face.
"Did you have anything to do with their deaths?"

Forrester reeled back. "Of course not. I had nothing to
gain, and money to lose."

"Maybe they blackmailed you." Winter eased closer. "And
you decided to get rid of them the same way you tried to get
rid of us."

"I refuse to discuss Tofteland. The man was fired. He
was sick and needed help. As for Lorelei and Phoebe, I liked
those two. Pretty and smart and not afraid to go after what
they wanted. I admire gumption. I was going to help them

expand their business. They did a lot for me with their club, and we had an understanding."

"What sort of understanding?" Chance asked.

"They make me money. I do the same for them in return."

Winter clasped her hands, an impatient look on her face. "Details and be specific."

"How do I know this conversation will remain private?"

"How do you know the video of you cheating the mob will remain private?" Chance smiled. "I guess you'll have to trust us. Start talking and make sure you're specific, like she said."

The governor's cheeks reddened. "A lot of development is going on in and around Bitterroot. Everyone involved in various projects is making serious money. I told them about plans to build a private airport. A site hadn't been picked yet. Lorelei floated the idea of a plot of land her uncle owned being chosen as the site. I agreed to help her make it happen. She bought it for pennies. I connected her with a city councilman to have it rezoned from residential to commercial."

"Who?" Chance asked. "Which councilman?"

"Bill. Bill Nesbitt. I told him to grease the skids, to make sure they didn't have any issues with the rezoning. I heard there was some kind of pushback at one of the council meetings. Some group that had been leasing the land, but their claim didn't have any legitimacy. I guess the lease was a verbal agreement."

Chance slid his hands into his pockets. "Did this group get violent or aggressive or make any threats? Did they ever threaten Brewer or O'Shea?"

"As far as I know, no one ever did. Bill told me they were a bunch of apocalyptic preppers who just wanted to be left alone. There wasn't any yelling or name calling or threats made at the meetings. It was civil. Once the situation was explained to those doomsday preppers, that they didn't have any legal grounds to support their claim, they simply left and didn't fight it anymore. I wasn't there, but you can always go back over the official transcripts for yourselves."

"Was the rezoning approved?" Winter asked.

"It was. There was no legal reason to deny it. The papers were drawn up for the sale of the land. They were all set to sign it next week. Two million dollars, that's how much Lorelei and Phoebe were going to make. Taxpayer dollars, not my money. Why in heaven's name would I kill them?" The governor straightened. "Now is that all you wanted?"

"No, it isn't." Chance took his hands out of his pockets and took two steps closer to him. Close enough to invade his personal space. "If you or any of your employees, previous or current, ever come for me or mine again, I will spend the rest of my days making you regret it. Starting by destroying your political career. Am I clear?"

The governor hesitated, surely weighing his options and balancing it with his ego. "You are. I hope I have nothing further to worry about regarding the warrant for the hotel security footage of the presidential suite."

"At this time, we won't be pursuing it," Chance said. "And I also expect you to stay away from Harper Jones. Consider her under my protection, too. There are a lot of copies of the video showing you brag about cheating the Russian mob. All in safe hands. For now. You need to make sure it stays that way."

A smug smile curled Winter's lips. "Enjoy the rest of your evening, Governor."

Chapter Nineteen

In the truck, Winter shifted in her seat and looked at Chance. "Bill Nesbitt confirmed everything the governor told us. Do you buy the story?"

It was almost the same recount as Forrester's regarding the land deal. With the clarification that the land had been rezoned for commercial use as well as Airport Impact Overlay zoning. Aside from that, nothing new from Nesbitt.

"The story about greed and government corruption, yes," he said, and she could see he was still thinking.

"But?" she prodded.

"I'll still have one of the guys pull the official transcripts and double-check them to be on the safe side."

"Both Bill and the governor seemed to think the preppers wouldn't be a problem."

"Maybe it's not them," he said. "Maybe the commando is someone who cares about them. Maybe they're his family. His friends."

"Autumn did tell us that this might be personal for him." Winter took a deep breath, and her ribs protested. Once they got back to the ranch, she'd have to take an over-the-counter painkiller to manage the discomfort while keeping her head clear. "I only wish Phoebe O'Shea had confided in us about what she suspected might have happened to Lorelei, so that we could've helped her. Saved her."

"It was probably complicated for Phoebe. Yes, her friend and business partner was murdered, but she probably wanted time to think about how to protect herself and still collect the two-million-dollar payday. I'm sure she would've tried to hide the deal with the governor."

Winter supposed he was right. It would've explained why Phoebe had asked for extra time before meeting. Not to get herself together but to get her own story straight.

"Don't worry." Chance reached over and put his hand on her thigh. "We're going to catch him."

Her gut told her they were closing in, and time was on their side.

Chance stroked her leg, and his fingers snagged on the thigh holster she was wearing. She'd picked it up at her house when she got her car to drive to the barbecue.

"Is that what I think it is?" His voice was low and husky. "Let me see."

Sighing, she pulled up the flowy skirt and flashed him her subcompact gun stuffed in the holster hugging her thigh.

"Please wear that to bed later," he begged.

She could only laugh.

His phone rang, and he put the call through on speaker. "This is Chance Reyes."

"Hello, Mr. Reyes, this is George Brewer. My daughter-in-law told me that you needed me to call you back. That you were following up on my niece's murder. Officer Keneke didn't have many details. Did you learn something new?"

Chance updated him on the relevant details, like Phoebe's death, leaving out the part about the land deal with the governor.

"Oh my, that's a shock," George said.

"Were you close to your niece?" Winter asked.

"Not really. I wasn't very close to my brother, so I wasn't around her too much, but she was a nice girl. Helped me out so I could afford to move to Boston to be near my son."

Chance changed lanes and took the off ramp from the interstate. "Did you have some sort of lease agreement with a group of preppers for the land that you sold to Lorelei and Phoebe?"

"They don't like the term preppers. Prefer to be called survivalists, and yes, I did. It was a verbal agreement sealed with a handshake. We've had it for many, many years. They paid me a few hundred bucks a month to live on the land, off the grid, and to hunt. I wasn't using it for anything. When the girls offered to pay me two thousand dollars an acre so they could turn it into a farm, I jumped at it. Needed that money to move out here to Boston and not be a burden on my son."

"Lorelei and Phoebe told you they were going to use the land as a farm?" Winter asked.

"That's what they said when I asked what they planned to do with it."

Chance turned down the road that led to his ranch. "Did you ever wonder where they got the money to buy it?"

"Not really. Lorelei was always a crafty one. I figured they were making good money at the Buckthorn Club, doing more than serving drinks, if you know what I mean. They're really pretty, and I've heard stories about what those rich guys get up to over at that club." He lowered his voice to a harsh whisper. "Probably have sex parties."

Chance shook his head.

"I accepted the offer, took the check and signed the paperwork on the condition that they honor the existing agreement I had with the survivalists. It's a group of four families that live out there, and they even use the land to feed themselves. I didn't want them displaced, and I've found it's best practice to keep your word with folks. Especially those people."

Winter took out her pad and pen from her purse. "Do you happen to know the surnames of those families?"

"Yeah, let me think. There's, uh, the Cooper family, Turner, Armstrong and of course Rogers. Joe and I, their leader, I guess you'd call him, Joe Rogers and I always got along. They didn't want a paper trail about the lease, and I didn't want to pay taxes on the rent. It was a win-win."

This was it. "Does Mr. Rogers have a son or a nephew by the name of David by any chance?"

"Sure does. His son David is a war hero. Navy SEAL if I remember right. Joe is really proud of him."

"Have you ever met him?" Winter wondered.

"Yeah. He would drop off the payments to me sometimes. David is a quiet fellow. The kind that's always taking things in. Helpful. Whenever he'd drop by with the money, if I asked him to move something or lift it, you know, anything that was too difficult for me. He'd simply grunt with a nod and do it," George said. "Is there something wrong with the lease now that the girls are gone? I mean, what happens to the land?"

"A probate court will decide," Chance said, "but if you're Lorelei's closest living relative, and she didn't have a will, then fifty percent of it will most likely belong to you once again."

"I hope I get the portion that Joe and the others live on then. So they don't have to relocate."

"Can you tell us how to reach the camp?" Winter asked.

George gave them directions from a main road as well as taking a trail that led from his house. "Make sure you stay on the trails."

Winter's stomach tightened, and she stopped writing. "Why is that?"

"Don't know. Just what Joe always told me, so it's what I always did. They're a paranoid bunch. Best to follow the rules."

"Thank you for your time, Mr. Brewer. If we have any

further questions, we'll be in touch." Chance disconnected. "We've found our guy."

Winter pulled down her skirt, covering the holstered gun. "Which means we have a long night ahead of us." She took out her cell phone. "I need to call Director Isaacson. I want a warrant and a SWAT team ready to raid that camp first thing in the morning."

EARLY MORNING LIGHT was just breaking through. The black sky was turning gray, and patches of fog wafted through the trees. A SWAT team of seven from the Bitterroot County sheriff's office crowded around the rear of a massive, armored vehicle, already wearing their tactical gear and dragging out weapons.

Chance and Winter were in the huddle. She had given him one of her ballistic vests. The other one she strapped on herself. With Director Isaacson's assistance, she had gotten Chance clearance to be included in the raid as an investigator working for the BFPD.

They were about a mile down the road from the camp. A solid camouflaged gate barred the entrance.

"Thirty acres," Sergeant Fallow said to everyone. "Looks like the area where they live is near the gate that we'll breach with the tactical vehicle." Everyone peered down at the satellite map on his tablet. "We count twenty-six heat signatures. The chopper did a pass earlier and—"

"I told you not to fly over the camp," Winter interrupted. "It would only alert him."

Chance glanced at the SWAT team leader. "David Rogers is a former SEAL with eighteen years of active-duty experience. If he gets the slightest whiff that we're coming for him, he'll go underground and disappear."

"We have one chance to get this right," Winter said. "If that chopper pass blew it, then he's gone."

"Air support for this kind of raid is essential. We know how to do our job. The bird didn't hover overhead too long, and the pilot didn't go too low." Sergeant Fallow brought up a picture of their perp. "This is Rogers, but every single person inside that camp should be considered armed and dangerous."

"George Brewer," Winter said, "the man who had a verbal lease agreement with these people warned us to stay on the trails when going through the land they use."

Fallow nodded. "Be on the lookout for booby traps as we search."

"If we get into a standoff," said Janson, the crisis negotiator, looking at Chance and Winter, "I'll take the lead. The goal will be to talk him down and bring him in alive."

"Load up," Fallow said.

The SWAT unit jumped inside the armored vehicle and two police SUVs. Chance and Winter climbed into his truck parked behind them, and the convoy took off down the road. She rolled down the window, letting the fresh cool air rush over them.

Once they reached a half mile out, they picked up speed.

Chance glanced over at her. She was tense, Glock in hand, and focused with an intensity he'd never seen in her before. Even out on Main Street, when they'd been under fire, she didn't hesitate, didn't show any fear, but this was different. Quiet. Calm. Almost detached.

"Are you all right?" he asked.

"Something's going to go wrong. I can feel it." She tightened her grip on her weapon. "Rogers is too good. We're not good enough, and we're outnumbered, going onto land they all know like the backs of their hands. One mistake, one wrong move on our part…" She shook her head.

A steady *thwump*, *thwump* filled the air, the telltale sound of a helicopter.

They both peered through the windshield, craning their

necks skyward. A black tactical chopper buzzed overhead, swooping in toward the interior of the camp.

Dread washed over Chance. Any advantage they had, their stealth ingress, it was all toast. Their risk level had just sky-rocketed.

Winter slapped the dash. "They should've waited to use the chopper until after we breached. We're almost there, and it's not much of a heads-up, but it might be enough."

Chance agreed. If Rogers didn't know they were coming, he sure as hell did now. No doubt the former SEAL was either getting ready to move within sixty seconds flat or he was preparing to dig in and fight.

Both scenarios were bad for them.

They rounded a bend, and a big black gate came into sight. The armored vehicle zoomed ahead, gaining momentum, and blasted through the gates, knocking one side off completely. The convoy barreled inside the camp, rolling over the downed metal gate. They all came to halt, hopped out of their vehicles, weapons at the ready.

A bald man in his seventies, tall and sinewy, with a beard, a weathered face and hardened eyes, stood in the middle of the dirt path that continued through camp as far as the eye could see. He had a rifle slung over his shoulder, but his palms were raised high.

"Down on the ground!" Fallow said to him.

The rest of the team fanned out through the camp.

To either side of the path were green and camo-colored tents of varying sizes, woodsheds filled with firewood and small cabins. There was a pavilion made of logs and stones, a long table and benches running through the middle. The structure was covered with camouflage netting, along with a few vehicles. To hide them from aerial surveillance. One vehicle looked like the Chevy Blazer they'd been looking for.

Keneke had confirmed late last night that David Rogers and two other men on the list owned older model Chevy Blazer K5s.

"This is the Bitterroot County SWAT, executing a warrant," a booming voice came from the sky. "Come out slowly, place your hands on the backs of your heads and get down on your knees."

"I'm Joe Rogers. We have women and children here." The bearded guy got down on his knees. "I want to see the warrant. We've done nothing wrong."

Fallow removed his weapon and forced the man face down on the ground. "David Rogers, where is he?"

"My son's not here."

Seconds ticked by. People began to emerge from the tents. Slowly. One by one.

"Runner!" a SWAT guy said. "We've got a runner!"

Off to the west, one hundred yards out. A man wearing a dark ball cap, woodland green flannel top and dark brown pants was fleeing through the woods, rifle slung across his back.

Four SWAT members bolted after him along with Winter.

"Damn it." Chance took off right behind her.

The chopper rose higher above the trees, trying to track the chase.

A hundred yards stretched to one twenty, and the man, presumably David Rogers, was moving like lightning. Weaving and bobbing in between trees. Running so fast in clothes that blended in with the forest he was a blur. Running like he'd navigated that route a million times, knowing when to duck and when to jump. Running through grass and small brush.

Not in a straight line.

Not on a trail.

To their right, someone screamed, an anguished cry that rent the air as a man dropped. "Oh God! Trap! My leg is caught in a trap!"

Bear traps. Chance's stomach filled with acid. His knee throbbed, the pain blooming. His heart pounded like it was trying to fight its way out of his chest.

The lone tactical medic changed course and made a beeline to the wounded. But no one else slowed down. Not even Winter.

What was wrong with them? Who knew what else was out in those woods?

The need to catch Rogers was the motivating force overriding everything else inside those cops. But with each second, the former SEAL pulled farther away, putting more and more distance between them. Getting harder to see.

They were all being baited and lured. Chasing that man was a grave mistake.

"Winter!" Chance needed to get her to stop, to let Rogers go for now. They weren't going to capture him this way, not on his territory. They'd only end up hurt or dead. "Winter!"

Up ahead, the assistant team leader dashed between two trees. A loud click echoed. Then a concussive explosion—a sudden flash, deafening sound, a hot wave of air pressure—knocked them all backward to the ground.

Chapter Twenty

A bitter, acrid taste saturated Winter's mouth. She tried to swallow it down but failed. Bested and beaten yet again by David Rogers.

It'd been five hours since the former SEAL got away from them in the woods, no one at the camp was talking, and all they had to show for it was one dead—the assistant team leader—and another severely injured. The crisis negotiator might lose his foot.

Winter should be glad, grateful, that she and Chance were alive. A part of her was, but it was a small, distant, silent part. At the forefront, there was only frustration and fury and the determination to find Rogers eating away at her.

She reviewed the CCTV footage of Rogers tailing Brewer and O'Shea again. Looking for anything she might have missed previously.

"Tak and Bo found a guide to lead them safely through the thirty acres," Chance said, walking back into his office at IPS where she was working. "They're going to start combing the woods to look for Rogers."

"They won't find him."

Chance sighed. "They might. The guy didn't vanish into thin air. And if they don't, Autumn and Eli might find a lead."

Her sister and the other IPS investigator were interviewing the hotel housekeepers no one had questioned yet. They'd divided the remaining list of room attendants between them to save time.

"They might." Winter looked up from the laptop. "I feel like we have twelve hours. Eighteen max before Rogers regroups and disappears for good."

Chance put a hand on her shoulder. His touch was warm and comforting, but she didn't want to be comforted.

"I'm going to meet the nurse from the tip hotline at the hospital. Give her a little cash and see if she has any credible information. Want to come with me?"

"No." She shook her head. "Do you have any hard copy maps of the area?"

"Yeah." He went to a cabinet and rifled through it. "Why?"

"I rewatched the CCTV footage of Rogers following the two victims. Afterward, he took Lake Shore to Briar Woods."

"So, what?" He set a folded map on the desk.

"So Briar Woods would take him in the opposite direction of the survivalist camp. Where was he going, day after day, and why? I want to go out that way, look around."

Frowning, he tilted his head to the side like she was spinning her wheels. "If it'll make you feel better."

"Catching him will make me feel better." She grabbed the map, her things and marched to the parking lot.

A message came in, followed by another, on the IPS group text chain everyone was using to provide updates.

Tak: We got a second guide. Splitting up to cover more land faster.

Autumn: Realized a housekeeper has the surname of one of the survivalist families. Cooper. Bo already questioned her. Trying again. Heading to Sugar Hill Lane.

Shoving her phone in her pocket, Winter grabbed the door handle to her Bronco.

Chance took her arm. "Hey." Putting a hand to her cheek, he stared at her. "I know you feel like we lost him."

"Because we did."

"We flushed him out from a safe space. He's on the run. We'll find him."

"How do you know?"

"Because you and I have something else in common."

"Oh yeah, what's that?"

"We don't fail."

CHANCE GULPED DOWN a bottle of water while waiting outside Bitterroot Valley Hospital for the nurse to get a break from her shift.

A woman in pink scrubs, a sweater and Crocs finally came out. She made eye contact and waved to him. He went over to meet her next to the emergency room doors.

"Nicole Gleason?" he asked, and she nodded. He extended his hand, and they shook. "I'm Chance Reyes."

"I know who you are. Do you have my money?"

He took out an envelope and passed it to her.

"This feels light." She peeked inside. "How much is it? Four hundred?"

"Five. That's my daily ATM limit."

She handed the envelope back. "I guess we'll talk on Monday after you go to the bank."

They didn't have that long to wait. "You only get paid if your information leads to the capture of the individual that we're after. The five hundred is a gesture of good faith. You get to keep it even if what you tell me doesn't pan out."

"I don't know." She folded her arms and rocked side to side. "What if you catch him because of what I have to tell you and then the cops or the government or whatever decides not to pay me because they don't have to any longer?"

"First, that would make the concept of offering a reward

ineffective in the future. Second, I'm personally offering and paying the reward. I'll keep my word and pay you if your information is solid."

Nicole pursed her lips. "Okay. I guess I'll have to trust you."

"Tell me about your neighbor."

She looked around. "I live next door to Megan. She has a boyfriend. A big guy. Drives a Chevy Blazer. I think it's a K5. It looks like the one in the picture on the poster, always dirty like he does a lot of off-roading. Never saw the license plate, not that I ever looked for it. Anyway, he's always there at her place, but after the shooting, I haven't seen him again. Until this morning."

"He was back in the Blazer?" Maybe Nicole had gotten the tag number this time.

"No," Nicole said, shaking her head. "I saw him trudge out of the woods like a sweaty mountain man with a big ol' rifle slung across his back. He was huffing and puffing like he'd just finished a marathon."

"This morning?" Chance's brain was spinning as the details fell into place. "Around what time? What was he wearing?"

"Um, I was leaving for my shift, it was the only reason I even spotted him. So it was around seven thirty. He was wearing a green, woodsy-colored flannel shirt, brown pants and boots. Maybe combat boots. He used to be Navy."

His pulse spiked. "Your neighbor's full name and address?"

"Megan Cooper. She lives a 5511 Sugar Hill Lane."

Winter swerved onto the shoulder of Briar Woods Road and skidded to a halt. Pulling out the map again, she scanned the area. She looked at the survivalist campsite she'd already circled and then examined firebreaks and any possible egress routes that might have led to Briar Woods.

None.

But there were a couple of other roads off Briar Woods that led to the backside of the wooded area a few miles from the campsite. Bear Creek and Sugar Hill Lanes.

Sugar Hill.

Winter took out her cell, pulled up her sister's text and reread it. Sugar Hill. Cooper. Couldn't be a coincidence. She hit the phone icon, dialing Autumn.

Straight to voicemail.

What the hell? Worry slithered through her. She tried again. Same thing. Her sister's voicemail message played. She brought up the locator app, searched for Autumn's icon.

Her profile picture was no longer in color and had turned gray. That only happened if the phone was powered off or the battery had been removed.

The last location was on Sugar Hill. At a house that sat adjacent to the woods.

Then her phone rang. It was Chance.

"Hey," Winter began, "you're not going to believe this—"

"Rogers is at his girlfriend's house. Megan Cooper. That's where he ran to when he fled the camp. 5511 Sugar Hill Lane."

"Autumn went there." Winter threw her car into Drive, peeled out into the road and sped off.

"I'm already on the way."

"She's not answering her phone. Goes straight to voicemail. I'm headed there now."

"No, wait for me."

"My sister is in trouble. Rogers feels threatened, cornered. We don't know what he's going to do to her." What he might've already done. Whether it was already too late.

"Listen to me, I'm twelve minutes from Cooper's house. I'm speeding, I can possibly make it in eight."

"I can be there in three."

"Wait for me!"

"I can't." No way was she sitting still, doing nothing, while her sister was in the hands of a murderer.

"Winter, just give me five minutes. You need backup. Think this through. Don't rush into it. You can't go up against him and get your sister out, get yourself out, *alive*, if you're alone."

He was right, but backup was on the way. "Rogers has her. He's armed and cornered. What if he's feeling desperate, too? His instinct might be to kill her. Make her disappear. Then go to ground."

Rogers was a man who not only planned but made split-second decisions in combat situations. He might not weigh the pros and cons of killing one private investigator. Waiting could mean the difference between life and death for Autumn.

"Please, don't do this. I can't protect you, either of you, if you do this. Listen to me. For once!"

"I'm not your responsibility. Autumn is. Getting her away from Rogers alive," she said, her voice turning shrill, "is all that matters."

"Not true. You matter. You matter to me. Let me keep you safe."

"It's not your job to worry about me. Or to keep me safe. But this *is* my job. This is my sister."

"Winter, please," Chance said, anger mixed with a plea so powerful in those two words it tugged at her heart.

She could barely breathe. "I'd never forgive myself if I waited and anything happened to her. I don't have a choice."

THERE WAS ALWAYS a choice.

And Winter was constantly going to make the same one. Duty over her safety. Chance had witnessed it over and over.

Out on Main Street. Out in the woods at the survivalist camp. Now again, and she was doubling down because Autumn had found Rogers, had stumbled right into him.

Chance cursed, speeding down the street. As soon as Winter hung up on him, he called Logan and the others and told them everything. The police were coming. Declan and Eli, too. The SWAT team was still in the area as well because they'd lost one and had another in the hospital, and those guys were fired up.

Backup was on the way, in full force.

His knuckles whitening on the steering wheel, Chance only prayed they all got there before it was too late. Because Winter mattered more than he realized, more than anything else in his life. If he couldn't protect her, couldn't keep her safe when they were working together, then who was he?

For years, he'd been searching and waiting, in no rush, for the right woman to come along. Finally, he met her. Finally, he decided it was time to make a move, regardless of naysayers and drawbacks because it felt like a clock was ticking and he might miss his opportunity. Finally, he got her to lower her wall and let him in.

Like hell was he going to lose her now.

He reached into the back seat and grabbed the ballistics vest she lent him. Set it in the passenger seat. Opened the console. Pulled out two extra loaded magazines.

A light up ahead turned yellow. He gunned the accelerator. The light blinked red, and he ran it, barreling down Briar Woods Road as fast as the truck could go.

WINTER SPOTTED HER sister's car. Parked in front of 5511 Sugar Hill Lane.

Fear churned in her stomach as she passed the house and stopped two doors down. Popping her trunk, she took off her blazer. She grabbed her armored vest, strapped it on and drew her weapon.

She hustled down the street. There was no vehicle in the driveway. Winter couldn't tell if Megan Cooper was also in the house. Or if Rogers was in there alone with Autumn. What if he had moved her? Taken her into the woods to kill her? To dispose of the body? How would Winter find them?

Creeping up the driveway, she shook off the thought. The fact Autumn's car was still at the house was a good sign. He'd want to get rid of it and the body as quickly as possible. Maybe transport the body in the trunk.

She came up alongside the single-story house and peered in through a crack in the drawn curtains of a window. The living room was empty. She shuffled to the back of the house. In the kitchen, there was a body on the floor.

Autumn!

Her sister was tied up and gagged but moving, wriggling on the tile floor. She was alive.

But where was Rogers?

There was no other movement in the kitchen. A sinking sensation dipped in her belly. She eased under the carport, across the covered back porch and crept up to the back door. Tried it. The knob turned. She pushed it open quietly.

Waited. She ducked inside, scanning every step of the way. Expecting him to be hidden anywhere. To pop out when she least expected it.

The Mk 12 SPR was resting against the cased opening between the kitchen and living room, the butt of the rifle on the floor.

Autumn's gaze was locked on Winter as she crept closer. Winter knelt beside her sister, keeping her Glock up and her head on a swivel, her back to a row of cabinets. All entry points to the room within her sights. She reached down and ripped off the duct tape covering Autumn's mouth.

"He knows you're here," Autumn whispered. "Rogers tiptoed out the back door. The same door you came in."

Ice water ran through Winter's veins. They needed to get out of there. She grabbed a knife from the counter and cut the zip ties binding Autumn's wrists and ankles. "Listen, carefully. Help is coming. But I need you to go to your car and get out of here."

Fear and worry wrinkled Autumn's brow. "I'm not leaving you."

"We have to separate. Go in different directions." Rogers couldn't get them both if they weren't together, and if he decided to run, Winter was going after him. She couldn't let him get away with this and disappear forever.

"He has my car keys." Autumn's voice was low and shaky. "He was planning to take me somewhere."

Kill her away from the house.

Winter dug her car keys out and put them in her sister's hand along with the knife. "Two doors down. To the right. Don't look back. Don't stop moving."

"I'll wait for you at the car."

Winter shook her head. "Just go. If you argue, we both die. Understand?"

Autumn hesitated, her eyes glassy and wide, her jaw trembling, but she nodded. "I'll give you a sign I made it."

Winter helped her sister up from the floor and shoved her toward the living room. *Go*, she mouthed.

Autumn ran to the front door, looked back once, and Winter nodded. Her sister opened the door and raced across the yard.

Winter eased outside through the back door, needing to keep him from going after her sister. "Rogers! Come out and let's talk!" She scanned the yard and the tree line of the woods, gun at the ready, and listened as she moved along the covered back porch. No sign of him, but she sensed he was there. Close. "I understand why you killed Lorelei Brewer and Phoebe O'Shea. That you were only trying to protect your people, make sure they kept the land."

She went totally still, didn't say anything and stayed silent. All she heard was the rustle of dry leaves blowing across the yard, the creak of branches in the trees swaying, the frantic thumping of her heart in her ears. She had no idea where he was.

A car peeled down the street, tires screaming, horn honking. The sign. Autumn was safe. Her sister made it.

Tipping her head back, Winter glanced at the roof above the porch. She redirected her aim and fired two bullets in different sections. Light poked through the holes.

Still, no movement.

Winter needed to find him before he got to her. Going up against him one-on-one would be a no-win scenario for her. *Flush him out.*

"Your father is sitting in a jail cell." Winter stepped off the back porch, weapon trained on the detached garage farther down the driveway next to the backyard. "Your family. Your friends, your girlfriend, Megan Cooper, could all be in a lot of trouble. Charged as accomplices for aiding and abetting you. But you could help them by giving yourself up without hurting anyone else."

A soft thud.

Fear slicked her belly as she froze. Rogers was behind her. Close. So close, she could hear him. Feel him.

She spun.

A stunning blow smashed down on her arm. Another into her face. She staggered back into the yard, blood pooling in her mouth as Rogers wrested her weapon from her hand. He whirled with a low kick, sweeping her legs out from under her.

She slammed into the ground. Air rushed from her lungs. He was on her with her gun pointed at her head, but she kicked and punched and clawed at him. She managed to scratch his face, her bootheel striking his knee.

But he kept coming, kept moving, like a machine. A stunning punch to her head left her dazed. He flipped her onto her front, throwing her face into the dirt and jammed a knee into her spine. Pain burst through her injured side.

"I'm sure I broke some of your ribs the other day. Or came close." He added pressure, and she would've screamed if there was air in her lungs. "This can be painful or painless. Choice is yours, DCI Agent Stratton. We're going to get up and go get your sister."

Not happening.

Rogers twisted both her arms behind her back, cinched a zip tie around her wrists and hauled her up from the ground. She raked in a painful breath. He swung her around like she weighed nothing, and they turned.

Then they both stilled.

Chance swept across the back porch with his gun aimed in their direction. He dropped to a knee, ducking behind a large grill, gun locked on them.

Rogers shifted her in front of him like a human shield, her arms wrenched behind her, and pressed the muzzle to her temple. "Step aside."

"No can do," Chance said.

The *thwump, thwump* of a helicopter drawing close resonated in the air.

"Drop your weapon and move," Rogers ordered, "or I'll shoot her!"

Blinding fear struck her that Chance might comply, and if he did, Rogers would shoot him. If Chance held his ground, there'd be a standoff when backup arrived. It wouldn't be bloodless. She'd probably end up shot dead along with Rogers.

"Don't wait for him to do it," she called to Chance. "You shoot me."

"What?" both men said in unison.

"Do it. Shoot me! Right where your scars are." She hoped Chance would understand what she was asking him to do. To shoot her in the chest. In the vest. The impact would take her down and give him a clear shot at Rogers. "Shoot me!"

The helicopter swooped in overhead, kicking up wind and blowing dust and dirt.

A deafening bang ripped through the air. Agony blasted her chest. The power of the bullet flung her backward and to the side with so much force there was nothing Rogers could do.

As she fell, with darkness closing in, another gunshot cracked.

ROGERS DROPPED TO the ground. A bullet to the head. Chance jumped up and ran to Winter.

She was down. Not moving. Her eyes closed. Had he done the right thing listening to her? His heart jumped into his throat. He dropped to his knees and hauled her into his lap.

"Winter." Chest tightening, he cradled her in his arms. He pulled the knife from his pocket, flicked it open and sliced through the zip tie around her wrists. Looking her over, he cupped her cheek. The bullet was lodged in the vest, but she wasn't moving. Wasn't breathing. He unfastened the straps, pulled the ballistic vest over her head and tossed it to the side. The risk was too great. He never should've fired at her. Even with the vest, the shot could've caused bruising, broken ribs, internal damage. Death. "Winter!" he said, shaking her, terrified of losing her.

Winter sucked in a breath, and her eyes fluttered open.

Relief swamped him. She was going to be okay.

Her gaze found his. "Never been happier to see you." Her voice was a ragged whisper. "Did we get Rogers?"

Tears stung his eyes. He held her, looking at her and wanting to say a million things. To tell her how stubborn she'd been, to apologize for not giving her the latitude to do her job as a cop—a dangerous job he couldn't protect her from, to say how he regretted not making a move and asking her out and kissing her sooner. They'd wasted six long months that they could've been together. To let her know he didn't know what he would've done if anything happened to her because she was it for him, *the one* he wanted to be with, no matter what.

But as he held her in his arms, with blood on her lips, her body trembling and no doubt hurting like hell, only four words came out of his mouth.

"We got him, honey."

Squeezing her eyes shut, she nodded and clung to him tighter.

Chapter Twenty-One

Sixteen hours later

Sunlight peeked through the curtains of Chance's bedroom. Tangled together with him, Winter ran her fingers through the curls on his chest, tracing his scars, soaking up his warmth and the feel of him wrapped around her.

"Morning," he said, his hand stroking her arm.

"Sorry. I didn't mean to wake you."

"You didn't. I just wanted to hold you a little longer before I got up and made us some coffee." He kissed the top of her head. "How are you feeling?"

Her entire right side and the center of her chest were covered in bruises. She ached, riddled with bone-deep pain. But she was alive. They both were, and they had somehow found this bubble of warmth and acceptance and affection. "I'm fine."

He kissed her shoulder and planted more across her collarbone. "I don't believe you." He ran his hand over her hair, his fingers caressing the scar on her head.

"I know what happened to you," she said, stroking the jagged lines on his chest. "Summer and Autumn told me at the barbecue."

"Oh, I thought I was *he who shall not be discussed*."

She smiled. "Don't make me laugh. It'll hurt too much. Yes, you were, but Autumn figured it out about us. She told me about the Beast of Bitterroot County. You've been through so much ugliness and horror and pain." Putting a hand to his cheek, she kissed him. Softly. Sweetly. "I'm sorry."

"I'm not. I helped stop a killer, and we found bodies that had been missing for years. Families were able to lay loved ones to rest. It's all made me who I am. The darkest, most wounded parts of us are just as important as the light," he said, looking at her like he could see straight down to her soul.

The sense of exposure, the vulnerability didn't scare her.

"I don't want to hold back with you," she said. Life was too short. She didn't want to play games. Didn't want to pretend not to feel deeply for him when she wanted to feel everything with him.

"Me, either. I waited to tell you about the scars because I don't like it when people look at me like I'm a victim."

"A broken thing," she whispered. Sometimes she wondered if that was how people, her sisters, looked at her because of her history with men. "I don't."

"I know."

"I see a hero who made sacrifices to save others."

"That's what you do all the time, honey."

Honey.

Smiling, she liked that. To be thought of as sweet and not bitter. She slid her hand over his chest. Over his scars. If anyone could ever understand what she'd been through, personally and professionally, it was him. "We're survivors. Like attracts like."

"When I look at you, I see beauty and strength and courage." He brushed his lips over hers, and she shivered from a warm tingle. "I'm in awe of you."

"Well, I am like an unfriendly, treacherous mountain pass. I'm sure Lewis and Clark were in awe, too."

They both smiled.

He held her gaze. "I love you, Winter."

She stilled. Didn't blink. Didn't breathe. The smile frozen on her face.

"I've wanted to say it since our first night together, but I didn't want to scare you off. I know *fast* frightens you, but I've never felt this way about anyone. Never been so certain." Chance searched her face. "Don't push me away or run from this."

Her throat tightened. "Wow." She took a breath. "I thought you were going to let me set the pace."

He lowered his head. "Yeah. I should've held that back."

Snuggling closer, she slid her leg between his thighs and kissed him. "I'm not running. Your pace is scary but in a good way. You push me out of my comfort zone. I'm done letting fear hold me back."

"Really?" He slid his hand over her thigh, and she shivered again.

"Really."

"Then I'm going to push a little more. Move in with me. You've got the codes to the front gate and the door. Just bring your stuff over and make this home with me."

She stiffened, surprised how big the push was, though it was good and beautiful.

"Keep your house, if you feel like you need an escape plan. Let's jump in with both feet and see where we land." He tightened an arm around her waist. "I'm sure about you, about us, but I'm scared, too. I've never done this before, fall in love, live with someone. There's going to be smack talk from Logan, and Summer is going to give me that side-eye of disapproval, but I don't care. I'm aware of the pitfalls, the endless unknowns, the compromises, and I want this. Because you're the best thing in my life."

Her mind whirled with possibilities of a future with him. She knew fear all too well, the taste, the smell, the corrosive nature of it eating away at hope, and she was also capable of facing it head-on.

This gorgeous, charming, incredible man understood her, *saw* her—the darkness and the light and the bits in between—and still wanted to take a leap of faith with her. He wanted to love her.

Deep down, she wanted all that with him, too. To embrace his warmth. To take comfort in his strength. Cherish this intimacy. What they shared was rare. Precious. This felt right, he felt right, and she was going to hold on to him.

She met his gaze. "I love you, too."

"But..." he said, his tone tentative, like he was waiting for her to add some caveat.

This was an opportunity she wouldn't squander. "But there's a secret between us."

He flinched. "What secret?"

"Who snitched I wasn't working an active case when we met for coffee?"

He grinned and let out a breath like he'd been holding it. "Heather."

Her office manager. Caressing the stubble on his cheek, she pressed her forehead to his. "No other buts. I promise."

"I'm happy to hear it."

"It's fast and scary, but I want this. *I want you.* No escape plan necessary."

She was going to take a chance on him, jump in with both feet, holding his hand, happy to land wherever, so long as they were together.

* * * * *

CHRISTMAS BANK HEISTS

R. BARRI FLOWERS

In memory of my beloved mother, Marjah Aljean, a devoted lifelong fan of Mills & Boon romance and romantic suspense novels, who inspired me to excel in my personal and professional lives. To H. Loraine, the true and dearest love of my life and very best friend, whose support has been unwavering through the many terrific years together; as well as the many loyal fans of my romance, suspense, mystery and thriller fiction published over the years. A special shout-out goes to a wonderful group of talents whom I have long admired: Carol, Peggy, Krista, Lisa, Charmian and Olivia. And last but not least, a nod to my great Mills & Boon editors, Denise Zaza and Emma Cole, for the wonderful opportunity to lend my literary voice and creative spirit to the Heroes series, as well as Miranda Indrigo, the wonderful concierge, who serendipitously led me to success with Mills & Boon.

Prologue

The white GMC Savana passenger van drove at the speed limit down the street that was covered by a light sheet of snow. It came to a stop after turning into an alleyway. The four occupants methodically covered their heads with ski masks that matched dark clothing and leather gloves and got out. Two were wearing long overcoats, shielding what lay beneath. Without uttering a word, the quartet marched down the alley and onto the sidewalk, where they picked up the pace before reaching the bank on Vernon Street in Leyton Falls, Colorado.

They went inside and quickly sized up the situation. There were two windows open, each with a customer doing business with a bank teller. Another two customers were waiting in line. At one desk, a crimson-haired female bank employee was working on a computer, while a tall, bald-headed male employee was walking in her direction.

As the four bank robbers spread out in a practiced process, two brandished handguns, while another pulled out a Palmetto State Armory Sabre AR-15 rifle. The male leader of the group and designated spokesperson opened his overcoat and whipped out a Lever Action X Model .410 shotgun, while stating in a no-nonsense tone of voice, "This is a bank robbery! Everyone stay right where you are. If anyone even thinks about alerting the cops or doing anything else really stupid—like trying to be a hero—we'll kill everyone in here and call it a day. Trust me! You don't want to test us," he warned, gazing up at a security camera audaciously and back, "if you know what's good for you. Or bad…"

The message seemed to register loud and clear as no one made a risky move.

The ringleader then ordered everyone but the bank tellers to come together and they were forced to zip-tie one another, then lay face down on the floor. The two tellers emptied their drawers of all the cash they had, as ordered, while being advised against slipping GPS trackers or dye packs in the bags—which were collected by the pistol-wielding bank robbers, as the other two robbers kept an eye and their weapons on everyone else.

With skillful precision, the bank heist seemed to go without a hitch like clockwork, and as the robbers were leaving, the leader glared at the those left unharmed inside and cautioned, "Don't try to follow us, or you'll get a bullet or two for your trouble—think about it!"

The bank robbers left the same way they came in and calmly made their way back to the getaway van, where the masks were removed and they drove off, laughing at once again having succeeded in their plan of action.

TAMMY YOSHIMURA HAD been reapplying her lip gloss in the bathroom when she heard the commotion. She had experienced a bank robbery once before in her three years as a teller at the Bradley Bank. It was in her first month on the job, when she was only twenty-three years of age. A lone armed bank robber had handed her a note that announced what was happening and demanded she hand him every bit of money in her drawer. Or else. Shaking like a leaf that day, she wisely did as she was told, while he was threatening her with a gun in her face.

Now it had happened again. She'd been ready to return to her window when she'd spotted the bank robbery underway. From what her hazel eyes could see, there appeared to be four armed robbers, all wearing ski masks. The way they moved about in systematic and confident fashion, it seemed clear to her that this was not their first go-round as robbers. *And probably not their last*, she imagined, were they to get away with it.

Ducking out of sight just before any of the robbers could see her, Tammy tried her best to backtrack to the bathroom to hide, while praying she didn't give herself away with the rustling of her wool blend pantsuit. Or the sound of her square toe booties softly but surely tapping the solid hardwood flooring.

She slipped inside a stall and crouched, as if they were already onto her, while wondering if the robbery would turn violent. The thought of one of her colleagues or a customer being injured, or worse—killed—turned Tammy's stomach inside out. Especially at this usually festive time of year, just three weeks before Christmas. Talk about putting a damper on the holiday season.

Lifting the cell phone from a pocket in her blazer, she called 911, and in a trembling, whispering voice reported that a bank robbery was currently underway. She had no idea if the authorities had already been alerted. The dispatcher assured her that help was on the way, while directing her to stay hidden until such time.

Doing as she was told, Tammy remained crouched inside the stall and tried not to make another sound while nervously running her fingers through her brunette pixie cut. Her mind turned to the one bank robber who did all the talking. His deep and resonant voice sounded familiar. Had she heard it before? Hadn't he tried to hit on her once at a bar, in which she rejected his advances? Or was it only her imagination?

These thoughts lingered in Tammy's mind like a throbbing toothache till the police arrived, at which point the robbers were long gone.

But that didn't stop detectives from the Leyton Falls Police Department Robbery Unit from investigating the brazen daytime bank heist and who might be responsible.

Or, for that matter, bringing in special agents from the FBI to lend their expertise in bank robbery investigations to help capture the culprits and hold them accountable for what Tammy saw as a horrible way to begin the Christmas season in town.

Chapter One

"We've got a bead on the suspect," FBI Special Agent Sheldon Montgomery relayed over his cell phone on speaker to Karen Muñoz, special agent in charge of the Federal Bureau of Investigation's Denver field office that he worked out of. He was in his black Ford Explorer SUV en route to a house in Leyton Falls, Colorado, where a bank robber was holed up after making off with nearly $40,000 in cash this Saturday afternoon from the Leyton Falls Credit Union on Third Avenue, in Hemton County, which was about thirty-five miles from the greater metropolitan statistical area of Denver-Aurora-Lakewood, Colorado. As a consequence of the deadly armed bank heist—a federal offense with a maximum penalty of life behind bars or the death penalty—the robber had shot to death, in cold blood, sixty-seven-year-old Doris Flynn, a customer and doting grandmother and great-grandmother.

"Go on," Karen urged him anxiously.

Sheldon trained his blue eyes on the snow-covered road and pressed down on the accelerator while staying just inside the speed limit as he dodged other vehicles making their way to wherever this afternoon, with less than two weeks till Christmas. "We've identified the suspect as fifty-one-year-old Arnold Cappellano, thanks in part to surveillance video of the man and the getaway car, a white Hyundai Sonata, that was registered in his name."

"Sounds like he really thought this through," she said facetiously.

Sheldon chuckled. "Gets even worse for him," he told her. "Turns out, a teller was clever enough to slip a GPS tracker into the bag of money, making it easy to track Cappellano right to his own house on Schaefer Street."

"That's good. What else do we know about the suspect?"

"Well, Cappellano's got a record for domestic violence, drug possession and a DUI for added measure. He's currently unemployed, going through a divorce and has an eleven-year-old son."

"Hmm," Karen uttered thoughtfully. "Hopefully you can get the suspect to give up peacefully. We don't need to make matters any worse at this time of year, if we can help it."

"Always the game plan," Sheldon said understandingly, wanting to stay in the spirit of the holiday season to the extent possible. Never mind that his own spirits had been dampened in that regard by his personal failures of late. He knew, though, that this would ultimately be up to Cappellano and any circumstances that might come into play, in what was presently a standoff. "I'll let you know how it goes."

"All right."

Sheldon ended the phone call as he continued driving to Arnold Cappellano's address. His thoughts immediately turned from the lone bank robber to the bigger picture of recent criminal activity. The Denver area had seen more than its fair share of bank heists in recent memory, coinciding with a surge in substance abuse and drug addiction, under employment and unemployment and, frankly, desperation by many offenders to get cash to deal with their various urgent needs. To say nothing of those individuals who barefacedly flouted the law to line their greedy pockets with money that didn't belong to them. This had led to the formation by the Bureau of the Rocky Mountain Money Grab Task Force—with members including diligent FBI agents such as himself, special agents from the Colorado Bureau of Investigation, and deputies and detectives from local police and sheriffs' departments—to address the pressing issue in the state.

But it was the recent spate of armed bank robberies in several small cities and towns in Hemton County, including Leyton Falls, that was Sheldon's chief concern at the moment as the lead investigator. Since the beginning of the month, a group of robbers wearing ski masks had brazenly robbed at gunpoint six banks and credit unions. Dubbed by the press as the Hemton County Bandit Quartet, surveillance video and physical assessment suggested the foursome was made up of three white males—or a combination of white and Hispanic males—and one white female robber. All were in good shape and seemingly in their twenties or thirties. Each wielded a firearm during the bank robberies and ostensibly dared anyone to put their threats to the test before possibly making their getaway in a light-colored vehicle.

Though thus far no one had been seriously harmed, the forceful rhetoric and brash nature of the crimes seemed to be increasing with each robbery, making Sheldon believe it was inevitable that the robberies would escalate in violence—perhaps resulting in fatalities. Unless they could catch the unidentified culprits first. To that end, the FBI sought the help of the public and was willing to offer a $2,500 reward for useful information that led to the identification, arrest and conviction of the Hemton County Bandit Quartet.

Maybe giving someone financial incentive to spill the beans will do the trick, Sheldon told himself, even if it wasn't exactly a pot of gold, per se. But that, of course, was relative, depending on the person. More likely, he firmly believed, it was the hard work of the ongoing criminal investigation that would ultimately nail the unsubs.

At least this was the tenet that had been passed onto Sheldon from his father, Foster Montgomery, a retired and decorated FBI special agent. Following in his footsteps, Sheldon had joined the Bureau a decade ago, receiving his training at the FBI Academy in Quantico, Virginia, before being assigned to field or satellite offices in Arkansas, South Dakota, and currently, Colorado. Prior to that, he had picked up his bachelor's degree in criminal justice from the University of South Dakota's College of Arts & Sciences in Vermillion, South Dakota.

That was where he'd met his bride-to-be, Lauralee Kettle, an international studies major. The marriage had lasted five years—which was probably five years too long, if Sheldon were totally honest about it—and ended in a divorce that was contentious but that both agreed needed to happen. Now thirty-four and on his own going on five years, he had not exactly given up on the happily-ever-after part of a lasting relationship, having dated a bit here and there, while keeping an open mind. But he sure as hell was never going to jump into anything headfirst and get burned again. Which was why he was treading carefully in that department these days. If that meant he'd have to be single forever, hard as that was to fathom, then so be it.

Sheldon put those uncomfortable thoughts away as he reached his destination, pulling up behind some police vehicles. Brushing a hand habitually through his thick, short dark hair, he glanced at the Glock 19 Gen5 9mm Luger semi-automatic service pistol in his leather hip holster and exited the car. Wearing an FBI jacket and body armor, he ignored the chill in the air, hitting his face like a slap, and quickly sized up the scene. The suspect's address was a one and a half story Craftsman bungalow. It sat on the corner of the street. Cappellano's Hyundai Sonata was parked crookedly at the curb nearby, as though he'd left it in a hurry to get away. The residence was surrounded by an FBI SWAT team armed with Colt M4 carbine semiautomatic assault rifles, along with other armed agents, and officers and deputies from the Leyton Falls Police Department and Hemton County Sheriff's Department, respectively, shielding themselves from the house and potential for gunfire.

After flashing his ID to perimeter police, Sheldon stayed low while making his way behind a black Ford F-150 Police Responder vehicle, where he found the man he was looking for.

Leyton Falls PD Lieutenant Nolan Valentine was African American and in his late thirties, with a solid build inside his uniform and closely cropped black hair with a shaved side part. "What took you so long, Montgomery?" he asked with a deadpan look. "These bank bandits are serious business."

"Hey, the roads can be dicey at this time of year," Sheldon explained with a straight face, while knowing Nolan was only teasing him. The issue at hand, though, was no joke for either of them. "So, what's the status?"

"Arnold Cappellano's holed up in his house," Nolan confirmed. "Been there for over an hour now. A neighbor noticed him go inside and he hasn't come out since. But he did make an appearance at the window, as if to say, 'Here I am, come and get me,' before ducking out of sight. We've evacuated all the nearby houses till this is over."

"Makes sense." Sheldon gazed at the suspect's residence. "Have you been able to make contact with him yet?"

"We've tried calling him, but he won't pick up." Nolan frowned. "We're not going to wait him out forever," he warned impatiently.

"I know." Sheldon understood that there was always a point of no return when they could wait no longer before going in and bringing out the suspect, one way or the other. Alive or dead. "Any indication that someone else is in the house?"

Sheldon got the impression that the lieutenant was going to say that they believed Arnold Cappellano was alone, before the suspect suddenly shouted out a broken window, almost on cue, "I'm not alone. My son Gregory is with me. Unless you back off, I swear I'll kill us both—"

"Damn," Nolan muttered under his breath. "Puts this in a whole different light."

"Tell me about it." Sheldon had hoped that the son was with his mother, Martha Cappellano, elsewhere. Instead, they now needed to deal with a possible hostage situation. Or worse.

Reading his mind, Nolan said matter-of-factly, "We need to get a member of our Hostage Negotiation Unit over here pronto."

Not disagreeing in the slightest, Sheldon responded, "Go for it." He added thoughtfully, "Probably a good idea to reach out to Cappellano's estranged wife as well, to get her input on his state of mind and just what we're up against in dealing with the situation."

"You're right. Maybe have her on hand, to make contact and try to reason with him, in case all else fails."

Sheldon nodded, concurring. "Yeah."

In the meantime, he took it upon himself to call the bank robber and murder suspect by cell phone, hoping Cappellano was ready to pick up and looking for a way out of this hole he'd dug for himself.

OFFICER KELLI BURKETT wore her second hat, figuratively speaking, as a trained hostage negotiator for the Leyton Falls Police Department's Hostage Negotiation Unit. Her collateral duties in this respect to her routine police work pertained to dealing effectively with crisis situations that included barricaded individuals, hostage taking and suicidal persons.

It was the last area that she was presently engaged in, after responding to a 911 call that a female was on the roof of the Welan Office Building on Welan Street in downtown Leyton Falls. Kelli was the first officer to arrive on the scene. She was aghast when she spotted the woman from the ground level among other horrified onlookers.

Moving quickly to avert disaster weeks before Christmas and the new year, Kelli took the elevator up as far as it would go, then needed to scale two flights of stairs to get to the rooftop. Every step of the way, she had prayed that she could get there before the woman took the plunge ten stories to her death.

As a widow, having lost her husband, Pierre Burkett, a US service member in the army, when the Black Hawk helicopter he was in crashed into the Mediterranean Sea three years ago, Kelli hated the thought of anyone's life being lost prematurely. No matter the circumstances. It was one of the reasons she'd entered the field of police work in the first place, after getting a bachelor's degree in communication from the University of Colorado Boulder and a master's degree in criminal justice from the University of Colorado Denver. She wanted to help people in dire straits and keep the public safe. Another reason for being in law enforcement was to do something positive with her life and be a good role model for her younger sister, Samantha Quinlan.

Kelli had met Pierre when both were in graduate school and he was out of the military. Before she knew it, they had fallen in love and would soon get married. She'd encouraged his desire to reenlist in the army, as Pierre had wanted to continue to serve his country in the way he knew best. The plans they had to start a family were put on hold, only to lose that opportunity when tragedy struck, leaving her alone and lonely at the age of twenty-nine.

When Kelli reached the roof, she was relieved to find that the suicidal woman had not yet taken her own life, but she was still hovering precariously close to the ledge.

"Wait—" Kelli gasped, getting her attention as the woman faced her, looking terrified.

She guessed the distraught female to be around her own current age of thirty-two. Assessing further, Kelli's bold green eyes saw that she was as slender as her and about the same height of five feet eight inches, and had a short two-tone bob. By comparison, Kelli had long, curly black hair, currently in a braided bun. The woman was underdressed for this time of the year in a white V-neck cotton shirt, wide leg jeans and tennis shoes—likely figuring with her game plan, it wouldn't matter if she was cold or not.

Wearing her uniform, a bulletproof vest and a body camera that was recording the scene, Kelli did not want to appear threatening at all. And therefore, she kept her hand away from the Smith & Wesson M&P 9mm handgun inside the duty holster on her hip.

"What's your name?" Kelli asked the woman in an even voice as she stepped a little closer.

"Alaina Rosen," the woman answered with a crack in her tone.

"I'm Officer Burkett, Alaina. Would you mind stepping away from the ledge just a bit, so we can talk?" *Please do it*, Kelli thought, wanting this to end well.

The woman hesitated, glancing down below, before seemingly having second thoughts about taking the plunge. She took a couple of tentative steps toward Kelli. Just as she was about to ask the woman what had brought her to this point in time, Alaina muttered despairingly, "My boyfriend left me."

"I'm sorry to hear that," Kelli said sympathetically.

"We fought all the time," she conceded, her voice trembling. "But still... I never thought it would end between us."

"Relationships come and go all the time." Kelli ventured a little closer, hoping she wouldn't inadvertently trigger a life ending exit. "But taking your own life is not the answer," she told her. Or was this really all about a cry for help?

"He's seeing someone else," Alaina remarked bitterly. "I gave him my whole life, and *this* is how he repays me? So unfair!"

"Life is not always fair," Kelli pointed out realistically. She should know, given her own tremendous loss, that she was still coming to terms with, in spite of moving on to the best of her ability. "But we all have to deal with that, for better or worse, and try to look at the bright side of every bad thing that comes our way." In her own life, that meant accepting that she was a young widow and not ready to give up on still making a meaningful contribution to society. And maybe even still finding love again at some point. "I'm sure there's someone else out there for you, Alaina. It may not seem that way at the moment, but if you just give it some time and not give in to the dark place that you're in right now, you can get there."

"You really think so?" Her voice rang with expectation.

"Yes." Kelli moved even closer to the point that they were now within arm's reach of one another. "Don't let a broken relationship break you. Trust me, he's not worth ending your life. Or wanting to hang on to the life you had with him."

Alaina stared at the words for a long moment of contemplation, before her shoulders slumped and she began to cry, while moving toward Kelli. She wrapped her arms around Alaina warmly and felt a sense of relief. Another crisis averted. Another life saved that could hopefully still have a bright future.

Other officers arrived and Kelli turned the troubled but physically uninjured woman over to them, knowing she would be routinely taken to the hospital for a mental evaluation as an attempted suicide—and would get whatever treatment she needed to try and avoid a reoccurrence down the line.

AFTER RADIOING IN the incident, Kelli got into her black-and-white Ford Police Interceptor Utility patrol vehicle to head back to the Leyton Falls PD building she worked out of. The roads were beginning to clear of snow, though she was expecting—maybe even hoping for—a white Christmas, as was often the case in these parts every year. She only wished so many people weren't driven to despair at such time, for one reason or another. Loneliness could be especially brutal during the holidays. She was thankful to have Samantha around to keep her company. And vice versa. Especially with their parents, Arthur and Nancy Quinlan, no longer alive to lean on when they needed them.

When her cell phone rang, Kelli answered, "Officer Burkett," as usual, and put it on speaker.

The caller was Trent Garcia, the hard-core tactical commander of the police department's Hostage Negotiation Unit. He uttered without prelude, "We've got a hostage situation."

"That doesn't sound good," she said in an obvious understatement.

"Never is," he muttered. "We need to make sure it doesn't get worse. A bank robber, who killed a customer in the midst of the robbery, and fled home, is using his own son to try and worm his way out of this. Or maybe die trying—while taking the son along for the ride."

"Give me the address and I'll do my best to try and end this peacefully," Kelli promised, knowing that being on call 24/7 as a hostage negotiator, she didn't have the luxury of taking a victory lap from one incident to another. Meaning that bragging about saving Alaina Rosen's life would have to be put on hold for the time being.

"I know you will," Trent said confidently, and then acknowledged, as though a mind reader, "By the way, good work in talking down the suicidal woman."

Kelli welcomed the praise. "Thanks. Sometimes all one needs is a listening ear." *And a hug*, she thought, while wondering if that would be the case with a distressed bank robber, in trying to safely separate him from his son, at the very least.

Within minutes, Kelli had arrived at the scene of the standoff. She was greeted by Nolan Valentine, the intimidating lieutenant for the Leyton Falls Police Department, who stood beside a tall and extremely handsome man in plainclothes beneath an FBI jacket, which were a good fit on his solid frame.

Nolan told her, "Kelli, this is Special Agent Sheldon Montgomery."

Meeting his arresting blue eyes with flecks of gray that were bearing down on her interestedly from a heart-shaped face with a five o'clock shadow beard, she said evenly, "Officer Kelli Burkett. I'm the hostage negotiator."

"Nice to meet you," he said in a baritone voice, and ran a hand through his short black hair. "We can definitely use your help here. A boy's life may well depend on it…"

Kelli didn't doubt that for a moment, putting even more pressure on her to get him out of the robber's lair, alive and well. "I can do this," she assured him coolly. Now she only needed to deliver.

Chapter Two

Sheldon studied the drop-dead gorgeous hostage negotiator. He found her captivating green eyes fit perfectly on a diamond-shaped face, along with a dainty nose, full lips and a dimpled chin. Jet-black hair with curtain bangs was in a twisted low bun for the job, but obviously fell well below her shoulders when down. He guessed her to be five-eight or -nine, which was a good height for him—and she was slender beneath her police uniform and leather boots.

When Sheldon realized that he was gawking at Officer Kelli Burkett and she was aware of it with her own solid gaze, he shifted his eyes, while hoping he hadn't made her uncomfortable. Or perhaps she wouldn't blame him one bit for being attracted to her, as any man with a keen eye for beauty would be.

He watched as she conferred with Nolan Valentine and Martha Cappellano, who had arrived on the scene moments after Kelli. She was informed about the nature of the Cappellanos' fractured relationship.

Martha, in her forties and thin, with short red hair, was clearly distressed when crying out, "Please, don't let him hurt my son."

"We'll do everything in our power to try to keep that from happening," Kelli said in a calm voice. "But I'll need your help. What can you tell me about your husband that would drive him to rob a bank and hold his own son hostage?"

Martha sighed. "Arnold recently lost his job and was angry about it," she explained. "He took it out on me—yet another excuse for being abusive—and became even angrier when I couldn't take it anymore and left him. I got a restraining order. He took Gregory against my wishes. I guess he'd hoped to use him to somehow get out of his current situation and as leverage in making me want to get back with him."

"Which, I take it, you have no interest in doing?" Kelli asked her, as though she already had the answer.

"Not if I can help it." Martha's shoulders slumped. "Arnold hates me for what I did. Now my son has to pay for it. Unless you can stop Arnold before it's too late…"

"How do you want to play this?" Nolan asked Kelli. "Do we let her try to talk some sense into Cappellano?"

"Probably not a good idea." Kelli wrinkled her nose. "In my experience, abusive and vindictive spouses, who just also happen to be desperate right now, could be pushed over the top in these situations, if provoked by hearing from the person he blames for his troubles."

Sheldon regarded the hostage negotiator and asked, "So, what's your move?"

Kelli faced him squarely and answered, "Let me call him and see where Cappellano's head is at the moment."

Sheldon glanced at Nolan and back, nodding in agreement. "Do what you need to." He cautioned, "Time isn't on our side here—or his…"

"Okay." Kelli nodded and got on the phone with Arnold Cappellano.

Nolan watched as she identified herself and began talking with the bank robbery suspect. Her expression meandered between even, to anxious, to one of exasperation, as it appeared as though Cappellano was not budging.

Looks like we may have to go in, Sheldon told himself, in spite of the nice-looking hostage negotiator's best efforts. Not that he would fault her any. Desperation often made criminals the most unstable—and dangerous. He'd learned this over time, no matter their best efforts to end any precarious situation peacefully.

When Kelli disconnected the cell phone, ending the conversation, she sucked in a deep breath and declared, "I'm going inside."

Sheldon's brows knit. "You're what?"

She stood her ground. "I think I can get Cappellano to let his son go if he has a better bargaining chip—me."

"I can't let you do that," Sheldon said adamantly. "The last thing we need are two hostages."

"I wouldn't be a hostage," she insisted. "Not really. But I can be a lifeline for the suspect and a lifesaver for the boy. Just let me do my job and trust that I can end this without bloodshed." She eyed Nolan. "Your call, I believe…"

Even if Sheldon felt this was debatable, he was willing to defer to the lieutenant in what was a joint operation, knowing that the SWAT team was already in place to swarm in and take Cappellano out at a moment's notice, if the need arose.

Nolan considered her game plan for maybe a millisecond or two before saying authoritatively, "Do it. But leave your phone on and give us a heads up if you get even the slightest indication that Cappellano is uncooperative and intends to harm you or his son."

"All right." Kelli regarded Sheldon and offered a soft smile. "I'll be fine," she said in a way in which he couldn't help but believe her. Even if against his better nature.

"If you say so," he told her respectfully, then watched as she moved from behind the Ford F-150 Police Responder vehicle that had been shielding them from any potential gunfire and approached the house coolheadedly. Sheldon turned to

Nolan and couldn't help but ask out of curiosity, assuming he had answers, "So, what's her story anyway—apart from showing some real courage under fire as a hostage negotiator?"

Nolan pinched his nose and answered. "Kelli's been with the force for a while now. She's a widow. Her husband died a few years ago after his Black Hawk helicopter went down in the Mediterranean during an army mission."

"Sorry to hear that," Sheldon remarked.

"Yeah, we all were," Nolan said. "You can ask her to fill in the blanks sometime, if you like."

"I just may do that." Sheldon's interest was admittedly piqued and he wanted to learn more about Kelli Burkett, if the opportunity presented itself. He zeroed in on her while she sought to enter the house with the permission of a bank robber who had already taken one life.

DON'T LET THEM—or him—see you sweat, Kelli told herself lightheartedly, although the situation was deadly serious for all parties concerned. Especially for a young boy, who was probably scared out of his wits by someone for whom he was supposed to feel most protected with in life. *It's my job to separate him from his father and reunite him with his mother*, she thought. While also trying to keep Arnold Cappellano alive—even if it meant having to answer for his crimes.

Sucking in a deep breath as she stood in front of the house, her arms raised as if to surrender, instead, she hoped it was the other way around for the suspect as Kelli voiced coolly, "It's Officer Burkett. If you don't mind, Mr. Cappellano, I'd like to come in and talk to you about the current situation we have." She paused, realizing she was still armed and, as such, could be rightfully viewed as a threat to him, sure he was watching her guardedly. "I'll remove my weapon slowly and we can chat—"

Though Kelli knew she would probably get some flak for making herself so vulnerable against protocol, this was a judgment call that might be the difference between life and death for the suspect's son, Gregory Cappellano. So, she took the firearm out of her holster and placed it on the ground. She knew that SWAT and others had her covered, should push come to shove, and her efforts fell flat. But she had to try. Especially during this time of the year when the season was supposed to be merry. Right?

"Come in," Cappellano muttered begrudgingly. "But only you and don't try anything…"

Kelli heeded his warning. She glanced over her shoulder and could see the show of force ready to step in at any moment. She caught a glimpse of Special Agent Montgomery from behind the F-150 truck and imagined that he wanted nothing more than to accompany her inside the house as a means of having her back. And though the thought was comforting, this was something she had to do on her own, the risks notwithstanding.

She walked onto the porch and stepped inside the door, leaving it slightly ajar. The first thing she noticed was that the place had been trashed, as if a child had thrown a temper tantrum. She suspected, though, that it was more likely an adult who took out his frustrations on the contemporary furnishings and accent pieces.

No sooner had she begun to wonder where the suspect was holding his son than the door slammed shut behind Kelli and she turned to find Arnold Cappellano standing behind it. A hulking man, he had gray midlength hair in an undercut and a boxed salt-and-pepper beard. She noted that he was wearing military clothing and holding a gun—recognizing it as a Springfield Echelon 9mm pistol—on the boy in front of him.

Gregory Cappellano resembled his father for an eleven-year-old and was slender with curly brown hair in a scissor cut. His blue eyes looked frightened, but he otherwise appeared unhurt.

She had to ask him anyway. "Are you all right?"

Gregory hesitated, then responded softly, "Yeah."

Kelli gazed at Cappellano, who stared back, and had turned the gun on her, while ordering her, "Over there…"

She followed his hard gray eyes and did as she was told, moving farther into the cluttered living room and away from the casement windows, where marksmen likely had a bead on the interior and were waiting for orders to strike.

Cappellano kept his son between the window and himself as he moved quickly to stand beside Kelli. He uttered admiringly, "You've got guts, lady."

"I suppose," she acknowledged calmly, even if it came with the territory, then stated bluntly, "So do you. Robbing a bank, for whatever reasons, took guts." *Just like pointing a gun at an officer of the law*, she thought, while keeping her cool.

Cappellano furrowed his brow. "I did what I had to do," he argued. "I needed the money."

"But at what price?" Kelli found herself challenging him. "A woman's dead—"

"That wasn't supposed to happen," Cappellano stated. "It was an accident."

"If true, then you can still get out of this without making things worse," she told him.

"I think it's too late for that," he said thickly, pointing the gun back and forth at her and his son. "I messed up and now I'm done."

Kelli peered at him and said, "Is this really what you want your son to remember you by—holding him hostage, and planning to do what? Have a shootout with police?" She didn't allow him to answer. "Why don't you let Gregory go… back to his mother. Whatever your differences with her, he shouldn't have to bear the burden of it. I'll take his place," she urged. "That way, you remove one major headache and your son will be safe, whatever else happens…"

Kelli could see that the bank robber and killer suspect was contemplating this, which would buy her more time to convince Cappellano to give himself up—before there was bloodshed. Including possibly her own.

"Okay," Cappellano finally said. He released the boy. "Sorry I screwed up with you, Gregory. Now get out of here." When his son appeared reluctant to leave, perhaps fearing this would be the last time they ever saw each other, Cappellano took a fatherly role in reiterating forcefully, "Go!"

Gregory headed toward the door and Kelli told him, "Raise your hands and let them know who you are and that you're heading outside—"

He complied and, after opening the door, stepped out slowly, closing the door behind him as his father had directed him to do.

This left Kelli alone with the desperate man, while knowing that her very life could depend on how well she could further diffuse the dire situation for them both.

NEEDLESS TO SAY, Sheldon felt relieved when Gregory Cappellano emerged from the house, safe and sound. He watched as the boy ran into his mother's arms, before both were whisked out of sight to safety by authorities.

But what was going on inside the Craftsman bungalow with Kelli still at great risk with the murder-robbery suspect? She had obviously succeeded in getting Cappellano to release his son. At what cost, though, to her own health and well-being?

This unnerving thought weighed heavily on Sheldon's mind. Though they didn't really know each other—not yet, anyway—he still didn't want to see a fellow officer of the law's life cut short, even in the line of duty, with Christmas just around the corner. He needed to do something to give Cappellano another person his own size to have to contend with. Then, just maybe, both he and Kelli could come out of this on their own two feet.

Sheldon made his way over to where Gregory and Martha Cappellano had been placed into the back of a squad car, a safe distance from the house and any foolish thoughts by Arnold Cappellano of trying to shoot them both dead from a window of the bungalow.

Crouching by the passenger window, Sheldon identified himself to Cappellano's son and then asked him, "Is Officer Burkett okay inside the house?"

"Yeah," Gregory muttered. "She's fine." He frowned. "I'm worried, though, for my dad. Can you end this without killing him…?"

Sheldon only wished he could give the boy that reassurance. But that wasn't possible, if he were being straight with him. The fact that Gregory Cappellano was more concerned about his father coming out of this alive, in spite of the serious crimes he was suspected of committing—including his own abduction—left an impression on Sheldon. This reminded him of the love for and loyalty he felt toward his own father, whom he'd had his own issues with over the years, but still looked up to at the end of the day.

"We'll make every effort to keep this from escalating any further," Sheldon promised the boy. "Now, I need you to tell me what's going on inside the house and exactly where Officer Burkett is being held by your father."

Once Sheldon was equipped with all the information he could gain from Gregory, this was passed along to Nolan Valentine, whose patience had already run pretty thin, and other law enforcement on the scene.

With no communication from inside the bungalow, the decision was made to go in and get Kelli out—and take Arnold Cappellano into custody. Assuming he was willing to give himself up, with no chance for escape.

But they were taking no chances. This standoff had to end, one way or the other.

To Sheldon, the notion of it all coming to a head in any way other than Kelli being rescued from the clutches of the armed and dangerous suspect was something he didn't even want to consider. As if there was any way of avoiding the unnerving thought of such a disastrous outcome.

Chapter Three

With some effort and just enough empathy, when Kelli learned that Arnold Cappellano was a veteran of the armed forces like her late husband and shared her own grief, she was able to talk Cappellano into laying down his firearm and giving himself up—along with the loot he stole. With her assurances that he wouldn't be taken out by law enforcement during his surrender.

Kelli intended to honor that as she took out her cell phone and called Lieutenant Valentine, informing him that she had defused the situation and that the threat was over. Her message was loud and clear: take the suspect into custody without incident.

When she opened the front door, Kelli shouted, "He's unarmed. We're coming out…"

She took the lead, with Arnold Cappellano following close by, his arms raised in surrender. The moment it was clear that the suspect no longer posed a danger, and Kelli had separated herself from him, Cappellano was quickly surrounded by the authorities, cuffed and taken into custody peacefully. Others stormed the house, where the stolen $40,000 was waiting in a green duffel bag to be recouped.

She was happy to see that all was well that ended well, not counting the fact that one woman had lost her life. And another had feared for the welfare of her son, till he was able to walk out of the bungalow uninjured.

"Nice job, Officer Burkett," Kelli heard the deep voice say. She turned and gazed into the blue eyes of Special Agent Sheldon Montgomery.

"Thanks," she said, downplaying it. "I only did what was expected." Never mind that it probably wasn't too smart to go inside the house unarmed and against the rules. But her instincts paid off. No one got hurt. Including herself.

"You had us worried for a while there," Sheldon said. "We were about the blink of an eye away from storming the bungalow had you not come out when you did."

She smiled softly. "In that case, good thing I was quick to the whip," she quipped, while imagining his worrying about her translating to more of a personal than professional level.

"Yeah, that's true." He grinned handsomely, then reached into the pocket of his jacket and removed a Smith & Wesson M&P 9mm pistol. "I believe this belongs to you."

Kelli colored at the thought that he had ended up with her duty pistol. She took the firearm from his hand. Their fingers touched and she felt an instant spark. Had he experienced that too?

"Thanks for holding on to it," she told him, and placed the handgun back inside her holster, where it belonged.

"Anytime," he told her, sounding as though he meant it.

"I'll try to remember that, Special Agent Montgomery."

"Call me Sheldon," he insisted.

"Only if you call me Kelli," she countered.

He smiled genuinely. "Deal."

"Well, I need to call this in," Kelli told him reluctantly, referring to the results of her latest hostage negotiation operation. "Catch you later, Sheldon," she told him in a routine phrase.

He met her eyes with a twinkle and said earnestly, "Hope so."

AFTER HER SHIFT ENDED, Kelli headed home. The adrenaline rush that typically came with dealing with potentially life and death situations—not once, but twice in the space of a few hours—had settled down, and now she only wanted to put it behind her as another interesting day in the life of a small-town police officer. Well, maybe she did want to hold on to meeting Sheldon Montgomery in the course of her hostage negotiator duties. She wondered if he was married. At the very least, she assumed he likely had a significant other in his life. If he'd wanted to be in a relationship. Even if he did seem to be flirting with her in a way. Or was this more wishful thinking on her part, as someone who had been on her own too long now and liked the thought of a nice-looking man being attracted to her.

Kelli pulled into the driveway of her ranch-style home with four bedrooms and three baths on Mohawk Way, on the west side of Leyton Falls. It sat on ten acres of rolling hills, with magnificent views, grazing meadows, cottonwood and ponderosa pine trees, and a pond that had fish, cattails and turtles. She had purchased the completely fenced property with her late husband, which included a barn with five stalls that housed two Colorado Rangers, an American Quarter Horse and two Appaloosas. Both loved riding horses and just spending time on the land with its rich environment.

Choking back the thought, Kelli eyed her personal vehicle in the driveway, a white Volvo V60 Cross Country wagon, and a blue Subaru Outback SUV that belonged to her sister, Samantha. After breaking up with her last boyfriend, with whom she'd shared a condominium, she'd accepted Kelli's offer to move in with her and help with the horses. The breakup had occurred three months ago, and the arrangement with her sister was temporary. Kelli knew that there was plenty of room in the house for the two of them. It would also allow her to keep an eye out on Samantha, who was seven years younger, at twenty-five, and hadn't always made the right choices in her life—including being attracted to bad boys, for whatever reason.

Kelli got out of the car and went inside the house, taking it in. Custom-built and renovated, it had dark hickory engineered hardwood flooring, with vaulted ceilings. The rustic cowhide and reclaimed barnwood furnishings sat in a great room that had a wood-burning stone fireplace and picture windows with vertical blinds. There was a formal dining room with a crystal chandelier, clerestory windows with custom drapes, and pastoral style furniture. A large eat-in kitchen had quartz countertops, stainless-steel appliances and a double oven, with a cottage-style breakfast bar and natural wood stools.

The only thing missing from the picture was Christmas decorations. Since Pierre's death, Kelli had found herself unable to carry on traditions she'd had since childhood, and she wasn't quite sure why. Yes, Pierre had died in the month of December, but he'd loved the holiday season as much as her and would certainly have wanted her to continue to enjoy the spirit of the season. She hoped to break out of the doldrums at some point. If not this year, there was always the next one. Or the year after that.

Walking past the formal dining room, Kelli went into the kitchen, where she saw that Samantha had taken out leftovers from yesterday's dinner—beef and cheddar casserole—to eat with sourdough bread, and red wine to wash it all down.

That's great and I'm starving, but where's my sister? Kelli asked herself, grabbing a slice of bread and biting into it.

"Hey, save some for the meal," she heard a familiar voice quip.

Kelli turned and watched as Samantha entered the kitchen. "I'll try," she said with a chuckle, and met Samantha's big blue-green eyes on a diamond-shaped face. She had long sandy blond hair in a flippy layered style. An inch shorter than her sister, she was just as slender as Kelli in a beige crewneck sweater, jeans and loafers. Samantha worked as a teller at the biggest bank in town, Leyton Falls Bank. The thought mildly concerned Kelli, given the recent spate of bank robberies in town. "How was your day?" she asked.

"Same old, same old," Samantha responded, and then promptly broke her own rule by grabbing a slice of the bread to nibble on. "Yours?"

"Interesting, to say the least," Kelli told her musingly.

Her sister arched a thin brow. "Oh...?"

"Hold that thought," Kelli told her, "while I get out of these work clothes."

"Okay," she agreed. "I'll set the table, and we can eat when you come back."

Kelli smiled. "Sounds like a plan."

AFTER CHANGING INTO a pair of comfortable jeans, a button-up pink cotton shirt and wedge slip-ons, Kelli went into the en suite bathroom of her bedroom, where she washed her face and let out her hair from the bun and put in a high ponytail.

Moments later, she was seated with Samantha on ladder-backed, cushioned-side chairs at the plank farmhouse dining table, having dinner.

Kelli summarized her day, which included talking a despondent woman off the ledge of a building's rooftop and rescuing a boy being held by his father, suspected of a bank robbery that resulted in the death of a customer. "I also got the father to surrender without incident," she added thankfully.

"Wow! Eventful day for you," Samantha remarked, digging a fork into her slice of casserole. "Mine was strictly routine—boring, by comparison."

"Sometimes that's a good thing, comparatively speaking," Kelli had to tell her, while grabbing a slice of bread from the loaf.

"Yeah, I suppose," her sister concurred. "I'm just glad you weren't hurt in the course of your duties."

"Me too." Kelli tore off a piece of bread and popped it in her mouth, while taking that much in stride as someone who chose to be in law enforcement. But Samantha didn't have the same benefit in her line of work, potentially exposed to danger. "I'm more concerned about you," she told her.

Samantha gazed at her. "Really?"

"There's been a rash of bank robberies lately in the county, in case you didn't realize," she told her, only half sarcastically.

Samantha grinned. "I think a certain police officer has kept me in the loop there," she kidded.

"This is serious, Sam," Kelli argued, using her nickname while regarding Samantha over a wineglass. "I hope you're keeping an eye out for anyone who seems out of place in or outside your bank."

"Of course." Samantha almost seemed offended by the question. "I'm perfectly safe at the bank. It has a security guard and state-of-the-art security system should anyone dare try to rob it. Trust me, they wouldn't get very far."

"Okay." Kelli relaxed on that thought, realizing that she was coming across as a mother hen, though they were only seven years apart. But the thought of losing her only sibling to a bank robber—or any criminal, for that matter—left Kelli slightly on edge.

Samantha must have sensed her sister was ill at ease—she leaned forward and said equably, "Don't worry about me so much. I can take care of myself if I need to."

"I know you can." Kelli gave her the benefit of the doubt, even if her sister had not always shown that to be the case— moving from one job to the next, in spite of having a bachelor's degree in marketing from Colorado State University, in Fort Collins. Not to mention Samantha's unstable history in relationships. But there was only so much Kelli believed she could do in trying to steer her sister in the right direction, without appearing to be overbearing.

Samantha was holding her wineglass when she stated, "You know, you really need to get a life, Kelli. For real."

Kelli cocked a brow. "I have a life," she countered. "A pretty good one at that."

"You know what I mean," Samantha shot back. "Being a good cop and all is great. But I seriously think it's time you started dating again."

"Oh, really?" The thought had actually crossed Kelli's mind after meeting the intriguing FBI special agent today. Even if she had no idea if he was already involved with someone. Still, she fixed her sister's face with a firm gaze. "How's that working out for you?"

"Not so good," Samantha admitted, frowning. "But this isn't about me. Pierre's been gone now for three years. You're entitled to move on…find someone else, if you'll allow yourself to."

Kelli immediately regretted being defensive and mean-spirited in her sarcasm, when Samantha was only trying to be a helpful little sister where it concerned romance beyond Pierre. "Sorry I snapped at you," she told her. "You're right, maybe it is time to see who else might be out there for me." Sheldon Montgomery's handsome face filled her head.

"Really?" Samantha's wide-eyed look expressed her shock.

"Let's just say I'm keeping an open mind." Kelli sipped the wine musingly.

"Cool. And while you're in the *open mind* environment, maybe we should put up a tree and other decorations for Christmas this year, while there's still time. It would be great to celebrate the holidays that way again, as a family—"

"We'll see," Kelli said, knowing this would be a way to

honor Pierre's memory, as well as perhaps start creating some new ones with someone else. "Do you want to watch a movie or something on TV?" she asked, to change the subject for now.

"Can't," Samantha answered tersely, dabbing a napkin to her lips. "I've made other plans."

Kelli was dying to ask what these plans were—suspecting that her sister had met someone new—but refrained from doing so. She figured that Samantha would be more forthcoming when she was ready.

"No problem," Kelli told her in a sincere tone. "Some other time."

"You're sure?" Samantha asked guiltily.

"Positive." Kelli showed her teeth, so as to reassure her that it was perfectly okay if she had things to do rather than hang out with her widowed big sister. "Have fun."

Only after Samantha had left and Kelli had put the dirty dishes in the dishwasher, did she take a moment to ponder where she'd been in life—and what could lie ahead in the future if she played her cards right.

SHELDON TOOK INTERSTATE 25 to Denver, after hanging around Leyton Falls for a bit in the follow-up on the arrest of Arnold Cappellano for the murder of Doris Flynn and robbery of the Leyton Falls Credit Union. Giving credit where it was due to Kelli Burkett for rescuing Cappellano's son and getting the suspect to give himself up peacefully, Sheldon wondered what other tricks the hostage negotiator had up her sleeve. He'd love to find out someday. Assuming she was open to the prospect of them getting to know one another better off duty.

He dropped by the Bureau's field office on East Thirty-sixth Avenue for a few minutes of briefing on the latest cases before heading home.

A short time later, Sheldon drove his Ford Explorer SUV into the parking garage of the condominium building on Sixteenth Street in Downtown Denver. He'd lived in the penthouse condo in a converted warehouse for the last two years. He pulled into the parking space right next to his privately owned vehicle, a two-row red Jeep Grand Cherokee.

After taking the elevator up to the top floor, Sheldon eyed the eucalyptus wreath he'd placed on the front door before unlocking it and going inside. He stepped onto the Brazilian cherry hardwood flooring and gave a cursory glance at the lower of two levels. With a modern open floor design, it had exposed solid brick walls. The spacious living room area had large windows with plantation shutters and a gas log fireplace; with the dining room elevated, and both fitted with contemporary urban furniture. He glanced at the gourmet kitchen that had granite countertops, smart home appliances and a faux marble island with V-backed farmhouse chairs for seating.

Up on the second level were three good-sized bedrooms—one that he had converted into a home office, another a gym—and two bathrooms, one an en suite to the primary bedroom. A rooftop terrace offered great views of the Mile High City, as Denver was nicknamed.

Sheldon turned his eyes to the artificial tabletop Christmas tree with ornaments and string lights that sat atop a walnut console table beneath the window. He had considered getting a real tree with all the trimmings this year, but time constraints had prevented him from doing so. Not to mention, with no one in his life at the moment to share the holiday tradition, it didn't seem worth the effort.

He removed and put away his duty pistol, took off the FBI jacket and body armor and stepped into the kitchen, where Sheldon took out a frozen pepperoni and cheese pizza from the French door refrigerator and tossed it into the slide-in range oven.

A few minutes later, he was seated at the island, eating while doing some work on his laptop. With any luck, he would nab the Hemton County Bandit Quartet before the year was through. Prior to Christmas Day would be even better.

After dinner, Sheldon settled onto a gray platform sofa in the living room and cut on his 75-inch HD TV and started watching the *Thursday Night Football* game that featured the Denver Broncos. He loved football, but would much rather have been cozying up to a romantic partner, if he'd had someone in his life. Kelli popped into his head and he couldn't help but allow her to stay there as a fantasy, if not more.

TAMMY YOSHIMURA SIPPED her daiquiri as she sat at the bar inside the Ninth Street Pub. It was precisely the place she had been a couple of weeks ago when the deep-voiced, tall and good-looking thirtysomething white male with sharp brown-gray eyes and brunette hair in a men's updo, had approached her.

He'd tried to work his obviously well-practiced charms on her, to no avail, and scooted away snubbed, while turning his attention to another woman.

She believed it was the same man who had robbed Bradley Bank last week, where Tammy worked, while she hid in the ladies' room. But not before she'd listened to him barking orders to her colleagues and customers, on behalf of the bank robber's quartet of robbers.

Though they were all wearing ski masks, and had otherwise gone to great lengths in trying to hide their identities, the leader of the pack's distinctive voice still resonated with her. But what if she was wrong? She hesitated to share her beliefs with the FBI, heading the investigation into this and several other recent bank robberies in Hemton County. The last thing she wanted was to mistakenly identify someone based on voice alone, only to have him falsely targeted by the authorities as her younger brother Bobby had been last year when accused of a robbery he didn't commit—before the police left him alone and turned their attention elsewhere.

But she was also loyal to her employer and the customers they depended on—both deserving to feel safe and secure in the business environment. So did she.

If the deep-voiced robber and the man she jilted were one and the same, Tammy wanted to see justice served and would do the right thing in that regard.

She took another sip of the cocktail, then ran fingers through her hair nervously, while hoping that the brown-gray-eyed man with the updo would show up and try to hit on her again. Then she would know, once and for all, by the voice and body language—and act accordingly.

Until then, Tammy sensed that she would continue to be ill at ease while the Hemton County Bandit Quartet remained on the loose—and just as capable of hitting her bank for a second time.

Chapter Four

On Monday, Sheldon had already made his way back to Hemton County, when receiving word that the blue GMC Sierra 1500 pickup truck belonging to a bank robber suspect had been spotted outside an apartment complex on Klagger Drive in Leyton Falls. Ex-con Marvin Mantegna, fifty-two years old, had been released last month from the United States Penitentiary, Florence High, just south of Florence, Colorado, in Fremont County, after spending nearly two decades behind bars. Mantegna had been part of a trio of bank robbers known as the Rocky Mountain Bank Burglars—having robbed multiple financial institutions in the Denver area at gunpoint. In spite of being the one calling the shots, he was the only member of the group currently out of prison, with the others having faced additional charges for incarceration.

Now Sheldon had to wonder if Mantegna was up to his old tricks again. Could he be the ringleader of the Hemton County Bandit Quartet?

Though they had no definitive proof that was the case, it was incumbent upon the Rocky Mountain Money Grab Task Force that each and every possible lead be checked out in the pursuit of bank robbers and closing the books on outstanding cases. As it was, with the high rate of recidivism among federal robbery offenders, it stood to reason that ex-cons such as Mantegna were more than capable of reoffending if opportunity knocked and desperation for cash kicked in.

Let's just see what you've been up to, Mantegna, Sheldon told himself, as he drove his Ford Explorer SUV onto Klagger Drive and approached the Wenfield Creek apartment complex. He pulled up to another Ford Explorer in the parking lot. Inside was fellow FBI Special Agent Joseph Eala.

They both exited their vehicles at the same time. Eala, a twenty-year veteran of the Bureau, was a muscular man in his midforties with a dark line-up buzz cut. "Montgomery," he greeted him tonelessly.

"Hey." Sheldon nodded. "So, any sightings of the suspect?"

Eala wrinkled his nose and gazed at Marvin Mantegna's pickup, parked haphazardly in the lot, nearly hitting a gold-colored Dodge Hornet GT next to it. "Haven't laid eyes on him yet," Eala said, "but Mantegna's likely here somewhere, though his current address is listed as a duplex in Denver."

Sheldon walked up to the pickup and looked in the window. He spotted what could be tricks of the bank robbery trade: a pair of black leather gloves, a dark ski mask, binoculars and a black backpack. There also appeared to be illicit drugs inside the pickup. "Hmm…" he said interestedly. "Where are you, Mantegna?"

They headed to the apartment complex in search of the suspect, whom Sheldon surmised could be armed and still dangerous.

KELLI WAS DOING her normal rounds when dispatch reported that a man was seen loitering around the Wenfield Creek apartment complex on Klagger Drive that was in the vicinity. She took the assignment to check it out, welcoming her sometimes mundane duties as a cop to the often more stressful responsibilities as a hostage negotiator. But she understood that it was the latter that ultimately proved more satisfying and was key to her moving up the ranks in the police department. She even had a fantasy of one day joining the Colorado Bureau of Investigation and putting her skills to use on a statewide level. Which would hopefully give her more flexibility on the home life and tending to her horses.

She spotted a fiftysomething, slender white male with slicked back brown hair in a short man bun, wearing baggy clothes and black tennis shoes. He was prowling around, looking both lost and keenly aware of his surroundings.

After stopping and shutting off her squad car, Kelli got out and saw that the man was suddenly teetering, as if high on alcohol, drugs, or both. She wondered if he was armed as she cautiously approached the suspect, while keeping a hand close to the Smith & Wesson pistol in her holster.

"Hey!" She got the man's attention. "What do you think you're doing…?"

Without answering, he simply glared and then took off, running away from her. She ran after him, recalling that she had run track in high school and still liked to jog.

"Stop!" Kelli ordered him, while continuing to pursue and closing the gap, as he tried to dart across the sidewalk and around thick bushes. As she was now within reach and about to use her momentum and adrenaline to tackle the man and quickly handcuff him—he ran smack-dab into, of all people, Sheldon. Along with another tall and fit man wearing an FBI jacket. Both seemed just as surprised to see her pursuing the loiterer, while keeping the suspect firmly in their grasps.

"Just the man we were looking for," Sheldon told him knowingly. "Are you Marvin Mantegna?"

"Yeah," he admitted, voice slurred, while struggling to break free of them.

"I'm FBI Special Agent Montgomery," Sheldon said, "and this is Special Agent Eala."

Mantegna regarded them warily. "What do you want with me?"

Sheldon began to frisk him. "Do you have any weapons on you?"

Mantegna hesitated, before saying, "No."

This was verified by Sheldon, and then Eala responded to the suspect's question bluntly, "We just need to ask you a few questions about a recent string of bank robberies around the county."

"Know anything about that?" Sheldon asked suspiciously, peering at the suspect.

"No!" Mantegna said flatly. "I gave up that life a long time ago."

"You sure about that?" Sheldon appeared dubious at best, and favored Kelli with a look of curiosity. "Mind if I ask why were you chasing him?"

"We received a call that someone was loitering at the apartment complex," she responded. "Seems like the suspect lived up to the accusation. I caught him prowling around. When I tried to get some answers out of him, he took off like a jackrabbit."

"In that case, you're free to take him into custody on suspicion of loitering—or whatever you choose to charge him with," Sheldon told her. "It might include possession of the narcotics that appear to be inside Mantegna's pickup truck." He took the liberty of removing his own hinged cuffs and putting them around Mantegna's wrists after placing his arms behind his back. "We'll follow you to the PD and complete our questions to the suspect there."

"Sounds good to me," Kelli said, offering Sheldon a smile, as Eala led the suspect to her patrol car.

"WE HAVE TO stop meeting like this," Sheldon said to Kelli, after Marvin Mantegna had been interrogated at the Leyton Falls Police Department on Eighth Street for any possible role in the Hemton County Bandit Quartet bank robberies. He was eliminated as a suspect, but was still arrested for loitering and drug possession, which also happened to be a parole violation and would likely result in reincarceration.

"I know, right?" She chuckled, and Sheldon found the ultrasweet sound of it to be music to his ears.

This might be a good time to ask her out—or something to that effect, he thought. "Would you like to have lunch with me?" Sheldon tossed out tentatively. "Today…tomorrow…or whenever you like…?"

Kelli's face brightened and she answered, "Yes, lunch is good. Today works. I just need to do a little paperwork and I'm all yours." She checked herself, blushing. "You know what I mean."

"Of course." He smiled back, while imagining her truly being all his for the taking. "You pick the place, and we'll eat there."

She nodded in agreement. "Works for me."

Half an hour later, Sheldon had driven them to the Leyton Falls Grill on Burnsten Road. They sat at a table by the window, where he ordered a grilled pastrami sandwich and lemon chicken soup, while Kelli chose a turkey club sandwich and ranch fries. Both ordered huckleberry coffee, to go with water.

After a couple of minutes of small talk, Sheldon looked at Kelli and said straightforwardly, "In the interest of transparency—or maybe more of an excuse to learn your marital status—I asked Nolan Valentine about you…"

She looked surprised—or was it perturbed, as if an invasion of privacy?—over her mug of coffee. "Did you now?"

Sheldon hoped this didn't get things off to the wrong start, but wanted to come clean, knowing his heart was in the right place in the inquiry. "He told me that you lost your husband in a Black Hawk helicopter accident while he was serving with the US military."

Kelli's expression became sullen. "Yes," she said sadly. "It was due to mechanical failure while on an army assignment in North Africa."

"I'm sorry about that," Sheldon said sincerely. "It must have been tough on you."

"It was." She rubbed her nose. "I always knew that anything was possible in Pierre's line of work. But when the worst-case scenario actually happened, it took me a while to come to terms with it."

"That's understandable." Sheldon could only imagine her grief in having to deal with something of that magnitude. How might he have handled it had he lost a wife so soon in life? At the same time, he had known his fair share of tragedies both in his own profession and on a personal level.

At least Kelli's indicating that she's moved past that dark stretch of her life, Sheldon told himself, tasting the coffee.

"What about you?" She broke the reverie. "Are you married, have a girlfriend, or whatever? Never mind that we're here for lunch—as fellow members of law enforcement…"

Sheldon realized that the last part was for Kelli to protect herself, in the event that the meal invitation was more of a professional courtesy than a genuine interest in her. That couldn't be further from the truth. He leaned forward and told her assuredly, "I'm not married—not anymore. Been divorced for five years now. I met Lauralee in college, and we were married for five years." He paused, thoughtful. "There hasn't been anyone serious in my life since then."

Kelli met his eyes contritely. "Sorry things didn't work out between you and your ex-wife."

"Me too," he had to admit. "I'm sorrier that I wasn't able to read the tea leaves in advance, to know we simply weren't right for each other. But that's the way life goes. Live and learn."

"That is how it's supposed to be for all of us and our life experiences," Kelli stated perceptively.

Sheldon was glad to know they were on the same page there. He wondered if they were on another level when he said to her, "For the record, the lunch invite was more than just from one member of law enforcement to another."

"Good to know." Kelli grinned. "I was hoping you felt that way—I do too."

Sheldon grinned as well, believing they had turned the corner in getting to know one another as the food was served.

So, he's not married after all—albeit divorced, Kelli thought, as she bit into her turkey club sandwich. Seemed as if they had both experienced heartbreak where it concerned relationships that ended prematurely. She felt there was hope yet for the two of them. Perhaps with each other.

Kelli eyed Sheldon as he took a bite out of his grilled pastrami sandwich. "How did you end up working for the FBI?" she asked, both out of curiosity and wanting to get to know him better. She had to admit that being a Bureau special agent seemed to suit him.

Sheldon swallowed food and responded, "I suppose you could say it's in the blood. My dad was a special agent—till he called it quits a few years back. Not sure if I was trying to win his approval or do him one better, but this was the path I chose after going to college and picking up my criminal justice degree."

"Maybe a little of both led you to where you are," Kelli reasoned, and grabbed a ranch fry.

"Maybe." Sheldon spooned some lemon chicken soup. "And what drew you into a career in law enforcement?"

"After college and two degrees, one in communication and

another in criminal justice, I wanted to do something useful with my life," she explained. "Police work and helping to ensure public safety and deal with crisis situations seemed a good way to make use of my communication skills."

He grinned at her. "I'd say you made the right choice."

She blushed. "Thanks."

"What do you enjoy doing outside of work?"

"That's an easy one," she told him, sipping coffee. "Riding horses would have to top the list."

"Really?"

"Yep. I live on a ranch, currently with my sister—along with five great horses." Kelli gazed at him. "Do you ride?"

Sheldon grinned sideways. "As a matter of fact, I do." He drank water. "I grew up in and around horses in South Dakota. After retiring from the Bureau, my father and stepmother bought a horse ranch in Rapid City, where he raises Arabians, Morgans, and quarter horses. I try to pay him a visit and get in some riding, if only as an excuse to get out of the big city life in Denver, where the field office is located and I have a condo, whenever I have the time—and patience…"

"Nice." She smiled, impressed with his familiarity with horses, while sensing some friction there with his father, but nothing out of the ordinary. "Maybe we can go riding sometime?"

"I'd love to ride one of your horses with you, anytime," Sheldon agreed enthusiastically.

"Cool." Kelli found herself looking very much forward to that. It would be the first time she'd ridden with anyone other than Samantha since Pierre's death.

Sheldon leaned forward. "So, apart from riding horses, any other pastimes?"

She lifted another fry. "I like to jog, hike, go to art museums, watch movies and read books, mostly fiction. And you?" She tried to predict what he might say.

"I love to work out, mostly in a home gym, go rafting and cycling… What else? I've done some international traveling for the Bureau—been to parts of Africa, Europe, Asia and Australia—and a bit of sightseeing, when the opportunity has presented itself."

"Sounds good." Kelli liked his activities and was impressed with the locations for his travels, regardless of the circumstances. "I've been abroad too—actually lived there for a while," she told him. "We spent time in Japan, Turkey and Italy when my late husband was on active duty the first time around. I've also visited England and Scotland. The latter is where my maternal grandparents came from, and I still have some distant relatives there."

"Well traveled," Sheldon said with a rapt smile. "As for bloodline, my ancestors are from all over the place—in the States and overseas."

"I see." She sipped the coffee and looked at him curiously. "Is your mother still in the picture?"

Sheldon shook his head. "She died when I was eight years old. It was a hard pill to swallow, but I got through it over time." He met Kelli's eyes. "What about your parents?"

"They're dead too," she answered, feeling sentimental at the thought. "I was older than you were when they passed away in different years, but it was no less difficult to come to terms with."

"I'm sure it was." He put the coffee mug to his mouth. "And you only have the one sibling?"

"Yes. Samantha works as a teller at Leyton Falls Bank," Kelli noted, while trying not to think about the flurry of bank robberies to hit the area recently or Sheldon's investigation into them. "Honestly, we've had our differences over the years, but we've pretty much agreed to disagree, when necessary, while maintaining a strong relationship."

Sheldon smiled. "That's the way it should be between sisters."

"Do you have any siblings?"

"Not that I know of," he quipped, sitting back. "Seriously, I would have loved to have had brothers or sisters, but it didn't work out that way." He paused. "Maybe I can make up for that by having children of my own someday, who can count on each other throughout their lives when all is said and done."

Kelli beamed. "That sounds nice." It also told her that he wanted to have a family of his own. That was something she could very much relate to. "I'd like to have some children too, if I ever marry again," she told him. "We were never able to start a family before Pierre died."

"That's too bad." Sheldon waited a beat. "Maybe you'll get another crack at it."

"Hope so." Kelli left it at that, even as her head was already spinning at the thought of him being the father of those future children, presumptuous as that seemed for someone she was still getting acquainted with. But that didn't stop her from thinking that Sheldon was a good catch. Perhaps a very good one.

Chapter Five

After driving Kelli back to the police department, Sheldon almost hated to depart from her. He had enjoyed spending time with her. And had no problem admitting this to himself. He liked Kelli Burkett and could tell that she liked him too. Now all that was left was to see where they went from there. And just how far.

Before she could get out of his car, Sheldon did the polite thing by asking Kelli first if he could kiss her. "It would be a nice way to thank you for having lunch with me," he added adorably.

Kelli's eyes lit up. "Yes, feel free to thank me with a kiss," she agreed eagerly.

"Will do." He laughed. Then leaned over, placed his mouth upon hers and found her lips to be incredibly soft. Or perfect for kissing.

Though he could have kissed Kelli for the rest of the day, were she amenable to this, Sheldon didn't want to overdo it. He decided it was best to save some of the smooching—and then some, hopefully—for later.

Once he'd pulled back and they both allowed the kiss to sink in, Kelli grinned, blushed, and said, "Ticklish from your designer stubble—nice." She left the vehicle. "See you later."

With a smile on his face, Sheldon drove off, heading back

to Denver. Suddenly, he had more on his mind than working some bank robbery cases and other investigations. Now he had to consider that he just might be on the verge of getting into a relationship again. And one that held more promise than other times he'd made a half-hearted effort to go down this road since his divorce.

Sheldon backtracked from that pleasant thought to the recent bank heists, thinking about the fact that Kelli's sister worked at the biggest bank in Leyton Falls. It had yet to be hit by the Hemton County Bandit Quartet, or other bank robbers. He hoped that continued to be the case. The last thing he wanted was for Samantha to become an inadvertent target of overzealous bank robbers, resulting in another major tragedy for Kelli.

Especially when they were just getting started in a possible romance with lots of upside. Both deserved to see it through without the type of events that could put it on hold. If not derail it altogether.

Sheldon took out his cell phone, told it to call his father, and then put it on speakerphone, while slipping it into the car phone holder.

Momentarily, Foster Montgomery answered with a boisterous, "Hello." He was in his midsixties and, though he was still as tough as nails—including trying at times to micromanage Sheldon's professional and personal life, much to his chagrin—his father had mellowed a bit since retiring from the Bureau and devoting time to his horse ranch.

"Hey, Dad," Sheldon said, his eyes on the road.

"You're not ready to step away from the FBI and the potential your career has given you for advancement, are you?"

Where did that come from? Sheldon asked himself, unsure if he should laugh or be pissed at the unwarranted concern. Or was it a backhanded warning? "What gave you that idea?" he asked.

Foster replied tersely, "So I take it that's a no?"

"Yeah, it is. I'm happy right where I am," Sheldon said. "I'm not going anywhere at the moment."

"Good." His father took a breath. "Heard about some other agents who were going into early retirement due to stress, money issues, unrealistic expectations, distractions, you name it."

"Each agent has to do what's best for him or her." Sheldon felt the need to defend his colleagues, respecting their choices, one way or the other. "Not everyone wants to make a long career of it, like you—or me, for that matter," he said with emphasis.

Foster, who had put in more than thirty years with the Bureau, made a grunting sound to indicate his disapproval on that score. Then he pivoted and said in a fatherly tone, "So, what's happening with you?"

Sheldon thought about Kelli, the kiss and a desire to move things to another level with her. But he knew that his father was more interested right now in the status of his latest investigation.

"Still working the Hemton County Bandit Quartet case," Sheldon answered, aware that his father was following this, "along with other bank robberies the Rocky Mountain Money Grab Task Force is looking into."

"Well, keep at it," Foster urged. "For each bank heist, they tend to get a little sloppier, which ultimately leads to the unsubs' downfall."

Once an agent, always an agent, Sheldon told himself, amused, as he switched lanes. "Agreed," he said. "We won't slow down till we catch them."

"Okay."

"How's Julia?" Sheldon asked about his stepmother. Though he'd already been an adult and in college when his father had decided to tie the knot again, Sheldon got along well with her and believed it was a good decision. He only hoped that the next time he got married—if there was a second marriage in the cards—it would be the last time, and they would grow old together.

"She's fine," Foster told him. "I'm doing my best to keep up with her, but Julia challenges me every day to hold up my end of the bargain."

"I'm sure you challenge each other in that regard, Dad," Sheldon said.

"You're probably right about that."

"How are the horses?"

"Some more ornery than others—but overall, they make it all worthwhile."

"I'm sure they do." Sheldon thought about Kelli and her horses. "I look forward to saddling up my favorite Arabian and riding her," he told his father.

"Come whenever you like," Foster said. "She's always ready and willing."

"Will do."

When he disconnected, Sheldon decided he should try to visit his dad and stepmom more often. Maybe bring Kelli along, if things worked out between them, sure she would feel right at home on his father's ranch.

After reaching Denver, Sheldon headed to the field office for some work, before calling it a day.

ON A COLD Tuesday morning and off day for them both, Kelli and Samantha, dressed warmly in riding clothes, cowgirl felt wide brim hats and synthetic leather boots, rode their horses on the grass of the property. Atop a Colorado Ranger named Cora—combining the two names of the horse breed—Kelli gazed at her sister, who was trotting on an Appaloosa named Fletcher and who was obviously deep in thought as the colloquial chat between them suddenly went silent.

Finally, Samantha looked at her and said, "So… I've started seeing someone."

"That didn't take long." Kelli couldn't help but to say it sarcastically, considering the recent breakup with her last boyfriend. Not that she was surprised, per se, in knowing that her sister was quick to fall for guys—if not necessarily in love with them.

Samantha said brashly, "It doesn't always have to take a long time. When you know, you know. His name is Chase."

"Chase, huh?" Kelli rolled her eyes. "And where did you meet this Chase?"

"We met online," she answered simply. "It was a few weeks ago. But we only got together in person for the first time on Saturday."

"I see." Kelli continued to ride, holding on to the reins. "Does Chase have a job?" she had to ask, not wanting to see her sister be taken advantage of financially. Not that her bank job left Samantha that well off.

"Actually, he's in college," Samantha told her. "Chase attends graduate school at UCLA. He's a business major."

"Hmm…sounds promising," Kelli had to admit. Maybe this time her sister had landed someone worthy of her.

"You think?" Samantha chuckled. "We'll see how things go."

Kelli looked at her. "So, he flew in from California *just* to meet you?"

"Yes and no. Chase's brother lives in Leyton Falls, which was how we connected in the first place. He's staying with him while Chase is on the holiday break from school. That gave us the opportunity to meet face-to-face…and take it from there."

"I see." Kelli glanced at the green grass before them. "Just don't rush into anything," she warned, as it related to thinking too far ahead, mindful that her sister was prone to doing just that.

"I don't intend to," Samantha insisted. "We're taking it slow, but still having fun getting to know each other in real time."

"All right." Kelli didn't want to go overboard in her concern and risk pushing her sister away. Still, she wanted to meet the latest man Samantha had started a relationship with.

As she weighed whether or not to bring that up, it was Samantha who beat her to the punch, as she said, "I was thinking about inviting Chase over for a late lunch today—and maybe go riding afterward. He says he's ridden horses before."

"Good idea," Kelli said, happy to see her take the lead on this one. "I'd love to meet him."

"So what else is new?" Samantha chuckled. "It's cool. I'm sure Chase won't have a problem meeting my big sister. Just as I hope to meet his brother one of these days while Chase is in town."

"Wonderful." Kelli grinned and imagined her sister following Chase back to Los Angeles for a whole new life there. Though she would definitely miss her, were that the case, Kelli would not stand in Samantha's way of living her own life—and finding true love—wherever that took her. Just as Kelli knew that her own romantic fortunes needed to develop a life of their own, apart from her past love and loss. As she was sure Samantha would encourage and, in fact, had been pushing her toward, even when Kelli had resisted.

Till now.

They rode a bit more, taking in the delightful landscape, before Kelli said tenderly, "On the issue of relationships, I've actually met someone myself."

"Seriously?" Samantha's eyes popped wide. "Who? When?"

"Calm down." Kelli laughed. "His name is Sheldon Montgomery. He's divorced and an FBI special agent. We only met recently, when I was called in as a hostage negotiator in a bank robber case he was working on."

"The one where you came to the rescue of the robber's son?" Samantha asked.

"That's the one," Kelli acknowledged. "Anyway, we went out for a bite to eat just yesterday, and it went well."

"I'm glad you're finally putting yourself out there, sis."

"Me too," she admitted. "It was only a first date, if you could call it that. We'll see if there's a second and third, and what happens beyond that."

"Why don't you start with the second date by inviting him for lunch today too," Samantha suggested. "That way, we get to meet the new men in our lives at the same time. Are you game?"

"Yeah," Kelli said without giving it much thought. "Sounds like a great idea. I'll ask Sheldon if he's available." Something told her that even if it was undoubtedly a work day for him—with probably multiple investigations underway—he would jump at the chance to meet Samantha and see where they lived. Kelli suspected that Sheldon would most likely even be up for some horseback riding, in showcasing his own skills on a horse.

"Cool." Samantha showed her teeth. She clutched Fletcher's reins and said challengingly, "Race you back!"

Kelli chuckled and squeezed her thighs so that Cora reacted in putting on the speed, as they took the lead, while Kelli pondered bringing Sheldon further into her world.

THAT AFTERNOON, SHELDON drove to Leyton Falls at Kelli's invitation to lunch and to go riding at her place. He definitely saw this as a positive development in their getting closer. It would be nice to meet her sister too, as an extension of Kelli herself, while reminding him of what he had been deprived of as an only child, with no one really to bounce things off of.

Beyond that, Sheldon saw this as an acceptable distraction from his work as an FBI agent, even with the Hemton County Bandit Quartet, in particular, and statewide bank robberies, in general, never far from his mind.

After arriving at Kelli's house, Sheldon got out of his Jeep, wearing black jeans, a plaid flannel shirt beneath a green quilted jacket, and brown chukka boots. He was greeted by Kelli and two others.

"Hey, you made it," Kelli told him spiritedly. She had her long hair down and was wearing formfitting bootcut jeans, along with a purple mock neck sweater, and Western leather black booties.

"Wouldn't have missed a great way to spend a mid-December afternoon," Sheldon remarked truthfully, taking her in and liking very much what he saw.

"This is my sister, Samantha," Kelli said, favoring her warmly with a smile. "Sam, this is Sheldon."

He eyed Samantha, who was attractive and bore some resemblance to her older sister and was around the same height—only with long blond hair, also hanging loose on her shoulders.

"Hi, there." She beamed at him with bold aquamarine eyes.

"Nice to meet you," Sheldon said, and meant it, as he shook her extended hand.

"You too." Samantha turned toward the twentysomething, tall and slender male who had dark hair in an Ivy League cut and a door knocker goatee, as he stood beside her affectionately.

Before she could introduce him, he took the liberty of doing so. "I'm Chase," he said evenly, sticking out a long arm to shake hands.

"Hi, Chase." Sheldon shook the hand of the college student

whom Kelli had already briefed him on as Samantha's new boyfriend, home from school for Christmas break.

"Why don't I show you around," Kelli said, taking Sheldon's hand, "then we can have lunch."

He grinned at her. "Sounds good to me." They separated from Samantha and Chase, and Sheldon was only too happy to have Kelli to himself, albeit only temporarily.

"So, what do you think of it?" Kelli asked him fifteen minutes later after they had toured the grounds and dropped by the barn to introduce him to the horses that easily warmed up to Sheldon as he petted them—before going inside the ranch house, where he checked out the spacious place.

"What's not to like?" Sheldon answered, and met her gaze. "It's great!" He was envious of her nice slice of heaven and wished he could give up his city life condo for a more rural down to earth setting and all the perks that came with it. In this case, starting with what Kelli herself brought to the table.

She beamed. "Glad you approve."

He grinned at her. "I'd be a fool to think otherwise. You've got everything one could ask for here."

"Maybe not quite everything." Kelli laughed. "I still need to put up a Christmas tree."

"Well, there is that." Sheldon laughed too, enjoying her quick wit. "If you need any help, just let me know."

"I'll do that," she promised. "I think we'd better eat now before the food gets cold—or Samantha and Chase decide to chow down without us."

"Wouldn't want either of those to occur," Sheldon said lightheartedly.

After a lunch that consisted of brown sugar glazed baked ham, walnut spinach salad, apple cider muffins and iced tea, the four went horseback riding.

Sheldon found himself right at home on the Colorado Ranger, as he rode alongside Kelli across the meadow. "I think I could get used to this," he told her candidly, while knowing riding horses was already in his blood.

She grinned. "The way Abigail has taken to you, Sheldon, I'd say the feeling is mutual," she quipped, saying the horse's name.

"That's good." He looked at his new Colorado Ranger friend, then gazed ahead at Samantha and Chase. They were riding side by side, when Chase leaned over and gave her a quick kiss. "Seems like things could be getting serious between those two," he half joked.

"Hmm…" Kelli sighed. "I'll reserve judgment on that for now. Let's see where things stand in six months or longer."

"Makes sense," Sheldon agreed, even if he knew that relationships could be totally unpredictable, regardless of the length. He only wished the best for them. Just as he hoped his own romantic fortunes were about to change for the better—with Kelli having something to do with that, if he played his cards right.

After they rode back to the barn, the horses were groomed and put in their stalls, before Sheldon and Kelli had a moment to themselves to exchange a kiss. It was slow and thoroughly enjoyable to Sheldon.

"Mmm…nice," Kelli murmured, in expressing the same sentiments, as she touched her swollen lips.

"There's a lot more where that came from," he told her, feeling his heart skip a beat and wondering what it would be like to make love to her. As if he needed to imagine how terrific that would be.

"Oh really?" Her smile was radiant. "Is that a promise?"

"Absolutely." He couldn't resist gleaming back at her, making it clear that he was definitely a man of his word in wanting to see more kisses pass between them and whatever evolved from that.

By the time he was back on the road to Denver, Sheldon found himself excited about where things seemed to be headed with Kelli. They had both been dealt a bad hand in previous relationships, albeit due to different circumstances. He didn't want to see their own burgeoning romance take a turn for the worse. Not if he could help it.

Chapter Six

On Wednesday morning, the Hemton County Bandit Quartet parked their white GMC Savana van on a side street, before exiting methodically, wearing ski masks, long overcoats, leather gloves and dark clothing. They were armed to the teeth with a high-powered AR-15 rifle, .410 lever action shotgun, a Taurus G2 9mm handgun and a Colt Cobra .38 Special revolver.

Without uttering a word to one another, the quartet of bank robbers marched like soldiers toward the bank on Brodgin Drive in Ekerly Heights, Colorado, a block and a half away.

They stepped inside and quickly got the measure of the bank. Three teller windows were open and all of them had female tellers doing transactions with customers—two of whom were middle-aged females and one, an elderly male. The female bank manager sat at her desk in an office. Another office was empty.

After the male ringleader motioned for the lone female member of the quartet to get the manager and for the other two bank robbers to spread out accordingly as they whipped out their firearms on cue, he then got the attention of everyone inside the bank by clearing his throat loudly. He then stated, with a decided edge to his voice, what had become his routine way of getting to the heart of the matter. "This is a bank robbery! Everyone stay right where you are—and I mean it! If any one of you behind the counter even thinks about alerting the cops or doing anything else really dumb—such as trying to be a hero for the day—it'll be a bloodbath in here. Trust me when I say that! We have nothing to lose. *You* do! Don't test any of us," he advised them strongly, and eyed the security camera recording the action, then looked back at the group. "If I have to repeat any of this, you won't like what comes next…"

No one inside seemed to be willing to put his threats to the test. Everyone obeyed the orders.

The female bank robber forced out the nervous manager at gunpoint and all the bank's occupants, aside from the tellers, were huddled together by the robbers, zip-tied and made to lie on the floor, face down—and then robbed of their possessions by the thieves.

The ringleader and another male member of the quartet rushed to the tellers' windows and made them hand over whatever cash was in their drawers—to which they complied—loading the money into two cotton canvas bags.

When another customer—a short, thirtysomething male—entered the bank and saw what was happening, he sought to pivot and leave. But he was met by the ringleader, who pointed his shotgun at the man's frightened face and said whimsically, "It's your lucky day! You've just landed in the middle of a bank robbery. Now hand over everything you've got in your pockets, then get down on the floor!"

When the customer balked, and boldly muttered an expletive, the leader of the bank bandits drove the barrel of his shotgun into the man's stomach and then slammed the butt against the side of the customer's head, knocking him out cold.

Another male robber then stole whatever the man had on his person.

Then the Hemton County Bandit Quartet quit while they were ahead and began to make their escape with the loot and other items.

As always, the ringleader was the only one to speak— apparently by design. He glowered at the occupants inside the bank just before leaving, and warned them, "Don't even think about trying to follow us, or otherwise being a hero, or you'll get his treatment—" he eyed the still-unconscious customer "—and probably much worse. Happy holidays!" He chuckled sardonically before leaving the establishment.

The quartet hurried to their getaway vehicle, removing their masks, then driving off, proud of themselves at having succeeded in another bank heist.

SHELDON ARRIVED AT the Ekerly Heights Bank just before noon, accompanied by Special Agent Joseph Eala, after receiving word that another bank heist had occurred. The unsubs, as described, and their modus operandi, made it all but a certainty that the Hemton County Bandit Quartet had struck once again.

Greeting Sheldon and Eala were members of the Ekerly Heights Police Department's Robbery Unit, Detectives Debra Bohrer and Len Hoyt.

"What do you have for us?" Sheldon asked.

Debra, who was in her thirties, tall and slender with brown hair in a flipped bob with Birkin bangs, pursed her lips as she responded. "The bank was robbed at gunpoint by four assailants wearing ski masks, overcoats, leather gloves and dark clothing. Taking money from tellers at all the open windows, the robbers made off with about twenty thousand dollars—and more, when considering that they also stole whatever valuables the customers had on them."

Sheldon blinked thoughtfully. "Anyone get hurt?"

"One male customer was knocked unconscious by what's

been described as the bank robber, also a man, who was apparently calling the shots," Hoyt answered. He was in his forties, around six feet tall, and of medium build with salt-and-pepper hair in a brush cut. "The customer is being treated at the hospital for a head contusion, but it appears as though he'll be okay."

"That's good to know," Eala said, furrowing his brow. "But it also illustrates that the propensity for violence is increasing—if we're talking about the same quartet of bank robbers that's been hitting the county all month."

"It's what I'm afraid of," Sheldon remarked, sensing that time wasn't necessarily on their side before the bank heists by the group turned deadly. Unless, of course, they could stop them and prevent this before such time ran out. "I'd like to talk with the bank manager," he said, wanting the person's take on what went down.

"Sure thing," Debra said. "She's in her office over there—" the detective pointed "—still trying to process this, after one of the robbers went in there, put a gun to her head and forced her to capitulate to the robbery, or else."

"Hmm." Sheldon bobbed his head musingly. "Okay."

"I'll see what the tellers have to say about this," Eala said. "Maybe someone picked up on something that we can work with."

Hoyt scratched his jaw. "We'll see what the bank's surveillance video shows on the robbery."

"Good." Sheldon eyed him. "Any security camera footage from surrounding businesses might also give us valuable info on the unsubs and what they may be using as a getaway vehicle."

"We're looking into that even as we speak," Debra assured him.

Sheldon nodded, figuring as much, and headed for the manager's office. In her forties and slender, with red hair in a cropped undercut, she was leaning against an L-shaped oak desk, deep in thought, when he walked in.

"FBI Special Agent Montgomery," Sheldon told her.

"Andie Zuniga." She stuck out a thin arm and they shook hands.

"I just need to ask you a few questions about what happened."

"I understand." Her voice shook. "Would you like to sit down?"

He accepted the offer, if only to make her feel more relaxed under trying circumstances. They both sat on armless guest chairs near the desk, after which Sheldon got to the nitty-gritty. "What can you tell me about the bank robbery this morning?"

"Where do I start?" She rolled her blue eyes. "Four masked and armed individuals came into the bank and one barked that it was a bank robbery, and threatened both the staff and customers alike should anyone try anything."

"And then what?" Sheldon asked.

"The robbers set about rounding up everyone, apart from our brave tellers, and used zip ties to bind our hands and took everything anyone had on them. Then they forced the tellers to empty their drawers and warned them not try anything that the thieves considered out of bounds."

Sheldon took this in and regarded the manager. "What can you tell me about the robber who came into your office and brought you out?"

Andie sucked in a deep breath and answered. "It was a woman. About my size, maybe a little taller. I couldn't make out much else with the ski mask and dark clothing she wore. I do know she held the handgun she was carrying to my temple and made it clear that she wouldn't hesitate to shoot me if I resisted her orders in any way."

Sheldon lowered his chin. "Glad you didn't challenge the

robber's authority in that situation." Beyond that, it told him that the female member of the quartet was potentially just as lethal as her male counterparts, had push come to shove. Which was disturbing.

"I wouldn't have," Andie insisted, smoothing an eyebrow. "Still, it was clear to me that she, like two of the other bank robbers, were following the lead of the one who was running the show."

Sheldon nodded knowingly. "I've gathered that much." The ringleader of the group evidently had the others under his thumb, which was consistent with other bank heists he believed the quartet had committed. Only question was just how far were they willing to go for him? Or he, for them, in presumably splitting up whatever loot they were able to confiscate from one bank robbery to the next?

"I hope you catch them soon," Andie remarked, clearly ill at ease. "The banking business seems to be very much under attack these days."

"I agree, and we will arrest the four robbers before they can get too comfortable." He sought to reassure her.

As for financial institutions being a risky enterprise right now, in reality, Sheldon knew that it had long been fraught with danger for both bank employees and their customers. Colorado in particular had the highest rate of bank robberies in the nation—constituting nearly one in ten of the total number of bank robberies in the United States per capita. Not that this did much for shattering the manager's weakened sense of security. The only thing that could do that would be for those responsible to be held fully accountable for their crimes.

It was something that Sheldon and his partners in law enforcement endeavored to accomplish, with the help of victims, witnesses and anyone else who could aide in the effort.

THAT AFTERNOON, IN a conference room at the Bureau's Denver field office, Sheldon provided the Rocky Mountain Money Grab Task Force with an update on the Hemton County Bandit Quartet investigation. Standing beside him at the podium was the special agent in charge, Karen Muñoz. The forty-seven-year-old Latina, with twenty-five years of service with the FBI—including earning her stripes as a criminal profiler—was tall and slender. She had blond hair in a pixie wedge cut and wore cat-eye glasses.

"Where are we, Special Agent Montgomery?" she asked formally, though he'd already briefed her on the basics. "Everyone in here is getting a bit antsy, while this quartet of bank robbers continue to run amok in the county with these daring heists."

"Everyone has a right to be anxious about making some arrests in the Hemton County bank robberies," Sheldon said understandingly. "Believe me, I want to close this case as much as anyone—as a subset of the Rocky Mountain Money Grab bank robberies occurring in the greater Denver metropolitan area." He held a stylus pen, using it to operate a large touch screen display, and brought up the exterior image of a commercial bank. "At approximately 10:00 a.m. today, the Ekerly Heights Bank on Brodgin Drive in Ekerly Heights was hit by four bank robbers. Every indication, including surveillance video, is that this was the work of the so-called Hemton County Bandit Quartet of serial bank robbers. The unsubs include three white or Hispanic males—one of whom appears to be the undisputed leader of the group—and one white female. All were wearing ski masks, overcoats, leather gloves and dark, somewhat baggy clothing, par for the course of their bank heists. This marks the seventh such bank or credit union robbery in Hemton County this month. Like the others, the robbers were well armed, with a high-powered

AR-15 rifle, .410 lever action shotgun, Colt Cobra .38 Special revolver and a Taurus G2 9mm handgun. We believe they made their escapes driving a white van or SUV."

Sheldon took a breath and said levelly, "Let's take a look at the financial establishments hit by the quartet to date…" He switched to a different image on the screen. "The first bank robbery occurred on Monday, December 1 at the Kiki Bank on Klinton Street in Leyton Falls. The armed group made off with just under $30,000." Sheldon put up another bank. "Two days later, on Wednesday, December 3, they were at it again—this time, robbing the Collens Credit Union on State Lane in Toppers Bay, where they escaped with $15,000 in cash."

The next bank appeared on the display, and he continued. "Three days after that, on Saturday, December 6, the East Side Bank on Twenty-third Street in Holbee Hills was hit by the group to the tune of nearly $50,000." Sheldon moved it along with the stylus. "Bank number four, Hemton County Savings on Ricard Avenue in Leyton Falls, was robbed of about ten grand on Tuesday, December 9," he said. "Two days later, Thursday, December 11, the foursome targeted the Jaspreine Bank on Preppin Road in Jaspreine, netting some $18,000 or so for their trouble at this bank."

Sheldon put on the screen a picture of the Bradley Bank on Vernon Street in Leyton Falls. After noting as much, he said, "Apparently not satisfied with their gain from the last heist, the next day, Friday, December 12, the Hemton County Bandit Quartet made off with upward of $30,000 in cash, before successfully engineering their getaway."

He came full circle to the most recent bank heist by the group, putting the Ekerly Heights Bank image back on the screen. "And so here we are, on Wednesday, December 17— just over a week before Christmas—where the bank robbing quartet struck again for the seventh time, after a five day pause in their criminal action. They got away with approximately twenty grand from the bank itself and a few hundred more that was stolen from bank customers, along with other valuables. One late arriving customer sustained minor injuries after being hit a couple of times with a shotgun by the apparent leader of the pack of robbers—but could easily have been seriously or fatally injured had he chosen to tempt fate with even more defiance."

Sheldon frowned at the thought and then used the stylus to bring up a map of Hemton County. He said evenly, "Given that the bank heists have all occurred within the county, albeit different towns and cities, we can assume that some or all of the unsubs live in Hemton County, where they are easily able to blend back into normal society—bank wolves under the cloak of sheep's clothing, if you will." Sheldon turned off the monitor and faced everyone. "This gives us a certain radius for which to concentrate our efforts in trying to track down the culprits, wherever they are holed up between bank robberies."

When Karen took to the podium at that point, she offered words of encouragement to Sheldon and the entire task force, then adjusted her glasses and stated in a level tone of voice, "As you all know, sophisticated security systems are a common apparatus in most financial institutions and their vaults in the US these days. And penalties for those who seek to skirt the law as bank robbers are harsh." She frowned. "Unfortunately, this is not enough of a deterrent to prevent bank robbery from occurring far too often. For whatever reason, Denver County and nearby counties, such as Hemton County, have become a magnet for bank and credit union heists. The FBI and its law enforcement partners, state and local, will continue to pursue the Hemton County Bandit Quartet and the money they illegally obtained—whatever it takes to find justice for the victimized financial institutions and their customers, along with the communities they operate out of."

Karen took a breath, before turning to her expertise as a profiler—meant largely for the press on hand for the briefing, and saying coolly, "Bank thieves come in all shapes and sizes, age and gender, and walks of life. Some are armed, others are not—but can still be a problem to those they choose to victimize. The robbers have multiple reasons for hitting banks and credit unions—financial straits, alcohol and drug addiction, relatively easy targets and risks with the obvious rewards and various escape routes, the lure for repeat offenders, you name it. But the unsubs' motivations are for them to figure out. Our job, plain and simple, is to make their lives on the run as uncomfortable as possible—till they either get tired of running or we box them into a corner, so to speak, and there's nowhere left to run…"

She eyed Sheldon and said, "Why don't you do the honors regarding the reward money adjustment."

"Will do." He gave her a smile in earnest and then announced to everyone in the room, "In an effort to give the public more incentive to loosen some tongues in helping to bring the Hemton County Bandit Quartet to its knees, the FBI has upped the ante in the reward money. We've increased it to $7,500 for pertinent info that leads to the arrest and conviction of any of the unsubs—if not all of them…"

Sheldon let that settle in for a moment or two and wondered if it would have any effect on the outcome of the case. Or would they need to flush out the culprits on their own, strong money incentive for public assistance notwithstanding?

THE LEYTON FALLS Police Department's Hostage Negotiation Unit coordinated their skills with the Bomb Squad and SWAT team in once-a-month joint exercise as part of the department's training and readiness in dealing with potential hostage situations and dangerous encounters with unpredictable offenders. In this instance, a simulated hostage scenario was staged, in which the hostage taker was armed with an unloaded Walther PDP Compact Steel Frame 4" 9mm Luger firearm, while claiming that he also had planted a bomb inside the rented, sparsely furnished building on a dead-end street at the edge of town.

In her role playing a hostage who was swept up in the workplace crisis situation, Kelli went along with being a victim this time of the desperate and vengeful-minded ex-employee. That role was occupied by fellow hostage negotiator and one of three negotiators for the department, Ronnie Whiteman. A member of the Ute Mountain Ute Indian Tribe, the thirty-eight-year-old husband and father of three was tall and solidly built, with brown hair in a curtain cut that grazed his shoulders, and brown eyes.

Ronnie played his part to perfection in Kelli's mind—perhaps a little too well in contrast to his real mild-mannered character. He embodied the role of an embittered former worker, looking for some payback after being wrongly terminated in his mind.

"Just let me go," Kelli uttered, the sound of panic in her voice, in portraying the former boss of the hostage taker, now caught in the crosshairs of his plan for retaliation.

"Sorry, no can do," Ronnie snorted, having already pretended to have shot and killed another coworker—actually a dummy. "You're not going anywhere," he insisted. "And if they try and barge in like gangbusters, you'll be the first one to take a bullet—make that the second one…" He glanced amusingly at the dummy and then pointed the empty gun at her, just for effect.

"Ouch." Kelli made a face. She then used her skills as a negotiator to try and calm him down, while he sought to play off this in reacting as a typical hostage taker would in this tense situation.

They went back and forth, where she made progress, then lost ground—before Trent Garcia, the tactical commander of the Hostage Negotiation Unit, took over. Operating outside, and backed by the SWAT team, who went through their drills on cue, Trent skillfully engaged the hostage taker and hostage—and managed to lower the temperature just enough to defuse the situation without anyone else getting hurt. The fake suspect was arrested peacefully and the Bomb Squad rushed in to successfully locate and detonate the bomb.

Trent, a Puerto Rican who was in his fifties and muscular, with a shaved bald head and steely gray-brown eyes, told Kelli and Ronnie, "Good job, you two."

"Hey, practice makes perfect, as the saying goes, right?" Kelli smiled at the tactical commander.

"Absolutely," Trent said with a chuckle. "Next time, you get to play the heavy, Burkett—figuratively speaking," he added, as he regarded her slender frame.

"Uh-oh." Ronnie raised his hands in mock surrender. "Don't go too hard on me now."

"Wouldn't dream of it." Kelli laughed. "Well, maybe just a tad hard, to keep you on your toes."

"I can live with that," he said back to her, chuckling. "Let's just hope when we're dealing with the real bad guys or gals, we can keep putting these interesting performances to good use."

"One can only hope," Kelli said, as she dusted off her clothes, before calling it a day.

En route to her home, her thoughts shifted to the Ekerly Heights Bank robbery that occurred that morning. One man had been injured and the robbers got away. She knew that Sheldon was on the case and would do whatever he could to capture the Hemton County Bandit Quartet, who were thought to be the unsubs. The sooner, the better, as far as she was concerned. Especially as long as Samantha was still potentially in the line of fire.

TAMMY YOSHIMURA SAT on the sofa in her studio apartment on Briar Road. Alongside her was her male mini schnauzer dog named River—or Kawa in Japanese, whenever Tammy received a visit from her grandparents, who lived in Hiroshima, Japan. She had yet to visit her mother's parents but hoped to do so in the near future.

At the moment, Tammy had other things on her mind. Training her eyes on the 24-inch television that was sitting on a walnut TV stand, she watched as the pretty, dark-haired female newscaster talked about the latest bank robbery to hit Hemton County.

"According to FBI Special Agent Sheldon Montgomery, at ten this morning, the Ekerly Heights Bank on Brodgin Drive in Ekerly Heights was robbed by four individuals," Alicia Vaugier said evenly. "It is believed that the bank heist was carried out by the so-called Hemton County Bandit Quartet. The same serial bank robbers are thought to have been responsible for at least seven brazen and armed bank robberies in the county in the month of December." The newscaster moved hair from her face. "Agent Montgomery announced that the FBI had upped the reward money for info leading to the arrest and eventual conviction of the suspects to $7,500. Not a bad piece of change for anyone who comes forward to help put the brakes on the bank bandits."

Tammy petted River's head while contemplating the bank robbery news. She could certainly use the money the FBI was offering, as her income from Bradley Bank was barely enough to make ends meet. But contacting them about a voice that she thought she recognized from the robbery of their bank—that probably was more common sounding than she wanted to believe—likely would have only resulted in Special Agent Montgomery ridiculing her for wasting his time.

No, she needed more to go on than a feeling based on a vague memory of a one-time encounter with a man at a bar.

Still, the belief that there could be more to her instincts than an overactive imagination continued to gnaw at Tammy like something that simply wouldn't quit. Not so long as the Hemton County Bandit Quartet remained at large.

Chapter Seven

A week before Christmas, the annual Leyton Falls Holiday Festival was in full swing. Apart from a dusting of snow to make the season that much merrier without being too much of a hassle, there were plenty of enchanting decorations and lights, activities galore, arts and crafts, musical performances by local artists and an array of appetizing food choices, along with hot cocoa and spiced cider to warm the soul for attendees.

To Kelli, that was more than enough to make attending this year's festival worthwhile. Especially since she had invited Sheldon to accompany her as her date and he had graciously accepted. They had come with Samantha and Chase—albeit in separate vehicles—who had quickly wandered off to be by themselves.

That worked for Kelli, as she was more than happy to take everything in with Sheldon by her side. The fact that he had started to hold her hand as they walked around made her almost feel as if they were a couple. She wondered if he felt the same way. Or were the two times they kissed not indicative of where things might be headed between them?

"Hey," Sheldon said, getting her attention.

Kelli smiled, blushing as though he'd read her thoughts. "Having fun?"

"Yeah." He smiled back. "Been a while since I've gone to

a Christmas festival, but being here with you reminds me of what I've been missing."

"Hmm…me too," she told him, immediately thinking that he meant that in two ways. As did she. Having someone special again to take in the holiday season was something she readily embraced.

"Hot chocolate or cider?" Sheldon eyed her as they approached the booth.

Kelli weighed that before answering. "I'll go with the cider."

"Two hot ciders, please," he told the young attendant dressed as an elf.

"Coming right up," came a spirited response.

After they began walking again with their drinks, Kelli asked curiously, "So, any news on the latest bank heist?"

Sheldon furrowed his brow. "Only that the quartet of robbers seem intent on hitting banks and credit unions in the county that offer the least resistance in terms of security or an escape route. But this strategy is doomed to fail—eventually. We continue to make inroads in trying to back them into a corner." He drew a breath. "It's only a matter of time before they slip up and we move in and make an arrest…"

"Good." Kelli couldn't help but think about Samantha's bank, hoping that being bigger and more secure would make the bank robbers think twice about trying to rob it—and endangering her sister. "Having these crooks be the grinches that stole Christmas—or money for the holidays—is so unfair to us all. Especially during this season that's supposed to be about *giving* and not taking…"

"Well said, and I couldn't agree more," Sheldon said, and squeezed his fingers around hers a little more.

She liked the feel of their hands pressed together. "Spoken like a true special agent with the FBI," she quipped.

He chuckled. "Yeah, I suppose."

They caught up to Samantha and Chase, who had his arm around her slender waist territorially, as they were enjoying a country music band's performance while sipping hot cocoa.

"Hey, you two…" Kelli got their attention.

Samantha smiled. "Hey."

"Are they any good?" Sheldon asked, glancing at the band that was playing "Santa Claus Is Comin' to Town."

"Yeah, they're giving some Christmas tunes their own spin that's working," Chase told him with a laugh.

"I was thinking the same thing," Samantha agreed, moving her feet to the music.

Sheldon chuckled. "I guess it's settled then."

"We'll see about that," Kelli said lightheartedly, wanting to judge for herself.

Half an hour later, after the four made their way across the grounds of the festival, passing by a group who were decorating ornaments, a Santa's workshop in full operational mode and a face painting booth, Samantha turned to Kelli and said, "We're heading out now…"

"Oh…" Kelli lifted a brow. "Where to?" she asked curiously.

"We're meeting up with Chase's brother and his girlfriend for drinks at a new club in town."

"Okay." Kelli smiled, happy to see that her sister seemed to really be making a concerted effort to make it work with her latest romance. "Have a good time." *But don't drink too much*, she thought, while feeling that Samantha was responsible enough in that regard.

"We will," she promised.

"Later," Chase said, glancing at Sheldon and then Kelli.

"Bye." Kelli gave a tiny wave at them both.

"They seem to be happy together," Sheldon commented after Samantha and Chase had left.

"I agree," Kelli had to admit. "I'm definitely rooting for

them. Samantha deserves to be in a relationship that actually works the way it's supposed to."

"Doesn't everyone?" He looked at her. "Such as you—and me?"

"Yes." Kelli felt a tingle in that moment, believing he had touched a chord that they both could relate to. "Definitely."

Sheldon grinned. "Glad we see eye to eye."

She was in agreement there, prompting her to say impromptu, "Do you want to get out of here as well?"

"Sure." He paused. "Where did you have in mind?"

"We could go to my place," Kelli said boldly.

Sheldon nodded willingly. "Your place it is."

THOUGH HE KNEW where he wanted this to go, Sheldon was keeping his libido in check as he stepped inside Kelli's ranch home. He certainly didn't want to be presumptuous that she was at the same place as him at this moment in time, as they navigated their way toward a real relationship. *All options are on the table*, he thought wistfully, while peering into Kelli's enchanting apple green eyes as they stood in the great room.

"Would you like a drink?" she asked him.

"Only if you'll join me in one," he answered.

"Deal." Kelli flashed a brilliant smile. "There's wine, beer, coffee—"

"Wine sounds nice."

"Wine it is."

Sheldon followed her into the kitchen and watched as she got out the bottle of red wine and half-filled two wineglasses.

"There," she said, handing him one.

"Thanks." He tasted the wine, savoring it. "It's good."

Kelli put the wineglass to her lips. "Yes, it is." She sat the glass on the counter. "But a kiss would be even better."

"I can't argue with that," he said, setting down his own glass after one more sip. "Not in this lifetime!"

Seizing the moment, Sheldon pulled Kelli closer and laid a solid kiss on her open mouth, tasting the wine on her lips, turning him on even more.

"I want you," she cooed inside his mouth.

"I want you more," he told her.

"I doubt that." Kelli kept the kiss going as they worked their way back toward the great room, triggering sexual impulses that Sheldon wanted nothing more than to fulfill.

But as much as he wanted to make love to her, he needed to be responsible about it. Prying their mouths apart, Sheldon said regrettably, "I didn't bring protection with me." He assumed she hadn't needed it of late as a widow.

"It's okay," she told him. "Samantha keeps some condoms in her bathroom, just in case they're needed." Kelli kissed him again. "I think this qualifies as one of those times," she added seductively.

Sheldon gave a desirous half grin. "I believe you're right."

She grabbed his hand. "Let's go to my bedroom."

"Lead the way," he told her.

They walked down the hall till they arrived at the primary suite. Sheldon gave it a cursory glance, taking in the double hung windows with pleated shades and rustic bedroom furniture. His gaze centered on the cedar log bed with its light blue comforter and two big sleeping pillows.

He turned back to Kelli and said desirously, "There's nowhere else I'd rather be right now than in here with you..."

"Nice to hear you say that." She licked her lips tantalizingly. "Especially since I feel the same way. It's time I give in to my feelings."

"Me too," Sheldon told her truthfully, as he cupped Kelli's cheeks and began kissing her again. Their bodies molded together perfectly in that instant, and he could feel his erection desperate to come out.

Kelli reacted to this mutual sense of urgency, backing

away and stripping off her clothes, while beckoning him to do the same. Sheldon happily obliged till they were both naked. He needed only one good look at her perfection in the nude, with small but firm breasts, narrow hips and long lean legs for Sheldon to know that Kelli was everything he had imagined her to be, and then some.

"You're gorgeous," he uttered, as if this was news to her.

"So are you," she stated, giving him the once-over and smiling, clearly pleased with what she saw. "Feel free to get in the bed. I'll be right back."

Sheldon nodded and did just that, slipping beneath the comforter and onto a soft burgundy sheet. He waited eagerly for Kelli's return to the room and what he anticipated would be an out of this world experience. *How could it not be?* he thought, his usually reliable instincts kicking into high gear.

KELLI WAS ADMITTEDLY a bundle of nerves as she released her hair from the ponytail holder, allowing it to fall freely across her shoulders while gazing at herself in the mirror of Samantha's bathroom. Though she was more than ready for this moment in being with Sheldon, it was natural to feel jittery about making love to a man for the first time since her husband died.

What if I've forgotten some of the basic steps? Or otherwise fall flat in pleasing Sheldon and his sexual appetite? Kelli thought.

She eyed her reflection again and thought, *He thinks I'm gorgeous.* That had to count for something, along with her own confidence in being naturally blessed with good features. To go along with keeping in shape through running and riding horses.

Kelli believed that would be more than enough to overcome any insecurities she might have. She opened a drawer next to the sink and pulled out the packet containing a condom.

When she returned to her bedroom and found Sheldon lying sexily in wait for her, Kelli's fears seemed to dissipate like magic, replaced by a burning need to be with him.

She slipped beside Sheldon's hard body and handed him the condom, which she had removed from the packet. Even as he was putting it on, Kelli could barely contain herself as she moved closer to him and started to kiss him.

Reciprocating in kind, Sheldon quickly pulled her into his strong arms and took over, using his deft fingers to roam through her hair and then slowly and agonizingly stimulate her body all over, working Kelli into a frenzy. When she could stand it no longer, she pleaded to him, "Make love to me, Sheldon. Now!"

"It would be my pleasure—and so much more, Kelli, believe me." He gave her one more succulent kiss. "Your wish is most certainly my command," he said huskily, before climbing atop her.

The instant that Kelli felt Sheldon go deep inside her, an orgasm coursed through her body, touching the nerves from head to toe. She clung to him like a second skin as the sensations lingered pleasingly for a long moment before rising again like the tide as Sheldon thrust himself into Kelli mightily with his own powerful climax following a few minutes later.

They both rode the wave of sexual intimacy like old lovers, while reaching for new heights, before finding the apex. Only then did things settle down and each fought to catch their ragged breaths in the aftermath.

Rolling off to the side of her, Sheldon said with satisfaction, "That was amazing!"

Kelli blushed. "You think?"

"Without a shadow of a doubt," he made clear. "You were incredible."

"So were you," she said in all honesty, still trying to regain her equilibrium fully.

He chuckled and gave her another kiss. "Guess that means we're the real deal when it comes to compatibility."

"Yes, I'd say we are at that."

At least in bed, Kelli told herself. Though it seemed to extend as well to other facets of their lives, she was sensible enough to know that a few kisses and one time in bed was not enough, in and of itself, to think they were the perfect match made on Earth. Or hear wedding bells ringing joyously in her ears.

But she certainly considered it a nice way to take what they had to a new and thoroughly enjoyable and passionate next level. Giving them a new point to build on as Kelli waited enthusiastically to see where things went between them from here.

Chapter Eight

On Friday, Kelli did her normal rounds in Leyton Falls, keeping an eye out for anything—or anyone—that seemed out of the ordinary. Though the rash of bank robberies lately had seemingly taken the wind out of the sails of other local troublemakers, there were still just enough of them to give law enforcement more potential headaches to stay apprised of. Juvenile delinquency, for one, was a problem that all communities had to deal with these days. Leyton Falls was no exception. Some youth apparently had too much time on their hands for getting into trouble.

Hopefully, not today, Kelli thought, as she drove around town. Most of the snow was gone, though the forecast was for more of the white stuff, just in time for Christmas, heading into New Year's Day and beyond.

Her thoughts wandered off to the mind-blowing sex she had with Sheldon last night. He certainly knew how to pleasure a woman, and she'd found that her desire to be with a man was still there. Maybe even more powerful than before, as Sheldon had awakened her sexual impulses in ways that Kelli could not have imagined. She wondered when there might be a repeat performance. And if there was the proverbial light at the end of the tunnel in store for them, as far as a real relationship.

One could only keep an open mind, along with a warm heart, Kelli imagined, as a request for backup came from a fellow Leyton Falls PD officer who was in pursuit of a teenager suspected of arson.

As it was not too far from her current location, Kelli took the call and headed toward Marjanne Street. When she arrived, she saw Officer Jolene Herrera attempting to cuff the female suspect, who was clearly resisting arrest.

Emerging from her squad car, Kelli pressed the record button on her body cam and readied herself to get in on the action as she approached the two. "Hey," she said, getting their attention.

Jolene Herrera was a few years older than Kelli but had been with the force less time. She had a medium build, a dark blond chignon and blue eyes. While out of breath, she said flatly, "I could use some help here."

"You've got it," Kelli said. She assisted the officer in getting the belligerent teen's hands behind her back and cuffing her. The girl looked to be no more than fifteen, and was slender, with messy light blond hair in choppy layers and a petulant scowl on her face. "What's she done?"

"She's suspected of setting fire to a shed behind a house on Sorrenta Street," Jolene answered. "The homeowner—who recognized the suspect as Merritt Rourke, a fourteen-year-old neighbor—spotted her running from the scene and called 911. I responded and caught the suspect trying to hide behind another house two blocks away."

Kelli lifted a brow, while wondering if the arson was personal, committed merely for attention, or a cry for help before the fire setting escalated to something more serious. She regarded the suspect and said, "Consider yourself fortunate that things didn't turn out much worse for you."

Merritt sneered. "Whatever."

Whatever, Kelli mentally replayed the sarcastic and defiant word out of the teenager's mouth, as they loaded her in the back of Jolene's patrol car. The suspect was facing charges of first-degree arson and criminal mischief and would be transported to the Hemton County Juvenile Assessment Center.

Back in her own squad car, Kelli headed to the café where she was meeting Samantha for lunch.

SHELDON SAT IN the courtroom of the Alfred A. Arraj Courthouse on Nineteenth Street in Denver, watching as United States District Court Judge Ryan Pagliaro was about to pronounce the sentence for serial bank robber Helena Estrada. The forty-seven-year-old career criminal had robbed half a dozen Colorado banks while armed over a twenty-month period, before finally being apprehended just as she was leaving a motel in Commerce City, Colorado, a year ago.

Having slapped the cuffs on her himself, after the joint efforts of the Bureau, Commerce City Police Department, Adams County Sheriff's Office and Colorado Bureau of Investigation finally paid off, Sheldon was only too happy to attend the sentencing. He had testified against the convicted bank robber, per his obligation as an FBI agent working the case. Glancing at Estrada, who was lean with brunette hair in a micro bob, it appeared as though she had reconciled herself to her fate after the string of brazen robberies.

Sheldon's mind switched briefly to last night's lovemaking with Kelli. She was everything he could have dreamed of in bed and a whole lot more. Though he was eager to continue their sexual relations, bringing her to even greater heights, he didn't want to overdo it to the extent that it seemed a physical connection was all he wanted from her. Quite the contrary. He yearned for a serious relationship with Kelli—one in which they could both challenge, learn from and grow with each other. Did she want the same thing with him, even if that was a road she had once traveled with another man?

Pondering that thought for a moment or two, Sheldon turned his attention back to the proceeding. Judge Pagliaro, who was in his sixties, heavyset and had a white horseshoe-shaped hairline, drew a breath. After touching his round glasses, he peered at Estrada and handed her, in a no-nonsense style, a sentence of nineteen years in federal prison and three additional years of supervised release. The judge further used the stiff sentence as a means to discourage other would-be bank robbers from following the same path.

Justice has been served, Sheldon thought happily, as Helena Estrada was promptly remanded into custody, with her conviction a victory for the rule of law. He looked forward to seeing the same results of a long incarceration for other bank thieves, including the Hemton County Bandit Quartet.

But first they had to capture them. This was front and center for Sheldon as he left the courthouse and headed back to the Bureau's field office. Though he knew that the longer the criminal quartet remained at large to hit financial institutions, the more comfortable they were becoming in feeling an aura of invincibility. This made them all the more treacherous in just what they might be capable of.

KELLI SPOTTED SAMANTHA at a table by the window inside Georgina's Café on Kletcher Street.

"Hey," she said, after walking over to her.

"Hey." Samantha smiled cheerfully. "I ordered us chai lattes, for starters."

"Great." Kelli sat down and grabbed her mug, taking a sip. "So, how's work been thus far today?" The bank robberies in Leyton Falls were never far from her mind, even if Kelli endeavored to think in positive terms where it concerned her sister being safe and sound.

"Nothing unusual," Samantha answered, as if to allay her fears. "Since online banking keeps many customers away from the actual bank, it's been pretty quiet. I guess that with Christmas less than a week away, people are too busy with last-minute shopping to take the time to go to the bank."

"I suppose." Kelli realized that she had yet to get her sister any Christmas gifts. Apart from never really knowing what to get Samantha, she suspected that not having a tree to place presents under probably had something to do with that. This obviously needed to be rectified.

They grabbed their menus, and Kelli went with a vegetable salad, while Samantha chose to order a veggie sandwich.

After the food came and Kelli tasted the salad, she lifted her eyes and noted, "You got in late last night." They had managed to miss each other this morning, en route to work.

Samantha smiled. "I'm surprised you even noticed, given that you were preoccupied with your guest."

Kelli colored. "Oh, that."

"Yes, that," her sister teased.

Kelli tasted her water. Though Sheldon had chosen not to stay overnight, she wouldn't have objected to that. They were, after all, adults and everything they did was consensual. But she respected his wish to leave in the early hours of the morning and not make things uncomfortable with Samantha. And maybe even Chase, had all four been present for breakfast.

"We're working our way through getting to know one another," Kelli explained.

"Yeah, I get that," Samantha told her. "And I'm happy that someone has finally broken through your walls and put a smile on your face again."

"Me too." Kelli forked one of the chopped tomatoes. She honestly believed that she and Sheldon had turned a corner after last night, even while still navigating what might be around the next corner—and beyond. Eyeing her sister, who had cleverly avoided talking about her own budding romance, she asked Samantha plainly, "Are things working out the way you expected—or wanted—with Chase?" *Though she seems happy enough, looks can be deceiving*, Kelli told herself.

"More or less," Samantha responded. "Not sure I had any strong expectations, other than simply going with the flow," she said. "Right now, it's going along smoothly. We get along great. Chase is a nice guy. And so is his brother, Preston… and Preston's girlfriend, Danielle."

"Good to know," Kelli said, remembering that Samantha and Chase got together with the other couple after leaving the festival last night. She thought it might be a good idea to invite Chase's brother and girlfriend over for dinner sometime early in the new year.

"Chase has some interesting thoughts on what he wants to do with his life," Samantha volunteered musingly, while holding her sandwich.

"Such as…?" Kelli once again chided herself for potentially overstepping her bounds. Maybe her sister wouldn't see it that way.

Samantha shrugged. "He wants to start his own business. Maybe get into real estate or the tech business."

"Those are good choices," Kelli said, sipping her latte. "Would his career aspirations be for California, Colorado, or elsewhere?"

"I'm not sure. We haven't gotten that far in our relationship as far as what his goals are, where either of us wants to live, or whatever."

"I understand." The last thing Kelli wanted was for her sister to try and force the issue. Any more than she wanted to with Sheldon. *Whatever happened, happened*, she told herself. The same was true for Samantha and Chase, assuming they intended to have a future together beyond the holidays.

Samantha gazed at her. "At least if things work out for you and Sheldon, you're both living and working in the same state."

"That's true." Kelli couldn't imagine trying to manage a long-distance romance. She wasn't counting the distance between Leyton Falls and Denver, where Sheldon lived—that was more than manageable. At least as far as dating was concerned. If things got serious between them—such as marriage—she supposed they would need to talk about where to live together. She loved her ranch and couldn't imagine giving up the horses for city life. On the other hand, finding love again would undoubtedly have to come first and would dictate everything else. She wondered if Sheldon lived by the same code of *romance conquers all*.

AFTER WORK THAT EVENING, Sheldon ditched his business attire for a dark red training tank top, gray sweatpants and black retro sneakers for a workout in his home gym. It was spacious with hardwood flooring, awning windows, mirrored walls and the latest in equipment. That included a treadmill, cycling bike, rowing machine and various weights for training and overall fitness.

Though generally speaking, he liked being in shape for himself, Sheldon had to admit as he worked up a good sweat on the magnetic rower machine, that he had a whole new reason for wanting to both look fit and keep up his stamina. He mused about Kelli and the incredible exercise they had been able to perform in making love. It was something he would gladly participate in time and time again with her, should the carnal instincts continue between them as though they were totally meant for each other.

But first things first, Sheldon told himself, his breathing measured. He needed to bring Kelli more into his world and see how she fit in. Or, at the very least, give him the opportunity to welcome her and be totally at her disposal. Maybe even cook her dinner, bringing his culinary skills out of hibernation and seeing if he could please her tastebuds the way he was able to please Kelli in bed.

By the time the workout was finished, and he'd hopped into the shower, Sheldon had settled in on that train of thought. He then forced his mind to switch to his current bank robbery investigation and just how long it might take to bring it to a close.

Chapter Nine

On Saturday, Kelli took Cora out for a morning ride. Her Colorado Ranger seemed to welcome the exercise as much as she did to help get her day started. She held on to the reins firmly and moved across the grassy hills leisurely, admiring the property while wearing her cowgirl hat.

She could imagine Sheldon fitting right in—as he seemed to when showing his comfort level around horses and country living in general. Even if working for the FBI would likely always be a priority for him, it didn't mean he couldn't embrace having a place like this to come home to every day. With her there to greet him, apart from her own duties in law enforcement—and future aspirations, to that effect.

Kelli continued to ride. Of course, she also wanted to check out Sheldon's condo and get a different perspective on Denver from his point of view. When would he invite her? *There's no hurry*, she told herself, while believing it was something they were surely heading toward. She certainly had no sense that Sheldon had a girlfriend in the city that he was keeping from her. He wasn't that type of man. Any more than Pierre was.

Maybe once things had settled down between the holidays and Sheldon's current workload, if not sooner, she decided.

Kelli was confident that she would get to check out his place and its surroundings.

After she finished the ride and let Cora out into the pasture with the other horses, Kelli's cell phone rang. She saw from the caller ID that it was the hostage negotiation commander, Trent Garcia.

Kelli answered evenly with, "Hi, Trent. What's up?"

"There's been a robbery and carjacking," he responded ominously. "Two armed men wearing masks approached the female driver of a Nissan Rogue at the First Bank and Savings drive-through ATM on Elfane Avenue. One of the men forced his way inside the driver's seat and the other got in the back seat—where they then robbed and kidnapped the woman and her young daughter—as the unsubs took off in the vehicle."

"That's awful," Kelli uttered, visualizing what the two victims must be going through at that moment, feeling totally helpless. She waited to see where things stood in this dangerous scenario.

"Not as bad as it could be," the commander said. "The stolen car was spotted on the move by one of our officers. The FBI has been notified, along with our SWAT team. As of now, the unsubs and their abductees have apparently been tracked to a shopping center parking lot, with the tense situation still in flux."

"All right…" Kelli said with expectation, knowing her services as a hostage negotiator were needed. "Where is the shopping center?"

Trent gave her the location and added, "Ronnie Whiteman is on the scene—but you should be there as backup, just in case…"

"I'm on my way," Kelli told him, though needing a quick change to her official clothing and equipment. She was hoping that Ronnie, another hostage negotiator in the unit, would not need her help in successfully securing the safe release of the kidnapped hostages from the unsubs.

SHELDON WAS ALREADY in Leyton Falls and hoping to ask Kelli out to lunch or maybe an early dinner, after conferring with members of the Rocky Mountain Money Grab Task Force, when the word came down about the First Bank and Savings ATM robbery, carjacking and kidnapping of a woman and her child. The unsubs had led the authorities on a wild-goose chase, before they hit another vehicle in the parking lot at the Leyton Falls Shopping Center on Teaton Drive and were at a standstill, with the abductees evidently still inside the stolen silver Nissan Rogue.

Racing to the scene in his Ford Explorer, all Sheldon could think of was that he hoped that this thing didn't end tragically for the woman and her daughter. He imagined them being his own wife and their little girl—Kelli came to mind as potentially the right partner for him and a possible mother of his children—and hated the thought of one hair being harmed on their heads. Much less, any other forms of victimization.

When he arrived at the scene, local and federal law enforcement were already surrounding the carjacked vehicle. Sheldon exited his SUV and met up with Nolan Valentine, the police department lieutenant in charge.

"Montgomery," Nolan acknowledged him with a glance.

"Where do things stand?" Sheldon asked.

"Two armed men—one African American and one Caucasian, commandeered that Nissan Rogue—" Nolan peered in the direction of the stolen vehicle "—from a drive-through ATM with the occupants still inside. One of the carjackers, the African American, identified as twenty-three-year-old Lloyd Johannesen, fled from the driver's seat to the mall, where we found him hiding in a clothing store and arrested the man without incident. The other, identified as nineteen-year-old Max Rosete—who has a record—is holed up in the back seat of the stolen car with the young daughter of the abducted driver. We've identified the driver—forced to remain on the passenger side of the front seat—as thirty-nine-year-old Carmela Egolf."

"Hmm." Sheldon stared at the vehicle. "Are you in communication with Rosete?"

"We have a hostage negotiator trying hard to get him to release the hostages," Nolan answered bleakly, and looked in a different direction. Sheldon followed his gaze and was expecting to see Kelli, but instead, he saw someone else. "Ronnie Whiteman will give it his best shot, before we're forced to move in to rescue them."

Sheldon watched as the hostage negotiator was on his cell phone, speaking with the carjacker…as the situation remained tense.

WHEN SHE ARRIVED at the shopping center, Kelli quickly made her way to the area where the action was taking place. She spotted Sheldon, who was talking to Nolan Valentine, and resisted an urge to get in on the conversation. Instead, she made eye contact with Sheldon as a flash of giddiness coursed through her—but pivoted toward Ronnie, who was standing beside a police van, talking on the phone.

"Hey," Kelli said, getting his attention.

Ronnie regarded her as he lowered the cell phone. "Glad you're here."

"What's the latest?"

With his brow creased, he answered, "Truthfully, I'm not getting anywhere with the suspect. He's still holding the mother and daughter as captives inside their carjacked vehicle." Ronnie narrowed his eyes at the Nissan Rogue. He briefed her on the current status of the crime scene. "Maybe you can talk some sense into him—before it's too late."

"I'll try," Kelli promised warily.

"Don't just try," she heard a voice say, and turned to find Sheldon standing there. "If anyone can work some magic here, it's you, Kelli—"

"No pressure, right?" She made a face, while feeling the weight of the hostages on her shoulders. Not to mention not wanting to disappoint Sheldon. Or the entire Leyton Falls PD, for that matter. "I'll get them to safety," she promised. Now she only needed to hold herself to this.

A crooked grin played on Sheldon's mouth. "Wouldn't expect any less from you."

"You wouldn't," she teased, but knew he was being serious.

"Here you go," Ronnie said, handing her the cell phone.

I've got this, Kelli thought with determination, with all eyes on her as she put the phone to her ear. "Hi. I'm Officer Burkett, a hostage negotiator," she said calmly. "You're Max Rosete, right?"

"Yeah," he muttered.

Kelli asked him nicely, "Do you mind if I call you Max?"

"Whatever."

I'll take that as a yes, she told herself, and said bluntly, "Max, let's just cut to the chase. How do we resolve this peacefully?"

"You tell me," Rosete said sardonically.

"All right, I will." Kelli steeled her nerves. "You need to let your captives go," she insisted.

"That ain't happening," he snapped back. "They're my insurance policy, till I can figure things out."

The only thing to figure out is how to keep them—and him—alive at the end of the day, she told herself. "I can help you with that, Max," Kelli said in an even tone. "But first, I need to talk to Carmela Egolf, the woman you're holding against her will."

After a moment or two, a shaky voice said, "I'm Carmela."

Kelli identified herself and asked, "Are you okay?"

She hesitated, before responding in a nervous tone, "Yes."

"What about your daughter?"

"She's frightened, but hasn't been hurt," Carmela answered.

"That's good to hear," Kelli said. "What's your daughter's name?"

"Wendy."

"That's a pretty name. How old is Wendy?"

"Five," Carmela said.

"I want you and your daughter to hang tight," Kelli told her. "This will be over soon."

Carmela sucked in a deep breath. "Hope so."

"Put Max back on the phone." Kelli considered her next move as she met Sheldon's steady gaze, knowing she had his full support. After a moment's pause, she said to the carjacker in straightforward terms, "Listen, Max, whatever your hang-ups are about what you've done and what comes next, I assume you have no more of a death wish than your friend Lloyd Johannesen, who quit while he was ahead. He knew that he wanted there to be a tomorrow—whatever it held— and deal with it. You have the same choice. Just let Carmela and Wendy go. Then lay down your weapon and come out with your hands up. No one has to die here—least of all you. But sharpshooters are already in position and ready to act at a moment's notice—meaning there will be no way out for you if something bad happens to either person you have in that car with you."

Max muttered an expletive, then said, "Why should you care what happens to me?"

"It's my job to care," Kelli told him matter-of-factly. "I assume you have family who cares too… Look, Max, no one has really been hurt, thus far. You're young enough that there will still be time to make a life for yourself after this is over. But you need to be smart about it. That starts with letting a mother and daughter go. Then come out yourself, leaving your handgun inside the vehicle. And this can all be over." She paused, tentative, while hoping she had been able to reach him. "What's it going to be, Max?"

Kelli waited for an agonizing long moment as she exchanged glances with Sheldon and Ronnie, before they watched the front door on the passenger side open and a tall, thin woman with blond hair in a short ponytail emerged.

Carmela Egolf, Kelli thought, as she saw her open the back door and remove her daughter Wendy from the booster seat before carrying out the five-year-old girl with blond pigtails, and quickly moving away from the vehicle. They were then met by law enforcement, who whisked the mother and her precious child away to safety.

All eyes turned back to the Nissan Rogue, while waiting to see what the carjacker's next move was. *Give yourself up,* Kelli thought, not wanting to see him decide to take the easy way out by committing police suicide.

After another moment or two, Max Rosete climbed out of the back seat, unarmed, his hands raised high. Tall and slender, with dark hair in a side part cut, he had removed his ski mask. Kelli couldn't help but think that he looked younger than his age, but in fact was an adult who chose to participate in criminal behavior that he would have to answer for.

After being ordered to lie down on the ground, Rosete complied, as authorities swiftly converged upon him, handcuffed him and placed him under arrest.

Kelli gazed at Sheldon, who said grinningly, "You got it done."

She downplayed it. "Did I have a choice?" she responded, knowing the potential alternative.

He laughed. "Not really."

"You took charge," Ronnie stated. "Maybe I need to learn a thing or two about the art of hostage negotiation."

"I doubt that." Kelli chuckled. "You started the process, I finished it. It was a team effort."

"I'll go with that," he agreed with a laugh.

"It's the only way we roll," Nolan insisted, coming up to them. "You both averted a potential catastrophe, and we can all take a victory lap that the young woman and her daughter will live to see another day and, hopefully, years."

"Amen to that!" Sheldon said, gazing at Kelli with a pleased look.

She waited till they had a moment to themselves before asking him, "Are you up for helping me to get a Christmas tree and decorate it?"

"Absolutely!" he responded, putting a hand on her shoulder. "Whatever you need, I'm here."

Kelli smiled, taking those tender words to heart.

THAT AFTERNOON, THEY drove to the Craxton Tree Farm in nearby Loughlin Hills, where there was an array of precut trees to choose from.

Kelli was admittedly indecisive, as she wanted to pick the perfect tree to help bring the Christmas spirit back to her ranch, in style.

"What do you think of this one?" she asked Sheldon as they sized up a six-foot Canaan fir tree.

"I like it," he told her, and moved to another tree at the farm. "Or, you might like this Eastern white pine even better."

"Actually, I think I do." Kelli smiled. "It's amazing."

"I agree. And it will look terrific in your great room," he declared. "Especially once you get the lights and ornaments on it."

"Then it's settled," she told him, excited at the prospect of putting it up together.

After getting the tree home, they placed a freshly cut pine wreath on the front door and were joined by Samantha and Chase in decorating the Christmas tree with classic snowflake and ball ornaments, along with mini string lights that Kelli had kept over the years, while adding new silver tinsel icicles and crystal and wood bead decorations.

"It looks wonderful," Kelli said enthusiastically, after they had completed the project, while eating oatmeal raisin cookies, sipping hot cider and listening to Christmas music to heighten the mood.

"Sure does," Samantha concurred, marveling at the tree. "Better late than never."

Kelli smiled. "True."

"I like it," Chase said, tasting the cider.

Sheldon nibbled on a cookie. "Me too."

"I'm so glad everyone approves," Kelli said with a laugh. "Especially since I thought that, with everyone here, it might be nice to decorate the outside a bit as well, beyond the wreath. I've kept a couple of boxes of lights, artificial poinsettias and an inflatable snowman, in the absence of a real one."

"Count me in," Sheldon told her.

"I have nothing better to do," Chase agreed. He looked at Samantha. "Or did you have something else on the docket for us?"

"Nope, sorry." She grinned at him. "I'm all for going all out this year in brightening the house for the holidays, inside and out."

Kelli smiled. "Nice to see that we're all in agreement," she said to everyone. "Let's get this done!"

By the time they were finished a couple of hours later, Kelli felt exhausted but grateful in putting out the Christmas decorations for some friendly competition again with her neighbors. Moreover, in the undertaking, she had managed to get over the hump in moving past her tragedy in los-ing Pierre and was embracing new and exciting possibilities with Sheldon.

When he invited her to spend Sunday at his condo, she gamely agreed, seeing this as another step forward in the re-lationship they were building.

Chapter Ten

The moment she stepped inside the downtown penthouse, Kelli was impressed. Its modern decor and open concept seemed a good fit for Sheldon, insofar as city living went. She imagined, though, that he could be comfortable living anywhere that he chose to.

"I like it," she told him after being given the grand tour that included a gourmet kitchen and huge primary suite with handcrafted solid wood furniture and dormer windows with plantation shutters. The room had an en suite bathroom. *How could I not be enamored with this place?* Kelli asked herself.

"You'll like it even more when we step out on the terrace," Sheldon promised her, and led the way to the rooftop.

He did not disappoint, as Kelli stood there and took in the incredible views of Downtown Denver. "Wow! This is nice," she said admiringly.

"I agree." He grinned, gazing at the skyline as their shoulders brushed. "I never get tired of this."

"Why would you?" Kelli regarded his profile. "How did you end up making this your home?"

"I got a pretty good deal on the converted warehouse, and went with it. At least until something better comes along."

"I see." She took that for what it was worth—which Kelli

suspected was a lot, coming from his mouth. "Well, lucky you that this incredible place fell into your lap."

"I suppose." Sheldon faced her and pulled them closer together. "I think I'd feel much luckier with you on my lap."

"Really?" She flushed. "If you play your cards right," she teased him, "you just may get that opportunity."

"Counting on it." He laughed. "I'm always up for a good card game, especially those where the winner takes all…"

"Hmm…" Kelli murmured. "Who says anyone has to lose?"

"Definitely not me," Sheldon insisted.

They shared a tender kiss that became harder, before one thing led to another, and they ended up back in his bedroom.

Both removed their clothing as fast as they could and, after some foreplay, Sheldon put on protection, before they got beneath the Jacquard cotton woven blanket on his king-size sleigh bed, and made love.

When it was over, leaving Kelli panting and thoroughly satisfied, as they switched positions more than once before coming together for one final burst of completion, she fell onto Sheldon's broad chest as he wrapped her in his muscular arms.

"This just keeps getting better and better," he whispered huskily in her ear.

"You think?" She felt a tingle in hearing the words. *I couldn't agree more*, she told herself dreamily. "I guess we must be doing something right."

"Yes—very right." Sheldon lifted her chin, and they kissed. "And I, for one, wouldn't have it any other way."

Kelli smiled. "Neither would I."

"Then we're on the same page."

"Even the same book," she said with a little chuckle, having no reason to believe otherwise, for which he didn't disagree.

About an hour later, Sheldon awoke and, sitting up, said, "I think I'll hop in the shower now."

"Care for some company?" Kelli rubbed her eyes.

"Only if you promise to behave yourself," he quipped.

She laughed. "Is that what you truly want?"

"No." He grinned desirously. "Not in the slightest."

"Didn't think so," Kelli uttered smilingly, as she followed him out of the bed.

THAT EVENING, THEY hung out in the kitchen together, moving about seamlessly like an old married couple—while making a dinner that included baked garlic butter chicken thighs, mashed potatoes, green beans and dinner rolls, with white wine.

As far as Sheldon was concerned, having Kelli in his life was starting to feel very real—something he hadn't experienced in a long time. Was this also how she saw it? Maybe this was the opportunity they had both been waiting for—to get beyond the difficulties they had both gone through in their romantic pasts and give the future a legitimate shot.

Bypassing the dining room, they ate at the kitchen island, sitting on farmhouse chairs.

"This is really good," Kelli remarked, using a fork to scoop up more mashed potatoes.

"It should be," Sheldon responded with a grin, grabbing a dinner roll from his plate. "You helped make it."

She laughed. "That's true."

"Guess we both know our way around the kitchen enough to be able to create some tasty meals."

"Having the right foods to work with always helps the cause," she teased him, sipping her wine.

He grinned. "Maybe just a little." A couple of minutes later, Sheldon asked curiously while lifting his own wineglass, "So, how long has Samantha been staying with you?"

"Just a few months now. Sam moved in after her last breakup. It's only supposed to be a temporary thing—till she's ready to get her own place. I haven't put any pressure on her to do that yet because, honestly, it's been good having her there for some sister bonding and relieving the loneliness I was feeling."

"I get it," Sheldon said sincerely. "I'm glad you two have each other—however long she chooses to live on your ranch."

"Maybe that won't last much longer," Kelli suggested, slicing a knife into a chicken thigh. "If things work out between her and Chase, who knows what comes next?"

"Think she could want to relocate to California or somewhere else?"

"She hasn't indicated as much." Kelli tasted the chicken. "But I wouldn't put it past her. Sam has always tended to jump into relationships headfirst, for better or worse. Why should this be any different?"

"Maybe this time she would have met her match with Chase and, as such, would treat it with more seriousness," Sheldon stated.

"Maybe." She smiled thoughtfully. "We shall see."

Not that I would object to having you all to myself, he mused, but certainly didn't want her to think he was trying in any way to push her sister out. Sheldon ate some green beans. There was room in Kelli's life for more than one person. Especially since she indicated a desire to have kids someday, something that he shared.

Kelli lifted her wine and inquired, "How are things between you and your dad?"

Sheldon sat back, sipping his own wine. "Good," he answered with a catch to his voice. "We've had our issues from time to time, like most fathers and sons—do as I say, not as I do, that type of thing—but it's gotten better since my father retired from the Bureau and the stresses of his life at the time lessened."

"Happy to hear that," she said, pensive. "Not having my parents in the picture has been a drag. I only wish one or the other was still around to get on my nerves. Or vice versa."

"I get where you're coming from—and feel grateful to have one living parent," Sheldon told her. "Though my step-mom has been like a birth mother to me for most of my life," he said.

"That's good." Kelli dabbed a napkin to her lips, gazing at him. "What are your thoughts about relocating to another field office, should the Bureau ask you to?"

A loaded question, Sheldon thought, but an honest one, nevertheless. Before meeting her, he would have likely jumped at the chance to move elsewhere for the career. Especially if it came with a promotion. But now, the thought of going anywhere, as long as things were going good between them, was something he couldn't imagine. Unless, of course, she was willing to leave Colorado too.

"I would tell them that I'm not interested in transferring to someplace else," he answered straightforwardly. "At least not before I carefully weighed the pros and cons, with respect to what I wanted most out of life."

"Which is…?"

Sheldon met her eyes. "Just being happy and having some-one in my life to share that happiness with."

Kelli smiled softly. "Good answer."

"What about you?" he asked. "Do you see yourself being more focused on your nice ranch and horses? Or do you have career goals that take priority?"

She waited a beat and then replied contemplatively, "Truthfully, I love the horses and property, but would rather have someone special to share my life with—whatever the setting." Kelli tilted her face. "As for my thoughts on my career—I love my current job with dual lanes that always keep me on my toes. But I have a dream of maybe someday working for the Colorado Bureau of Investigation as a step up the ladder of law enforcement—if such an opportunity would present itself, without compromising my other goals in life."

"I see," Sheldon said interestedly, finishing off his wine. "It all sounds good to me. If you ever do decide to give the CBI a go, I have a friend on the executive team there and would be happy to put in a good word for you. They are always on the lookout for great talent."

Kelli's smiled. "I'll remember that and just may take you up on the offer one of these days."

"Please do," he said forthrightly, and leaned over for a sweet kiss and felt her reciprocate in kind.

Sheldon was sure that she would be just as great with the CBI as what he'd seen with the Leyton Falls PD. And even better as a beautiful woman who seemed to have a lot of love to give—something he was more than open to receiving from her.

TAMMY YOSHIMURA WAS at her teller's window in Bradley Bank, trying to keep busy on this Monday morning, three days before Christmas. As it was, customers were trickling in, one at a time, with most undoubtedly preferring or able to suspend their banking business till after the holidays. Her own plans were to spend Christmas Day with her parents, who lived in Ogden, Utah, then return to Leyton Falls with time to spare before the new year began.

Just as she was about to wave an elderly woman with short snow-white hair over to her window, Tammy watched in utter disbelief, mixed with horror, as four persons wearing ski masks, long coats, gloves and dark clothing, entered the bank, brandishing firearms.

She recognized them as the bank robbing foursome that had been given the Hemton County Bandit Quartet moniker.

Are you seriously here to rob Bradley Bank a second time this month? Tammy thought to herself, wishing this was nothing more than a bad dream, but knowing she was very much awake. And that what she was witnessing was as real as real could get.

She listened as, like the last time, the distinctively deep-voiced male robber who seemed to be calling the shots, pulled out a shotgun and stated chillingly, almost verbatim to the last time, "This is a bank robbery! Everyone stay exactly where you are. If any employee has thoughts about notifying the police or FBI or doing anything else really dumb—like trying to be a hero—we'll kill every single person in here and won't lose a day's sleep because of it. Trust me! Don't test any of us," he warned, and gazed up at a security camera coolheadedly and back, "if you know what's good for you..."

Tammy resisted the urge to activate her silent alarm, for fear that the robbers would somehow know instinctively, thereby endangering herself and everyone else. Instead, she stood frozen as two of the robbers, whom she believed to be male, started rounding up the few customers and ordered them down to the floor, before zip-tying their hands behind their backs.

The deep-voiced robber briskly went to the office of Julian Souza, the bank manager, and forced him out at gunpoint. Julian, who was fifty-seven, short and a widower, with gray hair in a business cut, was brought to the others being held against their will and zip-tied.

Tammy watched as the lone female robber went to the teller two windows over. It was occupied by Lori Winslow, a slender thirty-two-year-old divorcée with strawberry blond hair in a stacked cut, who had been with the bank for ten years. As someone who had been robbed previously by the same robbers with a gun in her face, Lori had vowed to resist were she ever to be in the same situation again.

It was Tammy's hope that her colleague was simply blowing off steam at the time and wouldn't do anything foolish, such as show defiance.

But when Lori did just that, even admitting to triggering the silent alarm, the female bank robber shot her once in the head and Lori fell to the floor in agony.

She shot her, Tammy thought disbelievingly, putting a trembling hand to her mouth, wanting nothing more than to assist her fallen coworker. It was only then that she realized that standing at her window was the deep-voiced leader of the pack.

His tone was even more acerbic when he said cruelly, "It didn't have to be that way, but she wouldn't follow orders. Hope you're a lot smarter than that."

Tammy swallowed thickly, before saying to him, "I'll do whatever you want."

"Good girl." He peered at her through the ski mask, tossing a black leather satchel on the counter with one hand, and still aiming the shotgun at her with the other. "Put everything you've got in your drawer in there—and make it snappy!"

She followed his orders, knowing that he and his fellow bank robbers meant business in their willingness to hurt anyone who stood in their way.

After sliding the bag filled with money to him, he said coldly, "Maybe we'll be back for a third round!"

On that note, the bank bandits hurriedly made their getaway, warning them not to follow. Or try to stop them.

Only then did Tammy rush to the aide of Lori, but knew by the looks of her fallen colleague that it was too late to save her.

THE HEMTON COUNTY BANDIT QUARTET left the bank somewhat flustered with the deadly turn of events. This carried on once they loaded into their white GMC Savana van and made an escape from the area. Only then did they remove their ski masks while charting the road ahead.

When the dust settled, all were in agreement that it had only been a matter of time before their actions resulted in someone being killed, making no apologies to that effect. But even that stark reality and its potential implications—with all of them equally liable in the violent consequence as the female shooter—was not enough to keep them from plotting their strategy for the next target to strike.

Given that the haul at the latest bank was less than they bargained for, since the foolish teller chose not to obey the rules, the Hemton County Bandit Quartet resolved to be more successful in their efforts the next time to make up for their shortfall.

And continue as a solid group what had proven to be worth their while in going after what they believed they were entitled to in a county where the opportunities were still ripe for the picking.

Chapter Eleven

Kelli was patrolling the area, her thoughts still on a high after spending yesterday with Sheldon in Denver. She loved his penthouse condo and could see herself spending lots of time there. As if their general and sexual chemistry wasn't enough to put a smile on her face, the fact that they were even in sync while preparing and eating dinner told her that they could truly have something special. She, for one, couldn't wait to see what came next for them.

When dispatch reported that a holdup alarm had been activated at Bradley Bank, Kelli headed toward that destination. It wasn't lost on her that the bank had been the target of a recent heist. What were the odds?

Better than even, she told herself, knowing that it was hardly uncommon for the same banks to be hit by robbers. Especially if the word spread among criminal elements that it was a soft and inviting target. But the truth was most bank alarms turned out to be false, for one reason or another.

Kelli sensed that wasn't the case here. With the rash of bank robberies in Hemton County of late, any suggestion of such a crime had to be investigated for the seriousness it deserved. Her incentive went even beyond that. As Samantha worked at a bank, it gave Kelli reason to be concerned—and

she'd pass on whatever she learned about bank heists and protecting oneself to her sister, to be on the safe side.

She took a cursory glance at the white GMC Savana passenger van that passed her on Alery Avenue. It was traveling well within the speed limit, and there was no cause for
concern as she turned her attention back to the possible bank
robbery. Per the department's protocol, she waited for dispatch to confirm that the code word preestablished with the
bank to verify that the robbery was legit and, if so, whether
it was currently in progress or not.

It's not a false alarm, Kelli told herself a moment later, in
that the bank robbery had indeed taken place—and the robbers had apparently since vacated the premises.

She turned onto Vernon Street and, shortly thereafter,
pulled up outside the bank, behind another squad car.

Officer Jolene Herrera waited for her to get out, and Kelli
said tonelessly, "Hey."

"Hey." Jolene lowered her chin. "I was just about to head
inside."

"Have you learned any details about the bank robbery?"
Kelli asked.

"From what I'm hearing, the bank heist involved four
armed and masked unsubs—and one fatality."

"Oh, no." Kelli's brow creased. It was always the last thing
one wanted to hear, even if it was something that was never
far from her thoughts where it concerned armed robberies.
The idea of a life being lost during the course of this crime,
though, saddened her, to say the least.

"Seems like the Hemton County Bandit Quartet has struck
this bank again," Jolene muttered. "Has all the earmarks of
it."

Kelli was inclined to agree, but said, "Let's see what they
have to say inside."

She nodded. "Yeah."

In the bank, Kelli quickly sized up the situation, took a look at the deceased, which truly unnerved her, and spoke with the manager, Julian Souza, about the robbery. As expected, he was torn up about what happened to his bank teller—and hoped that the culprits were brought to justice.

Kelli wanted the same as she phoned this in, before calling Sheldon and briefing him about the latest bank robbery in Leyton Falls. "Hey," she said evenly when he came on the line.

"Back at you," he said in a calm voice. "What's happening?"

"Bad news, I'm afraid…" Kelli waited a beat and then laid out what she suspected had already been relayed to him. Beyond that, she found her mind wandering back to the van she had passed earlier—and couldn't help but think that the quartet of bank thieves could have been inside of it while distancing themselves from their deadly heist.

As far as she was concerned, the van needed to be located and anyone inside it brought in for questioning.

BY THE TIME Kelli had phoned him, Sheldon had already received the unsettling news about the second robbery at the Bradley Bank in less than a month—with the unsubs matching the descriptions of the Hemton County Bandit Quartet. Only this time, the daytime heist had come with tragic results. A bank teller, apparently uncooperative, had been shot to death by the lone female robber after the teller activated the silent alarm. Unfortunately, by the time help arrived, the unsubs had managed to make a clean escape.

But definitely with blood on their hands, Sheldon thought angrily, as he entered the small bank with the investigation underway. He was missing Kelli, who was back on patrol and trying to track down a vehicle she believed the unsubs may have used for their getaway. He met up with Special

Agent Tabitha Hammill, a petite, blue-eyed, thirty-year-old with brown hair in a deconstructed bob, and a Leyton Falls PD Robbery Unit detective, Neil Ormond, who was in his forties and thickly built with gray hair in a short crew cut.

"The quartet decided once wasn't enough," Tabitha muttered, wrinkling her nose. "They had to rob this bank again."

"Only this time, they went too far," Ormond stated, his brow furrowed. "The victim, thirty-two-year-old Lori Winslow, likely never had a chance to react when she was struck by the bullet."

"Through no fault of her own," Sheldon said sternly, placing the blame for her death squarely where it belonged. The idea that she was murdered in cold blood at this time of year had struck a nerve in him. "The fact that the robbers chose to target this bank again has me concerned that they might look for a repeat performance at some of the other banks and credit unions the unsubs went after as well."

"Yeah, it occurred to me too," Tabitha remarked. "They're either getting desperate or just plain reckless. That makes them more dangerous than ever, especially after what happened this morning in this bank."

Ormond echoed this sentiment, when he said stridently, "The quartet seems to be targeting and retargeting soft marks, while taking full advantage of the holiday season where banks and their customers are more likely to have cash on hand, or other valuables where it concerns the customers— and using the busier street traffic at the time to make it easier for the unsubs to escape."

Sheldon couldn't agree more with the assessment and said soberly, "They crossed the line in committing murder—upping the ante for us all…" Not the least of which were the unsubs themselves, whom he believed had to know that once a homicide occurred during the robbery, there was no turning back or undoing the crime of violence. With more to lose and less incentive to stop perpetrating the robberies, they were more likely to intensify their actions.

Sheldon went to take a look at the victim, who was lying in a fetal position on the floor of her workstation, wearing a maroon pantsuit and dark gray booties. Her blond hair was stained from blood from the bullet wound to her forehead. His heart went out to the bank teller and anyone she left behind.

He turned to Ormond and asked, "Do we have the spent shell casing?" Or had the bank robbers been smart enough to have collected it?

"Yeah," the detective answered. "Our Crime Scene Unit found what we believe to be the shell casing from the gun used by the unsub to kill the victim. It's been bagged and will be processed, and hopefully it will lead us to the Hemton County Bandit Quartet."

"Good," Sheldon said, knowing that this could be an opening that they were looking for toward solving the case. He just wished it didn't have to come at the expense of Lori Winslow.

He went to have a talk with Tammy Yoshimura, the teller who was nearest to her colleague when she was shot.

Tammy was sitting on a swivel task chair near a walnut workstation when Sheldon walked into the office. She looked visibly shaken. Just as she did when he had taken her statement after the first robbery of Bradley Bank, in which, as he recalled, she had managed to stay hidden from view as the bank heist was taking place, but was able to witness just enough to add to what others present had experienced.

Sheldon met her eyes and said in an amicable voice, "I'm Special Agent Montgomery."

Tammy nodded with recognition. "I can't believe *they* did it again," she said adamantly.

"I wish I could say the same," he told her regretfully, "but sometimes bank robbers will hit the same bank, time and time again, for different reasons." *With perhaps the biggest incentive being the element of surprise, followed by a level of confidence in pulling it off successfully*, Sheldon told himself, as he sat in the chair next to hers.

She wrinkled her nose. "I feel so badly for Lori. There was so much to live for. Now they've taken that away from her."

"I'm sorry for that." Sheldon thought about Kelli losing her husband so unexpectedly. While there was no comparing the death of a spouse to that of a coworker, the pain Tammy felt was evident. "You were nearest to her when it happened. Can you tell me about it?"

Tammy sucked in a deep breath and recounted the moment that Lori had been confronted by the bank robber and chose to defy her—only to pay the ultimate price when being shot at point-blank range. "I—I couldn't believe that the robber just shot her in the face like it was no big deal," she stammered.

"And you think the shooter was a female?" he said, needing to hear this from her.

"Yes." Tammy wiped her nose with a tissue. "Though she was wearing a ski mask and baggy dark clothing like the last time, I could tell from her physical makeup. If that wasn't enough, I heard her voice this time—and it was definitely a female's voice—when she was threatening Lori…before what came afterward…"

Sheldon took note of that, while having no reason to believe otherwise, given that it corresponded with other indicators and witnesses that this was the same quartet of bank robbers that included one female and three male unsubs.

"I understand that one of the robbers demanded money from your window," Sheldon said to the pretty bank teller.

"Yes." Tammy gave a thoughtful nod. "He threatened me with having the same fate as Lori, if I didn't do as he said."

"Which was…?"

"To fill his bag with all the money in my drawer…and not

try anything…" She ran a hand tensely through her hair. "I did what he wanted."

And likely saved your life in the process, Sheldon thought, now that it was clear that the robbers were no longer making empty threats, if they ever were. "You did the right thing," he assured her.

Tammy hesitated, as if something was weighing on her mind, before she said, "There is one other thing."

Sheldon met her eyes. "I'm listening."

She paused. "The robber who came up to my window… his voice…" she said on a breath. "I could swear that I've heard it before—"

"Really?" Sheldon sat back. "Where?"

She wrung her hands. "At the Ninth Street Pub a few weeks ago," she told him. "This guy with a distinctive deep voice was hitting on me." Tammy sighed. "He sounded an awful lot like the bank robber who stuck a shotgun in my face. Honestly, I felt the same way when I heard his voice during the first robbery, but second-guessed myself…and didn't know what to do with that. But now, with it happening again…well, I just thought you needed to hear this."

Seriously? Sheldon mused. His first instincts were to consider her words with a grain of salt, believing it to be a stretch in connecting the masked bank robber's voice to that of a man she met at a bar. Where she had likely been drinking, further calling her interpretation into question.

But still. Sheldon had to take every possible lead in earnest. Especially when the bank robbers still remained at large. Moreover, the fact that Tammy never mentioned anything about the reward money spoke volumes as to her motivation in coming forward.

Sheldon gazed at her. "Did you happen to get the name of this man at the pub?"

"Wish I had." Tammy fidgeted. "He never volunteered

it. Guess I never gave him the chance to do so, since I just wasn't feeling it with him."

Sometimes you do, sometimes you don't feel the vibes, Sheldon told himself. He was definitely feeling it himself, when it came to Kelli and making a connection.

"Can you describe the man from the pub?" he asked.

"I think so." Tammy contemplated that. "He was white, tall and handsome, I'd guess in his thirties and in good shape," she said thoughtfully. "His long, brownish hair was in a top knot updo, and I think his eyes were grayish brown."

"Hmm." Sheldon made a mental note. He supposed that this description could correspond to the height and body shape of one or more of the bank robbers. It was still a long shot that the two men were one and the same. But a possibility, nonetheless. "Would you recognize him if you saw the man from the bar again?"

"Yes, I think so," she answered. "I actually went to the bar to try and find him, but struck out."

"Probably best that you did," Sheldon said. "If this guy was someone who robbed your bank, he might have gotten suspicious, had you suddenly shown an interest in him."

"I wouldn't have," Tammy said steadfastly. "He's definitely not my type."

"All right." Sheldon stood. "We'll look into it." They would get a sketch artist over there, for starters. Then see if this potential suspect could be tracked down at the Ninth Street Pub. And, if so, they might find those he might be associated with, who could also be spending time clubbing with him when they were not robbing banks.

Members of the Hemton County Coroner's Office arrived to collect the body. This included Dr. Johnnie McIntosh, a fortysomething forensic pathologist, who was African American, tall and lean with a shaved head.

Furrowing his brow after an initial glance at the decedent, McIntosh muttered, "Sometimes, I hate this job."

"Tell me about it," Sheldon said in a commiserating tone after making his way back to the dead woman. Unfortunately, bad things were part of what they both had to experience with their professions, like it or not. He knew that McIntosh would go about his duties and perform an autopsy on the victim to confirm what had been established through eye-witnesses. Sadly, Sheldon was all but certain as to what to expect. The cause of Lori Winslow's death would be a fatal gunshot to her head, with the manner of death being murder as committed by a firearm.

Chapter Twelve

Sheldon spent the night at Kelli's place. He was beginning to feel as comfortable there as he was at his condominium. Something told him it had a lot to do with the woman he was lying next to in bed, cuddled comfortably in his arms while asleep. Or maybe it had everything to do with that.

Whatever the case, he only knew that having her in his life had given it a whole new meaning, and Sheldon was excited to see where things went from there. *I'm definitely up for going on a journey with Kelli that can allow us to bring out the best in each other*, he told himself.

At the moment, though, there was still the matter of the string of bank heists that had Sheldon feeling both frustrated and determined as ever to solve, one way or the other. With the Hemton County Bandit Quartet's crimes having escalated to murder, it was apparent that any possibilities of drawing a line not to be crossed in their armed robberies had gone out the window. Meaning that they were now more likely than not to settle any resistance to their crimes violently—for as long as the foursome remained on the loose.

When morning came, Sheldon had managed to get a little sleep, in spite of his mind being preoccupied on different fronts. He saw that Kelli was no longer in bed and found her in the kitchen after he had put his clothes on.

She flashed him a bright smile. "There you are."

"Here I am," he said with a soft grin, while noting she was wearing riding clothes.

"I made breakfast—French toast and crispy bacon, with orange juice and coffee."

"Sounds great." Sheldon sat on a stool at the breakfast bar. "Sleep well?" he asked, and sipped orange juice. He assumed Samantha was still in bed, with or without Chase, or had gone to work—with her bank having been spared thus far the robberies hitting the county. Knock on wood.

Kelli ran a hand through her hair. "Yes, I did, actually. That is, once you allowed me to." She blushed. "Or maybe it was the other way around?"

He laughed. "Both work for me." *Neither of us can help it if we find it hard to keep our hands off each other*, he told himself salaciously, while slicing off a chunk of French toast, coated with warm maple syrup.

"Thought it might." Kelli chuckled and sat beside him, then grabbed a slice of bacon.

The conversation became more serious as they spoke about the ongoing bank robbery investigations, including the latest to rock Leyton Falls. To Sheldon, the tragic death of the bank teller would only drive them harder to stop the quartet in their tracks. It was not a matter of if, but when. While that would do nothing to bring back Lori Winslow, it might make her rest a little easier, knowing that those responsible for her death had been taken into custody.

To that end, it was Sheldon's hope that Kelli's belief that a white van she passed by could have been used by the Hemton County Bandit Quartet might eventually yield some fruit in the search for the unsubs.

AFTER DRAGGING SAMANTHA out of bed and watching as she had breakfast, Kelli talked her into taking the day off and going horseback riding with her. Besides feeling a need to unwind in the midst of the tragic death of someone in Samantha's profession, Kelli found herself wanting to keep her sister from being in a similar situation—in spite of a greater security setup at her bank than some others.

They rode their horses across the meadow, which was blanketed by a light snow that had fallen overnight. Below her cowgirl hat, Kelli glanced at her sister, cute with her own similar hat on, and said thoughtfully, "You do know that you're welcome to stay with me for as long as you like, right?"

Samantha smiled. "Thanks," she told her. "I love it here and certainly love riding Fletcher. But you need your own space—especially with Sheldon in the picture—and I'll need my own. Eventually."

Kelli smiled. "Fair enough."

"Besides, I think we could both use a little more privacy, don't you?"

Kelli flushed, conjuring up images of intimacy with Sheldon. "I suppose you're right about that," she admitted, even if feeling there was more than enough space inside the house for them to coexist in their respective relationships.

"Thought that was something you could relate to," Samantha quipped with a laugh.

Kelli pivoted things back to her. "So, where does Chase fit into your future space?"

Her sister paused, then responded, "He may fit in nicely. We've started to talk about some possibilities, such as living together or relocation. Right now, we just want to get through the holidays and see which way the wind—or maybe in this instance, the snow—blows."

Kelli laughed. "Good way to put it." She had faith that Samantha would do what was in her best interests, even if this hadn't always been the case.

"Apart from that," she said thoughtfully, "I may even check out some other employment opportunities."

"Oh?" Kelli turned to her. "Didn't know you were thinking about changing careers."

"I wasn't." Samantha took a breath. "But since banking isn't exactly the safest occupation these days—at least not in Leyton Falls—it seems like a smart idea to explore my options."

"I couldn't agree more," Kelli had to concur, considering the dangerous workplace environment her sister found herself in—over and beyond the general risks of working in the banking industry. "You've got my full support in whatever direction you choose to go in."

"I feel the same way about you," Samantha said, surprising Kelli. "I'm sure that you're in your element working for the Leyton Falls Police Department—and studied for the opportunity. But honestly, I do worry about your safety too, in having to deal with crime and unpredictable people."

"Good point." Kelli favored her with an earnest look. "I'll be fine," she said, seeking to reassure her. "I take extra precautions in every move I make with the department—and have capable coworkers who have my back."

"Nice to know."

Samantha had a catch to her tone, which suggested to Kelli that her sister wasn't altogether convinced that she too shouldn't still consider other options. This prompted her to admit, "I have been thinking about joining the Colorado Bureau of Investigation."

"Really?"

"Yeah. It's actually something that's been on my mind for a while now," Kelli confessed. "It would be a step up the law enforcement ladder—and arguably be less hazardous from day to day. Sheldon has even volunteered to put in a good word for me with a contact he has with the CBI."

"Cool." Samantha's eyes lit up. "Go for it."

"I just might." Kelli grinned at her, while contemplating the possibilities. "Right now, I was thinking that maybe we could do some last-minute Christmas shopping this afternoon. Maybe get a gift or two for the new men in our lives, and anything else we wanted to give each other."

"Sounds like a great idea." Samantha tilted her face beneath the cowgirl hat. "Count me in."

"Consider yourself counted," Kelli said with a chuckle. "Now, I'll race you back to the barn."

"You're on," her sister agreed, as the two got their horses to cooperate in the challenge.

AT THE TASK force meeting that afternoon, Sheldon briefed those present on the latest news on the Hemton County Bandit Quartet case. "We have our first homicide directly attributed to this group of bank robbers," he remarked with regret. "It was inevitable that the armed bank heists, brazen and threatening as they were, would escalate to murder." Using the stylus pen, Sheldon brought up an image of the Bradley Bank on the large touch screen monitor, and said, "Yesterday morning, just after ten, this Leyton Falls bank was hit for the second time in less than a month." He played video footage from the bank security camera, capturing the bank robbers entering the bank and spreading out accordingly. "The four armed unsubs, wearing ski masks, appear to be three males and one female—fitting the characteristics and modus operandi of the Hemton County Bandit Quartet, which, as you know, is responsible for a string of robberies across the county."

Sheldon sucked in a breath and continued. "Sadly, a thirty-two-year-old teller, Lori Winslow, was killed during the robbery." He homed in on a still shot of the armed female unsub. "The shooter is believed to be this robber...who shot Ms.

Winslow at point-blank range, killing her instantly, according to the autopsy report from the Hemton County Coroner's Office. The victim was killed with a bullet from the Taurus G2 9mm Luger handgun that the female unsub was holding, as has been the case in each of the eight bank heists attributed to the quartet. We were able to recover the spent shell casing, bullet fragments and the bullet itself from the victim's head, and send them to the crime lab. The forensic examination of these found that the distinct markings, lands and grooves, were a match and makes it all but a certainty that they came from that same Taurus G2 9mm pistol."

Sheldon waited a beat, then said tensely, "Equally disturbing is that, according to the Denver Crime Gun Intelligence Center—" which was established by the Bureau of Alcohol, Tobacco, Firearms and Explosives "—and supported with findings from the National Integrated Ballistic Information Network, the shell casing was matched to spent shell casings found at two other crime scenes in the Denver area from earlier in the year. One of these resulted in a homicide, with the victim being a sixty-eight-year-old man, during a home invasion. As such, the same weapon was used in the commission of these crimes, with the shooter likely being either the female unsub or one of her three cohort bank robbers.

"Or, in other words," Sheldon stressed, "the Hemton County Bandit Quartet has given us more reasons to want to bring them in. Particularly with an increase in their aggression during the bank heists—meaning that they have no qualms in taking out anyone who dares to get in their way."

Sheldon put on the display a forensic sketch of a male. "A person of interest has emerged," he said, and spoke of Tammy Yoshimura's physical description of a deep-voiced man she encountered at a bar, who may be the masked unsub that spoke to her while robbing the bank. "We're trying to track down this person and see if he is, in fact, the apparent leader of the robbery quartet."

Sheldon then showed an image of a white passenger van that was similar to one Kelli thought might be the bandits' getaway vehicle. They would work to narrow down any such vans that fit the bill, who they belonged to, and go from there.

Special Agent in Charge Karen Muñoz offered a few comments on the investigation and an increase in resources, including upping the reward money to as much as $10,000 for information that resulted in the arrest and conviction of one or more of the robbers, to help track down the culprits and solve their crimes. As far as Sheldon was concerned, any and all assistance was more than welcome if it helped them achieve their objectives. Especially since he had a bad feeling that the Hemton County Bandit Quartet may have even more fiendish schemes up their sleeves.

THE HAILEY SPRINGS MALL on Dexferd Avenue was Leyton Falls' biggest enclosed shopping center, and crowded with holiday shoppers, as Kelli and Samantha made their way from store to store on the Christmas decorated second level.

Both were holding bags with gifts, as Kelli commented with laughter, "Looks like we're all going to have a Merry Christmas!"

"Yeah, definitely." Samantha giggled. "And a Happy New Year seems likely too."

"I agree." Kelli wondered what was in store for her once January rolled around, and beyond. The prospects excited her, even if she was slightly unnerved by the unknown aspects of navigating a new relationship as a widow. But, as of now, she and Sheldon appeared to be perfectly in tune with one another and were committed to seeing just how far down the road they could take this.

"I can't wait to see who got what—and from whom," Samantha told her.

"Same here." Kelli grinned, knowing that she'd purchased a lovely red cashmere cardigan for her sister, sure she would love it. Sheldon was a bit harder to pick out something for, not yet having a firm handle on the small things that he might like. But Kelli was confident that she had picked out a nice gift that would work for him. *Of course, there were always return and replace policies should that not turn out to be the case*, she told herself.

Suddenly Kelli's train of thought was disrupted when she heard Samantha's frightened whisper, "Umm… Kelli, I think a robbery's happening in that jewelry store."

Following Samantha's wide gaze, Kelli shifted her eyes toward Bellwood Jewelers, which was in a corner of the mall, right next to a fashion boutique. She could see that there were two white males inside, and they were wearing surgical masks and hoodies. One was pointing a gun at a light haired, thin female employee and a large gray-haired male worker, both standing behind a counter. The other suspect was removing jewelry quickly from cases and loading the items into a dark-colored backpack.

"What are we going to do?" Samantha's voice shook.

Kelli's first instinct was to confront the suspects. But since she didn't have her Smith & Wesson 9mm handgun while off duty, she didn't think that would be a very good idea. More than that, she wasn't about to make any move that would endanger the employees inside the jewelry store. Or Samantha, for that matter.

After managing to hold some bags beneath her arm and others with one hand, Kelli grabbed her sister's wrist and ushered her toward a designer shoe shop several stores away, and said sternly to Samantha, "You're going to go inside there and shelter-in-place, along with anyone else present!"

"What about you?" Samantha demanded.

"I'm going to call this in, alert others to get out of the area or shelter-in-place and keep my eyes on what's happening during the robbery," Kelli answered. "But I need to know you'll be safe in the meantime. Now go!"

"Okay." Her sister swallowed thickly. "Please be careful."

"I will," Kelli promised, and then said, "And take these with you." She handed off her bags and watched as her sister successfully juggled them with her own bags, then ran toward and inside the shoe store.

Satisfied that she was out of harm's way, Kelli got on her cell phone and reported that an armed robbery was in progress, gave the location and requested backup. She peered inside the jewelry store long enough to see that both robbers were now busy loading items into the bag, while the two employees stood there, offering no resistance.

Wise move, Kelli told herself. Even then, she knew that was no guarantee that the suspects wouldn't still shoot them or otherwise inflict bodily harm. *I have to try to prevent that*, she thought.

But first, she needed to warn those passing by and in nearby stores, to avert a potential bloodbath. She did this swiftly and then retrained her focus on the jewelry store. How should she play this?

Out of the corner of her eye, Kelli spotted movement heading toward her. She whipped her eyes in that direction, and they landed squarely on the firm gaze of Sheldon.

With somewhat of a start, she said, "Hey." Then asked, "What are you doing here?"

"Same thing as you, I suspect." He glanced at her intuitively. "I knew you had taken the day off, so I thought it might be a nice time to do a little shopping on my own for Christmas—then swing over to your house and put something under the tree."

"I see." Kelli smiled and noted that he was holding a single bag. She was curious as to what was inside. But now was not the time to ask. "You showed up at just the right time..." she had to admit, her heart skipping a beat.

Sheldon locked gazes with her and asked, as if sensing something was wrong, "What is it?"

"Not it—but *them*." She shifted her focus to the jewelry store, where the armed robbers were preoccupied with bagging their stolen items. But still remained a threat to the employees, who were still standing there, no doubt on pins and needles. "I'd say we have ourselves a big problem, Sheldon..."

Chapter Thirteen

"Mind holding this for now?" Sheldon asked Kelli, sticking his bag into her arms.

"Sure," she told him, her voice tense.

"No peeking," he warned her lightheartedly, knowing he had her Christmas gift inside the bag.

"Okay." Kelli smiled softly. "Promise."

Sheldon turned his attention back to the Bellwood Jewelers store, where a brazen robbery was underway. Assessing the situation, he saw that the robbers were wearing surgical masks and pullover hoodies. They seemed to be taking their sweet time in stuffing jewelry into a backpack. At least one of the suspects was armed with a handgun. He had to assume that the other robber carried a firearm too.

Sheldon felt it was good fortune that he still had his Glock 19 9mm duty pistol in a hip holster beneath his quilted jacket. He could see that there were two employees inside the jewelry store, standing behind the counter. Neither one appeared to be hurt and were clearly cooperating with the perpetrators. Given that their faces were partially obscured with the masks, Sheldon decided that they were likely not concerned about their identities being exposed, which actually worked in favor of the employees' health and well-being, so long as they did not resist the robbery.

"What are you thinking?" Kelli asked him anxiously. "Should I put on my hostage negotiator shoes to at least keep the robbers distracted?"

"That may not be necessary in this instance," he told her. "Probably best to hang tight and let them come out."

"All right."

Sheldon looked at her. "I assume you've already phoned this in?"

Kelli nodded. "Help should arrive at any moment now."

Maybe one moment too late, he thought, but said, "Okay."

She asked, "What's next?"

"We wait," he told her. "Unless conditions warrant a change of plans."

Just as Sheldon pondered a desire to get Kelli to safety, knowing she was off duty and unarmed, he watched as the jewelry store bandits emerged into the mall and headed toward the nearest exit.

"Why don't you check on the employees and make sure they're all right," he suggested to Kelli. "I'll go after the suspects."

"Okay." She touched his arm. "Be careful."

"Count on that." He flashed her a tender smile. *I can't allow our magical journey thus far to be threatened by these offenders*, Sheldon thought with determination, as he walked away from her, before losing sight of the men.

Sheldon kept his distance as he trailed the robbers past unsuspecting shoppers and out the door. Only then did Sheldon unholster his Glock. Following the men toward the parking lot, he spotted the police car crossing it. The officers inside seemed to instinctively find themselves suspicious of the suspects as they approached a gray Chrysler Pacifica minivan.

Before the officers could get out of their vehicle and the suspects could get inside their own, Sheldon felt that he needed to make his move. As such, with his pistol aimed at them, he confronted the two men and barked out, "FBI. Put your hands up!"

In an instant, one of the men turned around and whipped out what looked to be a SIG Sauer P320 9mm pistol, and pointed it at him. Sheldon never gave the robber a chance to fire, as he shot the gun right out of the perp's hand, quite literally.

Before the suspect or his partner in the jewelry theft could react, the two tall and muscular male officers had exited their squad car, drew their own weapons and demanded that the suspects surrender. Or else.

Weighing their options, both thieves wisely gave themselves up and were cuffed and placed under arrest, with the officers confiscating the backpack containing the stolen merchandise.

After putting his gun back inside its holster, Sheldon told the officers what he knew and witnessed, before allowing them to take over the investigation.

Going back inside the mall, where other officers had emerged and were questioning the jewelry store employees and securing the crime scene, Sheldon rejoined Kelli, who was with Samantha. He acknowledged her, then said, "We got them." He indicated that officers had taken the suspects into custody.

"That's good to hear," Kelli said, showing her teeth. "Even better is that, apart from being a bit shaken up, the employees are fine." She drew a breath, glancing at Samantha. "So are we."

"Thankfully," Samantha added, "frightening as it was."

"Great." He grinned at them both. "I'll take that back now," he said to Kelli, and grabbed his bag from her, assuming that she had kept her word and didn't satisfy her curiosity till Christmas Day. As it was, he considered the gift only a down payment to what he hoped would be showering Kelli with many gifts for years to come. "So, if it's all right with you two, I'll tag along, if you have more shopping to do."

"I think we're set," Kelli said, gazing up at him.

"Yeah," Samantha told him, switching bags from one hand to the other. "Let's get these gifts home, wrapped and put under the tree."

Sheldon grinned in agreement. "I'll walk you to your car."

ON THE MORNING of Christmas Eve, Kelli was called into service as a hostage negotiator after a disgruntled former employee took hostages at the office building where he had previously worked in the Central Business District. The suspect claimed that he had a bomb and was threatening to detonate it at any time.

"Not the best news a day before Christmas," Kelli moaned as she drove her patrol car toward the location on Granger Boulevard, after being briefed on the crisis.

Sheldon, who had spent the night and activated the FBI for the mission, sat alongside her. "You're right, it isn't," he told her. "Unfortunately, ill-timed as it is, these things can happen at any point in the year. We just have to deal with it—and hopefully get a good outcome when things come to a head."

"I suppose," she acquiesced, knowing that crime almost never took a day off. Even the holiday season was fair game to those who chose to violate the law. All they could do was react in the best way possible and hopefully save lives in the course of action.

They arrived at the Leyton Falls Center Plaza, a ten-story building that had offices from a variety of companies. On hand in the first-floor command center were Nolan Valentine, Trent Garcia and members from the Leyton Falls Bomb Squad and SWAT unit, along with the FBI's Hostage Rescue Team and special agent bomb technicians.

Filling them in on the details, Nolan said in an even voice,

"The suspect has been identified as Oscar Sewell, a forty-nine-year-old former information systems manager for an IT firm called Noctinn Technologies. He was fired last month after being accused of stealing sensitive data, for which he's currently under federal investigation."

Trent eyed Kelli and said, "Sewell's holding ten or more hostages, including the company's supervisor, in their eighth-floor office. Everyone else has been evacuated from the building. The suspect is on edge, by all accounts, and we need to get him to release the hostages unharmed. Can you make it happen?" he asked her point-blank.

There's that serious pressure of the job again, Kelli told herself humorlessly. "All I can do is try," she answered honestly, and glanced at Sheldon. "Do we know if the suspect has a real bomb? Or any other weapons?"

"Until proven otherwise, we can only take a bomb threat at face value," Sheldon said matter-of-factly. "If it is a fake, the suspect more than likely has a real weapon or more to back up the threat."

Officer Kraig Pennington of the Bomb Squad, who was in his thirties, tall and sturdy, with brown hair in a flat top, stepped over to them and said in earnest, "We're prepared to deal with any hazardous devices we come across. If real, hopefully we'll be able to disarm them before they detonate."

Kelli nodded to that effect, and said coolly, "Let's see if this can end on a high note."

Sheldon moved up to her ear and whispered, just to stay on the same wavelength, "If at any time you start to feel otherwise—and there seems to be no safe way out of this jam for the hostages—let us take it from there and we'll need to go in there and get them out…one way or another."

She offered him a soft smile, knowing he had her best interests—and theirs as a couple that seemed to be going places—at heart. "Will do," she promised, before gearing herself up to deal with the disgruntled hostage taker head-on.

SHELDON WATCHED INTENTLY as Kelli got on the cell phone and put forth her best efforts to reason with Oscar Sewell, described as a wiry thin man with a brunette quiff hairstyle and wearing round eyeglasses. His claim of having a bomb in a brown bag had yet to be established conclusively, but was being taken very seriously, given the stakes. As she went back and forth with the suspect, in an intense give and take, Kelli was finally able to talk him into releasing all but one of the hostages, who were whisked away by the Bureau's HRT and out of harm's way.

The remaining hostage, Walton Levinger, forty-one, was the supervisor at Noctinn Technologies, and apparently the person responsible for Sewell's firing and being under criminal investigation. Sewell was said to be holding a fixed blade hunting knife to the throat of Levinger, threatening to kill him and showing no signs of backing down.

When the situation became dire and it seemed as though the hostage's life was in serious jeopardy if action were not taken, the order was given to take out the perp. Sheldon, wearing protective gear, had gone up to the eighth floor, where he observed as the SWAT sniper used an Accuracy International AT308 rifle to fire a single .308-caliber bullet into Oscar Sewell's head, killing him. The knife fell from his hand as Sewell went down like a lead balloon.

Levinger, who was short and bald-headed with a sparrow goatee, ran quickly away from his assailant and out of the office, where he was taken to safety.

Only then was an explosives detection canine sent inside to examine the bag purported to contain the bomb. With the K-9 appearing to indicate it was a hoax bomb, an FBI special agent bomb technician was sent in to verify that.

It was quickly determined that the item in the bag was a facsimile device—or one that was constructed to look like a real explosive device.

Special Agent Stan Gonzaga, a fifty-one-year-old veteran with the Bureau and built like a brick wall with a shaved bald head, left the office as the Crime Scene Unit took over. He regarded Sheldon and remarked to him, "The perp pulled the wool over our eyes with the mock bomb."

"Yeah, looks like suicide by cop," Sheldon told him, using the term that refers to assisted suicide, where a suicidal person provokes a lethal response by law enforcement as a result of criminal behavior that was life threatening to them or others.

Gonzaga scratched his pate. "At least he wasn't able to take anyone else down with him."

"There is that." Sheldon credited Kelli to a large extent for saving lives. "Another crisis averted."

"True," the special agent concurred.

Back on the first floor, Sheldon caught up with Kelli, who looked distraught over being unable to get Sewell to lay down his weapon and surrender. "You can't save them all—no matter how hard you try."

"I know." She nodded. "If there had only been more time."

"It was Sewell who made the decision to threaten to cut the throat of the supervisor," Sheldon pointed out. "It was clear that he was determined to finish what he started on his own terms, one way or another."

"You're right." Kelli stuck her chin out. "I only wish he had chosen mental health services instead."

"Me too," Sheldon said, though knowing that was all too often the last path taken by distraught and vengeful-minded individuals. "But at least, thanks to you, all the hostages will get to spend Christmas or whatever with their loved ones."

"True." Kelli flashed him a smile. "And I get to spend it with you."

He grinned. "Absolutely." *If I have my way, it will be the first of many such Christmas holidays we get to spend together*, Sheldon told himself. But first, there was enjoying the merry season at hand.

AFTER DOING SOME paperwork at the field office that afternoon, Sheldon went home to his condo. It now felt empty without Kelli's warm presence. But he didn't want to crowd her or take away from her Christmas Eve plans to hang out with Samantha. If their relationship continued to progress, there would be plenty of time for him to be with Kelli and vice versa.

Sheldon went inside the kitchen and made himself a romaine salad, topping it with vinaigrette dressing, to go with canned white bean chili and beer. He sat at the island and had his dinner.

Afterward, he grabbed his laptop and rang his father and stepmother for a video chat. Momentarily, both appeared on the screen. Foster Montgomery reminded Sheldon of an older version of himself, with deep blue-gray eyes. He had a full head of gray hair in a façon cut and a salt-and-pepper Olde English beard and was in good enough shape to still work for the Bureau had he wanted to.

His stepmother, Julia Montgomery, was ten years younger than his father, slim and attractive with platinum blond hair in a curled in and out cut and hazel eyes behind oval glasses.

Sheldon grinned at them and said a bit prematurely, "Hey, Merry Christmas."

"Back at you," his father said spiritedly.

Julia gave a big smile while touching her glasses. "Merry Christmas to you, too, Sheldon."

"Thanks." Sheldon couldn't help but think that she was a good woman, and he was happy to have her as his stepmother.

He imagined that she and Kelli would get along great. "How are things at the ranch?"

"Same old, same old," Foster told him. "We're doing our best tending to the horses and each other."

Sheldon laughed. "Maybe it's the horses that are tending to you instead."

"Yeah, maybe," his father said, cracking a grin.

"It would have been great to have you visit for Christmas," Julia told him.

"I know," Sheldon agreed, feeling guilty that he didn't visit as often as he would like. "Maybe next year."

"We'd love it," she insisted.

Foster was more subdued when he said, "You're always welcome, when time permits."

"The same is true in reverse," Sheldon said, knowing that they rarely seemed to leave their ranch these days. Not that he could blame them, as it was beautiful country there in South Dakota.

"We'll get there again one of these days," his father told him, though not too convincingly.

"Promise," Julia said, sounding more positive about it.

"Okay." Sheldon paused. "There's a new woman in my life," he told them proudly.

Julia burst into a smile. "Oh, really?"

"Yeah." He looked at them thoughtfully. "She's a hostage negotiator."

"That so?" Foster said, and Sheldon could tell that this info had made a favorable impression on him. "We'd love to meet her."

"You will," Sheldon promised, sensing that his father was being on the level in wanting to become a bigger part of his life these days. His romantic involvement with Kelli was a big step forward for all parties concerned. Even better was if he could give his dad and stepmom grandchildren to dote over and have another place to get comfortable with and ride horses.

Foster gave a sideways grin. "Good."

Sheldon updated him on his latest investigations, specifically the Hemton County Bandit Quartet and the challenges and frustrations in trying to solve the bank robbing spree. "We're at it every day," he pointed out, "taking on every lead that presents itself. But still…"

Foster narrowed his gaze. "You've obviously got your hands full there. That's how it goes sometimes. The Bureau, though, is made for these types of investigations. I have the utmost faith in your team that you'll get the breakthrough you need—and soon—to nail the unsubs and move on to other cases."

"Thanks, Dad." Sheldon grinned at him, appreciating the support more than he could possibly express, given the ups and downs of their relationship over the years. *I won't let you down*, he told himself.

Beyond that, as part of the Rocky Mountain Money Grab Task Force, Sheldon was wholly committed to putting out of business any and all perpetrators of bank robberies under his watch. However long it took and whichever direction they needed to go in.

Chapter Fourteen

On Christmas morning, Kelli opened the front door to find Sheldon standing there. A cute little grin played on his lips as he said to her, "Merry Christmas."

With her hair hanging loose, she beamed. "Merry Christmas to you, too."

He whipped something out from behind him and handed it to her. "This is for you."

It was a single red rose, encased in a glass cloche for preservation. An even bigger smile formed on Kelli's face. "It's lovely," she said. "Thank you, Sheldon."

"You're welcome." He gazed at her. "Seemed like a nice way to break in the holiday."

"I couldn't agree more." She welcomed him inside, where Samantha and Chase were standing by the Christmas tree, holding mugs of hot chocolate.

"Hey, everyone," Sheldon said cheerfully. "Merry Christmas."

"Same to you," Chase said, raising his mug in a toast.

Samantha exclaimed, "Merry Christmas, Sheldon!"

Kelli lifted the rose and said, "Look what I got." As they marveled over it, she poured some eggnog into two glasses and handed one to Sheldon.

Tasting it, he said, "Mmm…delicious."

"There's much more where that came from," Kelli told him, sipping her own eggnog. She had already put into motion a tantalizing Christmas Day early dinner that included stuffed standing rib roast, baked sweet potatoes, creamed spinach and red velvet cake.

He showed his teeth. "I can hardly wait."

She laughed. "I'm afraid you'll have to. First things first. Time to open the gifts,"

"Let's do it." He spoke with eagerness, taking her hand and walking her toward the tree.

Kelli hoped he liked the red button-down gingham Oxford shirt she got him for Christmas, believing it to be a perfect fit. Or at least as much as she adored the gift that he'd given her, having resisted the temptation to take a look at the gorgeous Italian box chain sterling silver necklace in its little black box beforehand.

"I love it!" Sheldon declared, holding the shirt up to his body like a dashing model.

Kelli's eyes lit up. "I'm sure it will love you back once you wear it."

He chuckled. "No doubt about it."

After the gifts were opened to everyone's satisfaction, they took the horses out for a ride across the snow-covered grass. As Kelli expected, it went without a hitch as she rode comfortably alongside Sheldon, with Samantha and Chase off on their own.

During a brief silence, Kelli considered the hostage situation from the day before that had ended with the death of the hostage taker. She wished she had been able to elicit his surrender, but the man's intentions were obviously elsewhere. The fact that she had been able to secure the release of most of the hostages—with the last one managing to survive as well—was something for Kelli to take pride in. She wouldn't allow that accomplishment to be diminished in the scheme of things.

"I told my dad and stepmom about you last night," Sheldon said, breaking into her reverie.

"Oh really?" Kelli faced him curiously, wondering how they felt about someone new in his life.

"Yes, and they can't wait for us all to get together."

"I feel the same way," she assured him, a smile lifting her cheeks.

Sheldon, who looked good in the brown wide brim Western cowboy hat that fit snugly on his head, said confidently, "So do I."

"Wonderful." In Kelli's mind, nothing was more important than a sense of family and belonging. She was starting to feel both with Sheldon and clearly the feeling was mutual. It made her that much more excited about what good fortunes might fall their way in the year ahead. And the years beyond that.

AFTER ENJOYING A nice ride on Abigail, the Colorado Ranger that Kelli owned, alongside her horse, Cora, Sheldon was happy to chill back at her house. With Samantha and Chase having gone to hang out with his brother, Preston, and his girlfriend, Danielle, they had the place to themselves.

Sheldon joined Kelli in putting some logs into her great room fireplace and lighting it, before they sat on the rustic barnwood sofa and sipped white wine, while listening to soft Christmas music. He didn't presume to believe he could ever fill the shoes of her late husband, but Sheldon was sure he could stand on his own two feet, in terms of being able to make Kelli happy.

"You know, being here with you—like this—on a holiday, no less, really agrees with me," he told her unabashedly. "Just thought I'd throw that out."

"It's nice to hear." Her smile was generous. "I feel the

same way, Sheldon," she said, and sipped her wine. "Having you to spend Christmas with is giving me the second chance I've so craved, but wasn't sure I would ever find with someone special again."

He couldn't help but blush in being thought of by her as special. While he might not have necessarily attached that label to himself, he would take it every minute of every day, coming from her.

"You're pretty special in your own right, Kelli," Sheldon told her sincerely, tasting his wine. "I think we've both been in the market for something that gave our lives more meaning. I think this is it."

She smiled again. "It just may be at that."

He took the moment at hand to lean over and kiss her, giving them both something to appreciate as the day began to wind down. When tomorrow came, they could both get back to the grind, which, for him, was still the bank robber quartet that persisted in keeping the Bureau engaged in a hide-and-seek, catch them if they could, kind of game. Only this one was for keeps. And only one side could come out on top.

That had to be the side of justice.

But for now, Sheldon was feeling good about being right where he was—with Kelli, who never failed to amaze him, given the qualities she embodied through and through.

On Friday at noon, the Hemton County Bandit Quartet drove their GMC Savana van slowly as they approached the armored truck at the Leyton Falls Bank on Raytenne Avenue. They observed as a slender, red-haired female guard with a short ponytail was loading money into the back of the truck. A husky and bald-headed African American male guard was standing watch dutifully, his Glock 22 .40-caliber S&W service pistol in a waistband holster.

After the foursome donned their ski masks, to go with

gloves and dark clothing, they geared themselves up for the bank heist. When the male in charge gave the order, they proceeded to exit the van in proficient fashion, while carrying two large water-resistant duffel bags and wielding an AR-15 rifle, a Lever Action X Model .410 shotgun, Colt Cobra .38 Special revolver, and a Taurus G2 9mm handgun.

Without commotion, they quickly approached the armored truck guards and demanded the money the truck was carrying.

As the male guard immediately went for his firearm, before he could fire off a shot, the leader of the bandits promptly aimed the shotgun at him and shot the guard at point-blank range, rendering him helpless as his legs gave out from beneath him before he lost consciousness.

The shooter barked at him cheekily, "Bad move!" He glared at the female guard and said, "Unless you want to get the same treatment, I suggest you cooperate."

"I'd do as he says, if I were you," the lone female robber warned in earnest, pointing her handgun at the woman before the compliant guard was relieved of her firearm and ordered to lay face down in the parking lot.

While the female bandit kept the gun on her, the other bandits quickly loaded the cash into the bags, filling them to the brim before preparing to leave.

It was only then that one of the male robbers took note of the slender and attractive blond-haired woman who happened upon them. Before she could retreat toward the bank, she was forced at gunpoint to accompany the quartet as an insurance policy, as they hopped back inside the van and made their getaway.

THE MOMENT SHE received the notice from dispatch that four armed assailants had robbed an armored truck at Leyton Falls Bank, shooting one of the guards in the process, and abducted at gunpoint a blond-haired female bank employee, Kelli's heart sank. Before she could even confirm that Samantha had been kidnapped—between the timing, when her sister liked to take afternoon walks during her lunch break and the fact that Kelli had been unable to reach Samantha by phone—her instincts went into overdrive, telling her all that she needed to know.

By the time she arrived on the scene, the hard truth had substantiated Kelli's worst fears. Samantha had been kidnapped in broad daylight by the so-called Hemton County Bandit Quartet, who had once again managed to escape capture.

"How could this happen?" Kelli cringed at the notion, as she was being comforted by Sheldon who—along with other FBI agents, detectives and crime scene investigators from the Leyton Falls PD—had gotten there ahead of her in pursuit of their duties.

"Appears as though it was entirely coincidental." His face looked weary. "Samantha just happened to be in the wrong place at the wrong time," he explained. "For whatever reason, in going against their MO, the robbers decided to take her with them. Maybe Samantha saw something she shouldn't have, and they panicked."

"What happens when the kidnappers have no further use for her?" Kelli asked with dread, while knowing the answer. She glanced at the dead guard, lying in a pool of his own blood while they waited for the arrival of personnel from the Hemton County Coroner's Office to remove his body. "Will Samantha end up like him?"

Sheldon squeezed Kelli's shoulders caringly and answered calmly, "Don't go there. We'll do everything in our power to get your sister back alive."

"With all due respect, your power has its limitations," she told him candidly. "The fact that they did this out in the open—" her gaze again shifted to the dead guard "—with evidently no qualms about doing so, means they're capable of doing all kinds of things before Sam can be rescued." Kelli tried not to even think of what her sister's abductors might inflict upon Samantha over and beyond ending her life.

Seeming to read her disturbing thoughts, Sheldon said, "As far as killing Samantha, the unsubs would have already done so, had they wanted to go down that road. Abducting her buys us—and them—time." He took a breath. "Speculating on anything beyond that will only drive you to distraction. Let's just hope for the best and not get ahead of ourselves."

Easy for you to say, as it's not your sister who is most definitely in harm's way, Kelli thought. But she kept this to herself, knowing that he was only trying to keep her grounded to the extent possible while the investigation to locate Samantha was underway.

"We've put out a BOLO alert for the white GMC Savana passenger van that the unsubs are believed to have used in both the abduction and escape, after killing the guard and robbing the armored truck," Sheldon said. "They couldn't have gotten far…"

But maybe just far enough to continue to elude the authorities, she told herself, frustrated as she realized that the unsubs' getaway vehicle was almost certainly the same one that had passed her during a previous bank heist and had been difficult to track down. "Hope not." Kelli remained skeptical that the kidnappers hadn't found a way to get past the dragnet yet again for whatever they had in mind in choosing to take her sister against her will. She thought of Chase and the need to inform him of the perilous situation. "I have to tell Chase what's happened," she told Sheldon anxiously.

Kelli noticed a strange look on his face, as he responded measuredly, "Yeah, about that… I'd like to talk to Chase."

She cocked a brow, while reading between the lines.

"Surely you don't think he had anything to do with the armored truck heist…or Sam's abduction."

Sheldon paused while pinching his nose, then answered ambiguously, "I certainly want to believe that Chase isn't in any way involved." He paused again. "But you know as well as I do, that every angle needs to be looked at, especially when someone such as Chase is relatively new in the picture and hasn't been thoroughly checked out and eliminated as a suspect, routine as that may be."

Much as she hated the thought that Chase would be involved in bank and armored truck robberies, to say nothing of kidnapping and murder, Kelli had to think as a police officer and not someone who desperately wanted to give her sister's boyfriend the benefit of the doubt.

In reality, though, Kelli knew precious little about the person whom Samantha was dating, aside from some very basic information. And even less about Chase's brother, Preston, which Kelli suspected went into Sheldon's thinking as a special agent, wanting to leave no stones unturned in the case.

Kelli took out her cell phone, eyed him and said earnestly, "I'll ask Chase to meet us at the police department." She wanted to make it clear that she intended to be present for any interrogation of him, in needing to hear what Chase had to say as much as Sheldon did.

He nodded. "Okay."

Kelli had Chase on her contact list, after Samantha volunteered to give her his number, just in case it was ever needed to get in touch with her.

I only wish it were as simple as that, Kelli told herself, ill at ease as she waited for him to pick up.

When he did, Chase said coolly, "Hey."

Swallowing, Kelli got right to the point. "Samantha was abducted outside the bank—"

"What?" His voice seemed appropriately shocked.

"An armored truck was robbed, and the robbers took her," Kelli said, while gazing at Sheldon, who was looking back intently. After Chase muttered an expletive, she told him straightforwardly, "I need you to come in...to see if Sam might have said anything that can provide any clues as to her state of mind or why she was taken."

Kelli wondered if Chase would be rattled as a guilty person. Or otherwise refuse to be questioned as someone with something to hide. But he responded smoothly without prelude, "No problem. Just tell me where to go."

After she disconnected, Kelli said to Sheldon thoughtfully, "He'll meet us there."

"All right." Sheldon drew a breath. "Let's go."

Chapter Fifteen

For any armored truck robbery, Sheldon had to consider that it could be an inside job, given the timing and other dynamics needed for pulling it off successfully. Indeed, in one such case that he investigated just last year, a Denver bank branch manager, heavily in debt, was found guilty of conspiring with the robbers in supplying them with critical info, resulting in the theft of more than two hundred grand.

Though such a scenario had yet to be established in the current armored truck heist investigation, the thieves had made off with around $350,000—a substantial increase in the amount taken from the Hemton County Bandit Quartet's previous bank robberies.

While Sheldon had no reason in particular to believe that Chase Pomeroy was actually involved in Samantha's abduction—not to mention the robbery and murder—he needed to be convinced otherwise. So too, Sheldon believed, did Kelli want to have peace of mind that her sister's boyfriend had not set her up to be kidnapped as a member of an armed quartet of bank robbers.

The fact that Chase fit the general characteristics of one of the culprits, behind the dark clothing, and happened to have a brother with a girlfriend who could also have been part of the team of bandits, was troublesome to Sheldon, to say the least.

As he sat in a trapezoidal backed, armless chair next to Kelli in the interrogation room, Sheldon peered at the suspect, who sat on the other side of a stainless-steel interview table.

After a moment or two of gauging him while in the hot seat, Sheldon said in an affable tone, "Thanks for coming in, Chase. As Kelli—Officer Burkett—explained, we're trying to locate Samantha Quinlan. Do you have any idea where she could be?"

Chase ran a hand across his mouth, then replied, "No, I don't. We were supposed to meet for lunch, but she never showed up." He checked himself with a frown. "Now I know why."

While contemplative, Sheldon never took his eyes off of him, before inquiring bluntly, "I have to ask, did you play any role in Samantha's abduction?"

"If so, you have to tell us now!" Kelli insisted, peering across the table.

"Absolutely not!" Chase's voice lifted an octave. "I would never have done anything to hurt Samantha. And I'm certainly not into robbing armored trucks…or banks."

Maybe so, maybe no, Sheldon told himself. He had already checked to see if he had a criminal record. Chase was clean. But not all criminals had a rap sheet. "Where were you meeting Ms. Quinlan for lunch?"

"Veralyn's Steak House on Maremore Street."

"And you can verify that?"

"Yeah," Chase insisted. "I sat at a table and the place was packed."

Sheldon could see that, as people loved to be out and about during the holiday season and, as such, his story could easily be checked out. He leaned forward and said coolly, "Let's talk about your brother. What's his name?"

"Preston… Preston Pomeroy." Chase made a face. "My brother has nothing to do with Sam's abduction."

Ignoring this assertion, Sheldon asked, "Has he ever been in trouble with the law?"

"Not that I'm aware of," Chase argued, his jaw tightening.

"What about his girlfriend—what's her name?" Kelli asked him intently.

"Danielle Hamili." Chase sighed. "Danielle's never committed a crime in her life." He spoke with conviction. "Her dad's a cop in Hawaii. She wouldn't do anything to dishonor him."

Sheldon glanced at Kelli, both having a healthy respect for anyone in law enforcement, if Chase's statement was true. "What's his name?"

"Sean Hamili," Chase responded matter-of-factly.

While making a note, Sheldon got back to the brother and his girlfriend, asking, "What do Preston and Danielle do for a living?" He couldn't help but think about the quartet of bank robbers that included a female who wasn't afraid to kill while stealing money to keep them going.

"My brother's a successful playwright," Chase answered succinctly. "Danielle's an actress. They both keep busy with theater productions locally and throughout the state. You can check it out."

"We will," Sheldon said. He gazed at Kelli and detected the relief on her face that neither Samantha's boyfriend nor his brother and girlfriend appeared to be involved in Sam's abduction.

Inclined to agree with this assessment, Sheldon gave Chase permission to leave. He rose to his feet and, favoring Kelli with a concerned expression, told her, "I want to get Samantha back as much as you do. Whatever I can do to help. Let me know."

Kelli nodded. "You've already been a big help," she said

sincerely. "But any prayers for getting Samantha back safely will always be appreciated."

"Count on that," he promised.

No sooner had Chase left, and Sheldon began pondering the next move, than word came that the van believed to be the robbers' getaway vehicle had been located.

KELLI RODE WITH Sheldon to the Beaubier Junkyard on Quein Street near Tenth Avenue. She was on edge as to what they might find, as eerie thoughts of Samantha's bullet-riddled corpse left behind with the van danced darkly inside Kelli's head. That was countered somewhat by the knowledge that Chase was not involved in her abduction or the deadly armored truck heist. Much less, the armed bank robberies attributed to the gang of four. *But right now, I'm still scared out of my mind for Sam's safety,* Kelli told herself, fidgeting.

As if to settle down her troubled thoughts, Sheldon told her soothingly, "Don't get bent out of shape prematurely. My guess is that, knowing the van was red-hot at the moment, the unsubs simply dumped it for something less noticeable."

"Even if true," she complained, "where does that leave my sister?"

"Not in a good place," he conceded, a catch to his voice, "but still alive. Right now, we have to operate on that premise and the belief that Samantha is being held as a bargaining chip, if needed—till proven to the contrary."

"All right." This did little to pacify her as Kelli squirmed in the passenger seat of his Ford Explorer SUV. But freaking out would do nothing to get her sister back alive and well. Instead, she needed to focus on being able to use her skills as a hostage negotiator, if need be, to secure Samantha's release from her captors.

When they arrived at the junkyard, Kelli could see the apparently abandoned white van, with members of the Crime

Scene Unit on hand to collect evidence. There was no sign of Samantha.

After leaving the van, Special Agent Joseph Eala greeted them and said sourly, "This is definitely the same GMC Savana passenger van that surveillance video picked up at the bank. According to the owner of the junkyard, Victor Dudoit, it was dumped here, without him being the wiser till later—with no one inside…"

While Kelli took some solace that her sister was not in the van, it was just as unnerving that she was still being held by her abductors.

Sheldon glanced at Kelli and back to Eala, before asking him, "What's the word on the van itself?"

"We ran the VIN with the National Crime Information Center and found out that the van had been listed as a stolen vehicle last December." Eala rubbed his nose. "As for the license plates, they too were stolen, but from a Nissan Pathfinder."

"Why am I not surprised?" Sheldon shook his head with dissatisfaction. "What about security video at the junkyard?"

Eala furrowed his brow. "Dudoit claims his security camera has been broken for a while, and he hasn't gotten around to having it repaired."

"Figures," Kelli muttered, staring at the van that Samantha was forced into.

Sheldon said, "We need to see if any surveillance systems nearby can give us anything on other vehicles that were in the area around the time the van had to have been discarded."

Eala nodded. "Already looking into that." He gazed at Kelli. "The CSU will go over the van with a fine-tooth comb in hopes of finding DNA, prints, or anything else that can identify your sister's kidnappers—and lead us to her and those responsible for the cold-blooded execution of the armored truck guard."

"All right." Kelli was sure that they would do their best to help the cause. She simply feared that it might not be enough to bring Samantha back safe and sound. Eyeing Sheldon, Kelli sensed that he was on the same wavelength, which made the coming hours or even days that much more taxing.

THAT EVENING, TAMMY YOSHIMURA sat on her usual bar stool at the Ninth Street Pub, sipping on a cosmopolitan cocktail. She had given up on ever laying eyes again on Mr. Deep Voice, who had failed at charming her another time she was there. She believed he was the same man who stuck a shotgun in her face and robbed her at her teller's window, while hiding his face behind a ski mask.

She had described the man from the pub to a sketch artist and was now leaving it to the authorities—including Special Agent Montgomery—to take the ball and run with it, in trying to catch him and the other members of his bank robbing gang.

Now they had struck again—and with more deadly consequences.

Tammy wrinkled her nose when thinking about the armored truck heist at the Leyton Falls Bank that left a guard dead, a bank teller abducted and the perpetrators still on the loose. She could only hope that the teller—Samantha Quinlan, whom Tammy had actually met once at a different bar and had enjoyed knowing that they had something in common as bank employees in town—could survive her ordeal.

After tasting the drink again, Tammy heard the familiar deep voice. She turned to her right and was given a start when she saw the handsome man who had tried to put the moves on her weeks ago. Only this time, he had a different look. His hair was now black and cut in medium-length layers with a side part.

He was talking in what sounded like a heated conversation to another white male in his thirties and of slender build, with a brown shag haircut with lighter highlights and a hipster goatee. If she were to put her imagination to good use, Tammy could well envision him wearing a ski mask and the dark clothing like the members of the Hemton County Bandit Quartet, though she had never heard him speak.

While the two men were preoccupied with each other, Tammy instinctively took out her cell phone and, with Mr. Deep Voice facing her, snapped a good picture of him. Before she could do the same of the other man, he turned and walked away.

Mr. Deep Voice suddenly approached her and stood in front of her, asking, in what sounded to Tammy like a tone of suspicion, "Have we met before?"

She froze. Did he recognize her from the bank? Trying to control her nerves, Tammy answered sardonically, "Aside from being the oldest pickup line around, you tell me. If I had to guess, I'd say no—sorry."

"Me too." He laughed. "You just never know."

"If we had met, I think I'd remember your name," she said, in going fishing for information. "But I don't, I'm afraid."

"It's Jack," he said simply. "What's yours?"

"Rosamund," she lied, borrowing a friend's first name.

"I like it." He flashed a crooked smile. Then his cell phone rang, and a frown formed on his face. "Have to get this."

"Not a problem," Tammy assured him as he walked away, while putting the phone to his ear. She took her own cell phone back out and looked at the picture she took of his face. It was good enough to send to Special Agent Montgomery. She took the business card he'd given her out of her handbag and sent the picture to him and a text that included the name Jack as deep voice and her belief that he was, indeed, the man who robbed her at the bank.

ON SATURDAY MORNING, with Samantha still missing, but believed by Sheldon to be alive, with her abductors hiding out or on the run—he took seriously the cell phone photo that was sent to him by Tammy Yoshimura last night of a deep-voiced man she saw at a pub, who went by the name Jack.

With Tammy being convinced that the voice was the same as the unsub who confronted her with a shotgun in the bank and demanded money, Sheldon was more than willing to give her the benefit of the doubt. Having brought his laptop with him while staying overnight at Kelli's as they worked together to try and locate her sister, he used the Bureau's facial recognition software to run "Jack's" photo—before finally getting a match to a driver's license photograph.

It was for a thirty-five-year-old man named Jackson Rockmore. Sheldon ran the name through the NCIC database and saw that Rockmore had a criminal record, with arrests for assault, various drug charges and attempted burglary. He'd served time in Oregon for attempted bank robbery and auto theft.

"What do you think?" Kelli asked keenly, looking over his shoulder as Sheldon sat at the breakfast bar.

"I'd say it's more than enough to bring Rockmore in for questioning related to the bank and armored truck robberies," he responded flatly. Though he was sure she understood, Sheldon deliberately chose to leave out the part that the genuine hope was that, in locating the person of interest in the case, it would lead to wherever the robbers had taken Samantha, and they could rescue her. The unspoken truth was that if Rockmore was who Sheldon now strongly suspected he was, the man and his cohorts were armed and very dangerous, with nothing to lose at this point in their attempts to evade the law. Meaning that they wouldn't hesitate to get rid of any loose ends, once proven to be of no use to them.

Samantha could be quickly falling into that category, should the perps find their backs against the wall.

"So, what are we waiting for?" Kelli sucked in a deep breath as she glared at him. "We both know that in kidnapping cases such as this, combined with being wanted for the deadly bank heists, time is of the essence in getting to Sam before it's too late—"

"You're right, it is." Sheldon felt the tension in the air, as thick as molasses, with Samantha's life hanging in the balance. He got on the phone to secure a warrant for Jackson Rockmore's arrest, as well as a search warrant for the premises of his last known address.

Chapter Sixteen

The raid on the town house on Suttree Lane came up empty. Or at least as far as being the residence of kidnapping and robbery suspect Jackson Rockmore.

As Sheldon painfully discovered—while leading the charge of FBI agents, police detectives, a SWAT unit and officers from the Leyton Falls PD, including Kelli, who insisted on being an active participant in the search for her sister—Rockmore had not lived at the town house since last October, but had not bothered to update the information on his driver's license. Nor was there any indication that any members of the Hemton County Bandit Quartet resided there either, after the young Asian tenants voluntarily agreed to a search of the premises.

Though Sheldon didn't consider them to be back to square one, he definitely saw this as a setback. But not one that couldn't be overcome, sensing that they had taken steps in the right direction toward closing in on the perilous robbers.

And, by virtue, the whereabouts of Samantha.

AT THE AFTERNOON task force meeting, Sheldon listened in as Special Agent Tabitha Hammill talked about the murder of armored truck guard Geoff Earhardt, who was forty-one years old and left behind a wife and four children. His photograph was put on the monitor to reflect the tragedy, while noting that fellow guard, Hedi Nolden, had survived the fatal robbery.

Twisting her lips forlornly, Tabitha stated, "After recovering the shell casing and matching it with the two point five inch .410 slug removed from the skull of the victim during the autopsy, forensics confirmed that Mr. Earhardt was shot to death with a Lever Action X Model .410 shotgun. It's consistent with the weapon surveillance video caught one of the quartet of robbers using to commit the homicide." She paused. "We believe that person to be the ringleader of the group, and quite possibly our wanted person of interest, Jackson Rockmore."

Sheldon took over from there, grabbing the stylus pen. He took a breath, then put side by side images on the large display and said matter-of-factly, "This is the sketch of the then-unsub and a photo of a man named Jack—both provided by Tammy Yoshimura, a teller at Bradley Bank, who was robbed by a man wearing a ski mask as a member of the Hemton County Bandit Quartet. She recognized the robber's voice from a previous encounter at a bar, where she ran into him again last night and took the picture.

"Using facial recognition software, it matched the driver's license photo for Jackson Rockmore." Sheldon put it up on the screen next to the cell phone photo of Jack. "Pretty good likeness, I have to say." He let that sink in for a moment, before switching to the suspect's mug shot. "Jackson Rockmore, who has a long arrest and criminal record, including attempted bank robbery, has emerged as our chief suspect in the Hemton County bank and armored truck robberies. Furthermore, between surveillance videos and witness accounts, including Ms. Yoshimura, Rockmore appears to be the one in command of the foursome. We currently have a warrant out for his arrest and—" Sheldon put a vehicle photo on the monitor "—believe that he may be driving the car registered in his name, a blue Honda CR-V, like the one on the screen, and put out a BOLO to that effect."

Sheldon sighed and glanced at Kelli, who had accompanied him to the task force meeting. He thought that she'd been remarkably patient when dealing with the stress she was under at the moment, all things considered, but seemed to rely on staying coolheaded, which was in her best interests. He displayed the photograph of her sister, knowing that everyone needed to put an image to the name.

"This is Samantha Quinlan," he said evenly. "Ms. Quinlan's a bank teller at the Leyton Falls Bank. She also happens to be the sister of Officer Kelli Burkett, a member of the Leyton Falls PD's Hostage Negotiation Unit." Sheldon gazed at Kelli for everyone to see and she acknowledged this in a show of unity, which for both of them went much further than professional cooperation. "Yesterday afternoon, Ms. Quinlan was abducted at the bank by the unsubs in the midst of the armored truck heist that netted the abductors approximately $350,000 of stolen money from the truck. We believe that the kidnapping was coincidental as a possible bargaining chip should the perps run into trouble during their escape." His chin projected. "The getaway vehicle—a white GMC Savana passenger van—was found a short time after the robbery in a junkyard. It's being analyzed even as we speak. In the meantime, the robbers remain at large. Our top priority is to find them and rescue Samantha Quinlan before it's too late."

KELLI LISTENED IN, hanging on Sheldon's every word, as if her life depended on it. In fact, it was her sister's life that was very much at stake. She was certain that everyone in the room could relate to one degree or another. Definitely Sheldon, who believed in happy endings. At least where it concerned them. She wanted that too. But losing Samantha to these ruthless kidnappers was not the way to close out the year. Much less, have another tragedy for Kelli to deal with in her life.

"I appreciate everyone's support," she told the task force members in attendance. "Bringing my sister home, safe and sound, would mean the world to me. And catching her abductors and putting a stop to their robbery spree would be a nice bonus for all of us."

Sheldon, who stood next to her, gave Kelli's elbow a gentle squeeze, and said hearteningly, "We're totally committed to making that happen on both fronts."

Afterward, Nolan Valentine and Karen Muñoz, announced that they were increasing jointly the reward money to as much as $20,000 for information resulting in the arrest and conviction of the bank robbers who came out of this alive. Or otherwise led to their discovery or solving of the crimes.

An hour later, Kelli was back at home, having been dropped off there by Sheldon, who gave her a kiss, as if to let her know that whatever happened, he would still be there for her. This gave her comfort, as having someone strong enough to withstand the trying times was just what she needed in her life now and into the future.

Kelli fed the horses and cleaned out the stalls, knowing that these things weren't going to do themselves. She enjoyed sharing the chores with Samantha, even when she suspected that would soon come to an end as Sam charted a new direction in her life. Assuming her sister was still given a life to live after being taken against her will.

I have to believe that will be the case, Kelli told herself, as she gently stroked Cora's neck, while watching the Colorado Ranger respond favorably.

All the while, Kelli resisted the urge to hop in her squad car and try to find Samantha on her own, knowing that she could end up driving around in circles, only to come up empty and even more frustrated. No, the best thing she could do, as encouraged by Sheldon and her superiors, was to simply wait. Until she got news.

But that sentiment could only go so far.

Not when doing nothing wouldn't get Samantha out of the clutches of her abductors.

SHELDON WAS BACK at the Leyton Falls PD, having wished he could have stayed with Kelli and helped with the horses. But he didn't have that luxury at the moment. With her sister still being held captive—or so he wanted to believe was true—all hands needed to be on deck, as far as the Bureau was concerned, in doing whatever they could to find Samantha. That meant turning over every rock with the goal of making a solid breakthrough in the case. He was as determined as ever to achieve the results that would prevent another person from losing her life at the hands of an out-of-control gang of bank robbers.

Especially when the person who had come to mean more to him than anyone was hurting and Sheldon felt it was incumbent upon him to do whatever he could for Kelli and invariably himself—along with Samantha.

When he got a video chat request on his cell phone from the FBI Laboratory, Sheldon accepted it.

Appearing on the small screen was Judith Longshore, a forensic scientist in her thirties with dark hair in a baroque bob. She pushed up rectangle glasses over blue eyes and said, "Hi, Agent Montgomery. I've got good news for you."

"That, I can always use," he said honestly. "What do you have?"

"We found a treasure trove of forensic evidence from the GMC Savana passenger van used by the armored truck robbers," she told him. "DNA from an empty water bottle left behind was collected and run through CODIS—" the FBI national DNA database that Sheldon went to often in the course of investigations "—and came back with a hit." She drew a breath. "It matched the DNA in the Arrestee Index of Jackson Rockmore, as well as his DNA in the Convicted Offender Index."

Bingo! Sheldon thought, now being able to directly tie Rockmore to the getaway van and, consequently, the murder of Geoff Earhardt and kidnapping of Samantha.

"That's good," Sheldon told the forensic analyst, anticipating more.

Judith touched her glasses again and said, "There were two other forensic unknown profiles collected from the van we have yet to get hit on." She twisted her lips thoughtfully. "As for prints, we were able to recover a partial print on the dashboard. It was run through the Bureau's Next Generation Identification system and got a hit! The print belongs to a man named Javier Mínguez."

"Javier Mínguez?" Sheldon repeated, as if to himself.

"Yeah." She nodded. "I'll send over the info."

"Thanks." Sheldon got off the phone and immediately received the material, which he transferred to his laptop. He ran a criminal background check and saw that Javier Mínguez, who was twenty-nine years old, had a number of arrests in and out of Colorado for drug offenses, theft and attempted arson. He had served time in a Kansas prison for armed robbery.

Sheldon felt that this was the break they were looking for. Mínguez and Rockmore were almost certainly two of the culprits in the armored truck robbery and abduction of Samantha. The other two unsubs were probably the individuals behind the two unidentified DNA profiles found inside the GMC Savana van.

Now we need to find Javier Mínguez ASAP, along with

Jackson Rockmore and the other presumed members of the Hemton County Bandit Quartet, Sheldon told himself, feeling a rush of adrenaline at the prospect. He got the suspect's last known address from his driver's license and put in motion an arrest warrant and another to search the premises, where Samantha could be being held prisoner.

THE RAID ON the single-story colonial-style house on Coptone Road in Hemton County was a risky one at best. And outright nerve-racking at worst.

Sheldon wasn't sure which one best applied as he and other agents, a SWAT team, Hemton County Sheriff's Department deputies and a K-9 Unit converged at the location. There was a silver Buick Enclave parked next to the house. A run on the plates determined that it had been reported stolen two weeks ago by someone living in Denver.

After assessing the rural landscape that included a forested area behind the residence, Sheldon gave the order to go in. As they stormed the house, armed and ready, he hoped against hope that Samantha was inside, still alive and well.

But as they went from room to room across the parquet flooring, in and around a clutter of contemporary furnishings, there was no sign of Kelli's sister, much to Sheldon's chagrin. Where were they holding her? He had to believe she was still useful to her captors as a hostage.

Just as troubling was that it appeared as though Javier Mínguez had managed to escape apprehension, with no sign of him anywhere.

"We've got something…" Sheldon heard from behind in the hallway and turned to face a slender female deputy with short curly red hair. Wearing nitrile gloves, she was holding a brown duffel bag. Opening it, she said, "Looks like this could be some of the money stolen from the armored truck."

Gazing at a combination of exposed cash and an unopened

money bag, Sheldon was inclined to agree. He told her, "We'll be able to determine that quickly enough and process it for any evidence that might be gathered from it."

She nodded and he moved past her and into one of the two bedrooms in the back of the house. It was unfurnished, aside from a wooden table that had drug paraphernalia atop it. Noting that the window was slightly ajar with the vinyl blinds pulled up, Sheldon walked up to it and gazed out. It faced the forested area behind the place. Peering, he detected rapid movement between the trees. His instincts kicked in.

Javier Mínguez.

He's making a run for it after giving us the slip out the window, Sheldon thought. He wouldn't get far. Not on his watch. Or in this lifetime.

Within moments, while wearing his bulletproof vest, he was out the door and informed the K-9 Unit about his suspicions. They released two of the canines to go into the woods to get and detain the suspect.

Not wanting to leave it to chance that Mínguez could somehow evade the K-9s—and avoid answering hard questions on the whereabouts of Samantha—Sheldon took a different angle into the wooded area, wanting to cut off any means for an escape. He, along with others from the team, got there just as the K-9s had cornered the short and slender Hispanic suspect.

Sheldon recognized Javier Mínguez from his mug shot. He had brown hair in an Edgar cut and brown eyes. When the man suddenly managed to break free from the canines and removed a Colt Cobra .38 Special revolver from a pocket of the hooded windbreaker jacket he was wearing, Sheldon gave him no opportunity to use it. Or be taken out before Mínguez could be interrogated.

Sheldon quickly tackled the suspect to the ground, knocking the gun from his hand. While cuffing him, he said firmly,

"Javier Mínguez, you're under arrest on suspicion of kidnapping and armed robbery."

And that was just for starters, Sheldon told himself, as he considered other charges Mínguez could be facing.

Chapter Seventeen

In the interrogation room, Sheldon sat impatiently across the table from the suspect, Javier Mínguez. After glancing at the video camera that was recording the session, he got right to the heart of the most pressing issue at the moment, asking him sharply, "Where is Samantha Quinlan?"

Mínguez wrinkled his nose, playing dumb. "Who's that?"

"She's the woman you and your three colleagues abducted outside the Leyton Falls Bank during an armored truck robbery," Sheldon snapped.

Mínguez pursed his lips defiantly. "I have no idea what you're talking about."

Sheldon was not about to let him off the hook that easily. Not by a long shot. He leaned forward and said knowingly, "We found some of the stolen money from the heist in your house with your fingerprints on the duffel bag it was in. Your prints also showed up in the white GMC Savana getaway van that was dumped at a junkyard." He let that sink in for a moment. "We also have DNA from one of your partners, Jackson Rockmore, on a money bag from inside the duffel bag and in the van." Sheldon watched his reaction to Rockmore's name, indicating Mínguez's familiarity with him. "In other words, we can tie you both to the armored truck robbery, the murder of guard Geoff Earhardt and the kidnapping

of Samantha Quinlan. By extension, there's enough circumstantial and direct evidence—including the Colt Cobra .38
Special revolver you had in your possession when arrested,
and surveillance video—to link you to the string of bank and
credit union robberies in Hemton County. In one of those,
bank teller Lori Winslow was shot to death by the female
member of your quartet." Sheldon peered at him. "There's
no turning back for you at this point, Mínguez," he told him
frankly. "These are all federal crimes and, unless you want
to go down alone, I'd suggest you start talking—and fast!"

The suspect rubbed his nose nervously, seemingly weighing his options, and then responded haltingly, "Okay, you...
got me on the robberies—but I never...killed anyone."

"Unfortunately, it doesn't work that way," Sheldon told
him matter-of-factly. "In the commission of such homicides,
each and every one of you is liable for any deaths. That means
you're in deep trouble. If you cooperate, I'll see what I can
do to help you," he told him, more than happy to put in a
good word on his behalf, if it meant achieving the objective
when the smoke cleared on this case. "Otherwise, you're on
your own."

Mínguez set his jaw. "What do you want to know?"

Sheldon went back to where he began, reiterating intently,
"Where is Samantha Quinlan?"

"I don't know," the suspect claimed, lowering his chin.
"After robbing the armored truck, I took my share of the
loot and decided to go my separate way from the others..."

"When you say *others*, are we talking about Jackson Rockmore, in specific, and another male and female?" Sheldon
posed to him.

"Yeah." Mínguez sighed. "Jackson has been running the
show."

That confirms what we already strongly suspected, Sheldon thought. He probed further in asking straightforwardly, "What are the names of the other two bank robbers?"

Mínguez waited a beat and answered. "Glenn Evigan and Sandrine Kripke."

Sheldon nodded. As it was, they had already deduced this information from Mínguez's laptop but wanted to hear it from him.

"Glenn is Jackson's cousin," Mínguez volunteered. "Sandrine and Glenn are romantically involved."

They had also pieced together these details before his validation as the parts began to fall into place like a deadly puzzle. Sheldon regarded the suspect across the table and asked again, with the sense of urgency growing with each passing second for the safety of Kelli's sister, "Where would they have taken Samantha Quinlan?" He added, in pressing the issue and upping the ante, while knowing just what Jackson Rockmore and Sandrine Kripke in particular, had proven capable of with their cold-blooded fatal shootings, "If any harm comes to her, you're still on the hook as one of her abductors—"

Mínguez stared back ill at ease. "I'm guessing either Jackson's place or Glenn and Sandrine's apartment."

Sheldon drew a breath. Agents had already been dispatched to these residences, only to find that—apart from retrieving evidence relevant to the investigation—neither Samantha nor the suspects were anywhere to be found. Arrest warrants had been issued for Glenn Evigan, who was thirty-four, and Sandrine Kripke, twenty-seven; while BOLOs were put out for vehicles registered to the two suspects—including a blue Ford Ranger owned by Evigan and a red Toyota Camry driven by Kripke.

Sheldon feared that they could be using a stolen vehicle to get around. He frowned at Mínguez and considered how he might apply more pressure in getting solid clues from the robbery suspect on Samantha's possible whereabouts, while there was still time to work with. And before he chose to lawyer up.

KELLI WATCHED FROM the monitor room as Sheldon interrogated Javier Mínguez, getting valuable information regarding the bank and armored truck robberies. But not what she needed most to hear: the location where Samantha was being held by her abductors.

Please still be alive, Kelli prayed strongly inside her head, fearful of what her sister's captives might do, if cornered. The fact that there had been no indication that Samantha was dead gave her hope that there was still time to locate her.

Kelli gazed again at the video monitor as Sheldon continued to grill the suspect but came up just short in gathering intel on where his partners in crime currently were. She turned to Nolan Valentine, who was similarly riveted to the interrogation, wanting answers just as badly from the suspect.

"You want to take a crack at it?" Nolan asked her.

Kelli raised a brow. "Interrogate the suspect?"

"Yeah. See if your hostage negotiation skills can work on him to help fill in the blanks."

She seized the opportunity, if it could help in any way to find Samantha. "Yes, I'm ready to do what I can."

Nolan nodded. "Then, go for it."

Kelli walked with him toward the interrogation room, as Nolan gave her a smile of encouragement before she entered.

She met Sheldon's surprised blue eyes and said, "Lieutenant Valentine thought I might be able to help."

Sheldon stood and expressed support. "Of course."

Kelli gazed at the suspect and said coolly, "I'm Officer Burkett." She sat down where Sheldon had been sitting and decided to be straight with Javier Mínguez right off the bat.

"Samantha Quinlan is my sister," she said bluntly. "Why did you kidnap her?"

Mínguez squirmed. "Wasn't my idea," he argued.

"That didn't answer my question," she told him.

He tilted his face. "Jackson wanted to do it. He recognized her from the bank, after checking it out ahead of time. Thought she could come in handy."

Sheldon narrowed his eyes at him. "How was that?"

Mínguez swallowed. "They're planning one more big score, before fleeing the state and maybe heading for Mexico," he explained, as if describing a resort vacation. "Your sister was taken in case a hostage was needed to help them get away."

Kelli peered at him and demanded, "When and where is this score—robbery—going to take place?"

"Probably Monday." He shrugged. "I think it may be another armored truck robbery. Jackson thought it could bring in enough for them to live comfortably somewhere, along with what they already had stashed away from the other robberies."

Sheldon pressed his hands on the table in front of Mínguez and said forcefully, "So, where else could they lay low till readying themselves for this armored truck heist?"

Kelli added tersely, in wanting to keep the pressure on, "Anywhere at all that could buy them some time…?"

Mínguez ran a hand across his mouth, then answered. "Come to think of it, Glenn's uncle has a cabin in the mountains. I hung out there once with Glenn, Sandrine and Jackson. They might go there—especially since the uncle apparently only uses the cabin during the summertime."

Kelli exchanged glances with Sheldon. Reading his thoughts, she knew that this was something he was ready to jump on. As was she.

While hoping it wouldn't lead to a dead end.

When the stakes couldn't be higher, with Samantha's fate on the line.

SHELDON AND KELLI walked into the Evigan Café on Nopley Street, where they were looking for the owner, Otis Evigan, the uncle of kidnapping and robbery suspect Glenn Evigan. Sheldon hoped that he didn't attempt to stonewall them, knowing that there was no time to waste.

A medium-sized man in his sixties with slicked-back brown-and-gray hair and a musketeer mustache and goatee approached them between patrons, near the front door, and asked, "Can I help you?"

"Are you Otis Evigan?" Sheldon asked.

"Last time I checked," he responded humorously.

Sheldon flashed his ID. "Special Agent Montgomery and Officer Burkett. We need some information about the cabin you own in the mountains."

Otis cocked a thick brow. "What about it?"

Kelli peered at him. "We have reason to believe that your nephew, Glenn Evigan—who's a suspect in a string of deadly robberies and a kidnapping—and two others he's aligned himself with, including his cousin Jackson Rockmore, may be hiding out there," she said toughly.

"Glenn… Jackson…robberies…kidnapping…" Otis furrowed his brow in disbelief. "Are you serious?"

"This isn't a game," Sheldon stated in no uncertain terms, sensing that the man likely knew full well that his nephew was no angel. But maybe not to the degree of the very serious crimes he was suspected of. "We think they could be holding a bank employee there against her will—and to evade capture. Your cooperation is needed in pinpointing the location of the cabin, so we can check it out and act accordingly."

Otis appeared to have resigned himself to the hard reality of the situation, and said, "Of course, I'll cooperate." He paused. "I just hope you're wrong about Glenn…and Jackson. Both have had their problems, and Glenn especially has had a tendency to get in with the wrong crowd—but this…"

Sheldon narrowed his eyes. "I'm afraid this is what it's come down to," he told him straightforwardly. "But it can still get much worse for your nephew—and his cousin—if we don't get to them before things get out of hand."

Without his delving into the worst-case scenario, which Kelli didn't need to be reminded of, Sheldon watched as Otis Evigan gave them the location of his cabin and permission to enter.

Afterward, Sheldon got on his cell phone and immediately passed on the info to other agents and the SWAT team.

KELLI—WHO REMAINED on the clock in an official capacity as a hostage negotiator, in spite of her personal connection to the case—drove with Sheldon along the icy road in the mountainous region of the county, where Otis Evigan's log cabin was located on Grotler Road.

Though she tried her best to think positively, Kelli was finding it almost impossible to do while imagining what ordeal the kidnappers could be putting her sister through. The one saving grace was that if Javier Mínguez was correct, Samantha's abductors had an incentive to keep her alive as they plotted another robbery.

Beyond that, Kelli knew that she had Sheldon's rock-solid support and equal determination to bring Samantha—whom he had developed a fondness for as her sister and vice versa—back to them, come hell or high water. This was something she would hang on to for dear life, as they arrived at the cabin forty-five minutes after leaving the café.

They were met by other law enforcement, including

Hemton County Sheriff Isabella Granados, who was in her early forties and slender, with brown hair in an uneven lob. "Though there are lights on inside the cabin, and definite evidence—such as tire tracks and trash left behind—that someone's been here recently, we have no indication that anyone's in there right now," she said.

"Maybe they left for a while, but plan to come back," Sheldon suggested. He amended his own thoughts by saying, "If the kidnappers were here, they likely panicked and left, taking the back roads—upon learning that Javier Mínguez, one of their team of robbers, had been arrested and may have given the authorities their possible whereabouts."

Kelli frowned while wondering if Mínguez could possibly have led them astray deliberately. But what would he gain in doing so at that point?

"Has anyone gone inside yet?" she asked the sheriff.

Isabella responded, "We waited for your arrival and for the SWAT team to get set up in case they're needed."

Sheldon nodded, then after glancing at Kelli, conferred with FBI agents and SWAT members, who were carrying Colt M4 carbine semiautomatic assault rifles, before the single story, two-bedroom cabin nestled among pine trees was raided.

Inside were empty beer cans and a couple of pizza boxes and wrappers from fast food sandwiches strewn about the oak hardwood floor and rustic furnishings.

But no Samantha. Or her abductors.

Kelli flinched at the notion that her sister had been held prisoner there. They needed to be sure of this. She gave the handler with the Sheriff's Department's K-9 Unit an article of Samantha's clothing that Kelli had brought with her, so the female German shepherd named Greta could take in the scent.

It didn't take long for Greta to move about the cabin and

bark repeatedly while focusing on a log chair to indicate that Samantha had sat there at some point.

"She was here," Kelli said, ill at ease, looking at Sheldon.

"Yeah," he conceded. "Now we just need to figure out where they're headed and hopefully be able to cut off any escape routes."

"I'll radio it in," Isabella said. "They couldn't have gotten far."

Don't give up on us, Sam, Kelli pleaded internally to her sister. They wouldn't give up on the mission at hand, daunting as it was in a harsh wintry environment.

The search was back on to find the fugitives and their captive, wherever they had fled to.

ON SUNDAY MORNING after a mostly sleepless night, with Samantha still missing and her abductors nowhere to be found, Kelli was up early to feed the horses and get back out there in trying to locate her sister. Thus far, their efforts had come up short, though she believed in her heart of hearts that Samantha was still with the three armed robbers and, therefore, alive.

Sheldon had spent half the night at her house, but was up even earlier to get a head start on the investigation and pursuit of Samantha and her assailants.

Under other circumstances, Kelli would have rather he spent the entire night—every night—snuggled with her after making love. In this instance, though, she applauded him for his dedication to the task at hand. And wanting her to get some extra shut-eye after a trying day before tending to her chores and continuing to do her part in the armored truck heist that had bridged their worlds even more than before.

When her cell phone rang for a video chat while she was in the barn, Kelli saw that it was Chase. She could only imagine what he must be going through as Samantha's boyfriend, who had briefly been considered a suspect in her abduction, and likely now felt helpless while awaiting word on Samantha's status.

Accepting the call, Kelli watched his face appear on the small screen and said to him tonelessly, "Hi, Chase." She wished there was good news to share.

"I think I may have found a vehicle belonging to one of Samantha's kidnappers," he said matter-of-factly.

She arched a brow. "You what?"

Chase sucked in a deep breath. "I know you told me to stay out of it, but I had to do something to try and help out, with Samantha in trouble."

Though this probably was a bad idea, deep down inside Kelli knew they could use all the help they could get in this case. "Go ahead…"

"Okay. I've been driving my rented Volkswagen Jetta around all day and night, trying to see if I could spot any of the armored truck robbers or their rides." He waited a beat. "Then I was passing by the Birch Trees Motel on Sixth Street and Fullermore Road, when I saw this red Toyota Camry—like one I used to own—parked in the lot. I know there's a BOLO out for a car matching that description, so I checked it out." He sighed. "I think they might be holding Samantha inside their motel room, but I didn't want to make things worse for her by barging in to try and rescue her—so I called you."

"I'm glad you did," Kelli told him. "It wouldn't have been smart to go in unprepared and unarmed against dangerous opponents. Stay out of harm's way till I get there."

"All right," Chase replied. "Hurry—in case they decide to leave…with Samantha."

"I'm leaving right now," she told him, "and will notify Sheldon and my own department about this."

"Okay."

Kelli disconnected and immediately called Sheldon. Without prelude, she dove right in. "Just got a possible lead on Sam's whereabouts," she told him tersely.

"From who?" His voice was flat.

"Chase. He believes that a Toyota Camry he saw in a motel parking lot is one of the vehicles described in the BOLO alert."

"I'll meet you there," Sheldon told her succinctly.

"All right." Kelli ended the conversation, knowing that if Chase was correct, there was no time to spare if they hoped to catch the kidnappers off guard and save Samantha.

Chapter Eighteen

Kelli arrived at the motel in her squad car and spotted Chase as he stood by his beige Volkswagen Jetta in the parking lot. She pulled up beside him and got out, while expecting backup at any time. Including Sheldon.

"Hey," Chase said, his voice subdued.

"Hi." Kelli scanned the lot, till her eyes landed on the red Toyota Camry. It was parked in front of a set of rooms on two stories. She looked around for a blue Honda CR-V and blue Ford Ranger that were registered to Jackson Rockmore and Glenn Evigan, respectively, and the two suspects were believed to still be driving. The cursory search came up empty.

"I kept an eye on things, but maintained a safe distance," Chase pointed out.

She nodded, while still coming to grips with his playing the role of an amateur sleuth and being somewhat effective at it. "See anyone come in or out of any of the rooms?"

"Only an elderly couple from a first-floor room."

"Okay." Kelli glanced at him. "Wait here…" She walked over to the Camry and peeked inside. There were some food wrappers and a leather bomber jacket on the back seat. *Nothing criminal about that*, she thought. But she was suspicious, nonetheless, all things considered.

She took out her two-way radio and ran the Toyota Camry's license plate. Moments later, it was confirmed that the vehicle was, in fact, registered to Sandrine P. Kripke.

Got you—hopefully, Kelli told herself, regarding the female robber and kidnapping suspect. She scanned the motel rooms, realizing that Samantha could be in any one of them. Along with at least one of her armed captors. Assuming that finding Kripke's vehicle hidden in plain view wasn't merely a subterfuge.

And even if every nerve in her body wanted to charge into one room after another to find her sister, Kelli knew that—apart from being totally against police protocol—she wouldn't be doing Samantha any favors by acting recklessly in a misguided attempt at rescuing her.

So, instead, Kelli retreated back to where Chase was and waited for help to arrive, while making sure that no one would be allowed to get into that Camry—with or without Samantha—and leave the scene, unchallenged.

THE BIRCH TREES MOTEL was crawling with law enforcement, including FBI, SWAT team, K-9 Unit and police officers, along with emergency medical technicians, if needed, as Sheldon took stock of the situation. With the Toyota Camry confirmed as belonging to fugitive Sandrine Kripke, it concerned him as to the whereabouts of the vehicles driven by the other two robbery and kidnapping suspects.

Had they ditched the Camry to cover their tracks? Or was it the other way around, and this was now their sole means of transportation as they remained on the loose?

Either way Sheldon sliced it, as long as they still had Samantha, Kelli's sister remained in grave danger if her abductors found themselves boxed in with no apparent way out.

"We need to find out if the suspects simply discarded the Camry at the motel to throw us off the trail or if they've been holed up here," Sheldon said, gazing at Kelli.

"You're right," she agreed as they stood by the suspect's vehicle. "Those same thoughts crossed my mind."

"Let's see what the motel desk clerk or whomever can tell us."

"Yeah," Chase said, standing with them.

Sheldon looked at him, impressed at his intuitiveness in locating the suspect's vehicle in the lot. But as much as he wanted to continue to be in on the action in rescuing his girlfriend, it wasn't happening.

Putting up a hand, Sheldon told him politely, "You've done a good job, but you need to stay out of it from this point on and let us handle things." When Chase grumbled with resistance, he told the college student, more firmly, "Am I making myself clear?"

"Yeah, got it," Chase responded.

"Good." Sheldon glanced at Kelli, whom he knew was in agreement, as at the end of the day, she too wanted to play this by the book every step of the way in locating her sister the right way.

They went inside the motel office and up to the desk, where a slim twentysomething female with brunette hair in a French girl bixie was sitting. She eyed them with curiosity behind oversize glasses.

Sheldon wasted no time flashing his ID while saying in an official tone of voice, "FBI." He then identified Kelli as a police officer. "We need to know if any of these people have checked into the motel recently..." He laid before her current photographs of Sandrine Kripke, Glenn Evigan and Jackson Rockmore.

The young desk clerk studied the pics, looked up and answered matter-of-factly, "Yeah, all three checked in yesterday, paying for one day."

"Was this woman with them?" Kelli asked, showing her a photograph on her cell phone of Samantha.

The clerk peered at the pic. "Yeah, she was."

Sheldon felt relief to know that Samantha was at least alive at that point, and he could sense this solace in Kelli too. "We need the room numbers they stayed in," he demanded without delay.

"Sure, no problem." The clerk gave them the side by side second-story room numbers. "I think they may have left earlier."

If true, the rooms likely haven't been cleaned yet, making it that much easier to collect any physical evidence that could be used against Samantha's kidnappers, Sheldon told himself. He also was forced to consider, painful as it was, that they could have left Kelli's sister behind in a room—either dead or barely alive.

When the two rooms were raided, aside from clear indication that they had been occupied, neither Samantha nor her abductors were present.

"Where have they taken my sister?" Kelli asked, her voice breaking with worry, as they left the motel rooms.

Sheldon hugged her affectionately and responded with determination, "Nowhere that they can't be found." It was a conviction he stood by, no matter that the clock continued to tick with each moment in time in that regard.

ON MONDAY MORNING, the Ford Ranger, carrying four occupants, pulled into the parking lot of the Potters Grocery Store & Pharmacy on Dottie Road in Leyton Falls.

They watched patiently as an armored truck pulled up to the store, right on time. Two muscular armed male guards got out and went inside.

When one of the guards came out minutes later, the male and female occupants in the front seat donned ski masks and left the Ford Ranger truck—armed with a Palmetto State Armory Sabre AR-15 rifle and Taurus G2 9mm Luger handgun.

They quickly approached the tall, curly haired thirtysome-thing guard, overcoming his resistance when disarming and pistol-whipping him into unconsciousness.

Before the other armored truck guard could come from the store, the two robbers were able to remove from the truck six plastic bins of cash and eight deposit bags, filled with money.

They quicky returned to the Ford Ranger, tossed the sto-len money into the back seat—alongside the male and fe-male occupants—and took off out of the parking lot and onto the street.

WHEN A 911 call came in that reported an armored truck heist had occurred at the Potters Grocery Store & Pharmacy, Shel-don raced to the scene, sensing that the Hemton County Ban-dit Quartet—minus one—had struck again. Before bringing this to Kelli's attention, he needed to get some details first.

He pulled his Ford Explorer SUV into the lot and emerged to meet up with FBI Special Agent Joseph Eala, who was standing beside a bloodied armored truck guard.

"It was definitely them," Eala said unwaveringly. "Speed camera video showed a blue Ford Ranger barreling from the parking lot, with a license plate that's registered to Glenn Evigan."

"I figured as much," Sheldon hated to say, but had strongly suspected—especially given the one last big job that Javier Mínguez believed his former cohorts would try, while the going was hot.

The guard, identifying himself as Kent Urpanil, wiped blood from his nose and confessed, "They got the jump on me before I even knew what was happening. Though they wore ski masks, I think one was male, the other female. The male robber hit me several times with the rifle he was car-rying and the female may have gotten in a pop too with her handgun or fist…" He creased his brow. "They probably made off with over half a million dollars."

Sheldon wondered about Samantha and the other robber, asking the guard, "Did you see anyone else besides the two thieves who attacked and robbed you?"

Kent's chin protruded. "Looked like there might have been people in the back seat of the getaway vehicle, but I didn't get a good look at them."

Sheldon eyed Eala. "We need to see the store's security video—and fast."

He nodded. "Let's check it out."

A few minutes later, they were watching inside a back room with surveillance equipment. Sheldon saw the two armored vehicle robbers get in and out and back in again of the Ford Ranger. Then, upon zooming in on the inside of the back seat of the truck, he could clearly see a frightened Samantha, alongside an adult male who looked a lot like Jackson Rockmore.

"Damn," Sheldon muttered out loud. "They're keeping Samantha close to the action in case she's needed as a human shield."

"I was thinking the same thing," Eala said. "At least we know she's still alive."

But for how long? Sheldon could only wonder as the reckless and unpredictable kidnappers might soon find Samantha of no further use to them. And where would that leave Kelli? "Yeah, that's a positive thing," he said tonelessly.

The store manager, Rachael Deloach, who was in her fifties with blond hair in a collarbone cut, informed them that a GPS tracker had been placed inside one of the deposit bags. "It's been activated, and we can see in real time where they're headed."

"That's good," Sheldon told her, thrilled to hear this, as they were able to get a bead on the Ford Ranger carrying Samantha that appeared to be on a beeline toward Aimee's Inn, which happened to be two blocks past the Birch Trees Motel.

Sheldon quickly got on his cell phone to put the wheels in motion toward catching up to Samantha's abductors, rescuing her from their grasp and holding the deadly robbers accountable for every one of their deliberate actions.

"SAMANTHA'S ALIVE," SHELDON told Kelli on her cell's speakerphone, as she drove her patrol car through town, frantic in wanting to find her sister.

"Really?" Kelli's heart skipped a beat in that moment of clarity, after hearing about the latest armored truck robbery that all signs pointed toward being perpetrated by the remaining on the loose members of the Hemton County Bandit Quartet, who made off with hundreds of thousands of dollars for their trouble.

"I saw her on the security camera footage from the Potters Grocery Store & Pharmacy," he said. "She was in the back seat of the Ford Ranger her captors used as the getaway vehicle after robbing the armored truck. Though undoubtedly unnerved, Samantha appeared to be alert to what was going on."

That's a positive sign moving forward, Kelli told herself, but as long as her sister remained a hostage, her life was still in jeopardy. "So, what's the status of the investigation and the whereabouts of the robbers?"

"There was a GPS tracker in one of the stolen money bags. We've tracked the getaway vehicle to Aimee's Inn. The rescue and arrest operation is centering on the location even as we speak."

"That's just around the corner from where I am," Kelli told him, increasing her speed in wanting to be there when Samantha was successfully separated from her abductors. Or do the job as a hostage negotiator, should that become necessary.

Sheldon told her evenly, "Meet you there."

They disconnected and Kelli understood that between the lines they both knew that nothing was guaranteed in the dangerous rescue mission, no matter their best wishes. Or appropriate resources in achieving the goal.

Still, was it asking too much to want to get her sister back in one piece? Or to love someone who could give her back the same in return?

She pondered this while racing toward Aimee's Inn.

As FBI AGENTS, SWAT members, police officers and support personnel converged on the scene, the focus was on the Ford Ranger used by the armored truck robbers to make their escape. It was parked in the lot, away from other vehicles.

To Sheldon, this was to make it easier to make a run for it later. Or because the kidnappers had ditched it for another vehicle.

Another thought occurred to him—that the trio of robbers may still be inside the truck, needing a place to lay low for just enough time to divvy up their stolen loot. And maybe get rid of their captive before trying to get out of town.

They may also have gotten a room to wait it out, foolishly believing that they could.

Whichever scenario presented itself, Sheldon knew it was crunch time and they needed to flush out the kidnapping bank robbers, once and for all.

When the order was given to rush the Ford Ranger, with firearms out and ready to react to any threat that came their way, it was discovered that the truck was empty. The abductors and abductee were nowhere to be found.

When Sheldon went into the Aimee's Inn office, with Kelli having joined him, it was determined from the desk clerk that at least two of the suspects had gotten a first-floor room and requested one on the back side of the inn.

"Do you think Sam's in there?" Kelli asked, a shakiness in her voice.

Sheldon paused. "Only one way to find out," he answered succinctly, and relayed the information to the team.

The room was raided by overwhelming force as robbery and kidnapping suspects, Sandrine Kripke and Glenn Evigan, appeared startled and offered no resistance, in spite of them both carrying handguns when placed under arrest. The Taurus G2 9mm pistol Kripke was packing was almost certainly, in Sheldon's mind, the same weapon used to murder bank teller Lori Winslow. Forensics would undoubtedly confirm this by matching it with the bullet that killed her.

Also confiscated at the scene were some of the plastic bins and deposit bags of cash, along with a rifle.

There was no sign of Jackson Rockmore. Or Samantha.

While still inside the room, Sheldon peered at the handcuffed Sandrine Kripke, who was tall and slender, with blue eyes and reddish-brown hair in an asymmetrical bob, and asked her tersely, "Where is Jackson Rockmore?"

Kelli pitched in with a harsh tone of gravity, "And Samantha Quinlan, the bank teller you abducted?"

Sandrine sucked in a deep breath and answered frostily, "Jackson took her when we split up after robbing the armored truck. I have no idea where they are."

"Yeah, right." Kelli snorted, clearly with misgivings in her response.

Sheldon wasn't sure she would come clean even if the suspect knew their whereabouts, given Kripke's proven loyalty to Rockmore as the alleged ringleader of their criminality. Not to mention the depravity she had demonstrated in the cold-blooded execution of bank teller Lori Winslow.

Sheldon turned his attention toward Glenn Evigan, who was cuffed and being held firmly by a tall, bald-headed, muscular police officer. Evigan was smaller and not as tall, with highlighted brown hair in a shag cut and a goatee.

"Where is Rockmore and his captive?" Sheldon narrowed his gaze at the suspect. "If you have any relevant information and the unthinkable happens to Ms. Quinlan, you'll be subject to the same weight of the law as Rockmore—to go with the many charges you're already facing."

Evigan wrinkled his nose and said, "Jackson is trying to get out of Leyton Falls with his share of the loot—and her as his hostage till he no longer needs her. That's all I know, I swear."

"Is he driving his own Honda CR-V?" Sheldon asked pointedly.

"Yeah, last I saw," Evigan responded. "It was his fallback, once the other getaway vehicles got too hot."

Sheldon had heard enough for now from the two suspects, and said testily to officers, "Get them out of here."

As the kidnapping, murder and robbery pair were led away, Sheldon got on his cell phone and reissued the BOLO alert on Rockmore's Honda CR-V, along with the kidnapper and his captive, while considering Jackson Rockmore as armed and dangerous.

No sooner had Sheldon completed the call and consoled Kelli over the understandable frustration that her sister was still being held against her will than he and Kelli received word of a carjacking on Hegler Street. The elderly victim reported that the carjacker and the woman he was with matched the physical description of Jackson Rockmore and Samantha Quinlan.

It renewed the sense of urgency for Sheldon and Kelli in rescuing Samantha from her abductor's clutches, before he could succeed in escaping the dragnet for his capture.

Chapter Nineteen

Jackson Rockmore was desperate when he forced the white-haired woman from her dark green Mercedes-Benz GLS 450 SUV at gunpoint outside a convenience store on Hegler Street. He had threatened her with the Smith & Wesson M&P 2.0 10mm pistol he had bought on the black market as a backup to his Lever Action X Model .410 shotgun.

The same intimidation had been used to keep the bank teller captive in line after he had been forced to ditch his Honda CR-V for the Mercedes-Benz, to buy some time. After loading up the cash he had collected from the bank and armored truck heists—and smartly separating from the other two members left in his gang of robbers while he still could—Jackson took off, hoping to avoid capture.

He glanced over at the bank teller, whose hands were zip-tied, as she sat glumly in the passenger seat. While not bad on the eyes, truthfully, she wasn't really his type. Not like the pretty Asian woman he'd met at the Ninth Street Pub. If they'd had more time to get to know one another, they might have hit it off.

Turning his eyes back to the road, Jackson continued to drive faster than the speed limit while maintaining control of the SUV. He hoped to make his way to New Mexico and eventually Mexico, where he could disappear and start over.

He liked robbing banks with Glenn and Sandrine—and even Javier, before he turned on them.

But at the end of the day, Jackson knew that he had to always look out for number one, first and foremost. He loved his freedom too much to want to do time again. Whatever it took.

Glancing again at his captive, she batted her curly lashes at him and said nicely, "Just let me go—please…"

"No can do," he responded flatly. "You're my insurance policy in case things go south." He paused. "For your sake, you better hope that doesn't happen."

She turned away from him and sulked like a bratty child.

Grinning, Jackson felt she was entitled to that much. Just as he was in wisely kidnapping her outside the Leyton Falls Bank when she happened upon their armored truck heist. Her misfortune.

Everything else would play itself out, for better or worse.

SAMANTHA QUINLAN COULDN'T believe that she was in this uncomfortable situation—right out of a horror movie. Only it was her real life on the line. And the most terrible bad luck she could imagine.

How could she have possibly known that she would walk right into a robbery of the armored truck servicing her bank?

Or that, by happenstance, the robbers would abduct her at gunpoint, forcing her to accompany them as they made their getaway?

Why couldn't she have left sooner—or later—for her planned lunch date with Chase?

Would she ever get to see him again?

Not to mention Kelli. Her sister had already known enough tragedy in her life. She didn't need another major one to have to deal with.

Am I going to die and never have an opportunity to bond

even more with her? Samantha asked herself, as she took a peek at her kidnapper, who had separated her from the other kidnappers as the walls began to close in on them. She had little doubt that even if her hands weren't zip-tied, if she tried anything, he wouldn't hesitate to shoot her with the gun that was tucked inside his waistband.

As such, all she could do was hope that Kelli and Sheldon, along with their law enforcement partners, had a plan to rescue her. And could do so before time ran out.

"I NEED TO be there for Samantha—no matter what happens," Chase blared through the speaker of Kelli's cell phone as it sat in the dashboard phone holder in her patrol vehicle.

This came after he had admitted to following her in his Volkswagen Jetta ever since she'd left Aimee's Inn, where apparently Jackson Rockmore had forcibly taken Samantha with him after he abandoned other members of the Hemton County Bandits Quartet, Glenn Evigan and Sandrine Kripke, shortly before they were taken into custody.

Now they were in a full-scale search for the Mercedes-Benz SUV that Rockmore carjacked, with an FBI drone trying to zoom in on its location. Kelli was among those leading the way, with Sheldon a couple of vehicles ahead of her in his Ford Explorer SUV. Both decided it was best to ride separately to possibly cover more ground, in case it was needed to locate Samantha.

"I understand where you're coming from," Kelli said, sympathizing with her sister's boyfriend. Still, she had to caution him. "I'm sure that Sam will be delighted to see you, once this is over—" assuming she was rescued while conscious and unharmed "—but this is a dangerous undertaking and we don't need you to get hurt, in spite of your best intentions."

"I promise to keep my distance from the action," Chase told her, "till it's safe to reach out to Samantha."

"Okay." Kelli couldn't argue with his logic. Or his heart, for that matter, which was clearly in the right place. As was her own, where it concerned Sheldon and the direction they were headed in. She ended the call from Chase and then got a call from Ronnie Whiteman.

"Hey," the hostage negotiator said. "How are you holding up?"

"Ask me after I find my sister, and she's physically okay," Kelli answered honestly, pondering the nightmare of Sheldon seeing Samantha in the back of the getaway vehicle after the latest armored truck heist.

"I will," Ronnie promised. "Anyway, I'm on the move as well. Trent wanted me to be there as support for you, should it be needed, if the suspect refuses to let her go."

"Thanks, Ronnie," she said, grateful that the tactical commander of the Hostage Negotiation Unit had put family ahead of protocol, in this instance. "I can always use your help, should the situation call for it."

"Good," he said. "So, let's go get the son of a bitch who kidnapped your sister and finish this thing once and for all."

"All right." She disconnected and focused on the road ahead, while praying that Samantha remained strong in the face of adversity, as they worked to find her.

Kelli reached out to Sheldon by phone, needing to hear his reassuring voice at this moment. "Any news on the whereabouts of the carjacked vehicle?"

"Yeah, as a matter of fact," he told her, his voice lifted an octave. "The drone has hit pay dirt! It's on a surveillance mission and tracking the movements of the Mercedes-Benz, even as we speak."

"Where are they?" Kelli demanded, anxious to know the precise location of where her sister might be.

"On State Highway 56," Sheldon answered. "Appears as though Rockmore is trying to get to Albuquerque, New

Mexico." He paused. "We've got roadblocks up ahead and a SWAT team in place... We'll do what's necessary to rescue Samantha," he promised.

So will I, Kelli thought unwaveringly, as they raced to catch up to the fugitive who had her sister, knowing that every moment could well be Samantha's last.

"THE SUSPECT IS well within our sight," Sheldon reported over his cell phone to Special Agent in Charge Karen Muñoz, as the drone surveillance in real time showed the carjacked vehicle turning off State Highway 56 and onto a side street, in what Sheldon saw as a blatant attempt by Jackson Rockmore to evade detection and apprehension. Both would fail as they closed in on Samantha's last remaining abductor. "We'll put this to rest, one way or the other."

Karen voiced support. "That's good to know. It would certainly be nice to end the year on a positive note!"

"Yeah, I hear you," Sheldon agreed, pressing down on the accelerator, his adrenaline raised at the thought of putting Rockmore and his cohorts out of the bank, credit union and armored truck robbery business once and for all. Only with Samantha's safe return could they move on with their lives.

To Sheldon, that meant barreling ahead with whatever lay in store for him and Kelli, while leaving nothing on the table in terms of what they could be.

When Rockmore, under the cover of a spread of Colorado blue spruce trees, abandoned the Mercedes-Benz SUV, with Samantha being forced to accompany him as he attempted to carjack another vehicle—this one, a silver sage-colored Chevrolet Tahoe—the driver resisted, taking off to the sound of gunfire.

Rockmore had failed to hit his target and, before he could return with his prisoner to the Mercedes-Benz, heavily armed law enforcement had swarmed the area—making an escape all but impossible.

That didn't stop the desperate kidnapper from trying to make a run for it with Samantha into the woods.

With sharpshooters all around them, Sheldon and Kelli joined forces to go after her sister and Rockmore, knowing that they weren't about to let them out of their sight. Or give in to the dangerous perpetrator.

What happened from that point on would be entirely up to Jackson Rockmore.

KELLI FELT HER heart racing. She knew this was a make-or-break moment as Samantha's kidnapper tried to usher her through the snow-covered trees, as though there was daylight awaiting him at the end of the tunnel.

I won't simply sit back and watch it happen, Kelli told herself, while refraining from pulling out the 9mm Smith & Wesson pistol from her holster. Instead, she hoped to rely on her hostage negotiation skills in this situation. She glanced over at Sheldon, who had no such reservations in the use of firepower, if necessary, as he held his Glock 19 9mm Luger semi-automatic duty pistol in readiness. Both were wearing bulletproof vests. Kelli only wished the same were true for Samantha, in case bullets should start flying.

When they had essentially cornered the suspect and his hostage from all sides, Sheldon yelled at him in blunt terms, "Give it up, Rockmore. There's nowhere else to go!"

The suspect was defiant as he held the barrel of his gun to Samantha's head, and spat, "Back off—all of you—or I won't be the only one to take a bullet…"

As Sheldon motioned for everyone to stand down for the moment, apparently wanting to take no chances, he eyed Kelli thoughtfully and she knew this was her opportunity to make one pitch toward ending this thing peacefully.

She accepted the challenge, taking a precarious step toward the kidnapper and his surprisingly calm captive, and said levelly, "I'm Officer Burkett, a hostage negotiator." She paused then continued, "I also happen to be the sister of Samantha, the bank teller you kidnapped." Kelli watched him react with surprise. "Let her go and let me help you get through this situation."

Jackson Rockmore took a ragged breath, but kept the gun aimed squarely at Samantha. "You can help by making them give me safe passage out of here," he demanded.

Kelli peered at him, knowing there was no way to sugarcoat this in giving him a false read. She said straightforwardly, "That's not going to happen, Jackson. There's no way that you're getting out of here—not with the crimes you're accused of—and that's a fact. Continuing to resist by holding my sister as a hostage will only make things worse for you. You're surrounded by overwhelming, heavily armed manpower. They're never going to allow you to leave. It's not in their DNA as law enforcement. Shooting my sister will only guarantee your own death. Is that what you really want?"

As the kidnapper mulled over this stark reality—and Kelli made eye contact with Samantha, telling her mentally to hang tough—she gazed back at Rockmore and said, in further hoping to reason with Samantha's abductor, "Listen, the other members of the Hemton County Bandit Quartet, Javier Mínguez, Glenn Evigan and Sandrine Kripke, have all been arrested and did not put up a fight that they could not win. Be smart about this and surrender, Jackson, so you too can live to see another day and let the chips fall where they may…"

Kelli turned to Sheldon, who again took the lead and said sharply to the kidnapping and robbery suspect, "Which way will this go, Rockmore? It's your call."

Rockmore took a long moment of soul-searching, before

slowly releasing Samantha, who tentatively moved away from him as the suspect lay his weapon on the ground.

As FBI agents converged on Jackson Rockmore and placed him under arrest, while reading him his rights and tossing out a few more choice words at the captured fugitive, Samantha ran into Kelli's arms. Or maybe it was the other way around, as the sisters embraced.

"I've never been so happy to see and hug you," Kelli cried, feeling ever grateful for this moment.

"I feel the same way," Samantha said. "Honestly, for a while there, I thought I might never have this chance to be with you again."

Though the same thought had occurred to Kelli, more than once, she would never admit it to Samantha, who looked to Kelli to be in remarkably good shape, considering her trials and tribulation. But she would still need to be checked out by a doctor for a clean bill of health. "That was never on the table, as far as I was concerned," Kelli insisted.

"I'm with her," Chase said, approaching them. He embraced Samantha. "Seriously, you did have me going for a minute there, Sam."

Samantha grinned. "You weren't going to get rid of me that easily," she quipped.

He laughed and kissed her. "That's good to know, because I'm not about to let you go anytime soon."

"I'll hold you to that," she told him.

"You'd better," Chase insisted, and got a kiss from Samantha in response.

Kelli thought it was sweet that the two had their moment and reflection of how things could have taken a much different turn.

Ronnie joined the group and gave Kelli a thumbs-up. Sheldon said in earnest, "We were devoted to rescuing you from the kidnappers, Samantha. It may have taken a little longer than any of us ever wanted, but the end more than justified the means."

"I don't disagree." Samantha showed her teeth. "You guys were amazing! Especially my sister, who knew just what to say to him when I needed her most."

"All in a day's work," Kelli said, downplaying her role in what was a true joint rescue effort, from start to finish.

"Maybe more like a week—or even a month of exercising her formidable skills as a hostage negotiator," Sheldon joked with them. "The important thing is that we got the job done and the bank robbers will no longer be free to roam around Hemton County—or elsewhere when an opportunity to commit armed robberies presented itself—to pick and choose their targets as they saw fit."

Kelli beamed. "I'm pretty sure that's something all of us here on this wintry day in late December can wholeheartedly agree to."

There were no dissenters to the contrary as they made their way out of the woods, while investigators and crime scene technicians took over gathering evidence and incidentals that would be used in building the case against Jackson Rockmore and the other deadly robbers in his Hemton County Bandit Quartet.

AFTER DOING A bit of follow-up work on his laptop as he sat on a stool at Kelli's breakfast bar, Sheldon gave his father a video call to bring him up to date on the investigation.

"Hey," he said cheerfully, when his dad appeared on the screen.

Foster grinned instinctively. "I take it you have news?"

"Yeah. We got them," Sheldon was happy to report.

"That's good to hear, son. I never thought you wouldn't, frankly. Between the strength of the Bureau and your doggedness—just like mine—I knew the bank robbers were going to run out of steam, sooner or later."

"They did—and their train derailed," Sheldon said with a laugh in playing on the analogy.

Foster narrowed his gaze. "And what about the kidnapping…?"

"Samantha's fine," he told his father. "She came away with a few scrapes and bruises, but otherwise was unhurt." Sheldon didn't discount the psychological toll of being abducted and threatened repeatedly, as Samantha had been. But he also knew that she had displayed courage under fire and, like Kelli, had an inner strength that held up when put to the test.

"That's great to know," Foster said sincerely.

"Yeah." Sheldon grinned. "In fact, Dad, I have someone—make that two people—for you to say hello to…"

"Okay," Foster said, while waiting in anticipation.

Sheldon looked over this shoulder and signaled for both Kelli and Samantha to meet and greet his father for the first time. And vice-versa.

"Hi, Mr. Montgomery." Kelli flashed a grin at him and said, "Nice to meet you."

Samantha smiled brightly too. "Hey."

"Hey." His father grinned from cheek to cheek. "Glad Sheldon finally got around to introducing us. And, please, call me Foster."

"We will," Kelli told him with a chuckle.

Sheldon took delight in seeing them converse. Especially since he now considered Kelli and Samantha family. As such, it was important that they feel at home with his father and stepmother. And vice versa.

When his stepmother, Julia, also appeared on the screen, this made it a complete picture that Sheldon had longed for.

If Samantha's kidnapping told him anything, it was that family was more important than ever. When that was threatened from Kelli's end, he wanted to do his best to rectify this and it worked out.

With the love he felt in his heart for Kelli, Sheldon could barely wait for this year and its ups and downs to come to an end and the opportunity came to embark on a promising future together.

ON NEW YEAR'S EVE, Sheldon and Kelli stood on the rooftop terrace of his condo—taking in the spectacular fireworks display, intermingled with light snow falling in Downtown Denver—while holding goblets of champagne to mark the occasion.

"This is amazing," Kelli remarked, wide-eyed, as if witnessing what would culminate with a dramatic ball drop for the first time.

"I agree." Sheldon grinned, turning his attention to her. "But from where I'm standing, the fireworks can't hold a candle to the excitement I feel whenever I'm in your presence."

She turned to him, smiling. "I feel the same way about you," she confessed.

"Is that so?" he teased her, tasting the champagne.

"Absolutely. You've given me something I never thought I'd have again." Kelli paused emotionally. "A man I'm happy, able, and ever so willing to open my heart to."

Sheldon's own heart nearly melted in that moment. Which made what was about to happen next that much more perfect. "I'm so glad you said that," he told her, grinning. He took her goblet and set it, along with his own, on the table. "Because my heart belongs to you, Kelli, in every way imaginable. And that's why I wanted to give you this…"

As she kept her green eyes glued on him, he reached into the pocket of his wool sport coat and pulled out a yellow oval diamond engagement ring set in platinum. After taking her hand, he bent down on one knee, slid the ring onto her finger expectantly and said endearingly, "I've fallen madly in love with you, Kelli Burkett, and am more than ready again to share my life with someone as husband and wife for the rest of our lives—if you'll agree to marry me and make me the happiest man in the Mile High City. Not to mention the rest of Colorado. Hell, the entire planet!"

She laughed, then blurted out, "Yes, yes, I'll marry you, Sheldon Montgomery. I love you, too, and would like nothing better than to become your wife and take this magical journey into the future together!" Kelli chuckled while admiring the ring. "Now, you can get up and kiss me!"

Sheldon rose and laughed. "I'd love to do just that!" He put his hands around her waist, tilted Kelli ever so slightly and laid the most passionate kiss ever on her.

"Hmm…" she murmured enjoyably between their lips.

"Me too," he promised, loving every moment of this show of deep affection.

They came up for air just as the countdown had begun to ring in the new year, with the ball coming down, right on time. Grabbing their goblets, they clicked them in a toast and Kelli said, "Happy New Year, my love!"

"Back at you, a thousand times!" Grinning from ear to ear, Sheldon couldn't help but add, "And it's only just begun. Can't wait to do this again next year, the year after and for many more years to come."

Kelli's eyes lit up like the fireworks going off as she told him enthusiastically, "Why, I couldn't have said it any better myself!"

They kissed again to hammer home the point to their hearts' content.

Epilogue

At the Alfred A. Arraj Courthouse, Sheldon sat alongside Kelli, Samantha and Chase in the courtroom as Jackson Rockmore was about to pay the piper after being charged with numerous serious federal offenses, including aiding and abetting in armed bank robbery, kidnapping, possession of a firearm during the commission of a crime of violence, Hobbs Act Robbery that involved conspiracy to commit robbery and interfering with commerce, and use of a firearm in committing murder.

Sheldon expected United States District Court Judge Ryan Pagliaro to throw the book at Rockmore, who had been convicted on all counts, with a wealth of evidence against him in the robbery-related offenses supporting the guilty verdict. Especially after two other members of the Hemton County Bandit Quartet, Glenn Evigan and Sandrine Kripke, had faced similar charges and been convicted and sentenced earlier. Both robbers' DNA had proven a match to the two forensic unknown profiles found inside the GMC Savana passenger van used by the quartet.

Javier Mínguez, the fourth member of the bank robbing gang, pled guilty to various felonies perpetrated in the bank, credit union and armored truck robberies, cooperating with the Feds as he testified against Rockmore, Evigan and Kripke.

Assistant United States Attorney Wylson Millbern, a former FBI special agent and friend of Sheldon's, had prosecuted the case and pulled no punches in going after Rockmore full throttle, as though Millbern had everything to lose had he done any less. Tammy Yoshimura had been only too happy to testify against Rockmore, helping to secure the verdict.

When Judge Pagliaro sentenced a smug-faced Jackson Rockmore to spend the rest of his life behind bars, Sheldon looked at Kelli, squeezing her soft hand triumphantly, and then Samantha. Both sighed with relief that the last of the robbery quartet who had abducted Samantha nine months earlier, in a harrowing experience of courage and survival that she was still coming to terms with and trying to get beyond, had now been held accountable for his actions.

"Hope he rots in prison," Samantha said, seemingly satisfied, as Rockmore was led away in handcuffs.

"Me too," Kelli concurred. "He deserves no less."

"Like the others in his gang, Rockmore's getting what's coming to him," Chase chimed in, agreeing.

"That he is." Sheldon grinned with satisfaction, glad that this was finally over. "The system worked," he proclaimed.

Kelli smiled at him. "Thank goodness for that."

They all stood, and Sheldon said, more than ready to move on with their lives and whatever was in store for the future, "Let's get out of here."

"I think that's something we can all agree on," Kelli stated, and kissed him as they left the courtroom.

THE FOLLOWING SUMMER, Kelli and Sheldon saddled up their horses before taking a ride on their property in Leyton Falls. After marrying on New Year's Eve, a year after being proposed to, and honeymooning on Maui, Hawaii, Kelli loved being a wife to Sheldon and a future mother, with their first child barely on the way. Sheldon was thrilled as well that he was going to be a father and already started to make plans for the many things he wanted to do with their son or daughter.

In the meantime, Sheldon had settled in nicely on the ranch, after selling his condominium. They used the extra money to acquire a few more acres of land with plans to expand the house, as needed, down the line.

With Samantha having moved to San Francisco with Chase, both pursuing exciting new dreams and a future in matrimony, Kelli couldn't be happier that her sister had survived the kidnapping and gotten on with her life, not too surprisingly, away from the banking industry.

As they rode across the meadow on a warm afternoon, there was nothing but sunshine and blue skies. Her cowgirl straw hat fitting snugly over her head, Kelli gazed at her husband, looking every bit the handsome cowboy in his cognac-colored Stetson hat, perfectly tilted. She said jokingly, "If the Bureau ever decides they don't want you anymore, I'm sure there's a place for you with the Colorado Bureau of Investigation." She had joined the CBI six months ago, working out of a regional office, for the Investigations Section, as an agent in the Colorado Missing Person(s) Unit.

Sheldon chuckled and tipped his broad-brimmed felt hat. "You think so?"

Kelli laughed. "Absolutely."

"Well, if that means I get to hang out with my wife in a different law enforcement capacity, then I'll certainly keep my options open."

She showed her teeth playfully. "That's good enough for me." Though she was certain that being an FBI agent was right where he wanted to be, just like his father, Kelli still liked the thought of their working together—over and beyond the investigations that the CBI and FBI partnered on from time to time with other law enforcement agencies in the state.

As they approached a spot atop the hill, Sheldon took note

of the picnic she'd set up in advance and asked in surprise, "What's this?"

Kelli smiled. "Oh, just a little something I put together for my husband. Hope you like it."

Grinning, he answered, "That's pretty much a given where you're concerned."

"Good answer," she said with a chuckle.

They got off the horses and sat on the outdoor gingham picnic blanket, where Kelli had set turkey sandwiches, watermelon wedges, oatmeal cookies and a pitcher of iced tea.

After filling two tall glasses with the tea, Sheldon gave Kelli one of them, before offering her a prize-winning smile and, in toast, said lovingly, "To the best wife a man could ever ask for!"

With her heart very much in the right place, albeit skipping a few beats in the moment, Kelli responded with a thousand watt grin as she clinked her glass with his, "Aside from feeling the same way in reverse, that's a compliment I wouldn't mind hearing again and again and again for the rest of my life."

"And you definitely will," he promised her sweetly, sincerity in his loving eyes, leaving no doubt that they were in this for the very long haul.

* * * * *

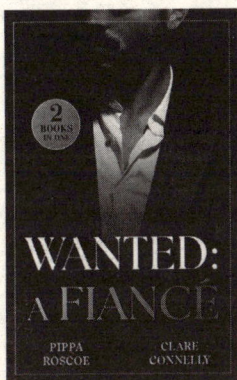

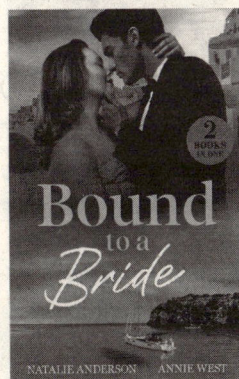

LET'S TALK
Romance

For exclusive extracts, competitions
and special offers, find us online:

 MillsandBoon

 @MillsandBoon

 @MillsandBoonUK

 @MillsandBoonUK

Get in touch on 01413 063 232

COMING SOON!

We really hope you enjoyed reading this book.
If you're looking for more romance
be sure to head to the shops when
new books are available on

Thursday 20th November

To see which titles are coming soon, please visit
millsandboon.co.uk/nextmonth

MILLS & BOON

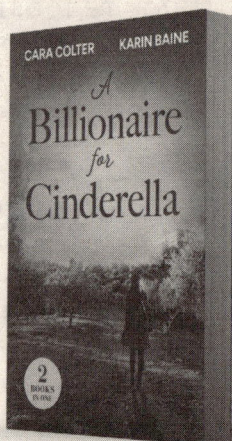